SUMMER SONS

SUMMER SONS

LEE MANDELO

A TOM DOHERTY ASSOCIATES BOOK
NEW YORK

SUMMER SONS

Copyright © 2021 by Lee Mandelo

Edited by Carl Engle-Laird

A Tordotcom Book
Published by Tom Doherty Associates
120 Broadway
New York, NY 10271

www.tor.com

Tor® is a registered trademark of Macmillan Publishing Group, LLC.

The Library of Congress Cataloging-in-Publication Data is available
upon request.

ISBN 978-1-250-79028-6 (hardcover)
ISBN 978-1-250-79030-9 (ebook)

Our books may be purchased in bulk for promotional, educational, or
business use. Please contact your local bookseller or the Macmillan Corporate
and Premium Sales Department at 1-800-221-7945, extension 5442,
or by email at MacmillanSpecialMarkets@macmillan.com.

First Edition: September 2021

Printed in the United States of America

0 9 8 7 6 5 4 3 2 1

Thx for the memories—
C. N.
1990–2011

SUMMER SONS

1

come home

i'll be waiting

Received 8/6 3:32 A.M.

The message sat unanswered. Andrew tapped from Eddie's hanging text thread to the brief obituary that had run in the local paper: *Edward Lee Fulton, recent graduate of Ohio State University, is survived by adoptive parents Lou and Jeanne Blur and sibling Andrew Blur as well as close friends and colleagues. Memorial services will be held at Streckler Funeral Parlor on Tuesday, August 10ᵗʰ at 11 A.M.* Andrew dropped his skull against the headrest of the driver's seat, free arm dangling out the open window. The impound office waited across a potholed blacktop parking lot, baked under dog-day sun to a shimmer. Sans air-conditioning, the interior of the Supra grew hot and hotter as he flicked through nothing on his phone. Del had left the I-65 rest stop right behind him, but she was late catching up.

He figured that might have something to do with the bitter exchange they'd traded over the hood of her sedan, when she'd said, "Come home with me after this, there's no reason to stay down here," and he'd replied, "There's no reason for me to go back up there, either." Her face had shuttered. The problem was he meant it. He was coming back to Tennessee, but there wasn't going to be a homecoming. He'd buried home two weeks past.

Del's trim red Focus crunched over the stray gravel scattered across the parking lot and jerked to a stop alongside him. He got out without rolling his windows up. If someone felt the pressing need to steal his trash bags full of clothes, or ransack a footwell crammed with books, they could help themselves. The estate letters in his back pocket were crumpled from the drive. He unfolded them as she joined him, sweat ringing the collar and armpits of her loose muscle tee, her mouth a rigid, bloodless line. Her crisp silence told him as much as he needed to know about the fallout of their sniping.

"Well, here we are," he muttered, to a hum of assent from Del.

The impound office was a glorified double-wide with a narrow service counter and dense safety glass barricading off the clerk in his reflective vest. Andrew said, "I'm here to pick up a car. It's been in impound a couple weeks, estate shit had to get sorted out first. I've got the paperwork."

"Okay, sure," the guy said without taking his eyes off his phone.

Andrew stuffed the letters and his license under the slot and stepped to the side with Del as the clerk heaved himself up to go searching. She said, "I'm serious, Andrew. I know your mom isn't going to say it, so I will. I don't think Nashville is where you need to be right now. Especially not alone."

He'd spent the past six weeks chafing to come south, waiting for the all-clear while Eddie put him off, and put him off, and put him off—May stretching to June, June to July, while he sat amongst his packed boxes wondering *what the fuck, man*. The excuses were bullshit, but they kept coming. First Eddie had a short research trip to finish at the close of spring term, then he needed to prepare every last perfect detail of the house for Andrew, and finally there was some old family business he said Andrew wouldn't want to be party to (he was right about that one). By the time Eddie drummed up a summer independent study that Andrew would "distract" him from if he showed before it was finished, Andrew figured he was being teased. After that interminable wait and the devastating payoff, he'd be fine if he never laid eyes on Columbus again.

He had to be in Nashville to find out what Eddie had done to get himself put in the ground. That wasn't a fight worth rehashing again with Del, though. She was as secure in her conclusion that he needed to cut his losses and accept Eddie's death as all the other people orbiting his life, watching and judging from the outside.

"I won't be alone. I'll be with what's-his-name, Riley, and all those folks," he said.

"Yeah, the friends he didn't introduce you to and that your parents didn't invite to his funeral, that sounds great. A super supportive system," she countered, measured but fierce.

Andrew scraped the sweat-drenched hair off his forehead, then ran his fingers through it twice to slick the whole mess out of his face. Four weeks past due for a trim. He wiped his damp hand on his jeans and wrangled the urge to say something: *you invited yourself, I didn't ask for support*.

The clerk interrupted: "I've got your keys, man, and there's a hold fee." He held out the twin red-and-black key fobs on a wire loop—one for valet, one for horsepower—and a thin sheaf of papers.

"How much?" Andrew asked.

"Looks like two hundred thirty-three, for the tow and storage."

Andrew clenched his jaw as his frustration abruptly compounded. It didn't matter that he'd summarily inherited the entire seven-point-five million dollars Eddie's late parents had left him a decade ago, not right then.

"You're telling me I have to give you two hundred bucks to pick up my dead best friend's car," he said.

"Hey, sorry, I don't make the rules," the clerk responded.

"Goddamn." Andrew slapped his card onto the counter. "Fucking charge it, then."

"Calm down," Del said.

"Leave it," he said through gritted teeth. The clerk passed him his card and the charge slip, along with the release forms and the key ring. He signed each dotted line with jagged, imprecise slashes of the pen. "Where's the car?"

"Head to row eighteen and hang a right, it should be about

three-quarters toward the end of the lot. Look for the sign at six-teen, though, the numbers fell off the rows after that. Just count your way." He took the signature sheets and stuck them into an accordion file. "Sorry 'bout your loss."

Andrew banged out the door; Del slipped through behind him. The pavement ended at the barbed-wire gate of the impound lot proper, giving way to gravel and, a handful of steps in, the crunch of pebbled glass. One fat grackle sat sentry atop the second numbered pole. Shreds of metal and plastic littered the ground underfoot.

Almost a third of the cars were mangled: doors crushed, paint scorch-ruined, windshields spiderwebbed with cracks. Those had permanent residence on the lot—*or were interred there,* he thought with a morbid humor. The sepulchral vibe ached in his molars, wreckage all around resting silent and still. The sign for row seven hung upside down from a single remaining screw. To his left at the head of row eleven, someone's sticker-splattered banana-yellow tuner—a Civic, maybe a 2010. He sidestepped to tap the hood in solidarity. Del snorted, and he flinched. Her hand caught his el-bow, thumb slipping on the sweat at the crook.

"Please just explain it to me, why you're still going forward with this after he . . ." she paused. The sun forced her to squint, chin tilted as he turned to stare her straight in the face. "After he did what he did."

"You aren't going to say it?"

"Do you want me to?" she asked.

Without answering, he shook off her grip and kept walking. The pale tops of his feet in his sneakers and the bare length of his arms had begun to sting, unsuited as he'd been since child-hood to the hot hand of summer in the South. A broiling tension pushed under his skin. The image of Eddie's corpse, emptied out and dolled up, remained stuck to the inside of his eyelids, a non-negotiable, fragmented picture. Under the sleeves of his funeral suit, fat stitches had closed Eddie's waxy forearms from wrist to elbow, black like tarred railroad ties.

No mistaking the ruined flesh and its bleak message, unless the obvious narrative wasn't the whole story. Maybe instead it was a palimpsest, scrawled in haste over the original draft to cover—something else. He wasn't sure what.

"I don't believe he killed himself. He had no reason to," he said against his better judgment to the sound of her footsteps crunching behind him, because he didn't have the fortitude to turn and look her in the face. "I don't know, Del. Does that sound like Eddie to you? He ever strike you as the type?"

"No, but that doesn't change the fact that he did it. I hate seeing you grasping for straws like this," she said.

Her pitying tone, the same he'd heard from the cops and his parents, pushed his temper over the edge.

"I wish you'd stayed the fuck home," he said.

The scuff of her shoes paused as he continued on. "Jesus, Andrew."

Naked poles stuck out of the ground like dead trees. He hooked a turn into row eighteen past a grisly, caution-taped SUV that leered with a dank stench. The hair rose on the nape of his neck. A shade loitered on the wreck's bones like a smear of night. The ghost reached toward him in the corner of his vision, but he resisted its gravitational force out of long habit, passing the wreck before the intrusive specter even had the chance to break his stride. Down the row he spotted a sleek and boxy black bumper. His heart tripped, squeezed.

"Look at me," she said desperately from behind him. He twisted on one heel, paused halfway between Eddie's car and Del standing with her hands at her sides, defeated already before she spoke again. "Why not defer a semester and come home, stay with me while you adjust? If you're still interested in the program come spring, then do it after all. I'm worried about leaving you here, not knowing what happened with him."

"Go home, Del," he said.

"What?" She balked.

"I've said it enough, we're done here. You didn't know him how I did. I'm going to find out what happened, and I don't give a fuck what you think about it, okay?" His shoulders heaved with the rising volume of his voice.

Deep red climbed across her olive-tan skin from collarbones to cheeks, a steel surety flashing as she spat back, "Don't be such a dick—he was my friend too. And I care about you. I'm trying to help."

Friends meant nothing in comparison to what he and Eddie were to each other.

He said, "You're not listening to me and you're not helping jack shit. The roommate said he'd meet me at the house at seven. I'm going to the executor's office before then, and I don't need an audience for any of that."

"God, you selfish fuck. The pair of you are such a mess, I don't even . . ." She trailed off as her words caught up: *are,* she'd said. *Are.* She jerked her head and pushed her hands out as if shoving the air between them apart.

The tiniest twinge of guilt flared in Andrew as tears spilled in a line across her cheek. The oozing specter from the crunched SUV lapped across her feet unbeknownst to her, clueless that she stood so close to old death. Under the high-noon sun, the alien shadow held his attention like a magnet; when her heels scuffed backward two steps, it retracted to the wreck once more, unable to reach her.

His distracted silence spoke for itself.

"All right, fine. I'll leave," she said.

"Delia," he murmured, closer to a concession.

"No, you said it yourself. Apparently it's more important for you to follow his lead even when he's *gone* than it is to be with your goddamn family, or your friends."

"I wasn't here with him," he said. Nashville held the last of Eddie, the unseen weeks. Andrew willed her to understand, even though she hadn't yet, not one time.

"And that's the reason?" She tossed her words out with a sky-ward gesture, frustrated.

"It's the reason I've got. I wasn't here when he needed me to be."

She shouted, "Because he left you behind with us! He didn't deign to *allow* you to be with him. He let the rest of us watch you mope around and—"

"Stop! Just, stop." The black car loomed, spiking longing through his chest. He said, "Let me be alone, Del. I didn't ask for help, and I didn't even ask for company."

Del scrunched both hands into her hair, yanking the ponytail lop-sidedly loose, a strangled shrieking sound tearing from her throat. No further emotion rose in him in response. He'd loved her once, or something close to it, years ago before the three of them had set-tled into their off-kilter unit. Now her paroxysm of grief and anger played out in front of him like a film, or the panic of a stranger, while he drifted in the void left where Eddie wasn't. After the outburst, she dropped her arms limp.

"Fuck you," she breathed out as she turned her back on him.

The sun-dappled straggle of her tawny hair bounced as she strode stiffly away without a final glance. An itch tickled the root of his tongue. He swallowed against it fruitlessly. Eddie had come to Nashville alone. He'd left in a box, a handful of weeks before Andrew was due to join him, without so much as a warning—leaving him a car, and a house, and a graduate program, and a fortune, but nothing that mattered as much as himself. Without Eddie, there was no point. He palmed the key fobs. Cicadas called as he crept the last few yards along the lot. The hulk of Eddie's car grew to meet him as he approached.

Slickly grim in the gold afternoon light, the black chrome and black detailing and cherry-red rims struck him to the core. The morning Eddie's trust fund spilled open, the pair of them had driven two hundred miles to pick up the absurd beast. *More muscle than the Aventador* went Eddie's argument; Andrew responded *and so American it hurts*. But the Hellcat fit him, reckless and extrava-gant, made to measure straight off the line. The brash white of Eddie's toothy smile and his muscled arm hanging out the win-dow, gunning the brutal roar of the engine at the first stoplight they'd coasted up to together, had lit him on fire.

The car could not be his. It belonged to no one but Eddie, this machine that had extended his churning life-large hunger from palm on gearshift and foot on clutch, glorious and unapologetic. The small bristling wolf decal he'd stuck in the corner of the back driver's side window flashed its teeth. Andrew pressed UNLOCK and crossed the distance in three stilted strides, jerking open the door to stand in the wash of magnified scent: *cigarettes cheap deodorant sweat-musk pot*. It lanced straight through his skull.

He laid his arm across the doorframe and his clammy forehead on top of it, breathing shallow. One scraping gasp hitched for a mo-ment before gusting out in an agitated burst. He hadn't cried for the last two weeks since he'd gotten the call from his own mother, Eddie's listed next of kin. When he thought too long about the fact that Eddie's big hand was never going to clap across the nape of his neck again, or that the brief, happenstance videos left on his phone had captured the final remnants of Eddie's human voice for endless stale replay, a nothing-numbness severed him from himself at the root. Self-preservation, maybe.

Faced with the real process of inheritance, Eddie's car reeking of summertime indiscretions, a terrible pressure constricted the soft muscle of his throat. Andrew clung to a thread of control as he collapsed into the grasp of the Challenger's driver's seat and pulled the door shut with a muffled slam.

One hundred thousand hours were packed on top of each other in Eddie's lingering scent: eleven years old and pressing cut palms with tears in their eyes, swearing brotherhood; thirteen and boxing up his bedroom for their move to Columbus, Eddie shell-shocked and silent over the loss of his mother and father and home; fifteen and smoking cigarettes under the back porch with the spiders;

seventeén and drunk, Del sandwiched half-nude between them in the back seat of a borrowed sedan under cold winter stars; nineteen and messaging each other across a classroom with grins tucked out of sight; twenty-one and putting in their applications for the same graduate program in the campus café. That's where it broke, when Eddie surprised him with an earlier admission and a request that Andrew wait him out. Their first and last extended separation. Andrew had promised to follow behind, toes at Eddie's heels.

He had, and he hadn't. This wasn't the way it was supposed to happen.

On the passenger side, Eddie had left a wadded-up tank top, a sea-green flat bill hat, and a crumpled straw wrapper. Andrew adjusted the seat out of habit to accommodate his lesser height, then pushed the clutch down and jammed the starter button. His thumb left a trace of his own sweat over the print that had been smudged there. The rumbling snarl of the engine waking shook him. The clock read 6:52. A Misfits song punched abruptly through the speakers as the media system replaced an absent Bluetooth signal with radio; the horrible jolt had him slapping his hand down on the volume knob to shut it off on instinct.

With nothing else waiting on him, he drove.

After a coasting trip around Centennial Park to the lawyer's offices, where he had to discuss investment accounts and multiple properties and cold cash funds, then an additional circuitous drive through campus, he rolled to a stop in front of 338 Capitol Street—Eddie's house, now somehow Andrew's property. The place was a sedate old Craftsman six blocks from campus, shaded by a looming oak that shed branches on the rooftop and yard in twiggy tangles. The photos Eddie had sent, framed over his shoulder with a grin or the corner of a crinkled, smiling eye in view, had made it look verdant and charming, not quite so summer-withered. Lights glowed through the front windows. He pulled out his phone to swipe through saved snaps from Eddie that spanned the past six months.

He lingered on a shot of the roommate, Riley, flicking a wave with a rillo between his lips and a dimple at the corner of his smile. He was wiry, sporting an undercut colored black on top and a shade of yellow too close to orange to be natural on the scruffy stubble beneath. A scar crossed from the bridge of his nose down to the top of his cheekbone, thin and pale pink. Andrew flipped through more photos of strangers, recalling their names where possible—Ethan, West, Sam, Luca, a handful more whose faces he'd glimpsed but couldn't place. The people who'd been around Eddie most, until the end.

Eddie's assurance that he'd introduce him around as soon as he arrived left him stumbling now. Over the past week, he and Riley had traded a few awkward, terse DMs about what time Andrew would be arriving, but nothing more. He knew that Riley was also in their American Studies program, and that Eddie had invited him to be their roommate after knowing him for two weeks, despite having absolutely no need to share expenses on the house he'd flat-out purchased: an incursion on Andrew's space that rankled. He pieced together the home from a series of stills: a foyer with a bike rack, leading through to the sprawl of the living room and kitchen; upstairs, three bedrooms and a bathroom off of a landing. It was close and charming. It was supposed to have been theirs.

Andrew cut the engine. The warm night outside blinked with fireflies while he sat adrift. Fatigue throbbed in the soles of his feet and in his tailbone. He would walk in and see Eddie's things, pace over his footprints like he was waiting for him to arrive—like he'd gotten held up after class and had Andrew pick his car up from the shop. He crossed his wrists over the steering wheel and dug the fingernails of his right hand into the blotchy bracelet of inked dots around his left wrist, then bowed his head between them.

Glowing red digits ticked out time, methodical, on the dash clock. He wondered if Riley was concerned that the mysterious stranger who now owned his house might be about to kick him out. The thought of mounting those front steps, crossing the threshold, and introducing himself to his inherited roommate made his skin crawl. Instead, Andrew fumbled for the seat adjustment and tipped into a recline, flinging the seat belt aside and tucking one knee over the other. The soft nap of the red leather headrest held a faint animal scent.

Enough minutes slid past that the interior displays cut out with a click and plunged him into streetlight-banded darkness. He counted his steady breaths, continuing to squeeze his own wrist. The underside of the steering wheel dug against the outside of his leg, huddled crooked as he was in the bucket seat. Weighed down by the shittiness of the interminable drive, the conflict-riddled afternoon, and the impending rest of his life, he allowed exhaustion to drag his eyelids shut for a brief rest.

Freezing pressure crushed his lungs. He woke with a heaving spasm less than a single blink from the moment he'd drifted off, or so it felt to his disoriented brain. His bones throbbed under his muscles, wracked with another shudder that torqued him against the seat. His right hand scrabbled at the divider; superimposed over his limp left arm was a headache-inducing vision of a skeletal limb dripping brackish blood.

Mist fogged in front of his face from the wheezing gasps of his breath. His own distorted, huffed yelps brought him further out of his stupor, enough to fling himself across to the passenger seat headfirst. The gearshift slammed into his calf. His temple cracked against the window. He scrambled upright, dragging his leg to the other footwell as if escaping a monster's claws. A hollow silhouette constructed out of negative shadow occupied the driver's seat in his stead, claiming the seat where it had belonged in life. He wasn't alone in the way Del imagined—far from it.

The enclosed space stank of summer-boiled earth, swamp-wet and fetid. Andrew snapped his teeth shut on a scream. The dead thing shifted through banded gold and black darkness, refracting the suggestion of a jawbone or a half-lidded eye, an elbow propped through the window without regard for the glass. It lifted a hand from the wheel to reach for him, uncanny as a marionette; searing cold fingertips tapped the tattooed bone of his wrist. The streetlight overhead popped at the instant of contact, bursting in a flare of light that left him part blinded—and when his eyes cleared, the thing was gone. Abandoned again.

It was the third time in fifteen days that the haunt had visited him.

He yanked open the glovebox and fumbled through junk for Eddie's spare cigarette pack: four left, lighter tucked inside in case of emergency. Three tries to light it, hands and lips shaking too ferociously to line up in the necessary order. He coughed out his first burning pull and sat with the glow of the cherry balanced between his knees while he caught his breath. Fragments of the nightmare drifted with the smoke curling tongues around his face.

Andrew had thought a near decade of persistent, life-starved haunts and their shredded memories prying into his dreams would be enough to prepare him for the shade he refused to name *Eddie,* but three times was not the charm. His hands continued to shake. Wounds he'd never had, only seen on his best friend's corpse and in his tortured imaginings, stung across his forearms—but on petrified second glance, he saw only unblemished lean muscle, dusted with sparse hair standing on end.

Dregs of primal fear clanged around the inside of his head with the dissolving remains of a nightmare: the specter's punishing gift to him, disorganized visions of pain, fear, cut wrists, desperation without structure or clarity. He'd sorted through the tattered remnants left behind by purposeful suicides before. This grisly, vicious miasma didn't remind him of those at all, though explaining that to another human being was a nonstarter. Only Eddie could've grasped his point, understood from experience the gulf between the two and the questions it raised.

A sour copper taste lingered on his gums. He lifted his unsteady hand to the dim moonlight and found fingerprint blisters frostburned around the base of his wrist, crossing the uneven dots of old ink. He stubbed the cigarette, crawled into the back seat, and tucked his body into the tightest ball it could make, the collar of his shirt stuffed between his teeth to grind. His wrist stung in starbursts where the phantom had marked him.

Eddie, he thought, *what happened, what the fuck happened to you?*

2

A knock on the window glass roused Andrew abruptly. He bolted upright with spit drying in a streak on the side of his jaw and twisted to face the driver's side window, but the tint obscured the person outside to a silhouette. He couldn't remember where he was. The seat leather stuck to his palms. Sweat dripped behind his knees and down the crack of his ass.

"Hey man," said a muffled voice, pitch light but husky. "Is that, uh, Andrew?"

He scrubbed his palms over his face, heart pounding with disoriented adrenaline, and croaked, "Yeah, sorry, give me a second."

There was no dignified way to maneuver himself into the front of the car again without the impetus of hysterical panic. He stuck one leg into the passenger seat and wriggled his body over the divider after it, banging his head and his pride on the roof of the car. He snagged the keys from the ignition and slid out, gulping down a cooler breath of night air as he planted a hand on the doorframe to haul himself upright. Riley the Roommate stood across the expanse of the hood. Eddie had either staged his pictures or gotten lucky, because Andrew hadn't noticed that Riley was even shorter than he was—at least six inches shy of Eddie's not-insignificant six-foot-one.

"So, this is fucking awkward," Riley said.

"Yeah," he replied. The cicadas screamed. "What time is it?"

"Hair after midnight," he said. His accent dragged out the vowels. "Guess you saw the car."

"That I did." A further moment of strained silence spread before he stuck his hand out. "Riley Sowell, second-year master's student, at your disposal. Sorry the circumstances are totally fucked."

Andrew clasped his hand, fingers bridging onto his wrist for more of a grip than a shake. Strain showed at the corners of the other boy's eyes and mouth, lurking beneath his welcoming smile. He must've spent the last two weeks alone, isolated in a house he'd shared with Eddie before—those six months unaccounted for to Andrew except through mediated digital snippets. Six months to sift for answers about Eddie's . . . habits, choices, the chances he took without his usual second-in-command on site. All the moments he'd missed out on while others, like Riley, had been present. Andrew grabbed a backpack containing a couple changes of clothes, his toothbrush, and his laptop from the rear footwell, then slammed the door with booming finality.

"Lead on," he said.

They crossed the summer-crackled yard rather than taking the footpath. Riley's grey T-shirt stretched taut around his shoulders, the swell of muscle wiry but clearly fought-for. His skinny jeans were black, cuffed once above narrow, bare feet. He jiggled the doorknob as he twisted it, glanced over his shoulder and said, "The door sticks sometimes, we still haven't fixed it."

Andrew caught his tongue between his back teeth to keep from speaking his piece too soon. There was no *we* outside of Eddie and Andrew. He'd left Eddie to these people's care, and they hadn't kept him well. Whatever had happened, Andrew didn't know these strangers from shit, and none of them were presumed innocent. The step across the threshold behind Riley was eerily unremarkable, identical to entering any stranger's house for the first time. Two bikes hung on the rack in the dim, cool foyer, with room for a third.

"Let me show you around," Riley said. He laughed mirthlessly. "It's like, your house now, right?"

Andrew paced after him through the living room, past a TV

playing ESPN on mute, glanced into the kitchen—dirty dishes next to the sink, a stack of beer cans and an empty bourbon bottle—then mounted the stairs. The landing creaked as they turned and took the last few steps up to the bedrooms. Riley jerked his thumb to the door immediately on the right, said "mine," then pointed to the one after it—"yours"—and finally pointed to the sole door on the left. "Ed's." The bathroom, directly in front of them, explained itself.

The whole place smelled like home, but with a discomfiting undertone of *old* home, home before Columbus. Even AC couldn't fight the thick green smell. Andrew's parents had moved the family north four months after Eddie's adoption had gone through—ostensibly for work, but since their surprise additional kid had gotten them rich, Andrew figured their move had more to do with running from what had happened to him and Eddie the summer before; the summer his life went wrong. He strangled the bare thought of *before* as soon as it wriggled loose.

Riley broke the silence to say, "No offense, but I don't think either of us wants me here for this part."

And he squeezed past Andrew to disappear down the steps in a cascade of thumps. All three doors were closed. Andrew laid his hand on the knob to Eddie's door and dropped his forehead onto the wood. He'd seen the room plenty of times, in picture and on video, from hundreds of miles away: a bed against one wall with Eddie's desk and gaming setup at the foot; an end table with a mirror propped on it crooked; curtains over the far wall that was almost all window. The streetlights outside would lend it a dim glow. There would be half-finished drinks on the shelves, a guitar and a battered amp in the closet that used to be Andrew's and were once again.

Instead, he turned to open the door to his own room—putting off the inevitable. The hinges squealed. Moonlight cast shadows across the warm mismatched spread of furniture Eddie had selected for him: a monstrous desk, so deep brown it might as well have been black, pushed into the far corner; a shelf stained bright gold with chips knocked out of its corners and a handful of books piled on the shelves; a luxurious king-sized bed that dominated the room, up against the wall so Andrew could tuck into the corner the way he preferred.

The framed picture on the bedside table, a twin to the one he knew waited in Eddie's room, nailed the final stabbing touch. Del had taken the original on her phone of Andrew's and Eddie's cars parked side by side, while she waited on the road ahead of them to serve as flagger. The photo immortalized the moment when Andrew had sprawled over his center console to reach out his passenger window and flip off a smirking Eddie, who had his shades pushed up into the unkempt mess of his hair. Their expressions were savage with joy.

Andrew hooked the door shut behind him with his ankle. He sank into a crouch and buried his face against his knees. When that proved insufficient, he tipped forward onto the floorboards and dug his fingernails into the seams. His mouth filled with spit, sick-fast. Eddie had put together a perfect room, a room that held all of him without the slightest effort. He'd done it without question, knowing Andrew's needs inside and out. The shelf yawned for his own books to be added to it, the closet gaped for clothes, the space waited to become home. No part of Andrew could conceive of the room as a goodbye offering. It was too much a welcome to the life in Nashville that Eddie had talked up on his calls, the impending reunion after their brief, uncomfortable separation.

Downstairs the TV cut on, the quiet murmur of a sportscaster piping up through the vent. After the vertiginous swoop finished twisting through him, Andrew pushed himself to his feet using the corner of the bed. The stairwell echoed noisily with the thump of his sneakers jogging down them. The television was on, but the living room was abandoned. He sank onto one couch—there were two, catty-corner—dropping his hands between his knees. How long had that room been ready? How early had Eddie prepared a place for him? If he'd been allowed to come down two or four or six weeks earlier, instead of being stalled by a series of petty reasons, Eddie might still have been with him to see it. A moment later footsteps approached and a cold bottle was pressed to his wrist, proffered wordlessly.

"I'm sorry," Riley said.

"No problem," he muttered in response.

"He talked about you all the fucking time," Riley continued. His naked foot and the coffee table formed the centerpiece of Andrew's vision. "Feels like I already know you, honestly."

It would've been proper to give as given: *yeah, he talked about you too.* Andrew tipped his bottle back and swallowed bracingly cold beer in long mouthfuls. When the bottle was half-finished, he eased off for a breather and glanced over to see Riley fiddling with the label on his own.

"Sorry," Andrew said into the awkwardness.

"Don't worry about it. I don't think anyone would be all right, the situation being . . ." he trailed off and gestured to the rooms above them.

Andrew caught sight of his tattooed forearm and asked, "What's that?"

Riley turned his arm obligingly to show inked, elegant, almost impenetrable script reading, *it's not about forcing happiness.* Andrew recognized the lyrics from a band Eddie had been a fan of. The straggling conversation laid itself to rest. Both boys drank. Andrew felt like a stranger in this city, this house, his own body. He'd made Riley into a stranger too, just by arriving on the doorstep. He had questions, but no sense of where to begin asking them.

Why didn't he let me come sooner?

"You want another?" Riley asked with a tip of his empty bottle.

"I'll get it," Andrew said.

Might as well begin to learn the house, alien as that sensation was. He stepped into the kitchen, surveyed the cupboards, opened the unfamiliar fridge. The bottom shelf held six different kinds of beer. He snagged two mismatched bottles and brought them back; Riley popped the caps with the carabiner clipped to his jeans. Wisely, he said nothing about his houseguest-cum-landlord exploring the other room.

Instead he asked, "You're starting our program, right? Orientation is tomorrow."

"Right, I am," Andrew said.

He hadn't thought about his academic calendar. Based on Eddie's prior reportage, the orientation had been a bore, a glorified social hour without the buffer of alcohol. Eddie had handled his first-semester registration for him already, as he'd done since freshman year at OSU. The screenshot-filled email with his login, password, and schedule languished in his abysmal Gmail inbox. Eddie had made those decisions for Andrew as a matter of course, keeping them paired together as much as he could—until his surprise early semester at Vanderbilt. Five months of separation that had stretched into eight over the summer, and now would never end. Eddie and his goddamn secrets. Andrew heard the teasing in his head: *I'll tell you what I'm up to when it's time for you to know, just sit pretty and be patient.* And he'd accepted that, dumb as a dog. No reason to torture himself sitting through an orientation he didn't care about.

Riley arched his back in a stretch. Joints popped with audible force. He stood and said, "I'm going to sleep. Obviously I'm complete shit at whatever it is I'm supposed to be doing to help with this situation, but you're welcome to the fridge or whatever else. Let me know if there's something you need?"

Andrew cast a long glance over him as he waited in the shadow of the stairwell for confirmation. While he'd been straining at his seams waiting for permission to toss his shit in the back seat and come home, Riley had slept across the hall from Eddie, maybe even spoken to him that final afternoon. Riley was connected. He wasn't a stranger.

"Don't worry about it, I'm good," he said eventually.

Andrew swung his feet up to lie down as Riley mounted the creaking stairs. He checked his phone. Past one in the morning; three missed calls and a handful of unread texts. Knowing the cozily arranged bedroom waited overhead sent a dull throb of pain through his temples. Those sheets could stay crisp and untouched for another night. Eddie wasn't going to care.

———

In the morning, he passed Riley opening his bedroom door as he exited the bathroom, wearing the same clothes he'd slept in. The shower kicked on as he stood in the center of the kitchen. His stomach grumbled and he ducked into the pantry, perusing canned soups, mysterious unlabeled containers, half-finished snacks. An open box of Apple Jacks seemed like the most expedient option. He pulled it off the shelf, uncrimped the rolled but not clipped bag, and ate three handfuls of stale, dry cereal. The shush of running water cut off, leaving him alone with the crunch. Sugar-grease coated his tongue.

"Hey," Riley said from behind him. He startled and spun on his heel. "Sorry, didn't mean to surprise you. I'm heading over to campus, do you need a ride to orientation?"

The expression on his thin lips and slightly furrowed brows hovered between earnest and awkward. His weight shifted to one foot as he cocked a hip, keys in his fist and messenger bag slung across his chest. Andrew swallowed against the crumbs tickling his throat, sat the cereal on the counter, and said, "No, I'm good. Thanks."

"Okay, cool." He had the door open and one foot out when he continued, tossing offhanded over his shoulder: "I'll be home late, so I'll catch you in the morning probably."

Andrew sagged as soon as the door shut. Out the window, he watched as Riley unselfconsciously bent himself into a stretch with his wrists braced on the roof of his Mazda, feet spread wide, head hanging and spine long. Andrew's neck and shoulders ached from the long drive plus a night spent on the couch. The other man slid into his car, and the coughing roar of an aftermarket engine rebounded off the house. Andrew tore his attention free and made a beeline for the fridge. The milk in the door was three days past its date, but it smelled fine, so he stole a swig direct from the carton.

The haunt that had visited him the night before, as brutally familiar as his own skin, was unimaginable in broad daylight. The absence stung somehow. Dust on the stairs stuck to his sweating feet as he ascended again. The door to Eddie's room was nothing remarkable, but that didn't stop his hand from stalling on the brass knob. He took the first two steps into the room with his eyes clamped shut, dragging his toes across the floorboards to avoid tripping. He nudged the door closed. Once it latched, he forced a breath out through his nose and opened his eyes again.

Rumpled sheets spilled onto the floor at the end of the mattress on its plain metal frame. Two pillows were crammed into a pile against the wall, and a third lay sideways in the center of the bed. Clothes lay in a scattershot circle around a full laundry hamper at the corner of the desk. A hideously neon-orange pair of boxer briefs and one sock with a giant hole in the heel dangled haphazardly from the edge of the pile. The chair was rolled back from the messy desk, covered in a scattered mountain of papers, pens, books, High Life cans, and a monitor with a headset hooked over it. A half-smoked blunt rested on the edge of a glass ashtray. A still life painting: *One Boy's Room, Summer.*

On autopilot, he staggered across the room to collapse into the chair, the same chair from their shared apartment in Columbus. He gripped the armrests and laid his head against the divot they'd worn into the upholstery through the years. The room felt so freshly interrupted he was surprised the chair wasn't warm to the touch. A snowdrift of loose-leaf paper drew his attention first— plain printer stock and ruled alike, covered with Eddie's cramped sprawling handwriting in multiple colors of ink—but the broken-backed composition book splayed open on top of the unkempt pile was obviously the last piece touched.

Andrew dragged it onto his lap, caught the most recent lines in a jagged scrawl that implied excitement or distraction:

the land itself is the thing in most of these stories, right, it's about people who are connected to the land in their inheritance (??) or blood or some shit. It isn't inert, it's the source—it's a battery? or a character?—to the inheritors. There's a cost the user has to pay to pick up the curse/gift. The earth *has to be paid*

He stared at the unfinished sentence. The hair on his nape rose in an abrupt wave, nerves tingling. He flipped to the beginning of the notebook, since Eddie had filled three-quarters of it already, and started reading.

Facts:
   (1) I see dead people
   (2) I didn't before that summer
   (3) The closer I get to home the worse it gets
   (4) Andrew too, but not as much as me
So time to find out: why?

—and scrawled in the margin next to the damning number four was the notation, *he's gonna be so pissed at me.*

Andrew hurled the notebook at the door as if it scorched his hands. It slapped the wood and thunked onto one corner, landing on its cracked back, pages riffling open. *Our ghost story,* Eddie called it sometimes when they were drunk, or partway asleep, or catching their breath after a race—whenever he thought Andrew would forgive him for bringing up the thing he'd promised to let lie. Andrew had sworn them to silence that summer, and pretended afterward unto amnesia that he'd never floundered through the grasp of revenants that crawled hungry from their graves at his passing step. Pretended that he hadn't spent most of his life ignoring desperate whispers at the limits of his hearing, and that his bones kept quiet under his skin instead of flaring to life with a terrible itch of *potential* during the blackest depths of night. Eddie hadn't ever wanted to pretend, from their first night to his last, judging from his fucking notebook and the stack of texts that, Andrew realized with a tremble, had titles like *Tennessee Folklore* and *True Ghost Stories of the South* and *Granny Magic*.

Through the past decade, Eddie had agreed over and over again to Andrew's demands for silence, but here he was, fucking up the moment he left Andrew's sight. He shouldn't have been in Nashville in the first place, considering the force with which Andrew had protested their application to Vanderbilt, far too close to the teenage past they'd skinned loose. But Eddie was a convincing liar with a long list of fake reasons; his decision had withstood Andrew's meager arguments. In hindsight, it looked a lot like Eddie had led him by the nose around his loathing for the prospect of homecoming, led him with promises of comfort, promises that he wouldn't get him into the same trouble again, promises that it was the best place for his research—not Oregon or California, states with more ocean and fewer hollers, none of their shared childhood ghosts.

"American Studies my ass." Eddie and his Southern gothics. How had he thought the inevitable reveal was going to go? Did he think there was any way Andrew would welcome the truth: that he'd brought them South to chase haunts? Was that why he'd kept putting Andrew's arrival off? "You fucking—fuck, fuck, *fuck*."

And he'd collected an unnecessary roommate in the interim, based on unspecified "shared interests." Andrew wildly wished Riley was home for him to tear into about this goddamn mess Eddie had made for himself, but the house was still and hollow, mocking in its brightness.

The colorful scrawl warped under the damp blur of his furious stare. He swept the pages onto the floor in a fit of frustration. He needed to go outside. He needed to be somewhere else.

The neighborhood unspooled as he strode away from the house on Capitol, leaving the door unlocked behind him when it occurred to him he had no keys. After forty minutes or an hour or more, he had no idea, he'd ended up in a more ragged area: smaller houses, fewer cars, sagging stoops. The pounding beat of his heart had cooled a fraction, but *he lied to me* ran on a cacophonous loop through his skull. Or *had* he been lied to? Eddie had steered him around the truth of his work at Vanderbilt with dissembling answers that passed for straightforward. Andrew had been misled, misdirected, misused. Now he had nothing left but to piece together the scraps. He reached for his phone and found nothing, then realized it was still on the table back at the house. His steps slowed. At first glance, the neighborhood street felt familiar as if he'd been there before, but on a closer look he recognized none of the road signs—and then nothing around him was familiar at all.

———

With the help of a handful of strangers giving directions, and a detour to a café for an iced tea and a giant cup of cold water, Andrew made it home in the late evening, footsore and sunburnt as hell. Riley was absent, as promised. An eerie hush settled over the house as he shut the door and flipped the dead bolt behind him, almost a pressure against his eardrums. The muffled sensation dogged him on his begrudging trip to the second floor. The bedroom door hung open, papers scattered across the landing. Andrew bent and gathered them, frowning, to drop on the desk once more. The old blunt sat exactly as Eddie had left it, half-smoked on the lip of the ashtray. Seventeen days had dried the wrap enough to crack. Andrew licked his thumb and smoothed the split in short strokes. The pinched end fit between his lips natural as breathing. He grabbed the purple Bic, flicked the fire to life, lit the charred end.

The initial drag tasted of burning dust and aged ash first, sweet earth and smoke second. He pictured Eddie in the same spot beside the desk, washed with white summer sun, rillo dangling from his mouth while he balanced on one foot to pull on his sneakers. Andrew kicked his off instead. He sat gingerly on the edge of the mattress, holding each drag until his lungs strained. There was no hand to pass to, and the only smoke in his face came seeping from between his own lips.

At the end he pulled so hard he singed his bottom lip, flinching. The roach fell to his palm and he scuffed it in the ashtray. That was the last blunt Eddie would ever roll him, and he hadn't been there to joke about Andrew getting it too soggy: *you slobber like a dog, man, I've got so much of your spit in my mouth,* as he'd said once. Every moment of his life that followed would take him further from Eddie, no matter his efforts to scrounge for the remains, but what else was there for him to do except draw what was left as close as he could? One thing: to find what or who had taken Eddie from him, since he was sure it couldn't have been Eddie. Not on purpose. He unbuckled his belt and kicked off his pants in abrupt jerks, head swimming, then crawled up the mattress to drag the pillows around his head. The musk of sweat and hair product filled his nose.

Fabric stuck to his damp cheek. The moment he realized that tears had begun to leak from the corners of his eyes, the dam broke; he tucked his knees against his chest as he heaved with sobs almost deep enough to make him retch. Delirious, he imagined his ribs might shatter from the force and spike straight through his lungs. The uncontrollable weeping stretched on endlessly, to the start of physical pain then far past it. Streetlights hummed outside. Muscles spasmed across his sides, throat, and jaw as eventually his tension waned and he began to snuffle more than wail. Snot clogged his nose and exhaustion swaddled him, but as sleep descended, a prick of stinging sensation flared at the root of his spine. He had no time to resist the ice-cold press of an ankle slipped between his, the weight of a broad arm and elbow pressing around his shoulder and over onto the mattress. Bones like fingers combed through his hair. Indistinguishable murmuring touched the shell of his ear. He had a moment to think, *Eddie,* before the dream took him under.

The night of the haunt-dream had never known starlight: black, sightless. Andrew wore the wrong skin, small and fragile, with the knobby knees and gangly arms he used to smash into doorframes, bedposts, all sorts of things before he'd grown into them. The pooling liquid under his hands and shins was cold and thin, then thick and slick-hot. He scrambled to find footing; stone bruised him when he fell. This was familiar, bad dream and memory both. It had happened something like this, and he had no power to stop it. The littler him pushed forward until his seeking, stinging hands found cloth. He dragged himself through primordial and crushing darkness over the prone, still, also-adolescent body beneath him.

The fingers that reached up to touch his face streaked his skin wet, nose to lip. He was speaking but couldn't hear himself. All he heard was a hissing sibilance that plugged up his ears. The fingers pushed into his open mouth and the iron poison of blood coated his taste buds. He gagged; the hiss rose to a chatter. The invasive hand dipped from his mouth, skated to his torn shirt and found the open edges of his flesh, pushed inside with questing, horrible tenderness, put him on his back. *Good boy,* he heard in his head with the force of a rung bell.

Ghastly fingers wrenching into his hair pulled him from the dream, wheezing and trembling. His shirt was rucked up to his shoulders, his own fingernails dug into his chest so deep that specks of blood dotted the pale skin. Salt gummed his eyelashes and the bridge of his nose, as if he'd continued to sob in his sleep. When he rolled flat into the freezing body-shaped dip in the mattress behind him he jolted away, teeth chattering, but didn't get up. The cold receded an inch at a time without another touch, another word. The thing that had been Eddie abandoned him to its bed.

Andrew hadn't dreamed about the night in the cavern in six years.

3

The front door slammed directly below where Andrew lay on the floor, bundled in a wad of bedsheets with a pillow wedged between head and shoulder. He flinched upright. The cast of the light coming through the curtain said *afternoon.* Masculine voices, boisterously conversing, filled the house. He pried himself off the ground, threw the sheets on the bed, and ducked into the bathroom to piss and wash the salt off his face. The nail marks on his chest had scabbed to four fine crescents; he tapped his fingers on them and swallowed at the recollection of his witching-hour visitor. One half of the loud conversation downstairs stalled, mid-sentence, as he turned on the sink.

Andrew paused on the landing as he heard a man say, "Hey, you all right?" The voice was familiar, at the edge of his brain, but he couldn't place it.

"Shit, I guess I just . . . spaced out, sorry," Riley said with an odd, unsettled tension to his tone. "Noticed something weird, don't worry about it."

Andrew remained frozen in place, remembering: the roommate Eddie had talked up, *so cool, shares so many interests, you're going to love him,* and those notes, chock-full of the topic Eddie was forbidden from looking into. Riley presented a set of questions on top of the ones he'd already had.

Before he made the decision to turn tail and retreat, the other voice called out, "We hear you loitering, dumbass, just come on down."

Caught out, he acquiesced, dropping a quick "hey" as he entered the room.

Riley had a rumpled, distracted look about him. His face was pale where it wasn't flushed a dull red, and a pair of matte black plastic-framed glasses perched low on the bridge of his nose. But the other man, standing with thumbs in his pockets and a crooked black-and-violet snapback shading his eyes, caught Andrew's attention in an instant. Andrew's eyes locked on to a scabbed scrape on the left side of his jaw. The voice clicked into place from a twenty-second Snapchat video Eddie had sent a month before, howling with laughter and spitting filth while Eddie chased him across a field, throwing firecrackers at his feet. Sam Halse, cousin to Riley. The oldest of the group Eddie had fallen in with. A savage compulsion had radiated from him in Eddie's stories; he was high on Andrew's shit list. The twinge that had pitched camp in his chest, late at night while he'd listened to Eddie rambling on and on about Halse, reared to life again.

"Heard so much about you, Blur." Halse strode across the room and offered his hand for a shake. Andrew moved to accept, right-to-right, but Halse hooked their thumbs and yanked their joined hands into a tight clasp between their chests. His knuckles jammed against Andrew's breastbone. He had a few inches of height on Andrew, and a couple more through his broad shoulders. "Some of it real good."

"Sam, be chill for once in your goddamn life," Riley said.

The exhaustion in his tone kicked the smile from Halse's mouth. The shift left his face wolfish, closed off. Andrew looked straight at him with his chin up.

Halse asked, "You treating my cousin all right?"

"Of course he is, he's been here like twenty-four hours," Riley said.

"Okay, sure." Halse dropped Andrew's hand and rounded the coffee table to sit next to Riley, shoving his feet to the side to make room. "Ed was a good guy, and he made it sound like we'd all hit it off. You into the same weird shit?"

"Define weird shit," Andrew said as his skin prickled.

Halse barked a laugh and took his hat off, tossing it onto the other couch. His buzz cut was a fraction too close-cropped to obscure the paleness of his skin, one stage past stubble. "That's a yes."

Riley kicked him in the hip. He frowned and scooted farther across the couch.

"It's probably a no," Andrew said.

"Whatever you say," Halse drawled. "But, hey, give me your phone. I'm going to put my number in there."

"I think it's dead," Andrew replied.

He listed to the side to lean against the living room doorframe, hovering outside the cousins' space. Halse took up too much air with his presence alone, and Andrew was too tired to muscle his way in. Restless nights, two in a row lost to his revenant visitor, and the stop-motion bedroom upstairs—he'd had the intention of questioning Eddie's new friends on arrival, but the reality of the situation tripped him over his own feet. He couldn't marshal his thoughts past his raised-hackles resistance to their being more at home than Andrew was in the middle of his own living room.

"C'mon, man," Halse prodded.

"You don't have my number, either," Riley said.

Easier to give in than to keep arguing. Andrew slipped the phone from his back pocket and tossed it into Halse's outstretched hand, satisfied when he pressed the home button and nothing happened. Halse grinned, showing a broad white slash of teeth.

"You weren't bullshitting," he said.

"I don't, much."

Riley stole the phone from his cousin and fished around next to the couch until he found a dangling charge cord.

"This is scratched all to shit," he said as he plugged it in.

"And the screen's cracked," Halse said.

The family resemblance was abruptly clear. Both of them looked at him with the same tilt to their heads, the same dimple-cornered mouths, identical cheekbones and deep-set brown eyes. The differences were telling as well. The bump of a past break on Halse's nose, his squarer jaw, the thinner, ginger-tinged stubble on the line of Riley's jaw—someone on that side of the bloodline was a blonde.

"Fuck, could you just sit down? Your hovering is making me anxious," Halse said.

"I'm good here," Andrew said, almost without meaning to.

The flat look Halse leveled at him in response spoke to how often people told him no. A flicker of a smile pushed at the edges of Andrew's mouth, his shoulders squaring up wider at the brief burst of tense contest, bringing the agitation stewing inside him to the forefront of their strange domestic tableau. Maybe he had the energy to fight after all. Except then Halse snorted and rolled his eyes.

"Down, boy. It's your house, stand all afternoon if you want to. I was being polite."

Riley pressed the power button on the charging phone, load screen lighting up. Mid-reach to set it down on the table, the phone started to vibrate and didn't stop, one missed message coming after another in an unending stream. The alerts went on and on with the phone balanced on Riley's palm like a snake that might bite at the slightest provocation. Chagrin was a delicate and scholarly look on him, paired with the glasses.

"Thirty-seven unread messages, eight missed calls. Six voicemails. Also, a software update needs to be applied," Halse said, peering over his cousin's shoulder at the screen.

"That isn't your business." Andrew crossed the room to take his phone from them, but at one percent, he hesitated to unplug it again. He was caught towering awkwardly over the seated men on the couch.

"Let me get this straight," Riley said. "You drove down here from Columbus, let your phone die, and haven't turned it on since yesterday?"

"Who am I supposed to be calling?" he said against his better judgment.

"I'm assuming whoever left you all those messages," Riley replied, incredulous.

Andrew fumbled for an answer he didn't have. *It doesn't matter* was staggeringly inappropriate, but also too close to the truth: *I don't care.* He had no excuse, aside from his weeks of constant shuttling between irritated exhaustion and dead numbness. His fingers tightened around the plastic casing.

Halse clapped a hand on Riley's shoulder and stood. "That's our cue to get out of here, kid. I need some help with the car before we go out tonight."

"Sam, I'm seeing Luca this afternoon when she gets off, I can't just—"

"You really can," Halse said.

The speed with which Sam hustled Riley into his shoes and out the front door was impressive. When the sudden silence of their departure descended on the living room, Andrew found himself standing stupidly next to the couch holding his phone. Halse had spared him from further interrogation, though he had probably been trying to save his cousin from an anticipated blowup. Andrew collapsed onto the warm impression of his roommate's ass on the couch and propped his phone on his knee to thumb the password in. The missed calls list—five from Del, two from his mother, one from a number he didn't recognize—he cleared. The voicemails he marked as read without listening. He could guess what was in them.

Most of the texts were from Del too. Instead of tackling those, he clicked through to his mother's thread, asking if he had made it safe. He typed back a brief *I'm fine, just busy.* Family brunch with him and Eddie, once a month for the past few years, was the extent of their usual interaction. Del probably spoke to his mom more than he did, and he briefly wished his mom luck with that, because Del's name on *his* phone had an impressive blue "24" in the alert bubble next to it. He halfheartedly scrolled through a wall of texts without reading. Another flick brought him to the bottom, where the last handful of messages read:

> Please please answer me
>
> You're such an asshole please text me back
>
> Are you dead
>
> This isn't funny I'm not laughing

He typed back, *I had to move in and take care of some estate stuff, please calm down.* Morbid curiosity about the paragraphs lingering hidden in the scroll was outweighed by the preemptive fatigue he felt just thinking about reading whatever she had thrown at him.

The phone vibrated in his hand a split second after: incoming call. He answered, "Hey."

"You're the most inconsiderate person I've ever met," Del said.

After eight years with Del, Andrew had a good sense of when he had pushed too far, and her brittle-bright tone was a strong indicator. But he had his own concerns to deal with. "Has it occurred to you that I might have some shit I need to work through right now?"

"I'm sure you do. So do I, you fucking asshole."

The line disconnected. Andrew sighed and pressed the phone to his forehead. Thirty seconds later, it rang again. He swiped to answer and didn't bother to say anything, just tapped speakerphone and set it on the table as he leaned back against the couch.

Cold with distance and fuzzy through magnification, Del said, "I thought you were dead. Literally, actually dead. I thought I was going to get a second call in a month from somebody telling me, *hey, that guy you care a lot about? He killed himself.*"

"I'm sorry," he said.

"No, you aren't."

Silence crackled between them. He slumped forward again, ran his hands through his hair, and stared at the phone display; seconds ticked past, then minutes. She was waiting for him to speak.

He said, "You don't need to worry. I wouldn't."

She laughed like crying. "Andrew, babe, I don't believe you.

Eddie spun all sorts of stories about how great he was doing. He didn't tell me something was wrong. Worse, he didn't tell you. So why would you tell me?"

He didn't do it warred with *he wouldn't have told you* and the impossibility of telling her what Eddie had been hiding from him—that fucking research—without exposing a host of other secrets.

So he said, "How am I supposed to argue with that?"

"Honestly, I don't know. Tell me the truth, are you okay down there?"

"I met his roommate, and the guy's cousin—the one with the WRX, I think." He paused. "He set me up a bedroom. It's a good bedroom. He was here without me for like six months, Del."

"Maybe you should leave the good memories, then, and stop looking to fill in the gaps. He's gone, you don't have to follow him into the trouble he made for you," she said.

Andrew flopped limp onto the couch, one foot hanging over the arm. The ceiling above him had a water stain at the corner; he stared at that 'til his eyes smarted. *He's gone*—she said it so simple, like a knife to his brain.

"Uncalled for," she said, quieter. "Sorry, I shouldn't have said that. I hate seeing him still doing this to you from . . . from beyond the fucking grave."

He couldn't stop himself from saying, "He would not have left me, Del. Not possible. I'm going to find out what happened to him."

"Andrew, come on," she said.

"You don't get it," he said.

"I get that he hurt you, and you're not accepting the truth about that," she said.

"I don't know what I think did happen, but I know it wasn't— *that*. He didn't fucking turn into a different person and kill himself for no reason without telling me a goddamn thing. He wouldn't do that to me." He ended on a choked note.

"He wasn't that good, Andrew," she said, her voice hitching to match, conflicting emotions swelling between them across the phone line. "He was always self-centered, and you know that. You can't argue with that. I don't think he thought about us at all."

He wasn't sure why he kept trying to convince other people, since their minds were made up from the start. To them, he knew, he came off as pathetic, distraught, grieving. They were all ready to let go, leave him in the deep end. He was alone with Eddie, or the remainder of him, as he'd always been.

He said, "I'll never be closer to him again than I am right now, and I'm staying."

"Shit. Please, this isn't good for you."

"Ain't going to convince me," he said.

"So you're going to go running straight down the same path he did, and *just see* what happens to you too?"

"I don't know what I'll do, but I'll figure it out," he admitted. He tapped off of speakerphone and held the phone to his face, warm like a broad palm. "I've got to go, Del. Take care of yourself."

"Don't hang up—"

He hung up.

———

The porch door opened behind Andrew as he stood at the sink, contemplating the pattern of ripples in his half-finished cup of tap water. The conversation with Del had left him numb and drowsy, and his new roommate's voice was slow to turn him around.

"Andrew, this is my girlfriend," Riley was saying as he turned to face them.

"Good to meet you," he blurted out, as stiff to his own ears as a telemarketer.

She smiled anyway. Kinked curls with a purple sheen the same color as her lipstick clouded around her face. The riotous combination of colors in her outfit—pink shoes, yellow blouse, white shorts—complemented her deep brown skin. She said, "Hi, sorry for the circumstances, but it's good to meet you. I'm Luca."

"We're dropping in for a minute, but I'm going out tonight," Riley said.

"All right," Andrew said, unsure why he was being told.

"I thought I'd apologize for Sam," he continued.

"Nothing to apologize for," Andrew said.

Luca laughed, leaning on the kitchen table with one hand on her hip. She said, "First time a person's ever come to that conclusion about Samuel Halse."

Riley shrugged expansively. "He can be a lot."

Andrew waved him off and sat his glass on the counter. "Seriously, it's fine. I'll be upstairs if you need me."

The sound of their murmuring conversation chased him up to Eddie's room, where he barricaded himself in against further socialization. The sinister spread of books and papers on the desk mocked him, still itching with betrayal. A cursory scan of the top layer of loose-leaf pieces revealed a printout about "the legend of the Bell witch," annotated heavily with doodles of birds and the occasional note on sensationalist reporting, and a tightly scrawled page of summaries of the old families in the state with a conspicuous blank under *Fulton*. There was also a barely legible set of purple-inked pages that appeared to be a short story about a haunted house. He figured that one had been an inebriated fancy of Eddie's.

Scooping those pages into a pile left Andrew with a stack of uneven sheets almost an inch thick. He stuck them on the shelf by the door and stacked a book on top to cover the handwriting. Without its explosion of research, the desk looked naked.

Someone knocked on the door and he said, exasperated, "What?"

"Got a second?"

It was Riley. There was no real out, other than a lie or pure petulance, so he said, "Yeah, do you need something?"

Riley opened the door and paused on the threshold. His chest rose on a long breath as his eyes swept the room, glance catching first on the rumpled sheets and second on Andrew, sprawled boneless in the chair.

"Before I head out, which courses did you register for? I thought we shared at least one, but I wasn't a hundred percent," he said.

"I'm not sure," Andrew admitted.

"It starts tomorrow, man. And it's Vanderbilt. I don't care if you're paying them out the ass, you'll have to at least try." Riley rapped his knuckles on the wall in a staccato pattern. The sound filled the quiet with a hollow, eerie echo. The moment he noticed, he stopped. "He bought the textbooks, at least, I think they're in your room."

"I'll get them," he said.

"I'm teaching a couple courses, so I'll be busy, but if you're lost or something . . ." He fidgeted again. "Okay, actually, want to come out with us tonight?"

Andrew fixed him with a baleful, exhausted glower. His patience had run out around the first time Del called him. Gathering up the remains of Eddie's unwanted research wasn't an improvement, nor was he pleased with the friends his companion had made, and that was without them prying into his business. Politeness was not his strong suit on a good day, and tonight he felt utterly raw.

"Message received—get some rest, dude," Riley said.

He disappeared again with a jingle of car keys and the thump of thick-soled boots on the stairs. A feminine laugh followed his exclamation below Andrew's feet, something that sounded like *let's get out of here*.

Andrew felt like he was losing traction around a steep curve, controlled for the moment in his cornering slide but half a second from a crash. The anticipation of impact tingled in his molars. On a masochistic impulse, he crossed the hall to his bedroom. Riley was right. The sole stack of books on the shelf seemed to be intended for his courses. He tucked them under his arm and took the university planner with his name written across the front in dripping silver paint-pen as well, trotting down the stairs to the living room. If he expected to keep hunting for the people Eddie had known, the places he'd been, the bullshit he'd spent his time on, he'd have to attend the program Eddie had selected for them. And also: breaking the habit of abiding by Eddie's plans was going to take longer than a handful of weeks. He still needed Eddie's direction, as much as remained to parse out.

Eddie was a hooligan, but an organized hooligan. His professors had found it charming enough to let him skate straight past the occasional missed deadline or lecture, a saving grace that Andrew often benefited from in turn. He would miss that luxury this time. Around midnight, after he had perused his course schedule and added relevant notes to the planner, his roommate staggered around the corner from the kitchen. Riley squinted against the glow of the overhead light and scuffed his forearm across his mouth. The center of balance he sought appeared to be skewed several inches to the left. Tires squealed from the alley, and the rattling roar of an engine sped off.

"Fucking Sam," Riley groaned.

His uneven stumble to the other couch ended when he caught his knee on the coffee table and pitched over it in a heap, rolling onto the floor on his back. The groan he let out was feeble. Andrew slapped the planner onto the table and leaned around to get a glimpse of his face. An unflattering, hectic flush glowed under Riley's pale splotchy skin. His glasses were gone. Either he'd changed before he left for the night, or they'd gotten lost in the interim. Andrew watched him fumble with the lacing on his boots long enough to get frustrated and start to curse, low and involved. He let that procedure continue until it crossed the line into pathetic before sliding into a crouch next to Riley and tugging the laces loose from the hooks. Riley covered his face with his hands, laughing, then spread his fingers to watch while Andrew pulled his boots off.

"I have to teach in the morning," he slurred. "This is dumb. Sorry."

Something about seeing a stupid, plastered boy laid out on a hardwood floor, regretful but no less pleased with himself, set Andrew back in time. In the better version of their lives that he didn't get to have, Eddie would've been getting the other boot, or throwing up over the porch railing. He missed him with fierce pain. The time-dislocation softened his spiny edges for a vulnerable moment.

"C'mon," Andrew said.

Riley hooked an arm around his shoulders and he levered them both up, catching what felt like fifteen separate elbows and knees in the process of forcing him up the stairs. He deposited him on the edge of the bathtub.

Riley said, "Get out, I need to piss."

Andrew had no intention of helping him with that. He waited outside the closed bathroom door until the toilet flushed and Riley slouched into the hall, using the wall for leverage.

"You got it from here?" he asked.

"Thanks, yeah, thanks. Hey—" Andrew cocked his head at the change in tone: clumsy with attempted delicacy. "I'm . . . I believe in it all, that dead people shit. Ed didn't tell you, I guess, but I'm on board. I don't think it's weird what you guys are into. Fuck Sam, anyway. Let me help you."

The air dropped out of Andrew's lungs.

Eddie had told Riley about them, about *him*. That was much worse than doing the research. They'd never even told Del—Del, who they'd known for eight years, who they'd each fucked and stopped fucking and once halfway tried to live with—but Eddie had come home south, picked up a kid who liked punk music and had a good car, and spilled their business like cheap beer. He'd shared their secrets while he kept Andrew waiting alone, then left him that way for good.

"Fuck off," he said, and slammed Eddie's bedroom door behind him.

4

The Mazda was gone by the time Andrew came downstairs the next day, saving him from having to address their nettling interaction the night before. He'd slept propped in the office chair wrapped in the comforter, and though it wasn't restful, he hadn't been treated to another morbid visitation. Time stretched strange and compulsive as he paced the corridors of the house on Capitol, making the circuit of rooms on repeat. Waiting for something to change, maybe. Once he had that thought, he shoved out the door and yanked it shut behind him. He could sit in Eddie's chair forever, but it wouldn't bring him home.

Routine was routine, regardless of the campus underfoot. He located a parking garage, loaded the school map on his phone, and set off for his first course with fifteen minutes to spare. Two on Monday and one on Thursday—an introduction to the program, then two subject courses, including a seminar on American contemporary music. The tiniest bubble of interest welled up when he considered it. He'd written his undergraduate thesis on murder ballads and folk-country, used that same thesis for his admissions writing sample, and had some intention of continuing with the research when he arrived. He'd cared about music, once, though he no longer had access to the emotion, which felt like it had happened inside a different person a long time ago.

The trees out front of Vanderbilt's three-story main hall cast inviting breeze-swayed shadows across the sidewalk and the stone staircases. The building carried a weight of age and respectability, something timeless that made him think of Eddie—bounded in his wildness, hunger that had never known privation. Old money, come home to roost. Eddie had always been the one with the passionate curiosity that drove them to college and more college. Andrew made a decent student, but his skill was first and foremost in adopting the directions Eddie gave him with equal parts dedication and cleverness. Eddie was gone, but he'd left a path for Andrew to follow, and that path might hold an answer to the questions he wasn't sure how to begin asking. Sticking to his set track wasn't a question of *want*.

The first course, his introduction, was slow and full of other first-term students. The professor didn't give any indication of knowing him by name or reputation, for which he was almost painfully grateful, and so he passed the time scribbling nonsense in his notebook and watching his classmates attempt to get a feel for each other. The cohort system seemed to be strongly encouraged, but he didn't see much of a point in learning these people; they hadn't been here with Eddie. None of them had anything to offer him. The second course, an hour later, was a literature seminar. When Andrew entered the room, three people were already there: two white women and a Black man, who was sitting on top of a desk near the front with his feet on the chair. He was smiling at his classmates, a blonde and a redhead, and the tail end of his sentence was, ". . . so I'm hoping the break went better for you guys."

The whole group turned to the sound when Andrew dropped his bag on a desk and slid into the chair. The man wore translucent silver acetate glasses that stood in handsome relief against his brown skin; his meticulously edged fade paired with short locs swept to the left on top. Andrew recognized the clean-shaven, aggressively square line of his jaw and polite smile from Eddie's photographic semi-essays on his life at Vanderbilt: the peer mentor, West.

The man lifted a hand in a desultory wave and said, "Hi, stranger."

"Hey," he said, unsure how to continue.

"This is Amy and this is Michelle." He nodded to the respective women.

"I'm a second-year, master's track," Amy said.

Michelle offered, "Second-year Ph.D."

"Good to meet you. I'm Andrew Blur."

Recognition dawned over the man's face and widened his eyes. He said, "I'm Thom West, sixth-year Ph.D.—"

Andrew cut him off. "Eddie's friend, yeah. Thought I recognized you."

"His peer mentor, and yours too. I didn't see you at the orientation, I wasn't sure if you'd come or deferred to spring." West bit his lip after he spoke, wincing at the implications of bringing up deferral. The two women watched with imperfectly concealed curiosity and pity. When Andrew didn't speak, he continued. "I ended up assigned to you both, thanks to our shared areas of interest. American Studies, research base in cultures of the Appalachian South, right?"

Eddie's Southern gothics. Andrew pursed his mouth. "I'm not so sure."

"Yeah, that's fair, totally. There's time to decide later. But we should trade numbers—I sent you a couple emails last week about setting up our first official meeting."

"Hadn't checked it," he said.

"I gathered," West said with the slightest edge of a grin, attempting to draw him out. "It's my job to get you acquainted with campus, the faculty, the process, all that stuff, so we should definitely set that up sooner rather than later."

Thom West had known Eddie too. Andrew racked his brain for more memories of the man in passing, and thought Eddie had mentioned a once-per-week beer meeting. More people had filed into the room while they spoke, taking seats in fits and starts, and some of them seemed to know each other. Conversations sprang up like small mushrooms after rain.

"Give me your number," Andrew said.

West hopped off of his desk, the pressed creases of his heather-grey slacks pulling tight over his thighs, and took a seat sideways in the desk next to Andrew's. "Here." He offered his phone. "Just put it in."

Andrew tapped the screen a few times, saved the contact, and handed it over. West immediately placed a call, and Andrew held up his phone to show it ringing. Satisfied, West nudged the toe of his leather boot against the side of Andrew's battered high-tops.

"Thanks," he said. "We should've met already, so, we could get something to eat after class lets out? I'll show you around the campus, do my job and all that. Make up for lost time."

"I guess you and Eddie spent a lot of time doing that?"

West said, "Should've done more, probably. He—"

"Well surprise, surprise," Riley said from behind him. He waltzed around the edge of their desks and sat on the one next to Andrew, dropping a proprietary elbow on his shoulder. The point of bone dug in. "We're all in this one together, looks like."

West's lemon-sucking face put wrinkles at the sides of his eyes. He lifted his phone in a farewell gesture and strode to the front of the room to take his seat with the women he knew, who rekindled their conversation after a few awkward glances in Riley's direction. Andrew shrugged off the weight of Riley's arm and the other boy kicked his heel against the metal leg of the desk.

"He doesn't care for me," he said under his breath.

Understatement, Andrew thought. "Eddie said he was kind of uptight, but all right otherwise."

"Well, West thought Ed was a nice rich boy who fell in with some nasty trailer trash," he said.

Riley stared across the room at West, radiating a dislike that Andrew found out of character, despite having known him for less than four days. West ignored him performatively with a dignified, almost effete slouch in his direction. The professor arrived, an older man with a grizzled beard and a salmon polo shirt. Andrew turned his attention to the class introduction, then the lecture, maintaining haphazard interest. When the professor dismissed them, he stood to go and found himself bracketed by

Riley and West. Bristling irritation radiated from his roommate and sloughed off of West's frown. A thread of curiosity twanged in Andrew. The two had bad blood, obviously, and the optics weren't great.

Eddie hadn't mentioned any of that, either.

"We're getting something to eat, then?" West asked, smile pleasant but chilly.

"If you'd rather, Sam's putting something together later." The lift of Riley's chin made an aggressive invitation. Andrew wasn't sure which of them it was directed to, or what the invitation implied. "He's grilling out at his place."

"Nah, I'm all right," Andrew said to his roommate as he ducked his head under his bag strap.

"Sure thing," Riley said. He clasped West's unwilling hand, the pair of them mismatched in stature but not disdain. Seeing his roommate standing with a colleague and wearing his teaching clothes—a black button-up and tan trousers that ended above a neat pair of grey suede Nikes—made his age jump from *young punk* to some indeterminate number in the mid-twenties. Riley was just releasing West's hand from a bruising grasp when he said, "Catch you at home later, then."

West waited for him to leave before he said, "So you're living with him."

"I inherited him along with the house."

"I see."

West didn't have to say it for Andrew to grasp the implication: *you could fix that.*

"Do you have some sort of mentor-intro speech for me?"

West grimaced and swung his own backpack over his shoulders. "Less a speech, more a conversation."

Andrew's messenger bag thumped the outside of his thigh with each step across campus, fast to keep pace with West's longer stride up the student-crowded sidewalk of 23rd Avenue. At the next corner, West gestured to a glass-fronted modern sushi bar. Andrew nodded his agreement and followed the other man in. The restaurant was expansive and loud. One end of the bartop seating had two chairs, so they took them, bunched more closely than could comfortably accommodate broad shoulders and spread knees.

"All right, so," West said, once he'd shifted his chair to put his back to the man eating next to them. Andrew leaned against the tight corner his chair fit into, one arm on the bartop. "It feels a little weird to start with the usual get-to-know-each-other spiel, since Eddie talked so much about you in our one-on-ones, but I guess we still should. Most people call me West, I'm doing research on occult fiction and the Southern gothic incorporating critical race theory, and my master's degree was in English. Born and raised in Massachusetts. I've been at Vandy for six years, hope to defend . . . any time, really, would be good."

Andrew opened his mouth to respond to the rote list of facts, but the waitress arrived to take their drink orders. West made a gesture toward covering them on one check and ordered two pints of Asahi; Andrew scrambled to organize his thoughts. Eddie probably had a hell of a "name, research, interests" elevator pitch for himself, but he had nothing.

"I did my undergraduate thesis on murder ballads," he offered.

"Awesome," West said. He leaned forward in his seat, gazing over the rim of his frames. Andrew noted the glasses were either non-prescription or so weak they might as well not have been. Andrew caught the sympathetic expression softening his smile, and braced himself for its inevitable follow-up. Lo and behold, West continued: "I'm sorry to bring this up, but are you certain you're good to start this semester? There's a precedent for deferred entry, like to spring if you need it. Ed was a mid-term start himself. My whole gig is to prepare you for success, and I'm sort of worried. I guess I already feel like I know you."

What else should I be doing, he wanted to respond, but instead he said with clipped courtesy, "I'll be all right. It's better to be occupied."

"If you're sure," West said with a winsome grin that fell flat on Andrew's dry affect. "The most important person to introduce you to is Jane Troth, his advisor. She used to be the graduate director of the department and she does research in our area, plus her husband is visiting faculty in folklore studies. She's my chair."

Andrew recognized the name: Dr. Troth, whom Eddie had spoken of with a mixture of respect and irritation. He didn't adapt well to being monitored or checked up on, which a faculty advisor was bound to do.

"Had she worked with him much?" Andrew asked.

"I guess they met as often as he and I did," West said, flexing his hands and popping his wrists. "I hope you don't mind my saying how weird I feel right now. You're different from how he made you sound."

"Different how?"

"Less energetic, maybe, but that's fair. I'm plenty depressed, and he and I only met once a week for a few months," he said. "I can't imagine your loss."

Eddie's goading enthusiasm had always provoked Andrew into a sort of rolling sociability that he couldn't put his heart into now. He'd only agreed to dinner because Eddie had spent time with West, another person who might be able to fill in a handful of the blanks he held in his head. A working dinner, in another sense than West suspected. It was all he could think to do for the time being.

"He had a way of bringing that out in people," Andrew said once the pause dragged on too long.

West traced a thumb around the mouth of his water glass, brows furrowed.

"I wouldn't know. He didn't spend much time on campus, or with me, or with his other classmates except—you know, Sowell," he said.

"I don't know much about his spring semester," Andrew admitted.

"I'm not saying Sowell is a bad kid, don't get me wrong, but he's got some problems," West said.

Curiosity reared its head again, eager for the slightest hint. He asked, "What sort of problems?"

"The men he runs with, that crowd Eddie got himself caught up in too," West said haltingly. "A word of advice: those kinds of guys don't mess around down here, Andrew. I'm not sure how much is performance and how much is real, but I'd suggest staying out of their way. Focus on your studies, make decent friends, and avoid taking the risk."

Andrew's stomach flipped, sank. "What do you mean?"

"A few times I saw Ed come in with bruises on his face, or very fucked-up hungover, and that's not the sort of thing graduate students are accustomed to at our level. I didn't want to say something, but . . . then he did what he did." West took his glasses off and ground the heel of his hand against his right eye. He wore his stress like a designer jacket. "He wasn't having trouble in seminar, he was doing research he cared about, and he was excited about his best friend joining him in this program. He drank too much, and he kept getting up to mischief that made him miss class and go off for days at a time, but I never thought there was anything seriously wrong."

None of that struck Andrew as out of the ordinary—less trouble than he'd expected, from the seriousness of West's tone. Mischief was Eddie's personal passion, the one he barely kept separate from his academic or professional life by using the occasional grease of money and charm to smooth over his mistakes.

Andrew said, "That just sounds like Eddie's usual to me."

"But if all this"—West gestured in the direction of campus— "was what he wanted, and he was having a grand old time with his charity-case roommate, why would he do it? Something must've happened, and he wasn't around campus enough for it to have much to do with our program, though god knows the graduate school has issues."

I don't know what happened to him. Desperation clamped onto the base of Andrew's skull like a vise. This campus, its manicured lawns and posh students with man-buns and topsiders, spoke to one specific and strange part of Eddie that Andrew hadn't shared. He didn't belong here. Clammy shock-sweat broke out on his palms; he moved on instinct to push his chair out from the bar and escape.

West's warm hand closed around his wrist and he jolted backward at the stark surprise of touch, chair thunking against the wall.

"God, that was exceptionally dumb of me," West said.

"I should go," Andrew said.

"I won't bring it up again." Without his glasses, West's face looked younger, spattered with almost imperceptible freckles across his cheekbones. "We're at dinner, debriefing after the first day, and I barely know you. I'm out of line. Tragedy does weird things to people, I'm sorry."

The ill-timed return of the waitress with their beers forced him to keep his seat. When West ordered, he did too. The dinner passed in stilted half-silence, Andrew out of small talk and his mentor struggling to recover their previous momentum. He was relieved to part ways and head back to the garage, but he considered the question West had posed with a dull thrill. *Why'd he do it?* Clearly, Andrew wasn't the only one with questions, but he was the one best suited to find the right answers.

How, though, he wasn't sure. It made him feel hungry all over again, filled with a secondhand emptiness.

The glow of the fuel light caught his attention when the Challenger purred awake. He sighed out a curse and coasted out onto the main street to search for a gas station. Even his bullshit car had better mileage than this monster. At a stoplight, late summer dusk heady and open across the horizon, he rolled the windows down and slipped Eddie's abandoned flat bill over the messy tangle of his hair. The cap shaded his eyes, ever-so-slightly too loose. Gripping the wheel until the stitching dug into the grooves of his fingers eased the hectic feeling seeping out from underneath the suffocating expanse of his numbness.

When he pulled into the first gas station he saw, his heart kick-tripped at the handful of cars spread out between the pumps and the parking spaces, a motley mix of livid colors and svelte frames—a fox-body Mustang in an eggplant purple, a green Civic with ugly red rims. Boys with too much time on their hands lounged with eager eyes, the kind of crowd that didn't happen by accident. Andrew's palms were damp when he parked and shut the engine off.

The unmodified Challenger was worth as much as any two of their tuned cars put together. The lazy bragging luxury of that fact was briefly uncomfortable to Andrew. No one spoke to him as he swiped his card at the pump. He hadn't decided if he'd approach them first when someone called out, "Blur, you got insurance on that thing?"

He wasn't about to answer Sam Halse, leaning out the driver's side window of a gunmetal WRX with black trim and a huge dent in the quarter panel, to say *we shared the insurance*. When Andrew failed to respond, Halse opened his own door using the outside handle and ducked between the pumps to come prop his hip against the Challenger. He crossed his arms, the fluorescent lights casting harsh peaks over his knuckles.

"Didn't think I'd see this baby out again. Riley give you the heads-up?" Halse asked.

"No, honest-to-god accident," Andrew replied, watching the tank fill.

His thoughts stumbled and tripped over one another while Halse observed him, a looming figure at the corner of his eye. The supposed *rough crowd* West had directed him to avoid was gathered around him, but, caught flat-footed without a plan for engaging them, Andrew's strongest urge was to retreat—to regroup after the strain of his awkward dinner.

"Coming with us anyway?" Halse said with a grin and a flick to the brim of Andrew's hat that unseated it, drawing his attention along with a glare.

Andrew tugged the bill into place again. The fueling stopped with a click and he jiggled the nozzle to shake loose any drips. Halse ran a hand over the hood of the car, watching him out of the corner of his eye.

"Not tonight," he said.

"Soon, though," Halse replied with unwelcome surety, clapping a hand on Andrew's arm for one brief squeeze around his bicep before he strolled back to his own car. Over his shoulder he tossed a parting, "See you later."

When he revved his engine, someone else laughed, a high, wild sound. The WRX rolled out first and the rest scrambled quick behind him, tussling for a place in the pack.

Andrew watched taillights disappear into the growing dark. If Eddie had gotten himself into trouble, as West suggested, he had a feeling he knew where to find more of the same.

5

The next morning, when Andrew returned from his brief trip to the impound lot to retrieve his Supra, he found a sticky note on the coffee table next to a packed but unsmoked bowl. It read *home after 3pm-Riley* followed by what Andrew presumed was Riley's phone number. His roommate had come and gone in the gap of time he'd spent picking up the car, at least for long enough to make him a weird little peace offering—which he did accept, taking the petite green glass pipe in hand. Eddie tended toward more outré paraphernalia, so he assumed it belonged to Riley. The lighter on the table sputtered at the first two flicks before it caught; he burnt himself a lungful or two, smoking with syrup-slow huffs. No reason to rush. After he cashed the bowl, he slipped out his phone and entered the number to fire off a quick *hey it's Andrew* text.

Once again, his inbox had a number of missed calls and messages that a person more concerned with participating in his own life might've been ashamed of. Several were from unfamiliar numbers. He listened to two voicemails from the executor about the processing of the estate, one explaining the massive plot of land he now owned out in the goddamn country and the other inquiring, *would you prefer the taxes to be paid from your accounts directly?* Becoming a millionaire something close to overnight had made less of an impression on him than he expected, since it wasn't much different than when Eddie had given him free reign over his cards.

Most of the texts were contained to Del's ongoing thread; he wasn't prepared to explore that. As he dallied in the inbox, a response from Riley came through: *cool. text is the best way to reach me, i never check messenger me neither* he responded.

The conversation with West kept popping back into his head. He'd eyeballed the stack of Eddie's notebooks again before bed, but his whole brain shied away from the thought of digging through the other man's research on their—supernatural horseshit. Ugly memories and the high likelihood of provoking his erstwhile haunting to pay him another grueling visit lurked down that avenue. And aside from those notes, he still had one more person to track down on campus.

He fired off a message to West that felt stilted but workable: *Can you introduce me to Dr Troth this afternoon*

With no attempt to delay for propriety's sake, West responded immediately:

> Perfect timing, I was about to ask if you would be free to meet her. Today she mentioned she has something she was going to give to Ed, and thought you'd maybe be interested in it too.

> Okay, how about in an hour

> I'll confirm with her.

> Meet me in front of the humanities building?

> Sure

Meeting the advisor would fill out the main cast from Eddie's unsupervised months, though he had to assume Vanderbilt and its esteemed faculty had played little role in whatever violence had happened. If Andrew got the chance to leave Eddie's hideous excavations half-buried, all the better.

He hopped in his Supra for the trip and found a close spot to park, striding purposefully to the assigned meeting spot and settling on a concrete bench to wait for West. Students bustled around him like disorganized cats, yowling and chasing each other. He propped his forearms on his thighs. The sun beat on the nape of his neck. A tingle twitched his fingers, recalling the scorching leather wheel grip and the thud of his heart in his mouth.

"Andrew," West called out.

His cream button-up reflected a blinding amount of sun, open two buttons over a few inches of russet-brown chest. He strode confident through a crowd of underclassmen, sporting a hassled grin, his silver glasses absent. Andrew shied away from eye contact, drawn by the flash of a cuff earring at the top of his left ear. West offered his hand for a firm shake before leading Andrew into the building.

"Come on, she should still be in her office. I think she's tried to email you, but you haven't responded." The crisply air-conditioned lobby turned Andrew's prickle of sweat to sticky gum in an instant. West tapped the UP arrow with his thumb. "As your mentor: have you checked your email at all?"

Andrew said, "Sort of."

"Okay, please fix that," West said.

The elevator opened with a tinny ping. Andrew leaned against the rail, thumb in belt loop, while West punched the button for the top floor. The hush of the enclosed space amplified the sound of their breathing. The door dinged at them again on opening, a touch accusatory. Andrew followed West across the hall to a warren of offices. Three were open, the rest shut for the afternoon. West rapped on the frame of one with his knuckles and lounged against the doorjamb without crossing the unmarked boundary. His pose spoke of casual deference.

"Oh, come in," a woman said from beyond the frame's edge. "I wasn't sure if you'd make it. I have a doctor's appointment with my husband shortly, so we'll have to keep things brief."

"Of course, no worries. This is Andrew Blur—he had to drive over to meet you," West said, glancing over his shoulder to confirm that he hadn't lost his charge.

Andrew followed him inside an office cramped with stacks of

folders in front of overflowing bookshelves and chose one of two chairs that would've fit better in a doctor's office in the seventies. West propped his hip against a shelf beside the professor's desk. She sat tall in her executive chair, a pair of reading glasses on top of her head and white-threaded red hair flopped over one shoulder in a loose braid. Her papery pale skin had a pinkish flush. Prominent collarbones winged above the scooped neck of her pine-green blouse, accented with a gold ring on a thin matching chain. She was understated but elegant; the hand she offered Andrew was thin and long-fingered.

"It's good to meet you, Mr. Blur—or may I call you Andrew?" she said.

"Andrew's fine," he replied.

"Andrew, then. First and foremost, I'd like to offer my condolences. I knew Edward as a fantastic student in the short time I had with him, and we're all grieving his loss."

"We are," West said, unobtrusively warm.

"Thanks," Andrew replied.

"How are you finding your first week? Has Thom been taking good care of you?" she asked.

Andrew caught West's eye and said, "As much as he's able."

She rested her wrists on the edge of the desk and leaned into the grasp of her office chair. Her gaze weighed him. He bet she found him lacking, but he affected ease, waiting for her to continue. What could she possibly have to give him?

She continued, "I understand this conversation will be difficult for you, and please let me know if you'd like to wait, but I thought it would be best if we got the messiest bits out of the way?"

"Which bits are those?" Andrew asked.

"To be frank, I wanted to discuss whether you intend to continue Edward's research into regional occult folklore, as he'd said it was an interest you both shared and would be pursuing together," Troth said. Andrew's jaw clenched in reflex; her eyebrows pinched in response, empathetic but cool. "I imagine it's stressful to consider following in that same direction right now, and possibly more so to think about doing anything else. So, please know that I'm your advocate. I'm still assigned as your advisor, but if your needs lead you to another faculty member, I'll be available to assist with that as well."

"I hadn't decided," Andrew managed.

Regional occult folklore. In truth, he'd begun to put the question of research out of his mind as soon as he met the raucous crowd Eddie had fallen into. The boys were the more obvious threat, and the scholarship made him more uncomfortable. He'd rather not face those notebooks with their secrets or the haunt stuck to the underside of his shadow, waiting for his guard to slip and allow it purchase. Letting his thoughts so much as drift in that direction made his heart stutter.

Troth continued, "I gathered a few texts from my partner's collection, and some from other colleagues, for Edward. Would you like to take them with you for now, and see if you're able to work with them?"

The ensuing silence pressed at his bones. West shifted, recrossing his arms as Troth waited for his response. Andrew's phone vibrated between his ass and the chair, and he jerked, saying, "Okay, sure."

Troth stood and looped the handle of a cloth tote sitting next to the desk over her wrist. When she lifted it, the sides of the bag strained with book-edges. "Here," she said. Andrew took it from her. "No expectations, of course, but it'd be a shame to see his work go to waste. His exploration of local supernatural folklore was already going in unique directions. There's so little source material that speaks to it sufficiently; he would've been able to publish. I was eager to see where it went."

Andrew stood as well, the weight of the books dragging his shoulder off-center. The bag thumped against his calf. West said, "He was doing some impressive fieldwork for a first-year, that's for sure."

"Certainly," Troth agreed.

"Fieldwork?" Andrew asked, unsure of their meaning.

West and Troth shared an impenetrable glance. Their delicate dance of implication and tradition remained alien to him, and it pulled the air out of the room. West's whole posture had changed in the presence of Dr. Troth, and Andrew figured his should've too, but he didn't precisely know how. He felt exposed by the expectations sailing over his head, close enough to prickle his scalp but beyond his reach.

"Yes, fieldwork. Over the summer he was collecting oral traditions from families in the area with significant histories," she said. "He started with me. The Troths have lived outside the Nashville area for seven generations. It's the reason I became involved in his research; it appealed to me, the way his work joined the Southern gothic and the ethnographic."

"Weren't you both originally from over on the route to Townsend?" West asked.

Another choked response crawled out of Andrew while cold sweat broke out under his armpits: "Yeah. Grew up outside town, haven't gone back."

"Edward said that his research was spurred by his own, how did he describe it, *spooky* childhood experience in the hollers," Troth said, her smile edged with invitation. Andrew's lips glued themselves together, chapped and sticky. No one was supposed to know about those childhood experiences, and "spooky" didn't begin to cover the horror crawling out of his memories like an oozing swamp. She carried on: "It's a solid foundation for you to build from, since you do share it."

"That was his business," he forced himself to say over the pounding of his pulse in his ears. The corners of the books bit into his shin again as he stepped toward the door. "Thanks. I've got somewhere to be."

"Andrew," West said, rising startled from his slouch near the door.

He ducked past the other man without acknowledgement. He

wasn't running, but he was close. His shoes slapped on the tiles. He burst into the stairwell and slammed the door behind him with both hands. The cold metal against his forehead, the quiet of the enclosed concrete staircases: he zeroed in on those things, those things alone, then on the strap of the cloth bag biting into his wrist. White specks floated at the corners of his vision. *I don't want to be here.* He swallowed the bitter acid crawling up his throat. Fuck going to class after that.

————

Riley's modest pipe sat on the coffee table in the quiet of the abandoned house, but his weed was nowhere to be seen. Andrew's lungs squeezed around nothing in a choking cramp. Troth's careless conjuring of the night of the caverns—*childhood experiences, goddamn*—had kicked his head crooked, especially with the dream so close to the surface after the bleak nights in Eddie's room. Sunlight warmed the stretched length of his calves on the couch, pouring through the front room's big windows, as he hunched over his phone. The air conditioner hummed along, struggling to keep pace with the dog days. His thumb hovered over the screen before he flicked it to scroll down and selected his thread with Eddie. The penultimate messages from August 6th, at 3:32 in the morning, read:

come home

i'll be waiting

And just below, his unknowing response:

keep it together I'll be there soon

A drag of his finger spun the thread further into the past, stopping on a handful of messages that he heard in Eddie's voice:

what're you doing right now biiiiiitch

I hope you're getting lit

but maybe not without me hmmmm not
too lit

are you already drunk

I mean of course

sam and riley treat a boy right

The photo he'd sent was blurred, taken at an outdoor table on a second-floor deck with fairylights strung up all around, which threw the shading off something fierce. Eddie had turned his chair and lifted the phone to an exaggerated selfie angle above his face, grinning so hard his eyes narrowed, shaggy curls askew, streaked with pale grey washout dye that had already disappeared by his funeral a month later. On the opposite side of the table Riley held a tall glass in one hand, the other tilting the straw to his half-open mouth, startled, no glasses.

Halse wasn't startled. He made strong, smirking eye contact with the camera—sprawled in his chair, one arm hooked over the back, T-shirt pulled tight over his full chest and the white lights casting a deep shadow into the divot of his collarbone. The table between them was littered with empty glasses and one sad tipped-over PBR tallboy. Andrew swallowed the knot in his throat. Eddie's next text just said *cmere,* followed by Andrew's response, *would if I could asshole.* He imagined the edge of a laugh in Eddie's voice as he teased, endlessly, always fucking with him. It was unfathomable that he would've abandoned Andrew of his own volition. The brackish wrist-cut gore in his haunted dreams remained a fact without explanation.

What next, he thought.

No classes for the afternoon. No one prodding him to come with them or speak to them or do things for them; no next steps implied in Eddie's leavings; no role to step into or space to inhabit. All he had were questions, with no idea how to begin looking for answers; he oscillated between a frantic crush of ignorance and a hollow exhaustion that turned him to stone. The combination of adrenaline crash and lack of direction provoked a miserable shiver. *What next?*

A wellspring of need dragged him up the stairs with the grace of a zombie. He froze as he turned the landing's corner. One sheet of notebook paper, filled top to bottom with purple gel pen, sat on the step above him. The end fluttered, dangling. He tracked the spilled sheets in visual slow-motion, skin crawling, to the point where the trail disappeared into Eddie's room. The door was still closed. The thought of sidestepping the pages and giving them his back flipped Andrew's nerves on end, so he gathered them as he ascended the final steps.

The floor of the room was no better. The book he'd used as a paperweight stuck out from under the edge of the bed as if someone had thrown it there. Pages were scattered in a whirlwind around the room, chaotic except for the trail that led out to the hall with utter disregard for the door—as if an immaterial hand had dragged the remaining sheets out like a trail of breadcrumbs to lead him inside. Andrew's shuddering hands collected the mess in a much messier pile than before. He cast around for a better hiding spot, and ended up stuffing it under a stack of towels in the dim, doorless walk-in closet.

How would a normal person explain that? *Just the wind,* he lied to himself. He knew better, and his knowledge had the taste of fear. Revenants appreciated the vital spice of terror when leeched from the living. If he hadn't been shaken before, he was now. Message received. The creature was not gone, nor resting.

He knelt next to the bed on instinct and reached beneath. Eddie only had one hiding place, it never changed. Sure enough, the antique wooden box carved with birds he'd gotten Eddie for his nineteenth birthday was right where he expected it to be. Andrew opened the box on its gliding, well-oiled hinges and snagged the respectable Ziploc full of weed from its nest amid Eddie's pipe and accoutrements. On second thought, Andrew tapped the grinder, found its catch partially full, and carried it with him to the living room as well. The bedroom felt a bit too—occupied.

The tan leather couch *whumped* with how hard he fell on it. Distracted and distraught, he packed himself a bowl and reclined against the arm, right foot on the cushions and the other trailing on the floor. The stretch ached in his hips. After the bowl burned to ash, he set it aside and lifted his arm overhead. His shirt rode up and his hip bones stood out like small hills, drawing an artificial holler between them above the band of his briefs. He turned his marked wrist to and fro, flexing a loose fist. The round dots of faded blue-black ink were uneven, a poor imitation of an organized line. Where the loop should've joined at the knob of his wrist, one dot overlapped another in a crooked Venn diagram. The glossy healing patches of the cold burns—the grave-touch—were almost gone.

Andrew remembered holding Eddie's wrist on his lap with his legs crossed and one knee propped against the sliding glass door of their postcard-sized campus apartment balcony in Columbus. The last cigarette drifted between them for a puff each, methodically fair. Eddie had bought the ink, bundled a set of needles together with string and electrical tape, then sterilized them with peroxide from the sparsely stocked medicine cabinet. Andrew finished off the cigarette and flicked it from the edge of the balcony.

Eddie locked eyes with him, grinning his best wolf's grin. Andrew fumbled for the needles sitting on a saucer at his knee, unable to unlock their gazes, not even to watch the first stab of ink. The corners of Eddie's smile flinched, eyes flicking down, then his mouth opened a fraction. His wrist twitched in Andrew's grip.

"Ouch," Eddie whispered.

"No shit," Andrew said. He inspected the welling spots of blood, a lively ruby red.

Eddie flexed his fist, forearm muscles bunching. "Can't back out now."

"Nope," he responded.

Finishing Eddie's bracelet tattoo took the better part of an hour; as soon as the last dot was fully marked, they smeared antibacterial ointment across the oozing mess of lymph and ink and traded places. Andrew offered his wrist, palm-up, his fingertips catching on the hem of Eddie's shorts. Eddie laced fingers through his and bent his hand over his thigh as he readied the needles, holding them like a fat pencil. The first poke pierced his flesh with a mix of ink and Eddie's blood, Andrew hissing long and loud through it and the next few as well. Eddie sat half in light and half in shadow, glancing up at him periodically while he worked, serious and quiet with his hands trembling minutely. There was something momentous, ritualistic, about the marking that surpassed the six beers, the bragging game that had led to *give me a tattoo, no seriously, we should do our first ones together.*

Del had broken up with Andrew the next day, and hadn't spoken to either of them for two weeks.

In the house on Capitol Street, Andrew touched the faded marks, stroked them and squeezed his own wrist in an unforgiving loop. He drifted, high enough to blur his vision, into a dream about a stag's skull rimed with lichen, hot mud between his toes. He buried himself in the dirt, digging his hands into the flesh of the land, filling his mouth and his nostrils and his veins up to bursting. If he dug deep enough, he might find—

He woke gasping, suffocating and disoriented, to the increasingly familiar slam of the front door. His fingernails ached with the pressure of digging into the leather couch. The dreams hadn't been so bad, so fucking *persistent,* up north. He wasn't sure he had it in him to blame that on coincidence. Adrenaline slammed his heart against his ribs, pulse thumping in his eyes.

"Andrew," Riley said abruptly, too loud.

"What?" he snapped, putting his face in both hands and swinging himself upright into a seated position on the couch.

"Uh, I just—" Riley paused and took a fortifying breath. "I noticed your Supra's out front, and it's got a bunch of your stuff in it. Do you need help bringing it in?"

"Shit," he said.

6

The ghost of his spectacular high lingered as a throb in his temples. The structural integrity of his skin was questionable; the inside of his head swam with partial memories and rootless homesickness. He dug his thumbs against the edges of his orbital bones and nodded to his hovering roommate. When he stood, he checked his phone out of habit and saw seven unread messages. He thumbed through them while descending the front stairs with Riley. Del had sent him a few, the last of which was *Are you going to pretend I'm dead too? Just let me know so I can set my expectations.* He released a controlled smoker's breath through his nose and responded, *stop doing this shit Del you know I hate it.*

An unsaved number had texted him as well, two messages: *Sup?* and *You there*

He frowned and tucked the phone back in his pocket to unlock the car. In the front seat, the spider plant Del had passed off on him sat dead from the heat, withered and limp. The symbolism was unpleasant. Riley hmm-ed at it and said, "Oops."

Between the two of them, garbage bags full of clothes strung over their wrists and crates of sundries in arm, the process took less than ten minutes. Andrew dropped his last load in the foyer and watched Riley stagger up the steps, loaded to his chin with boxes of books. The muscles of his arms strained, lengthened. Veins bulged at his wrists and the peak of his biceps. His roommate was sunset-glowing and all-American, a tightly bundled set of contradictions, same as all the young men Andrew had ever known, but none of those contradictions spoke to West's raw and obvious dislike. *Charity case,* he'd called him. Andrew didn't much appreciate that, but he wasn't comfortable with Riley either, given West's observation about the boys he ran with. The box thumped to the floor as Riley grunted with the effort.

Abruptly, Andrew asked, "Why help me?"

Riley sighed once, like catching his breath, and angled himself to face away from Andrew, scrubbing one hand through his sweat-spangled blond undercut bristle. The path of his gaze swept past the open door to land somewhere on the street.

"Because," Riley said finally. "He was my friend."

"But I'm not," Andrew said.

The response was weighed slow, one word at a time: "If he was here, we would've been. I don't see a reason not to be. I owe him that much, at least."

The statement hung in the air. Without another word, he followed Riley into the kitchen and they each got a glass of water. The tension remained, intimate and unfamiliar, while they cooled off together in the AC. For the first time, Andrew felt like he was co-habiting with Riley, as if he'd chosen his roommate and not simply inherited him.

Riley sat his empty glass on the table and said, "I'm thinking of how to ask you something, but I don't know how to say it."

Andrew braced his lower back on the edge of the sink, angled toward him, facing-without-facing. A few feet from them, above their heads, secrets within secrets in Eddie's messy scrawl sat stuffed under a pile of towels. How much did Riley know about what Eddie had been doing?

Andrew said, "Then maybe don't ask."

"Do you blame us for what he did?"

Andrew jerked, splashing himself and almost dropping his cup. Riley's narrow chest rose and fell with shallow breaths, his face angled to stare out the window instead of at Andrew. His jaw muscles braced tight like he expected a blow, literal or metaphorical.

"Should I," Andrew said. He meant for it to be a question, but it sounded more like a charge.

Keep out of the fucking crowd he got into, he rephrased in his head. Riley's crowd—Halse's crowd. If Eddie's lark of attending Vanderbilt and his burgeoning research posed no real threat, poisonous and horrible as it was for him to pursue without telling Andrew, then it had to be something else. Maybe something like the kind of trouble that tagged along after boys with fast cars and bad habits, who might protect themselves first and their new friend second if trouble arose.

Looking away, unable to see Andrew's control fraying thread by thread, Riley answered: "Maybe, fuck. I might. We're not great people, and I didn't even notice there was something wrong with him."

Riley thought he'd killed himself too. Andrew grunted with the impact of the words. The vertigo of his high returned with a vengeance as he moved to push past Riley, unable to scrounge up the right words. As he reached for the handle of the porch door, a hand fisted in his shirt. He whirled, furious. His better judgment shut off, leaving him standing in a kitchen that wasn't really his, in the heart of a place he'd tried to leave behind forever, thinking *is it your fault he's dead?* at a stranger who wanted to be his friend.

Andrew knocked the offending arm wide, the impact stinging his shoulder, and hauled his fist back to strike. But Riley caught the front of his shirt and shoved him against the fridge with a bone-jarring impact. The breath wheezed from his lungs. Riley immediately took three staggering steps toward the living room, hand held up for a pause. He scrubbed at his cheek with the other arm. Andrew's brain snapped into his body as he realized Riley had silent tears running from the corners of his eyes.

"No harm, no foul," Riley said with a wobble. "Shouldn't have laid hands on you. I'll go."

Andrew crouched where he stood as Riley left the kitchen. The front door slammed. A moment later, the Mazda coughed to life and growled into the distance. The question of who to blame, himself or the world or their lifetime of ghosts or the other boys Eddie had given his time, bared endless rows of teeth. Andrew snarled fingers into his hair and yanked until his scalp sang. He had come south certain of two things: first, that Eddie would not have killed himself on purpose. Second, that it had to be someone else's fault, though the question of *how* strained his credulity. His surety remained, but his questions had multiplied exponentially.

———

Maybe to punish himself, pacing the ground floor of the house while the sun set with mounting pressure outside, he checked Del's response to his previous text. The message read: *Hate being called out or hate being bothered? Because if I didn't know better I'd say you're cutting me out for fun.*

> it isn't for fun. I'm not cutting you out. you have your own life up there to deal with and I'm sorting out his business here

A response came back almost as soon as he finished:

> Okay, fine. Sorry, I didn't think Eddie was the sole reason we talked, but I guess I was wrong.

> you're being unfair

> And you're being a complete fuck

Andrew ground his teeth. Now that they'd come home, the eight years he and Eddie had spent in Columbus felt like the dream. He was already picking up Eddie's shit habits, acting as if *here* was where he belonged instead of *there*—or anywhere else. Home was where Eddie was; home was nowhere, now. Except the heat and the smells and the cicada-filled nights pulled him straight to his childhood, the summer before Eddie's parents died, the summer after the cavern. The imaginary fist he kept clenched around the haunted, *haunting* presence in his chest loosened bit by bit the longer he stuck around Nashville, and those cracks let out something other than light. He pictured a cold darkness seeping out, dripping free of the confines where it belonged, almost as tangible as the blood pulsing in his veins. He couldn't stand to let Eddie's research pry that fist any further open.

The phone lit up with another message. Del had continued: *Just because he was the only thing you ever gave a shit about doesn't mean that other people don't care about you.*

As his thumb hovered over the keyboard, weighing a diplomatic response against the lit fuse of irritation that pushed him to say something he couldn't take back, the unsaved number buzzed in twice more. *Text me back* and *Sun's down have some fun?*

"Who the fuck," he muttered.

He had one good guess and he didn't care to pursue that in the middle of the endless argument with Del. To fortify himself, he stole the near-finished bottle of bourbon from the kitchen counter and mounted the stairs, tapping the CALL button before he second-guessed himself.

She answered immediately. "Yeah?"

"Hey," he said.

"Hey yourself," she replied, the opposite of lighthearted. Andrew sat on the edge of Eddie's bed and took a swig from the bottle that burned his sinuses. "Did you call for a reason?"

"Yeah, because you're upset."

"Bullshit."

The sound of her breath on the other end of the line filled the silence. *Which of us did you love best,* he almost asked, but he knew the answer: no one who'd met them both could prefer him over Eddie. Even he didn't. Del should've given up on them both. So instead he murmured, "Because I'm upset."

"Bingo," Del said. He resented, childishly, the exhaustion he heard. "I figured you needed someone to talk to, whether or not

I felt like talking to you right now. Why come back to me? That crew he found getting to you or something?"

"I don't know, maybe," he said.

She paused, then started in. "Or is it the fantasy where you find a culprit, someone else you can blame for all this? Do you think someone else cut his wrists, Andrew, really? Is it starting to sink in that Eddie was just selfish, that he *abandoned*—"

Andrew hung up on her. *Do you think someone else cut his wrists,* said with such utter contempt, as if by chasing that possibility he was lying to himself about the person Eddie had been. But how was it any more implausible than offing himself out of the blue? The screen accused him with another incoming call, but he ignored it.

Their other friends hadn't tried to contact him. Del was the last straggler. He wondered if she hated him, and if he deserved it; she'd have been better off without their dead weight dragging at her heels, long after their frosty breakup as freshmen at OSU. He knew that the person he'd been with Eddie wasn't the person he would be without him, and neither version ultimately had much to offer Del. He tipped the bottle back, bitter and burning, for two short swallows. As he leaned to set the bourbon on the nightstand, he noticed it: the notebook lay open at the mouth of the closet, papers on top of it, like his hidden stack had been pettily upended.

Teeth bared, he thumped the bottle onto the floor. One more time, he scooped the papers and the notebook up, open to a page that began mid-sentence: *haunts are mediocre til you feed them & then you've got a fucking problem, moral of the story.* Disturbingly direct. He flipped it shut one-handed. The phone buzzed behind him again. He burst out, "Fuck, leave me alone!" With Eddie's notes in his other hand, he grabbed the phone from the bed and scrolled through his texts—a handful of apologies from Del, as he expected, but more from the unknown number.

> I thought Riley said you were treating him fine
>
> Don't make me fuck you up
>
> Poor you sure but you're walking a fine line here
>
> Riley says it's his fault but maybe you just need to get out of that fucking house for a night

The phone creaked in his fist, plastic protesting his grip. Not so unknown, after all, Halse taking up for his cousin and getting in where he didn't need to be. Another message flicked into the inbox, saying, *I'll ask you again: come out with us.*

Andrew dropped the phone on the end table, nerves skittering. *Don't make me fuck you up* was a hell of a thing to say to him, a total stranger. The sawed-through slashes on Eddie's wrists had bisected his tattoo; even if Andrew swallowed the suggestion that he'd been abandoned, Eddie wouldn't disrespect him so completely. *Do you think someone else cut his wrists?* Another man might, though, maybe someone like Sam Halse—for reasons Andrew couldn't begin to guess. All he knew of him was his brash reputation and the contained fury in his texts.

The dregs of bourbon called for him and he inverted the bottle, gagging down the last mouthful with eyes damp from the strain. His stomach rolled once in dizzy protest. Putting his fist straight through the drywall next to the closet door might have satisfied him, but he resisted the urge as he kicked the fallen stack of towels into the corner to unearth the remaining loose pages. One problem at a time.

"Stop doing this shit," he said.

His fingertips landed on a sheet of paper at the same second a horror-movie creak from behind electrified the hair on his arms. The bedroom door latched itself shut with a quiet click and the scalded patch on his tattoo shone in the dim light: a reminder for him, especially around these parts, that it was never just the wind. Foolish to pretend otherwise, for even a second. He braced his wrist on the doorjamb and sat on his heels, stone still with his face tucked against the crook of his elbow to hide. *It isn't him. It isn't really him.*

Floorboards creaked scant inches to his left, but he refused to lift his head and look. He wasn't asleep; he wasn't on the cusp of sleep; he was awake. Manifestations this physical were not supposed to happen while he was awake, gloaming light shining through the big bold windows in streaks of red-gold, but Eddie had always been an exception to the rules. *Don't,* he thought, but he reacted instinctively to the first brush across the knobs of his spine with a yearning, flexing shudder.

An icy burning gripped the back of his neck in the rough outline of fingers, their shape more familiar than his face in the mirror. Against good judgment and survival instinct he leaned into the too-solid hold. It hurt, but he missed that touch so much, even this noxious remnant.

"Stop," he whispered again.

The papers rustled along their edges. Crouching in the hidden hollow of the closet, scruffed by the revenant that dogged his heels, he felt terribly and paradoxically alive. Rank breath drifted past his ear and cheek. The punishing grip pushed until his head bowed forward, forcing him to stare unseeing at his shoes, but the haunt kept going. It pushed until his skin chafed and his vertebra cracked, until the boundaries between its false flesh and his skin gave out. The cold sank straight through the gagging constriction of his throat to the cavern of his chest, grasping at him from the inside out. Blood and dirt were all he tasted in his drooling mouth, choked on the phantom's invasive presence. His first sleep on native soil dredged itself up behind his eyes: wrists cut to exposed muscle, a frantic retreat from the fact of death. He echoed the vision's desperate call for survival: *I am awake I am awake I am awake—*

The loud rattle of his phone vibrating on the wooden table

pierced the film of the waking nightmare. The revenant disappeared as if a switch had flipped. He gasped like he was breaking the surface of a swimming hole and fell back onto his ass.

"Jesus fuck, holy mother of god," he whispered tonelessly as he flopped out of the dim closet to grab for the source of the noise. His hands shook so hard, swiping in the password took two tries.

> Why'd you come here if you're just going to be a bitch
>
> Eddie didn't make you SOUND like a bitch but you're proving him wrong
>
> I'm trying to welcome you with open arms

Andrew barked a ragged shout and kicked the metal bed frame, sending it skidding across the floor. He snatched up the loose papers, hands full of secrets, phone as maddening as the ongoing ordeal of his possessed fucking house. The phone buzzed again while he was holding Eddie's haunted research aloft, and he almost threw the papers out the window, blinded by a curtain of terror and rage. The documents rasped, page on page, in his shaking hands. Grasping for somewhere to stuff them back out of sight and out of reach, he yanked open the drawer of the bedside table, almost pulling it from its tracks.

He and Eddie had always maintained a handful of agreements. One was to never discuss their weird shit, as Halse had so eloquently labeled it. Another was no cocaine, based on lived experience. Eddie couldn't control his temper at the best of times, and he made terrible decisions when he had powder on his nostrils and keys in his hand; it made him a bad judge of his limitations and other people's patience. Which, for whole empty-headed seconds, made it hard for Andrew to comprehend the snipped green Starbucks straw, spare plastic gift card, and fold-over pill bag full of coke nestled in among

Eddie's spare change and receipts. *What the fuck else were you doing,*
he thought with flat hysteria.

He crammed the notes in the drawer, forced it shut, and dialed
the unknown number. The line rang three times before a rough
drawl answered: "Is it working? Am I riding your nerves hard
enough yet to get you to show up?"

"Did you sell Eddie coke?"

Halse snorted and said, "Of course, when he asked for it. I'm
here to help."

Andrew throttled his urge to shout. *Help* was a dangerous choice
of words given the context. Eddie hadn't needed *help* pursuing all
sorts of things he should've let be. He responded tightly, "Right,
sure. Yeah, let's meet, let's—I'll come out."

Off the line but audible, Riley said, "Is that Andrew?"

"Yeah, he's giving in to my charms," Halse said.

"Tell me where," Andrew said.

"The boys won't be around until—"

"Now. Where," he repeated.

"Hold your horses." To his cousin, Sam called out, "You good
to go now? Your roommate is in a hurry." Andrew missed the response, but then: "The gas station from the other night. That's your
game tonight, I'm assuming? You wanna drive?"

Andrew said, "I'll be there in fifteen."

"We'll be there after that."

The line went dead.

A struck match, blazing. The blended tangle of self-control and
apathy that had been smothering him caught fire in an instant,
charred to ash. Fifteen minutes earlier a haunt-remnant of his best
friend had fished around in his guts, and four minutes back he'd
still thought Eddie had only been hiding one shitty thing from
him. Impending night lurked with lush warning, creeping shadows
reverberating under his stalking feet as he crossed the front lawn
to the Challenger, recalling Halse's provocation a few nights past

about it being on the prowl again. Drunk enough to stop giving a shit and flayed to the bone, Andrew was as free as he'd ever been in his life. For once there was no firm hand holding his leash, ready to snap the lead choke-taut if he got too stupid on anger.

The familiar, roaring whine of the engine made him shake as he rolled the windows down, jerked a hand through his hair, and took off. Outdoor lights at the gas station buzzed halogen-blue in the gloom. He kept his hands on the wheel as he waited, counting to threes to restrain his breathing. The gunmetal gleam of Halse's car approached from the opposite direction an indeterminate amount of time later, bumping over the entrance curb and coasting to the space next to him.

Riley leaned out the passenger window and said, "Hey," with an eager edge.

Halse lounged in the driver's seat, his wrist on the steering wheel and his head lolled to the side to smirk past Riley. Andrew imagined him doing who knew what all with Eddie, while Andrew sat alone in his boxed-up apartment, none the wiser. Those teeth would split his knuckles if he put his fist through them.

"What's with that face, man?" Halse asked.

"Get fucked," Andrew said.

"Oh, well then," Halse responded with raised brows.

"Come on, guys," Riley cut in, flicking his fingers to draw Andrew's attention. "Aren't we gonna have a good time, let off some tension?"

"I don't think that's what the little prince wants," Halse said and stepped on the gas. The bark of the engine made all three men twitch. Halse laughed. "Follow the leader."

He reversed from the lot and Andrew followed, tunnel-visioned with the remaining dizziness of the shots he'd pulled. Halse took a handful of turns that led them out of town, coasting through the red glow of suburban traffic lights to the lesser authority of stop signs. Houses dropped off beyond secluded drives with gates across them, blockaded by foliage. Sam's blinking right turn signal pulled them onto a rural highway, two lanes twisting to mount a low hill, banked with old trees and overgrown culverts. The whole expanse was empty as far as Andrew strained to see. Halse drifted into the oncoming lane and stopped. Andrew braked alongside.

"On three-two-one-go," Halse shouted to him. Andrew rolled up his passenger window and toggled the engine setting to sport mode. Riley braced one hand on the roof of the WRX, the other lifted with three fingers up. Andrew braced his foot on the clutch, the other easing the gas to force the revs to climb with a grudging roar. Pressure boiled beneath his heel, threatening and seductive. Halse had provoked him into this; he might as well give it his strongest effort, from the seat that Eddie occupied before and better than Andrew. His chest cavity ached in time with the vibration of the car.

Riley ticked down one finger, then another, then the last—

He flagged his hand with a shouted, "Go!"

With Riley's cackling laugh and the Challenger roaring in his ears Andrew plowed off the line, the shrieking force smashing his body into the firm grip of the seat. The needle tapped six as the WRX nosed ahead and he shifted to second gear, tach rebounding as the Hellcat's MPH leapt, fractions of a second between shifts. The smell of searing tire rubber and hot clutch plate flogged him into third gear the moment the needle crossed redline, driving reckless to match the aftermarket liquid lightning of the WRX, Halse pacing him measure for measure. Elastic tension lashed their cars together across space, alone on the road, nothing in his head but grief and freedom.

Four seconds, four-point-five, five. Andrew slid through his bucking gearbox as he rode Eddie's big unruly beast toward triple-digit speed. It chewed the asphalt, heavier, louder, angrier than his own Supra. Andrew missed the bite point for fifth gear by a portion of a *portion* of a second and shouted an obscenity that disappeared into thin air under the raw noise of the engine, Halse's quarterpanel edging into the corner of his vision. Andrew smashed pedal to frame, devouring ground, letting the tach climb past the glowing digital six for longer than he'd usually risk. He hit the final gear and exploded into a screaming peak of acceleration that overtook Halse again; his eyes stung from remaining peeled wide open.

The rising grade of the road dragged them alongside, nose to nose, and he downshifted once out of necessity. Burning stench and euphoric, brittle anger poured through him. Factory standards capped the max speed just above 150, and he was willing to tap that edge, unsure of Sam's capabilities—

Oncoming headlights flashed at the crest of the hill. Instinct knocked his glance sidelong and it sparked against Halse's. Riley's mouth peeled wide with shock, sound swallowed in the bare yard between them. The moment hung like shivering glass about to shatter.

Halse tapped the brakes as hard as he dared without risking losing traction, leaving Andrew to maintain breakneck speed as he ducked across to the proper lane, grill terrifyingly close to kissing bumper. The offending stranger's car passed with an extended, accusatory honk. Halse downshifted as Andrew, too, let the speedometer slip, his pulse galloping with the cold premonition of a near-fatal collision. Of the hundred potential endings he'd almost written for himself over the last ten seconds—impact at triple digits, lost traction, crunched frames and windshield glass—none had come to pass.

Relief dumped over his nerves like ice-water. Andrew pumped his brakes to signal Halse into passing him, at last dipping below double the speed limit, to guide them farther from town. He led a circuitous and soothing chase that Andrew followed without thought, whipping around the curves of the hillsides with hints of understeer. With each dying burst of adrenaline, the debilitating furor that had driven him out of the house banked to a more manageable anger. Barely visible, Riley knelt up in his seat to drape his arms around it, flashing white teeth at Andrew. He made for an iconic, hungry gleam in the settling dark beneath tree shadows and open sky, more animal than boy. It was dumb, deliciously *reck-less*, and that compelling energy struck Andrew with the force of a punch.

Halse hadn't flinched, either.

If he'd been a half-second slower—

But he hadn't flinched. Riley had, his cousin hadn't. Death clipping straight past him hadn't broken through Halse's steady control; what else was he capable of doing without hesitation? Andrew slammed on his brakes and spun out into a sloppy, tire-smoking U-turn. *What the fuck were you doing, Eddie.* The WRX drove on in his rearview until the maw of the woods swallowed it. In the course of hours he'd learned that Sam Halse had cocaine and a fast car and apparently a goddamn death wish—inviting scabs on his knuckles, plus a mouth that could peel paint off a wall. The appeal was obvious. Eddie might have been fond of Riley, talked gothic bullshit with him and got drunk on cheap beer, but now Andrew understood where the hook had sunk in because it pierced straight through the meat of his cheek, too. He wanted to race Halse again, and that was a strange sensation: *want*. He also wanted to break his knuckles on Halse's jaw.

There were a hundred impulsive, destructive things Eddie might have chosen to do in the face of such heady provocation, without his other half riding shotgun. Andrew's heart maintained its hectic beat until he parked in the empty space behind the house on Capitol. For a moment, he'd seen a glimpse of a path that might get him answers, in a dead-cold stare and oncoming headlights.

7

No stranger to the post-bender sweating hot flash that woke him, Andrew scrambled from bed for the bathroom, seconds to spare before his stomach turned on itself. Vomiting before his brain had a chance to shift from *asleep* to *awake* made him shake like a kicked dog, acid burning his already-sore throat. He was setting a pattern for his mornings at Capitol Street. He spat a mouthful of drool into the toilet bowl with a disgusted groan before flushing and slumping to rest his overheated cheek on the cold tile floor. He'd passed out the second he got home and fell face-first onto the mattress; he didn't think Riley had bothered to return, which was a minor blessing.

Funhouse-mirror memories of bright headlights, flashing teeth, and crouching terrified in Eddie's closet clung in a scummy film to his brain. He wasn't ready to begin working through all that with his throbbing headache; he was in desperate need of some automatic tasks to ease his zombie-dull psyche back to full function. With the house to himself, he sat at the kitchen table to log into his school accounts, which seemed to occupy a separate universe from his recent tribulations. Troth had sent him three messages, two before their meeting and one after. The prior two dated back to the morning after the funeral—a brief set of condolences with an inquiry about his interest in deferral, same as he'd heard across the board, and following that, a request for a first advisor's meeting as soon as possible. The last one, timed to moments after he'd high-tailed it from her office, read: *I apologize for upsetting you, Andrew. I was attempting to be politic about an ugly and painful situation, and I understand that it was perhaps too much to spring on you at once. I*

would still like to discuss your path forward, and offer you the chance
to continue Edward's work with me if you would like to pick up his
legacy. I feel that it might be a powerful way to remember him—by
completing his project.

Andrew closed the email without responding. Something to
remember him by, sure, but the gruesome research Eddie was
bound to have been digging up was the one part of him he'd rather
forget. No matter how scholarly Eddie's interest might've seemed,
Andrew had spent the better part of his life in the shit with him.
The kind of haunts that dogged their heels weren't neat or clean or
well-contained as a campfire story. Troth had no clue the kind of
trouble she'd been stirring.

He checked the clock, found it was four minutes past the time
he should've left for his early afternoon class, and paused to consider if he cared. The answer was no. Once he let the window of
opportunity close for even a late start to head to campus, he picked
up his keys and two trash bags full of clothes, then stepped onto the
back deck. The house's strange design meant that he had to enter
the basement through a separate door at the end of a set of sunken
concrete steps under the porch. He wondered if it had been rented
as an apartment before. The solid metal door creaked inward at
his shove, catching on a floor mat and dragging it across bare concrete. He pulled the string of a naked bulb dangling overhead.
Harsh light cast shadows across the cracked and sealed floor, the
dirt-edged drain and sump pump at the far end, and a somewhat
battered washer and dryer. He kicked the floor mat aside and shut
the door behind him.

Hair rose on the nape of his neck. He didn't like basements—
even though he didn't think they were any more or less fucked up
than the rest of an old house, there was something about the tricks
of light, the coolness, the entombment. Made him remember wandering down the basement steps in Columbus at three-oh-five in the
goddamn morning to find Eddie crouched in a pitch-dark corner,
smiling an unwelcome smile at a smoky hovering *wrongness* that

scoured Andrew's eyes. He'd yelped and froze, but then Eddie had said, *don't you want to stay and chat, man?* Andrew had barreled up the steps, slid on the kitchen linoleum, and slammed his hip into the cabinet when he fell—hard enough to stun him momentarily blind. Their parents hadn't woken up. He'd limped for four days, bruised ass to knee, and Eddie had laughed it off like nothing.

The reminder of past sins tickled his aching head as he dumped his stale clothes in the washing machine and added detergent. And then, no surprise, a whisper on the air—wispy, ignorable. He bit his tongue and dropped the lid of the washer shut with a clang, staring at the options on the dial. He selected a timed wash. Wind tickled around his ankles from no particular source. He pulled the knob and water began to pour into the drum with a low roar. Something plucked at the hem of his shirt, and his hands twitched. He walked, sedate except for the wild flare of his nostrils as he managed his breathing, up the staircase and into the afternoon light.

The otherwise innocuous house loomed as he stood in the grass barefoot, sun prickling fresh sweat onto his brow to replace the cold sheen that lingered from his bourbon-sickness. Spent and exhausted but unable to secure a minute to himself without the shade dogging him, Andrew thought he might cry out of pure frustration. Acknowledging a revenant made it stronger. Despite knowing he should ignore the thing, he kept slipping—and the more attention he paid it, the more it would demand. Instead he chafed his hands over his arms, straightened his posture, and went back inside to stuff his laptop in his backpack for a strategic retreat.

———

Tucked into a corner booth at the coffee shop, sweating bullets onto the tabletop, Andrew nursed his continuing, ferocious headache and an iced Americano. His laptop and phone lay in front of him, each open to a different social platform. While Andrew had his own text threads and saved snaps—the ones he increasingly had to acknowledge Eddie had curated for him with a particular narrative in mind—Eddie's public feeds might tell a separate story of where he'd been, what he'd done there, and who with. After the prior night, he wanted to marshal his resources, confirm Eddie's movements, before he faced either of the cousins in a repeat performance.

Unasked for, the remembered sensation of a skeletal hand diving through the bones and cartilage of his throat rose up to gag him. The vent above his head kicked on; cool air wafted the smell of burnt-rubber smoke from his own hair to his nostrils. The remembered feeling of traction tearing off asphalt vibrated across his nerves. When he got home from the café, maybe he'd throw out the coke. Wash it down the sink. What was forty bucks to him? A cheap price to erase the evidence of Eddie's slipping further from him.

On the laptop he pulled up Eddie's derelict Facebook; on his phone, Instagram. Each digital record told a separate story. One narrated his home purchase, his birthday, his admission to Vanderbilt, while the other contained little text but constant bleeding splashes of photographic color. No posts across his social media in the two weeks leading up to his death—which in hindsight was unusual, a fact to consider further. Eddie thrived on attention.

The most recent and final photo was a shot of Eddie from behind, lounging on his front lawn. Someone else had taken it. He sat shirtless in jeans and Gucci slides, one knee cocked to rest his forearm across it, while the distant setting sun cast him in red and gold, streaking finger-width shadows across the flexed muscles of his shoulders and arms. Filter effects emphasized the depth of his summer tan, the pucker of his waistband gap revealing the top band of his briefs. Andrew let out a long breath, scrolling the comments—more emoji than words—but saw nothing out of the ordinary. Had Riley been his photographer? The picture had a vibe that made Andrew's skin itch, too intimate by far. Another swipe led him past more artful shots: the Challenger on top of a parking garage at night with the full moon high overhead; a lit firecracker in Eddie's hand; a bonfire circled by smeared, blurry bodies.

Andrew wracked his brain for the date of the bonfire and realized it had been the end of the spring term, or thereabouts. Eddie had mentioned a party. Another swipe led him to a throwback photo of himself in a headlock, glowering at the camera with squinting, irritable eyes in counterpoint to Eddie's huge grin, both of them washed in sunlight and sweat. Dampness burned across his eyes. His breath froze and expanded in his chest, fit to break him. He smacked the phone onto the table facedown.

The girl at the table across from him glanced up, frowned, and turned her attention back to her laptop. The whine of the barista's steamer cut through the haze. Andrew scrubbed the heel of his hand over his eyes and reclaimed another lungful of coffee-scented air. Nothing to find; Eddie's public feeds were even less detailed than his own, a performance of edgy charm and masculine competence. Dissembling, same as Eddie. If he wanted to find out what he'd got himself into, late-night lines or rough company, that meant looking into his private shit. His grim mood sank further as he thought of Eddie's laptop sitting on the desk at home, unopened and dusted-over.

Party tomorrow night at my place.
Celebrate the school kids coming back,
get the crew together
Show up and you could be the guest of
honor
Don't backslide on us now

Andrew idled in the parking space next to Riley's Mazda, which had reappeared during his coffee shop outing, thumbing absently up and down the text thread. One arm lolled out the window, with the other braced on his leg to prop the phone up. Overhead, a roiling mess of clouds pushed on the horizon. The afternoon air smelled like lightning in open spaces, dry grass wanting for sustenance. The door to the house swung open and his roommate stepped out onto the porch, provoking a pitiful twinge in the hollow behind Andrew's breastbone. The events of the past week left him feeling like tilled-up dirt: the earth's viscera showing, full of worms and rocks.

"Hey," Riley said as he planted his ass against his passenger door, one ankle crossed over the other. Andrew dropped his phone between his knees and slanted him a glance. "I'm sorry."

"For what?" Andrew replied.

Riley slapped his thighs and scrubbed his hands on his shorts, fidgeting. "I brought up something that it's real clear you're not interested in discussing, because I thought it was smart, but it wasn't."

Andrew parsed that. "But you're not sorry about what happened to Eddie, specifically."

"I don't know," Riley said. "I'd like to think I don't have shit to be sorry for, but who's to say? I might be worried I do; that's not your problem to solve for me."

The car door between them stood as a confessional partition.

"He was getting coke from your cousin. He shouldn't have been," Andrew said.

Riley shifted and straightened his legs. "Barely any, to be honest. But yeah, Sam sells people the things they ask for. He isn't going to be the one to tell you your business."

Andrew's phone vibrated. He glanced at the alert box and saw a portion of text—*How you like fireworks.* "I don't know if I believe that, man. Eddie knew better."

"If you're coming to the party tomorrow you can ask Sam yourself. Hell, you should come anyway. He'll treat us all good with folks coming back around. I know he's kind of a shit, but you've got to appreciate his dedication to rolling out the welcome mat," Riley said.

It was like having two separate conversations that happened to cross past one another. Andrew said, "I don't have to appreciate shit, though."

"C'mon, Andrew," Riley huffed.

"What?"

Riley swung his keys around his index finger, gnawing on his bottom lip. He shook his head. "Nothing, don't bother with my bullshit. Last night was fun, though. Let's do it again sometime."

Riley compounded the dismissal by walking around the hood to yank open his door and spill himself into the driver's seat. He spared one glance across the Challenger as he backed out, arm braced on the passenger's seat, and was gone. Andrew clambered free of the car, suddenly baking in the late afternoon heat. One beer from the dwindling supply in the fridge accompanied him upstairs. He kicked his sneakers off on the landing and, with a burst of trepidation, opened Eddie's door. For once there were no papers scattered across the floor.

Andrew sipped from his can on the threshold. Dust motes swirled in the gusts from the struggling vent. The lingering scent of that small universe wrapped him in its welcome funk. At the left corner of the pine desktop, Eddie's fat gaming laptop sat unassuming. Andrew dropped into the chair, which creaked under his weight, and slid the beastly thing in front of him. His grip left streaks through the accumulated silt on the sleek pitch-black casing. Guilty, he wiped it with his forearm until it was more presentable. Another crisp, wheaty mouthful of beer set his heart steady.

Face recognition rejected him, of course. He tapped through to the password screen and entered Eddie's usual combination of their birthdays and the word *boobs*. He'd used the same one for his main devices since middle school, and Andrew had a similar baseline, in case either of them needed to access the other's systems.

Except the password failed. Andrew frowned, altered the birthday order, and entered it again. Another failure; he tried Eddie's variant, rearranged the words and numbers, tried over and over until the system warned him it was about to lock him out for good. He smacked the lid closed with more force than he should've and got up to pace, stung.

Eddie was shit at remembering passwords. Where would he have recorded a new one, after breaking their ten-year streak? Andrew turned in place, one slow rotation. The clean desktop, the cluttered bedside table, the closed drawer containing too much of Eddie's callousness—he took them in once, then again, a thought rising like a slow bubble from a black depth of sea: *where is his phone?* It hadn't been among his effects when the hospital turned him over for the funeral: one of his lesser-worn gold rings and the thin platinum chain he wore *too* often, his wallet, the scuffed red Converse he'd been buried in.

Suspicion intensified, tripping up his spine.

He sat his beer on the desk and glanced over the bookshelves, then knelt to run his hand under the bed and the table beside it. He found a fistful of cobwebs and a quarter. His sinuses burned ominously while he pawed through the closet and the full laundry basket, doing his best to disturb nothing, with no result. Crossing the hall to his own room, he did a cursory inspection between the mounded pillows and inside the barren drawers of the handsome desk he ached to sit at with Eddie perched on the corner. Thin sweat prickled along his brow. He bypassed Riley's shut door and swept his hands over every surface in the living room and foyer, moving his own unsorted possessions as if there might be something hiding underneath. The phone remained elusive.

Andrew jogged outside to unlock the Challenger and crawl into the back seat, sticking his hands under floor mats, into seat pockets. He used his phone's flashlight to reveal a loose cigarette and a few crumpled receipts. On the one hand, he was surprised at how fucking clean the car was. On the other, a painful, frightened excitement stoked his nerves high. He fired a message off to his roommate:

have you seen Eddie's phone

no don't you have it?

no

shit i don't know. i can ask sam

no. thanks

Andrew collapsed onto the bench seat, legs hanging out the side of the car, and stared at the dome light. If he asked Del, she'd tell him the cops might've missed Eddie's phone in the woods, hidden in some tree-hollow, simple to brush past and buried there where he'd left it. She'd say the password change was another sign of him moving on, or some shit like that. She wouldn't see a pattern, only a collection of little hurts adding up to something bigger, another painful coincidence. And it did hurt, make no mistake.

Though he thought he'd been sure of Eddie before, and had defended that certainty in his arguments with Del, finding a real sign of outside interference made him realize: he'd begun to *doubt*. A thread of fear wound across the evidence of Eddie's secrets and lies, compounding from each day to the next. If he was wrong about so much, he thought with a gulping, panicked breath, what else might he have missed?

But the phone—that was a trail he could chase. He pressed his fists to his temples, willing himself to drop the bleaker line of suspicion he'd just unearthed. The laptop might be brushed off as more of Eddie's secret-keeping, but a missing phone felt like purposeful interference, covering tracks. If Eddie's phone—his whole life inside it, his book of numbers, names, photos—was missing, maybe something worse had happened to him than Andrew's current unspoken guess, a confrontation gone wrong in a split second. If someone had taken his phone, maybe someone planned to take his life. Once his breathing calmed, no longer wheezing through stuttering bursts, he read the most recent text, from Halse: *Answer me man, are you coming? I need to plan accordingly*

He typed, *yeah*

And hit send. If something *had* been done to Eddie, he had an idea of where to start asking: Sam Halse's arrogant, dangerous, seductively entertaining fiefdom.

8

"Riding with me tonight?" Riley called from his bedroom. "The place is kind of the middle of nowhere, so that might be easiest. It was our grandparents' house. I lived there with Sam till Ed asked me to come out here, be closer to campus for work and all that."

Andrew turned off the electric razor and ran a hand over the remaining stubble on his jawline. The bristle of it shaded out his cheeks, made the thinness of his face less delicate. He'd also shaved his undercut, setting the tousled, reckless disorganization of his ever-lengthening, increasingly wavy hair in a more purposeful light. His reflection stared at him, sunburn turning to a light tan that set off the muddled blue-grey of his eyes—the unwelcoming color and intensity of a winter lake about to suffer through a storm. When he moved down, he'd intended to stick around the campus and its city-ness, pretending the fresh buildings, bustling human life, and neat streets could be located anywhere in the USA. Crossing those borders to pass into the hungry hollers of his worst dreams was both inevitable and cruel.

Oblivious, Riley thumped into the hall in his boots and shrugged a jacket on over his tank top.

"Sure, I'll ride along," Andrew said.

"All right, good. I'll stay kinda sober and drive us back, so get as fucked up as your heart desires. Sam will provide. Ed was getting to be one of ours, so he'll treat you like you are, too."

Riley checked his product-styled hair in the bathroom mirror with a critical tilt of the chin, left and right. He crinkled his nose and shrugged, so Andrew supposed it passed inspection.

"He doesn't know me," Andrew said.

Riley grinned at him and said, "I dunno, you've gone head-to-head now. That counts for something."

On the way out, Riley snagged two beers from the fridge and passed one to Andrew. He cracked the pop-tab as he got in the Mazda. Riley took a few big swallows and started the car. In unspoken accord, both rolled their windows down. Andrew settled in with a gut-stretching breath. Hot asphalt and dirt, exhaust and old weed. Riley fiddled with his phone for a moment. The portable speaker stuck to his dash turned on, trying its best to blare MCR's first EP.

"Got no sound system, sorry. Money's under the hood," Riley said.

Andrew sank into the seat, stuck between the cold can in his fist and the heat of another boy's arm shifting through gears at his elbow. *Good-natured,* that was the phrase that kept popping into his head about Riley. Hard to square that nature with the conflict between him and West, his nonchalant acceptance of Eddie's eldritch obsessions, his uncritical kinship to his firebrand cousin.

The neighborhood transitioned to a familiar rural highway before Riley cleared his throat for Andrew's attention. After he grunted acknowledgement, Riley said, "Awkward question."

"What?" Andrew asked flatly.

"Household bills."

"What about them?"

"Eddie let me handle the electric, but he paid . . . legit everything else. I don't know how you'd want to handle that."

Andrew watched Riley's fingers drum on the wheel. He wasn't surprised. Eddie was generous with his cash, given that he had more of it than he needed and friends who could use it better. He responded, "We split the utilities, split the groceries. He already bought the house, so who gives a shit about rent."

"Okay." A notch of tension eased from Riley's shoulders. "I don't want you to feel like I'm taking advantage. I'll pay my fair share, whatever you think that is."

"It's just money. He didn't care about it, so why should I?" Andrew said.

"Okay," Riley repeated.

This is my roommate, Andrew considered as he sipped his beer. *I live with this guy. I'm going to keep living with this guy.* Eddie had left him this, all of this. These were his friends, or his enablers, or worse. The road climbed through hills. Riley ascended slower than their last breakneck climb, smooth and powerful through the turns. He took a branch road that passed farm fields and small houses, the occasional trailer. The itching pull at the beds of Andrew's fingernails increased as the sun coasted near the horizon. He scratched at the seam of his jeans, catching his nails against the stitching and tugging to ease the ache.

"Almost there," Riley said.

Andrew hung one arm out the window and caught a damp leaf from a branch that whipped past them. He crushed it between his fingers, grinding sticky green life into his knuckles. Riley was smiling when he glanced at him, a pleased tension to his posture, leaning forward to the wheel. Andrew chugged the rest of his beer. As he lowered the empty can, Riley turned onto a paved track cut through sparse trees, a mailbox hanging open, crooked on its post at the curb. The curving driveway opened to a clearing with a single-story ranch house and separate garage, cupped in the hands of the forest. Riley rolled up to the garage and parked among the startling number of ugly-livid cars splayed across the lawn. His engine idled while he finished his beer. Andrew thought about videos on his phone, firecrackers and gasoline. *Yeah,* he thought as Riley popped out of the car and slammed the door behind him, *yeah, it's a fire night.*

He threw his crumpled can in the yard and jogged behind Riley around the side of the house. The summer dusk settling on his shoulders propelled him into the soundscape of raucous voices and pounding trap music. Dull half-light washed out the features of the crowd. The congregation circled around an unlit bonfire, drinking from blue Solo cups and glass bottles, cigarettes in hand, and more bare feet and naked chests than was advisable for the thrum in the air. He knew a pack waiting for nightfall when he stumbled into one.

A welcoming shout went up from some corner of the crowd as the pair came into view, and a handful of curious stares slid past Andrew.

"Hey, kid," Halse barked from his precarious seat on the deck railing, where he'd been holding court. He hopped off clumsily, a blunt in one hand and a mostly full bottle of bourbon in the other. Liquor splashed over his wrist. "Welcome, welcome!"

He hooked one arm over each of their shoulders, sweat-sticky, dragging both along with him. Riley snagged Halse's wrist and guided the bottle to his own mouth, messily stealing a swig. Sweet smoke and heat curled under Andrew's chin. Halse flicked his wrist and proffered the blunt. Andrew took it between his thumb and forefinger. Halse's hand thumped onto his chest, encouraging, as he took a lung-straining drag.

"Oh, fuck yeah," Halse crowed. "I've been hoping you'd get that stick out of your ass, Blur. We all got our ways of coping, but I bet I know yours."

"Fuck off," he slurred through the smoke, voice milky.

"Riley, go make the boy a drink," Halse said. His cousin stole his bottle and left with a sideways grin, disappearing into the house through the open sliding door. Andrew tried to pass the blunt back. Halse slapped a hand to the side of his head and tousled his hair, yanking strands between his fingers. "Nah, you keep that. That's yours, guest of honor. Your prize for beating me the other night."

Andrew inhaled again, filling up his lungs. Halse released him; he swayed toward the retreating hand from old habit. One of the boys on the deck leaned over the rail. His hair was glossy black, combed in a tousled sweep off his forehead. The porchlights enhanced the gold-brown undertones of his skin, the rich depth of his dark eyes, and the painted-on maroon V-neck clinging to every ounce of his defined, slim torso. He gave off an air of willing trouble.

While Andrew took him in, the man said, "Sam, who's that?"

"Andrew Blur, Ed's friend," Halse replied.

"Hey there, I'm Ethan Jung," he said with a grin. Mirth narrowed his eyes as he smiled.

"Hey," Andrew said slowly in return, noticing Ethan's short-heeled leather boots as he shifted foot to foot.

Another round of introductions, a handful of unremarkable young men who could all use each other's IDs in a pinch, names like David and Jacob and Benjamin all forgotten immediately, finished before Riley returned. He leaned over the railing and passed Andrew a cup, bumping his hip against Ethan's. Ethan grinned wider and shoved him back, fingers splayed over Riley's shoulder at the line of his light farmer's tan. The jacket he'd arrived with had already disappeared while he was in the house.

"Welcome back," Riley said. He glanced over at Andrew. "Ethan here is in his second year of law school. He's going to be a goddamn lawyer."

"That's sort of what law school is for, dumbass," Ethan said.

Andrew snorted a slight laugh, looking into his cup. The liquid was a nondescript, tawny brown, fizzing gently. He kept the blunt going with a casual drag and blew a few sloppy rings.

"I hear you have a sick Supra," Ethan said.

Andrew stared up at him and took a sip: bourbon, soda, something bitter and tart—lemon, possibly. Riley glanced between them with an encouraging nod. Compared to the rest of the men on the porch, Ethan stood out, that was for sure.

"I do," Andrew allowed.

"Well, me too. We ought to test our builds out sometime."

A chorus of encouraging, derisive whoops broke from the crowd. Andrew's skin thrilled and his eyes narrowed. He sipped again, holding the stare over the rim of his cup long enough that Ethan's smile morphed into a sharklike challenge. His fingers drummed a beat on the railing.

"We'll see," Andrew said.

"Goodie," Ethan replied.

In another person's mouth it might've been a threat. In Ethan's, it held an edge of a laugh, partly mocking. Riley made a fist in Ethan's shirt and yanked him toward the stairs. The pair wandered off to the bonfire-in-progress, heads together to speak under the rolling crash of the music. Andrew flinched when a hand plucked the blunt from his fingers. He turned a fraction and Halse was in his face, the cherry glowing a few inches from his cheek.

"I can't figure you out," he said in a low voice. "Did you just need a good push to get you going, princess?"

"I don't know what you mean," Andrew said, though the truth was, *I needed to see for myself what kind of trouble you make.*

Halse blew smoke in his face and turned his wrist to stick the rillo back between Andrew's dry lips. Reflex closed them around the earthy paper, soft with spit, earning Halse's vicious grin.

"Finish that," Halse said as he pushed past him to rejoin his unruly guests.

Andrew ashed the blunt on the ground. The sunset hid behind the trees, grey light seeping around their edges. Milling groups broke into the occasional shoving scuffle or cackle of hyena-laughter. At the center, four boys and one young woman were breaking pieces of particle board and sticks with their heels to toss on the haphazard pile of material that Andrew assumed would soon be lit. The girl's hair was in a tight bun and her buff, thin silhouette reminded him of Del. Del wouldn't have been caught dead at one of these get-togethers. Sam approached the group and patted her on the ass; she smacked his with a piece of wood, which he danced away from with a laugh.

He checked his phone—no messages. No one had a clue where he was, or who he was with, or if he was coming home. Had Eddie been standing here three weeks before, talking to someone who ended up doing him harm? Maybe so. Andrew rolled the tension from his shoulders and put his phone in his pocket.

"Sorry, sorry," Riley said, stumbling up to him. "I shouldn't abandon you so quick, dude. I just hadn't seen Ethan in like a month and a half, he went to his parents' for break."

"It's fine," Andrew said.

Riley's hair was going flat already, dripping sweat and product down his temples. The pink scar stood out sharply on his cheek. He tugged Andrew's arm, saying, "Come inside, let me make you another drink."

The kitchen countertops were strewn with bottles and cups, and the sink was full of bags of ice. Riley popped the plastic safe-pourer out of a handle of whiskey and offered it over. Andrew swigged straight from the bottle. The burn scoured his throat from the inside, cheap and medicinal. They passed it back and forth until Riley choked a little and spit into the sink.

Andrew snorted. "Sanitary, spitting on the ice."

"Next to it," Riley corrected him. "You feeling good?"

Andrew's head swam pleasantly. He hadn't had much to eat before coming out. He'd dropped the finished roach somewhere outside, and he wondered if people often set the yard alight by accident during drought weeks.

"Maybe I am," he allowed. "Where's your, uh, your girlfriend?"

Riley wrinkled his nose and said, "Did you check the scene outside? I think Ethan is the only person at this party who isn't white, and Irene is the lone chick. Luca doesn't want to deal with that, and I don't blame her. Sam's parties are kind of . . . their own thing, you know? He mixes business with pleasure."

Andrew rewound his memory to check against Riley's explanation. He hadn't noticed the party's makeup, but on second thought, he guessed it was true. Most of the faces he'd passed were variations on his own—or, more accurately, Sam's. Scruff on square jaws, farmer's tans, high-top sneakers and blue jeans. West's initial warning took on a different significance in hindsight, with Riley's comment that his girlfriend wouldn't be caught in this white, rowdy crowd ringing in his ears.

"Hey," Halse bellowed from the deck. "Stop hogging the guest of honor!"

"Get fucked, Sam!" Riley hollered back, voice cracking.

Andrew glanced at his own shaking hands. He kept expecting to hear Eddie's voice in the cacophony outside, sliding between the gaps of the music when the track changed. Riley's palm slapped onto the back of his neck and squeezed. Andrew blinked down at him as Riley searched his face with drawn-together brows.

"Quit that pussy shit," Halse said from the doorway.

Andrew jerked free and Riley huffed, "Shut up, Sam."

Halse shoved aside a stack of cups and said, "Go grab me a book, oh cousin of mine."

"I don't think—"

"He doesn't have to, but I'm going to," Halse said.

Andrew sat at the kitchen table while Riley disappeared into the bowels of the house. Halse leaned against the counter. His black jeans rode low on his hips, baring inches of an electric green pair of boxer briefs. The muscle tank he wore had a grease stain on the side in the shape of a palm, smeared and faded. He expected Halse to speak, but the silence settled. The weight of the ticking clock dragged them both toward sunset.

"Here," Riley said as he returned, offering a large hardcover labeled *Algebra II*.

Halse fished a plastic baggie out of his hip pocket and tapped a snowdrift of cocaine onto the textbook. Riley handed him a credit card and he grunted his approval, cutting out three lines.

"Thanks, buddy," Riley said.

"I don't—" Andrew started.

Halse barreled over his objection with a smile: "Think it over before you say no. It's free, and you need to get out of your fucking skin tonight, don't you?"

All three men paused while Andrew drummed his fingertips on his knee. The ache of his missing half chewed at him. Eddie had left him this.

"Here's the plan," Halse said. He snagged a straw and flipped his pocketknife out, snipping it short with a fluid twitch of the wrist. "I'm going to do this line. Y'all are going to do yours. I'm going to go outside, fill a beer bottle full of gas, stuff a rag in it, and we're going to light that. And then you," he pointed at Andrew, "are going to start our bonfire in the most spectacular way possible."

Riley said, "And then we'll all be friends."

"If nobody goes to the hospital tonight, then we'll be friends," Halse corrected, prompting the thrill of impending risk.

Andrew scrubbed his hands over his face. His head pounded along with the music. He stood and took the two steps to put his hip against the countertop next to Halse, who punched his arm hard enough to jar his shoulder. He watched Halse bend down to the line, pressing one nostril shut, and thought, *Did someone here fuck Eddie up?*

The sweat on Halse's scalp glistened through his stubble. He snorted loud then reared back, nose scrunched and eyes squinted. He made a soft hissing sound as he passed the straw to Andrew.

"The last time I did coke, it was 'cause Eddie kept putting it in my drink," Andrew said.

"The bastard," Halse said with a fond edge.

"Yeah," he choked out as he bent to the textbook.

The straw edge cut into his nostril. He lined it up and tilted his chin, inhaling in one long burning go. Fire poured through his sinuses and dripped a liquid astringent rush down the back of his throat. He tipped his head up with a gagging swallow. His eyes watered. Riley stole the straw and muscled him aside, the lines of their legs pressed together. He finished his fast.

Andrew stared at him while he blinked and snuffled. Riley occupied two worlds but neither matched the other, and Eddie had straddled that same impossible divide without effort or concern.

The blistering noise of the crowd outside battered his screaming nerves as the leash around Andrew's neck slipped another notch looser.

"Let's light something on fire," Halse said.

"Fuck yeah," Riley growled back.

The pair hustled him outside with broad hands and toothy smiles. He found himself standing with Riley in front of the unlit bonfire, the thirty or so boys spread out in the yard around them hollering and carrying on.

"Ready?" Halse said from behind him, so close to his ear he felt the gust of hot breath.

"Give it," he said, sticking his hand out.

"Back up." Halse jerked him by the belt loop, and he staggered back a few more feet from the pit.

The sun set like a tether snapping. He felt the change, night coming in like a stinging slap on the soles of his feet. The woods loomed on the outskirts of the property, blacker than any city night. Eddie had been here too, without him. A lighter flicked. The soft *whoosh* of the rag catching set him ablaze inside, threatening raw orange glow kicking his heart against his ribs. The blur of chemicals and liquor and heat on his wrist all stung as drops of sizzling gas speckled him. He heard himself laugh, and then Halse said, *"Throw it."*

He pitched the bottle into the pile of wood and scraps so hard it shattered with a burst of flame and glass. The crowd roared. He staggered through a laugh that kept on going into wheezing giggles, and Riley jostled him with an elbow in turn. He tripped. Halse caught him around the waist to buffer his fall, his cackle closer to a snarl of delight in the flickering hot glow.

"You're totally fucked, good, awesome," he said.

"Halse," Andrew slurred.

"Call me Sam, bitch." He patted Andrew's cheek, almost a smack, then grabbed his chin in a squeeze that puckered his mouth. "I gotta go make friends and host and shit. Riley, keep him busy."

The support of his muscled arm and bony hand disappeared

at once as he withdrew into the crowd. Andrew wavered in place, spat a mouthful of bitter saliva on the ground. The roar and glow of the bonfire cast jumping shadows over anonymous faces and bodies. The lines of strong fingers haunted his stinging cheek. His eager pulse raced, teetering on the edge of nausea.

"Come on, let's go find Ethan," Riley said.

Tunnel vision. He placed his feet in the exact track of the other boy's, eyes on his heels, chaos spilling off around them. He wasn't certain if he followed for hours or minutes. When Riley abruptly whooped and leapt up onto another man, Andrew almost ran into them, staggering to a stop. Ethan's shouted greeting slipped out of Andrew's head in an instant, pushed loose by Ethan's hands clutching Riley's ass; Riley's legs locked around Ethan's waist. His dark eyes glinted in the ghost of firelight. Riley's lips slanted over Ethan's, sloppy, hungry, a flash of wet tongue—half on his mouth, half on his face. Andrew's hands hung loose at his sides. He swayed a step backward, and another, head blank. Riley's shirt rode up. He had dimples at the small of his back, divots for Ethan's grip to settle onto. Riley braced his forearms on Ethan's shoulders to lift his seat higher and press closer on his—*friend*. Ethan's hands squeezed at his thighs. Spit glistened between their moving mouths.

Andrew fled, and the crowd swallowed him up. He clapped a stranger's shoulder and took the bottle from his hand to pour half a lukewarm beer down his throat. The man shoved him good-naturedly and blustered about getting him another drink. Andrew floated like driftwood in a sea of crushing voices and unfamiliar faces. The bridge of his nose stung. A drip of heat rolled over his upper lip. He swiped his tongue out, tasting blood.

Behind him, a man said, "Can't believe Halse lets those faggots come around here."

Andrew bunched his shirt up and held it to his nose. Red spread across the fabric and behind his eyes.

Another man said, "I hear the last one he got all buddied up with cut his wrists. Guess that one's boyfriend is hanging around too, now. Can't get fucking rid of them."

"Well, one of them's his cousin—"

Andrew's heel slipped on the damp grass as his knuckles slammed into cheekbone and eye socket with devastating accuracy. The shit-talker's head whipped back. He dropped to the ground in a stone-still sprawl. One observer's shocked yelp ripped through the raucous music. The second man grabbed Andrew's shirt and cocked a fist, shouting "Fuck *you*—"

Andrew flipped his grip on the bottle in his hand and smashed it into the man's ribs with a sick-hollow thud. He crumpled around the blow and his raised fist foundered to a bruising grip on Andrew's arm. His stumbling weight took them both to the ground. Andrew saw nothing but flashes of color, air forced out of his lungs. He snarled and slammed his forehead into the bloodied face above him. The crunch of cartilage was unmistakable. He lost his bottle. An elbow glanced off his jaw and snapped his head into the ground. His skull bounced off the dirt. He jammed his fingers into the open mouth above him and yanked, so the man reared up with a yowl. He got on top without knowing how he did it, planting a knee in someone's gut. A second pair of arms came around his shoulder and throat, trying to choke him out.

"Hey, hey, *hey!*" Halse's voice rang out.

The pressure disappeared from his throat. Hands in his hair and shirt hauled him to his feet. His head lolled back onto Halse's shoulder, eyes rolling; he caught sight of Riley standing offside with his mouth hanging open in surprise. Halse snorted and popped him casually on the jaw, a disciplinary slap that made his vision go patchy.

"Blur, is there a reason you're trying to murder my fucking guests?" Halse asked.

Andrew considered the man on the ground, struggling to find his knees and sliding on the grass. The one standing, the one who'd been choking him, eye swollen ripe from Andrew's initial punch, spat on the ground. For a second Andrew was impressed with himself; he wasn't a big guy, and the one he'd knocked on his ass was built.

"Talking about Eddie," he slurred through an aching mouth.

"Man, who the hell is that," gasped the one whose ribs he'd tried to break.

"This young man is a good friend of mine," Halse said. His jovial tone set Andrew's survival instincts pinging. Halse lowered him in a controlled fall, and he sprawled on his ass while the other man paced over to the pair of strangers. The strangers drew together, sensing the same threat. "What kind of shit were you talking, and who invited you to my home?"

"Hey, you know us," the standing man said uncertainly.

His friend, though, stared silent at Andrew's face. His nose was crooked, a mask of blood painting him from hair to shirt collar. Andrew grinned. "Called Riley a fag," he offered without breaking the glowering eye contact.

"Oh, did he," Halse said.

The crowd had gone still around them, ripples of hushed conversation spreading through the circle. Andrew wiped his face again. His fingers bled sluggishly, split on someone's teeth. When he put his hand on the ground, pain and something *other* pulsed up his forearm from the grass, the earth he was oozing onto, clinging to his bones with a tar-stickiness. The surrounding forest rustled in an eerie cacophony of wind and leaves. Halse popped his shoulders and sighed, then hauled his foot back and drove it into the prone man's stomach. He gagged twice and balled up into a shaking huddle.

His friend stepped over him as if he were going to retaliate, but Halse pointed a finger in his face and said, "I'll kill you. I will kill you if you look at me again. Get out. Take your friend with you."

Andrew lay back, the starlit sky streaming and shifting above him. The damp grass on the side of his face let him know he'd collapsed. Music shrieked along without pause. A cold can slipped into his fist. He mumbled a thanks and pressed it to his forehead. Beer splashed on his skin. A boot skimmed over his ribs. He blinked up at Halse standing over him. Both his hands were tucked in his back pockets, drawing his jeans skin-tight over his crotch. Andrew dragged his stare up another couple feet to Halse's chin, tipped at a considering angle. Andrew focused on the sensation of bony ankles and the heels of shoes digging in on both sides of his hips.

"Are you concussed?" Halse asked.

"Holy shit," Riley said, and he appeared beside them, crouching. "I only lost you for like, ten minutes, dude."

Andrew let him tilt his head and observe his pupils. Halse waited. Riley reached for the hem of his tank, stripped it over his head, and wadded it up. The long, angry red scars under his pectorals were unexpected. Andrew stopped his hand halfway while reaching out to touch, to trace them with his fingers like he had with his eyes.

"Hold still, fuckass," Riley said and scrubbed at Andrew's face with the sweat-damp shirt.

Andrew dropped his hand to the ground, struggling to prop himself up on his elbows. Halse loomed, staring out at the surrounding revelers with his hackles up. Riley said, "For the record, don't defend my virtue, I don't give a shit."

"Eddie's," he corrected. The inside of his mouth was a wreck. He stuck his tongue into split skin along his molars on the left side. "They said Eddie . . ."

"Riley, take him home," Halse said.

He swung his leg over Andrew's torso and flicked a wave at them over his shoulder. The tall woman Andrew had noticed before fell in next to him and followed him into the crowd, which sorted itself out again in Halse's absence.

"I'm going to throw up," he said.

Riley tipped him onto his side and he puked, which was agonizing in the extreme. Adrenaline leaked out with the wet tracks of reflexive tears. The cold shiver that ran across his skin presaged another heave. He spat bitterness and blood. The rest was a blur, a cotton shirt shoved under his oozing nose, bare skin supporting him. Then he was in the bench seat, his feet propped out the open window, the breeze nipping him as they drove.

"I'm sorry," he said.

"Don't be. I wouldn't let someone talk shit about him either. And he was your—you know, he was yours, you were together."

"No," Andrew said. "It wasn't like that. We weren't like that."

"What," Riley said, twisting in his seat and glancing away from the road.

Andrew met his eyes for a split second before closing his own against the accusation he saw there, the hurt wedged like a splinter under a fingernail. "I'm not gay."

"Oh my god," Riley murmured. His laugh was forced and, Andrew thought, incredulous. "You've got to be fucking kidding me. You're serious?"

"The scars you've got," he said instead.

"Eddie helped me pay for it. Generous guy. We're not having that conversation while you're this fucked up," Riley said.

Andrew subsided. The night whipped past in silence. His knuckles hurt. And he kept hearing Riley say *he was your*—on loop. What word should he put after? On paper, a sibling; in practice, something else. If Eddie had been Riley's friend, he wasn't that for Andrew. That friendship was a muted fraction of the real thing, the marrow-thing, that tied them together. Through the cavern and their hauntings since, through a life spent with Eddie keeping him leashed but cared for at the same time, he couldn't find a label that fit where he needed it to go. Maybe instead, just a hard stop: *he was yours.*

9

Reminiscence carried Andrew into a fitful, drugged doze; in his memories, he sat perched on the rim of the bathtub, the cold ceramic making his legs tingle where it pressed into his hamstrings. His mom hummed and tilted Eddie's chin farther toward the ceiling, a damp wash rag in her other hand as she considered her angle of approach. Fat drops of blood rolled from his left nostril over his puffy lips, each rivulet cutting a path across the corded muscle of his throat to pool at his collarbone. While Andrew chewed his thumbnail, hunched over, the pool spilled down the firm swell of Eddie's recently acquired pectoral muscle.

"All right, hold on," his mom said with a kind but long-suffering sigh.

Eddie winced as she ran her thumb under his eye socket, across the bridge of his purple-black nose. His shoulders rounded inward, but he kept silent—stoic. Andrew tore his stare off of the wet red droplets mapping the contours of his torso and found Eddie watching him instead. The white light of the bathroom made his sixteen-year-old face look older, more angular. Something he might consider handsome.

"It's not broken, but seriously," his mom said as she pressed the cool compress to Eddie's bloodied nose, "you can't go starting fights every time someone else gets friendly with Andrew."

"Friendly is a weird way to put it," he replied, muffled.

"It wasn't that bad," Andrew said. "Marshall was like, messing with me, but it wasn't bad."

"Sounds as if he might've been pulling your pigtails to get your attention, hm? Eddie, you're going to need to learn to share your brother at some point," she chided gently.

Brother made his stomach squirm in rebellion.

"Mom, don't talk like that," Andrew grumbled, flushing under Eddie's relentless eye contact but unwilling to break it. Oblivious, she shifted the cloth and went back to humming, off-key.

"I'm allowed to protect him when he needs it," Eddie countered.

Andrew swallowed, remembering the relief when Eddie had ripped Marshall's hand from his hair and clocked him in the jaw, the beastly satisfaction that swelled in his chest when the pair of them dissolved into a tussle on the classroom tile. His recollection must've shown on his face, because Eddie's puffed lip spread in a small, proud smile. The weight of his unfiltered regard made Andrew float inside his skin as he listened for words that weren't being said. The funny, airy feeling he'd been drifting through since he watched the fight clung to him in wisps.

"Boys," his mother sighed in defeat.

Hidden together in his bed that night, a handful of inches separating them, Andrew tapped his fingertip to Eddie's eggplant nose and asked, "Was it worth it?"

"Of course. He shouldn't have touched you," Eddie said.

How come, he hadn't asked.

The night it really happened, Eddie had rolled over and gone to sleep, leaving Andrew to his curious lightness. He hadn't reached out to pinch his bottom lip between sharp fingernails as the shadowed room dropped abruptly to blackness, whispering in a ghoulish voice that hissed like static, "You're not his."

———

"Shit shit *shit,*" Riley yelped, frantic.

Andrew groaned. Vertigo punched through his sternum as he shifted. His hand thumped into the metal railing under the front seat and pain burst up his arm. The intrusive cold blanketing him from thighs to throat failed to register through his confused delirium until Riley slammed on the brakes, almost rolling him off his seat. His eyes popped open. The moonlight streaming through the windows revealed nothing out of the ordinary, but he felt a physical pressure creep up over his ribs in the shape of wide palms, disturbing the pattern of wrinkles on his shirt. His breath tripped over itself, bubbling panic. A lone cicada shrieked outside. Riley scrabbled noisily with his seat belt and the door, the car pulled over halfway onto the grassy shoulder.

The death-chill felt almost good for a second, cupping the side of his face over the swelling split skin, before it seared like an ice cube sticking to a wound. A strangled grunt punched from beneath his diaphragm. The suggestion of the revenant's hand passed over his nose and philtrum and fat bottom lip, burning despite its immateriality, sucking and gripping where real skin would've slipped on spit and blood. An atmospheric pop cracked in his ears, his brain, as the crusted remains of his blood absorbed into the *nothingness,* an offering lapped up by the ragged corpse-boned thing straddling him. His revenant settled heavier and hungrier, gaining an outline like exposed film. Andrew stopped breathing as it leaned in, its spine bending where spines had no joint or hinge, rot-stench breath gusting into his partially open mouth.

Riley fell out of the front seat in his haste to escape, tangled in his belt. Andrew stared past the haunt at his own bare ankles sticking out the far window, his shoes speckled with brown-red fluids, the old-growth forest and craggy sheet rock exposed by the highway cut into the hill. Roots tumbled from trees down the exposed stone. He stayed limp as the creature leaned in for another taste.

The door behind his head opened and rough hands hooked under his armpits. The revenant hesitated. Andrew struggled and twitched, kicking weakly as Riley dragged him out of the car, legs sliding through the specter's body with horrible resistance. His tailbone smacked the hot asphalt. Humid summer air slapped his freezing skin, and he grunted again.

"Jesus Christ, shut up," Riley gasped out.

"What the fuck," he groaned.

"Out of the road, get out of the road," Riley said, and the pair of them stagger-flopped to the grassy berm together.

The car dinged, doors hanging open, taillights casting a red glow. Andrew rolled onto his front and panted, shaking, his forehead on his own wrist. His heaving breath calmed in degrees as Riley's died down, an increment at a time. As the dregs of his dream faded, the bitter urge to allow the *connection* with his dead thing banked to a smolder, though the sensation it left behind after consuming part of him still vibrated through his cells—almost a communion.

"You knew. How'd you know?" Andrew said. His dry tongue felt twice its normal size.

"If you'd been willing to talk about it before *now,* you stupid little shit, you'd already have an answer," Riley barked at him.

"Fuck you."

Riley laughed in a staccato burst, almost a hiccup. "No, fuck yourself."

Another car roared past their sloppily parked vehicle without stopping to check on them, blue-tinged headlights blinding Andrew briefly. Wind whipped his hair around his face, clumped and damp with indeterminate fluids. The Mazda continued to ding, inviting them to return to its grasp. No unsettling shade lingered; it had disappeared as soon as it was interrupted. The first time he'd shed enough blood to take, there it was, ready and ravenous.

"Get up." A fist in the back of his shirt helped him to his hands and knees before Riley's shoulder dug into his ribs to haul him to his feet. "Passenger seat, in."

Riley pushed the door shut and Andrew slumped against it, elbow out the window. The metal edge bit into his tricep. The other doors slammed twice in quick succession. The interior of the little tuner was as mundane and oven-warm as it had been at the start of the evening. Riley put the car back in gear and pulled onto the road.

After a few miles passed in pensive quiet he said, "It's hard to miss the whole malevolent haunting thing. For a guy like me, at least."

"Never met someone else who could tell before," Andrew admitted, out of his head enough to be honest.

"It never occurred to you to ask why Ed brought me in on his research, huh?" Riley said.

Andrew tilted his head on his arm, seeking a position that didn't push his teeth into his wounds or put pressure on his cheekbone. The rush of air through the windows covered up his grunt of frustration. When Andrew didn't ask for clarification, Riley went silent again, but his wire-strung tension remained. They might be fighting, but Andrew's thoughts weren't organized enough to follow the thread of the argument. Noise and the absence of noise, but no structure. Clarity dissolved into chemical disorientation as he slipped away.

Gravel crunched in the alley behind Capitol as the car drifted to a stop in its usual place, rousing Andrew enough to sit up straight. They were home. Riley dropped his head between his hands on the steering wheel. The dash clock read 2:08, an early night given their original intentions. The entire experience took on an unreal cast, distorted with intoxication, fragments of memory scattered on the road halfway between Halse's place and home.

Riley said, muffled by his arms, "I know you're hoping I'll leave well enough alone, but for fuck's sake, Andrew, I can't ignore it."

"I do just fine."

"No, you for real do not," he said.

Andrew shoved the door open and levered himself out of the car, one foot ahead of the other. Dizziness nearly struck him to his knees. Too many revelations for a single night. He needed to get up the stairs and into the shower, close a door between himself and Riley, and find his bearings. The haunt-thing that wasn't Eddie had taken blood from him. That had no chance of being good, and he doubted the revenant coming after his first lonesome fire-night, one where he'd ended up with other men's hands on him, could be a coincidence. The bottom half of his face still tingled with unnatural cold. He tried to let go of the doorframe and ended up on his ass in the gravel.

"You're a wreck," Riley said.

He accepted a boosting shoulder one more time and let himself be guided into the house. Black patches laced the edges of his vision. His roommate sat him at the table in the dimly lit kitchen and put a glass of tap water in front of him. He picked it up with trembling hands, watched the surface ripple. The water soaked his parched, raw skin as he swallowed, the room wavering around him. Without knowing how, he made it to the couch, was manhandled and stripped to his boxer briefs, and passed out clutching the rough blanket that was dropped onto his chest.

———

Coming to was an experience not dissimilar to the initial impact of his skull on the ground: a reverberation in his teeth that made his eyes water. The taste of stale blood and vomit caked his tongue. He gagged, throat hitching as he swallowed dry to keep from throwing up again. Noise from the kitchen—water running, the clink of dishes—pierced his eardrums. The throbbing in his knuckles and wrists failed to eclipse the swelling agony of his face, but it was a close call.

After several minutes of twitches and huffs, Andrew pried himself up to a seated position and swung his feet to the floor. Liquor-stinking sweat grimed him from head to toe. The water cut off. Riley called out, "You up?"

He grunted.

Footsteps, then his roommate pressing a glass of tepid water into his loose grip. The room-temperature glass felt cool on his swollen mouth. The water stung as he drank. Once he'd taken a few swallows, he chanced a squinting glance up at Riley. The other boy's eyebrows raised as he whistled.

"How bad?" Andrew asked.

"Somewhere between 'got your ass kicked' and 'hit by a fucking car,'" Riley said.

Andrew grunted again. He had classes in two days. The pull of scabs and contusions gave him an idea of the damage when he worked his jaw. "Mirror," he said.

"Brace yourself," Riley responded.

Andrew pushed his unwieldy frame into a standing position and dragged himself up the stairs, shameless about hanging on to the handrail. The fight hadn't seemed long—he had flashes in his mind's eye of a punch here and a shove there—but when he took in the sight of himself he revised that assessment. Mottled yellow and green stretched from jaw to forehead, bridging a spectacular black eye. His swollen lip was a violent blueberry-purple. The stiff, puffy splits lacerating his hand had the look of a mauling, or horror-movie-grade torture. *What if Halse hadn't stopped them?* he thought unbidden, recalling the arm that had looped, choking, around his neck.

"Jesus Christ," he muttered to himself.

After Riley left, the hot shower sluiced over his scabs and bruises like cleansing penance. As he stood slack-jawed, he pieced together chunks of the night, from the cocaine to the fire to the Mazda on the side of the road, the terrified wheezing against his neck. Andrew had thought he knew himself and his business, but he apparently didn't know the first fucking thing about his roommate. Or who Eddie had been, when he was with him. Andrew scrubbed the filth from his face with punishing force.

On the landing he hesitated, towel around his waist, before heading into Eddie's room for clothes: briefs, a worn T-shirt from the stack in the closet, a pair of ragged tan cutoffs, low-heeled socks with a hole in the toe. He paused at the mirror to run his ruined, ugly hands through the mop of his hair, smoothing it to one side. The boy staring back at him, hollow-eyed and brutalized, was a stranger. The well-worn T-shirt that didn't quite hug his chest couldn't render him familiar.

Riley knocked on the wall and pushed open the half-shut door. His face twisted through several contradictory emotions and he said, "For fuck's sake, Andrew. Is there anything in this scenario that feels heterosexual or well-adjusted to you?"

His gesture took in the room, the damp towel on the floor, the outfit that felt suddenly alien.

"Used to trade clothes all the time," came out of his mouth without his permission.

"Of course," Riley said. He looped his fingers around Andrew's wrist, careful of the swelling joint, to lead him out of the room. Andrew followed him into the kitchen and sat at the table. There were cold pancakes. "Eat those, see if your teeth are all still stuck in your skull."

"Phone?"

"On the coffee table. The clothes are in the wash with some, like, color-safe bleach I found, but they're probably done for. Blood all over the fucking place. Blood on my seats." He waved an accusatory finger in Andrew's direction as he left the room.

Andrew picked up a pancake and tore off a bite. Dry and sweet, the cakey texture clung to the insides of his cheeks. He sighed and grabbed the milk from the fridge while he balled up the dough to swallow in lumpy pills. Riley dipped into the kitchen long enough to toss his phone on the table, then disappeared up the stairs with a heavy tread. Irritation carried in the thump of his heels.

One pancake forced into his queasy stomach, Andrew swiped the password in and winced: seventeen messages, most from Halse. He thumbed the thread open and read a chunk, skipping from *Where you at* to *Riley hasn't answered, you dead?* and *Make it home?* and *Jail y/n* and *Fucker that kid you broke owed me money I'm never going to collect it now.*

The most recent were from the morning, reading *If y'all don't answer me I'm coming to visit* and *Suit yourself.*

The ominous feeling in the pit of his belly jumped at Riley's voice from the stairwell: "FYI, we're talking about last night and the incident in the car now."

"No," Andrew said automatically.

"Yes, we are," Riley said, mimicking his tone as he sat on the stairs, visible from the table. The distance was the sort a person might leave for a feral dog while attempting to coax it to a meal. Andrew's hackles rose. "I took care of you all night, and I'm saying we talk about it. After the shit with Eddie, I don't care how awkward it is for me to ask what the fuck is wrong with you. I've been letting this weird shit go—"

"I said no," Andrew cut him off.

"And I said yes," Riley snapped.

The silence dragged.

"Points of order," he began, lifting three fingers. He ticked one down and said, "The—the *ghost,* I guess, you epic fucking idiot." The second finger dropped as he continued. "Your general brain state, centering the part where you're living in his bedroom." The last finger: "That shit about being straight, and about me, we cover all that too."

Andrew's jaw went loose as he tried to find his response. *How about the part where he hid all of this from me and he's dead now.* Gasoline and fire, humid nights, knuckles on the bridge of someone's eye socket. A shiver, indiscriminate between fear and vulnerability and anger, sparked in response. The Eddie he knew wouldn't have stomached anyone questioning their straightness, but apparently he'd left that shit up to interpretation once he got to Nashville. If the wrong person had gotten the wrong idea, said the wrong thing, maybe that explained his corpse.

He started out, "What the fuck did he do to make everyone think we—"

The front door banged open. Riley jerked upright with a curse as Halse rounded the corner into the kitchen. The purple hat had made a reappearance. He tilted his chin to give them each a long, judging stare from under the brim. Andrew plucked another chunk off of a pancake and popped it in his mouth, holding eye contact.

"This is domestic," Sam said.

Riley walked down the last two stairs. "Not a good time, Sam."

"I drove here from the middle of nowhere to check y'all were in one piece," he said, flicking Riley's nose hard. The other boy lurched and snorted, wrinkling his face in affront. "Since neither of you could be bothered to answer me after you drove home shithouse wasted and"—he pointed at Andrew—"potentially concussed. How's that brain doing?"

"Fine," Andrew said. He ate another bite and drank from the gallon of milk.

"So he's fine," Sam said. "What about you?"

Riley shrugged eloquently. Andrew kept his eyes on Sam to avoid his roommate's glower, the interrupted conversation echoing in the confines of his head. *After the shit with Eddie.* Had Riley thought of something, remembered something, about Eddie's last weeks? The daylight and the cold breakfast and Sam's grating concern all jammed needles into his temples.

"The two dudes you whipped the shit out of weren't important, by the way. Good riddance," Sam said.

He pulled out a chair and sat catty-corner to them both, knees spread, forearms draped over his thighs. The hole in one knee of his jeans was lopsided. Andrew continued the methodical process of feeding himself. Sam waited another beat, then jerked his thumb in Riley's direction. "So was it because they called *him* a faggot, or because they called *you* a faggot?"

Andrew pushed his chair out without finishing his final bite. Sam barred his path with an outstretched leg as he casually took off his hat. He occupied the room with an atmospheric pressure. Andrew's hands shook, throbbing with pooled blood and lymph. Again: if Eddie had been in his shoes, if Eddie had heard that kind of talk—

Sam continued, "I'm not complaining. I hear it was a good show, you wailing on 'em. I'm just curious about your motives, because you're half the size of that Mikey motherfucker."

"Stop it," Riley said. Sam opened his mouth again, but to Andrew's surprise, Riley cut him off: "I'm not kidding, shut up. Have some decorum, Jesus."

Sam subsided. The pressure of his presence decreased a measure. A path of bruises climbed the side of his neck, patches in the shape of tooth marks, but otherwise he seemed as fresh as a summertime boy could be: sweat on his temples, a sleeveless shirt hanging loose across the bumps of his ribs and the plane of his chest. Andrew stood next to him, words and silence battling in his throat.

"Okay, message received." Sam slapped his thighs and got up, pushed his chair in with his heel, then unlocked the porch door and opened it. "Y'all ain't dead, I'll head out. Good to see you, Blur."

Riley let out a tea-kettle-like whistle of a sigh when the other man clattered from the porch into the yard without shutting the door. The kitchen filled with the smell of grass and dog shit. The neighbor's mutt barked at Sam along the fenceline as he left.

"He just shows up sometimes. Thinks he's my fucking dad, swear to god," Riley said.

Andrew snorted. Standing tense and coiled had made the pulse in his temples vicious, almost powerful enough to provoke vertigo. He collapsed on the chair. For a second, he felt grateful to Halse for interrupting them. Impeccable bad timing.

"But seriously," Riley said.

Andrew said, "I'm not going to talk about it, no matter how much you ask. It's just things, happening, that don't concern you."

"I can't sleep, Blur." Riley's hands moved in an abrupt, agitated arc. "That *thing* came back with you, and you're not—" He paused, then plowed on when Andrew began to speak. "You're not doing anything about it. I didn't sign up for a haunted house."

"And you think I did?" Andrew said.

"I think you don't know what you're fucking doing."

That flensed him. Riley hit the nail on the head; he was talking ghosts, but he'd covered Andrew's sloppy investigation without trying. Clumsily staggering from one confrontation to the next, strung out between a campus he kept avoiding and a handful of men with questionable intentions he kept being drawn to—none of that had organized intention behind it. He was acting on one impulse after another, hoping he'd find the right direction while dodging the shit that he'd rather ignore. Andrew grabbed his phone as he stood. The floor swam. He tipped his chin and blinked at the pattern on the tile. Riley had exposed him on multiple levels, like he'd stripped off his topmost layer of skin. Andrew wasn't prepared to see himself, let alone show someone else.

"Please," Riley said as he approached the table. "Your ghost is like nothing I've ever felt before, my whole life, and I've seen my fair share of weird shit. You're dragging around a second shadow on your heels, I feel him all the time. It's awful. How can you stand it?"

"Because it's not really him," he said. "They never are."

"Then what is it?"

The juxtaposition of the dirty breakfast dishes on the countertop, their naked feet on the sun-warm tile, and the total lack of air in the room made for a claustrophobic pressure. Andrew's phone buzzed in his fist. He crammed it into his back pocket and winced at the drag on his scabbed fingers.

"It isn't Eddie," he repeated. "So ignore it, just—ignore it. There's nothing you can do that won't make it worse."

"That's so stupid. Ignoring it isn't going to make it stop. Doesn't he, doesn't *it,* need something from you or me or . . ." Riley yanked on his hair and let out a frustrated half-yell, spinning to face the wall instead of Andrew. His back flexed. "I hate this."

"It's not him," Andrew repeated. He swallowed the taste of souring milk and blood from the back of his throat. "It's a fucking copy of a copy, leftovers. The more of us it gets, the more it'll take, because it's dead and we're alive. Fucking forget about it."

"How are you so certain?"

Andrew said, "A lot of fucking experience, Riley," and pushed past him in a brush of shoulders.

He took the keys from the table and walked out barefoot to the sound of Riley calling after him, "Stop running off, goddamnit!"

Andrew walked as fast as his unsteady feet allowed, but Riley didn't chase after. Asphalt burned the soles of his feet, and the Challenger's textured rubber pedals flattened his toes out oddly under the pressure. He drove Eddie's car to the outskirts of the suburbs and beyond, found the highway from his sole race with Halse, and pulled off to the side. The engine ticked, cooling, as he sat surrounded by dim sun and nature noises, smelling the humidity like a rotten blanket. His phone hung lax in his fingers.

come home

i'll be waiting

He read it again, again. Halse had texted him to say *Put some ice on your face.* Riley had too: *why are you avoiding this when i already know your secret?* and then, a half hour later, *sorry.*

When he returned home, the television was the only light in the living room, washing out Riley's pale skin and two-tone hair into a ghastly blue-grey mask. He paused on the threshold. Riley said, "I don't get it. Eddie said you'd never talk about your . . . your spooky shit, whatever, but how do you not want to understand it? I do."

"I don't want to understand, I want it gone," he said.

And when he thought about the other half of the conversation, the things he didn't *need* to understand that had the magnetism and threat of a man's thumbs against the divots of Riley's lower back, his brain stalled out like a hung transmission. The research and his roommate's psychic bullshit weren't the only things Eddie hadn't mentioned getting closer to. The cavernous space of the house pressed all around them. Riley didn't push any further.

10

"Is there something you can do to track it?" Andrew asked.

He held Eddie's final phone bill crumpled in his fist. He'd waited until he had the house to himself to dig into the pile of abandoned mail next to the front door, sifting through junk and credit card offers and unpaid bills, all addressed to Edward Fulton.

On the other end of the line, the service rep said, "Unfortunately, no. If he'd had an app for tracking, it could be possible, but if the phone was turned off or out of charge, it wouldn't work regardless."

"All right," Andrew said, and hung up.

He traded the phone in his hand for the perspiring bag of frozen corn he'd snagged out of the freezer, leaving a wet splotch on the coffee table. The cold on the fucked-up half of his face lanced through the heat-daze of the afternoon and the stuttering disappointment of the call. He tilted sideways to lie on the couch, letting gravity hold the makeshift ice pack in place.

Asking Riley—or worse, his cousin—who Eddie had been spending time with in his last weeks was unthinkable, both because he wasn't certain of their personal culpability and because it would require an admission of ignorance. Attending the gathering had solidified his suspicions, though. The remembered thrum of the music, the coke, the liquor all carried recognition and temptation. Halse with his depth-charge grin holding court, one prince to another, magnanimous offerings hard to refuse. Andrew knew it without knowing it, how he and Eddie would've gotten on like a demolition. Halse had seemed in control of his scene, but Eddie had a gift for pissing people off when he felt the call to assert himself.

And aside from the danger presented by Halse, there were other violent men in his court. The split knuckles he flexed to feel the pulling skin were proof enough of that. From Riley's admission that Luca skipped Sam's parties for her own safety, to the fact that those two men had felt free to talk shit about Riley and Ethan, to the way they lumped Eddie in with their derision—aloud, where the whole crowd might hear—none of that was a good sign. More damning, no one had stepped in to deescalate the violence until Sam arrived to do so himself. Who would stop a fight that Sam wanted, stop violence the prince had ordained? Who there would have watched Eddie's back, if he'd dived into a fight without Andrew to help him?

Dangers stacked onto dangers, but provided no clear answers. The tomb of the bedroom above him filled him with a miserable, childish yearning: his head hurt, his hands hurt, his soul hurt, his hangover was monumental, and he missed Eddie. Face in his hands, Andrew shuddered through a few hard breaths. He didn't miss his parents, he didn't miss Del, he didn't miss his old apartment. Those gaps were all distant aches that didn't require filling, only an awareness of loss. Eddie's absence, though, cut a trough of tired need that no one else had the potential to fill up—

In a burst of confidence or cowardice, he tramped up the stairs and pulled open the drawer of Eddie's bedside table. Several of the loose-leaf pages were crumpled from his haphazard attempt at storage. He grabbed the composition book and sat on the edge of the mattress. The gentle bow of the notebook, warped from use, fit naturally into the curve of his hands. He remembered the devolution in handwriting from the neat introduction to the scrawl on the final page, either rushed or excited, talking about land and sacrifice. Eddie might've sat there too, bending it this way and that while he talked to Riley about his theories.

Riley, who had been aware of the phantom since the first moment Andrew had arrived, and yet had said nothing. The abrupt click of realization, that those monstrous haunted nights had all been followed by Riley's drawn, tired face in the morning, gave Andrew worse vertigo than his lingering head trauma. He hadn't said fuck-all. He'd lain in his room across the hall and let it wreck him and said nothing. Out of respect, or out of guilt? Andrew's crawling suspicion flitted between the two options. Since his arrival, he'd been struggling to find a direction to pursue, attempting to unearth what had happened to Eddie by grasping aimlessly at each sliver of a hint. Missing phone, grim research, strange roommate, a pack of boys with bad attitudes and worse tempers, uncorrected assumptions about himself and Eddie: all the lies and half-truths about Eddie's life in Nashville, without Andrew, spilled disorganized around his feet.

Those strangers had called Andrew a faggot with their whole chests. Once at some frat party, he'd started to pass out on Eddie's shoulder and slouched instead to push his face into the soft-solid plane of his stomach, one arm around his waist. Touch settled Andrew in a good place as his body shut down. Eddie had run a proprietary hand over the crest of his shoulder blade. When some guy had hooted derisively from across the room, Eddie had scooped Andrew onto the couch, walked over, and smacked him straight in his mouth with one big hand. "Say it again, you think I'm like that," he'd commanded with bass in his voice. Andrew remembered how he'd buried his face in the disgusting couch cushions to keep from throwing up, trying to remind himself and his sour stomach: they weren't like that.

He shied from that train of thought and flipped open the cover of the notebook, skimmed the initial page again. The second time, prepared for it, he didn't recoil from seeing their personal business laid bare. He didn't want to do this, not at all, but reading his familiar handwriting was as close to speaking to Eddie as he was going to get. Despite his advice to Riley, he was doing a piss-poor job of ignoring the haunting in his lonelier hours, and the visitations were getting nastier. He doubted there was a use for them other than jealous consumption.

He flipped a chunk of pages. The spread of smudged black ink was indecipherable for a split second, as if he was refusing himself comprehension, and then he read from the center of the righthand page: *the real interesting part is going to be seeing if it's better or worse when we're here together. Anecdotal evidence is all we've got but up north, separate, it was stronger for me. But together it was stronger for Andrew. So, is it actually me? Is he just getting the echoes? Except it feels like something's missing now that I'm home, there's this big looming pressure I can't stick my fingers into quite yet. Maybe it's him*

Andrew riffled forward further, skimming, his skin broken out in a chill sweat. He read chunks at random—*went to a graveyard yesterday and that was a fucking trip and a half holy shit* followed six pages later with *is it a nightmare or a haunt-dream let's play that game, they're happening with real fucking frequency these days* and *it's weird to meet a kid who's like, a little psychic or whatever and realize whatever I am is totally different.* He paused and tried to read the surrounding sentences—that was about Riley, clearly—but they weren't related.

Goddamn Eddie for his disjointed stream of consciousness. The result was a series of jabs that pricked randomly into Andrew as he read, suddenly and from different angles than he expected. On another page he read a single line, *but what if we'd died there?,* before slapping it shut and shoving it off of his lap. Cold light pulsed behind his eyelids. He shivered, a long and pitiful shaking from his toes to his scalp. His hands were trembling too. He packed a bowl, clumsy, and carried it into the stairwell. He tucked himself against the corner on the landing to light up, pulling an acrid lungful of smoke to settle his nerves. As he'd figured, not a single useful word about parties or conflicts or who he'd been meeting, aside from Riley and Andrew. And he'd had plenty to share about Andrew.

"Fuck you, Eddie," he muttered as he exhaled. The afternoon shadows ignored him.

Without Eddie's phone or a plan to find it, with the laptop locking him out and the journal being as much of a traumatic bust as he'd expected, Andrew sat in his private halo of smoke and breathed. He settled himself back into his skin. The shaking stopped, the cold flashes drifted to a halt. The sense of something straining against the creaking cage bars of his head, something he'd rather keep locked away, subsided.

The answers he needed weren't ever going to come from the ghost shit. He hadn't been able to explain it to Riley, and he hadn't wanted to, but the dead pressure of haunting was a strange constant in his life, a background hum, a thing he was never rid of as much as he tried to avoid it. The form of that truth wasn't different now, even if it was indescribably worse in intensity. Of course Eddie, monstrous as he'd been, had left behind a revenant that broke all the rules to cling to him, demolishing him one haunting at a time.

He still had other avenues to pursue, particularly given the adrenaline-pumping events of Halse's big get-together. He slid his phone out of his pocket and opened his message thread with Riley, then went back to his dead conversation with Eddie, then West, and finally Halse. He could tell Halse was more dangerous than the rest, but he had put far less effort into investigating West or the advisor, who might have more indirect information and wouldn't be as suspicious of his inquiries—might even expect them. He took another hit and let smoke seep slow from between his lips while he stared at the ceiling.

Even having had that thought, he still selected Halse's message and typed, *Next night out?*

The response came in almost an instant: *See you tomorrow*

He'd figure out approaching West or Troth later.

———

Andrew had nearly three hundred pages of reading to complete in the gap between his classes, thanks to his squandered concussed weekend and the one seminar he'd already skipped. Furthermore, he'd spent the entire night crashing from one hazy stress-dream through another, a stream of repetitive sensory input: blood in his mouth, cold stone under his hands, pitch-black dripping silence. It was almost predictable, after reading from that fucking journal, but entirely mundane. His phantom hadn't made itself known. Under all that stress, when West hollered his name across the courtyard of the humanities building, he almost ignored him.

"Andrew," West called again.

Andrew made accidental eye contact—no going back from that. He lifted a hand covered in mismatched Band-Aids to wave acknowledgment, and the pair met at the bottom of the short staircase. West's lips were pinched thin as he took in Andrew's mauled face.

Andrew preempted him and said, "I had an accident."

"What, you got hit by a car?"

Andrew snorted at the repeat of Riley's earlier phrasing and said, "Something like that, yeah. It's not as bad as it looks."

One sardonic lift of West's brows was response enough. The sight of himself in the mirror that morning, despite as liberal an application of ice as his body could handle, hadn't been pretty: not for him the aesthetic, fashionable black eye; instead, a visual reminder of the kind of uncontrolled violence that folks on Vandy's campus didn't see much. Another expressive glance raked him from head to toe.

"You don't have to tell me, but I see those hands. I told you that crew of Sowell's is rough. But how's your second week going otherwise? I still haven't gotten an email from you, and Dr. Troth nudged me to check up," he asked.

"Spent the last couple of days laid up, so I'm behind on reading. I should probably go work on that," he said.

West shook his head and offered, "Let me buy you a coffee, and I'll tell you what you missed? We should catch up."

Andrew clenched his sore fist around the strap of his bag, weighed the offer's sincerity, and said, "All right, but it better be enough detail to help me through the lecture."

"Pinky swear," West drawled.

Andrew followed him to the café, keeping pace with his long stride through the mid-afternoon hustle. Distressed jeans hugged his legs straight into a pair of well-kept leather boots with the tops folded over. Andrew was abruptly aware that West's whole ensemble—and West would've considered it one, he was sure—probably cost more than half of Riley's closet. One thick silver ring flashed on his index finger when he reached up to adjust his glasses in the café line.

"I'm assuming there's something you need in return," Andrew said.

West gave him a lopsided grin. "In a sense, yeah. I need you to let me do my job as your mentor, or it reflects poorly on me and the place I've earned here. I also thought I'd follow up on those books you borrowed from Dr. Troth, see if you're finding your feet. She's been asking."

"Give me the rundown for the lecture first?"

"Greedy," West teased him.

Like you even know me, he wanted to say, grumpy at being forced to socialize when he could have been planning the next move of his investigation. True to his word, though, West spread his own notes out on the tabletop; his handwriting was unexpectedly blocky and messy. Once they reached the end of his notes, after twenty minutes of unexpectedly empathetic teaching, West trailed off into silence. He sipped from his perspiring iced latte. Andrew took a long pull of his own cold-sweet-bitter concoction. The swelling in his mouth had started to recede, but the cuts stung fiercely when he drank anything other than water.

A few individual locs hung over West's forehead as he bent over his notes. They lent his expression a harried, professorial earnestness when he said, "Not to sound parental, but it's only the second week. You can't afford to get behind so soon."

"Special circumstances," Andrew answered with a gesture to his face.

"I'll say." Andrew watched him work his mouth around his straw, chewing the end, before he continued in a more subdued tone, "There were a couple of times it seemed like Ed might've had the same kind of accident. Sowell's friends, I'm guessing."

"No friends of his," he grumbled, one harsh word lodged in his hindbrain.

West hummed, unconvinced. "I don't know how Sowell hangs around guys like that, honestly. It must be difficult for him—you know, *considering*. God knows I'd be scared to head out into the country. You couldn't pay me enough to take on that risk, even if I was a *white* gay man."

Andrew shied from West's openness, which he felt invited a return admission, to ask, "You said Eddie got in some shit, though?"

West drew a wet line between the two puddles of condensation on the table with his thumb. "Once or twice he looked like he'd gotten into a fight. Scuffed up, stiff, all that. But, and no offense intended here, he never showed up to our meetings looking like he lost."

It wasn't worth asking if Eddie had told West who he fought with. Instead Andrew said, "He had a temper."

"I know," West said. "One semester with him was enough for me to see that, in class and outside it. Which made it hard to get a read on him otherwise—he was so butch, unlike Sowell. I couldn't figure him out."

West raised an eyebrow and left the implication open a second time. Andrew shifted in his chair, turning his cup in his hands. Was he being invited to say something about Eddie, or about himself? The continued questioning, from one man after another, provoked a sour bump of resistance. His interactions with West had a dynamic cast, an air of performance that attempted to welcome him in—but still held the unavoidable insincerity of strangers, laid bundled around an uglier truth: both of them saw his discomfort, his inability to move through the academic world as well as Eddie had.

Unsure of his response, given Eddie's apparent failure to correct people's assumptions about him and Andrew's own caustic guilt over it, he said without conviction, "Eddie was Eddie."

West let it lie, as if sensing he'd misjudged. "Well, how'd the books go?"

"How'd Ed spend his time on campus, with who else?" Andrew redirected.

West blinked, a catlike blankness slipping over his face for a second before he said, "You mean like, what was he doing while he was here?"

"Yeah. What'd he get into?" Andrew steeled himself to admit, "He left some stories out, the fights you say he got in. I need to know."

"Ouch, I'm sorry. And, well," he said, the vowel hanging long. He considered his answer over another sip. "I'm not sure I'm going to be much help there. He had a couple hours with me every week, a couple hours with Dr. Troth. You probably already know that he wasn't into extracurriculars. He didn't accept a teaching position, gave off the impression that he didn't need the money. He was friendly with his cohort, but he mostly . . ."

"What?"

"Entertained himself off campus," West finished, with a wince that said he knew it was inadequate.

Andrew nodded. He hadn't thought there would be much to glean on campus, but it ruled out another avenue of questions. If Eddie was close to his cohort, if he'd been spending his time with them, there might've been a point of interest. But West had admitted Eddie was fighting. Riley hadn't said shit about that, and it wasn't the sort of detail contained in a research journal.

"I'm sure some of his time with Sowell's friends outside the city was for research," West said. Andrew forced his attention back to the conversation. "He spoke more to Dr. Troth than he did to me about where he went and what he learned wandering. I've not got much for you there. Speaking of, I do need to offer her some sort of update, so, how did the books she picked work out for you?"

The bag Troth had given him was still in the back seat of the Challenger. He'd wedged it into the footwell and forgotten it as promptly as possible. "To be honest, I haven't had time for them yet. Sorry."

"Entertaining himself off campus" pointed straight in the direction Andrew was already leaning. He had to get closer to Halse's court if he wanted to find out what had happened—what *could've* happened, to set things so wrong. As he imagined confronting Halse, West reached over and plucked a stray hair off the scabbed bridge of Andrew's knuckles without touching his skin, flicking it off the table. The movement of his large hands remained delicate.

West grinned again, a tinge self-deprecating as he had been with the professor, and said, "Apologies if that was weird, it was bugging me."

"It's fine," Andrew muttered awkwardly, imagined heat prickling his fingers.

"Talk to Troth, once you look at the books. She has a better idea of where Eddie conducted his interviews."

He nodded, a noncommittal acquiescence, and stood with the watery dregs of his coffee. West followed suit and looped the strap of his bag over his head. Maybe he wasn't quite as done with campus as he thought—interviews meant strangers, difficult conversations. But compared to the danger of the three-digit speedometer and Halse's motley crew with its confirmed selection of bigots eager to start shit, that stood secondary.

"Class?" Andrew said.

"Sure," West replied, hesitating as if he had one more thought, but letting it drop.

Andrew had no intention of reading those books, regardless. His real research subject wouldn't make it into a dissertation; his subject was Eddie, and whatever Eddie had done to make all these guys so unsure of him, so enthralled by him. Creeping unease lingered in his memories—Riley's belief that he and Andrew were *together*-together, after six long months wherein Eddie could've corrected him; Halse and the boys tossing around the word *faggot;* West's careful insider warnings. How had Eddie made it so long without correcting them, if they talked like that in front of him? Denial rose to the tip of Andrew's tongue without an audience to hear it, a powerful reflex that Eddie had trained into him. Had the time apart from Andrew changed something fundamental in Eddie? Something that Riley and West had picked up on, and he'd missed by inches? The doubt scoured at him.

Eddie wasn't going to be answering that question, for him or anyone. His starving ghost was more than intimate, but not one for personal chats. Crossing the green campus with its frantic flush of youth, weaving between students on their bikes and a gaggle of kids attempting to tightrope walk on a strap they'd looped between two trees, death felt impossible. It had no place outside a romantic theoretical. After midnight on a pitch-dark stretch of road, tasting the finer edge of human fragility in the glare of wrong-way headlights, though—there death was a pressure on the sides of the neck, gripping where the pulse beat hardest.

The slump of his roommate's shoulders was the first thing Andrew saw on entering the classroom. Andrew took the desk next to Riley's and said, "Stayed at Sam's last night?"

Riley grunted his agreement and straightened his shoulders with an audible pop. He'd already opened his notebook and written the date at the top corner of the page, texts in a neat stack next to it. Compared to weekend Riley, the academic with his glasses riding low on his nose was a different person. He said, "Figured we could use some space, and I was behind on reading. Sam worked through most of the evening, and then his, y'know, second job after that. House was quiet."

"There's a first and second job?"

Riley rolled his eyes and said, "You fucking rich kids, I swear to god."

Andrew sat back at the frustration in his tone.

"Sam inherited the house, but it costs money to keep, and most of us don't have an unlimited supply. I guess hanging out with that prick—" he pointed toward West holding court at the front of the room, "makes it hard to remember the rest of us, huh?"

"He got me a coffee, like peer mentors do," Andrew said.

"Yeah, sure, that's all it is. Not a hint of trust fund solidarity. And don't give me shit about how I should be less of an asshole about him, we should be—on the same team, or something. But we're really not," Riley hissed.

Andrew, bewildered by his inclusion in an internecine argument he'd missed the important details of and had no desire to dig further into, asked instead, "Sam tell you I texted him?"

Riley sighed and said, "He did. Tonight, yeah?"

The professor called the room to attention, and Andrew cast Riley an agreeable nod before he put himself to it, joining the discussion when he could piece together a solid response from West's quick catch-up. Halfway through, his phone buzzed on his desk. He glanced at the screen and saw a text from Riley. *(1) Mechanic (2) drugs.* A moment later it clicked, and he swiped the notification off the screen.

The implication that he was closer to Thom West's *GQ* than the grease and sweat of Sam Halse stung him with something close to shame. He didn't have a rebuttal other than the fact that it insulted him, so he swallowed the urge to argue. Eddie's money hadn't changed how Andrew's parents had raised them, teenage boys making a ruckus in a lower-middle-class suburb. Except—

When he was eleven, his parents had debated whether they could afford braces for him and decided to leave his crooked bottom teeth alone. When he was fourteen, after the Fultons had had their accident and his parents had adopted Eddie per their willed request, when the reorganized familial unit had moved up north to accommodate his mother's job, they'd bought a house that was three times the size of the old one, no mortgage. Eddie hadn't once held a real job; when Andrew had worked part-time, it had been for a distraction.

He opened the message thread and typed back, *sorry.*

Riley opened it a moment later, cut a glance at him, and nodded.

II

Andrew coasted up the winding drive to Sam's place behind Riley, air-conditioning blowing over silence in the Challenger. After the last drive, he was eager to let the beast off the leash again—to occupy the driver's seat that Eddie left behind, be closer to the living man than to the terror of his remnant. His school bag sat on the passenger seat; he grabbed the strap and tossed it in the back, out of sight alongside the tote full of books West had been asking after. A handful of other cars lined the drive, two wheels in the grass and two on concrete. One was a blacked-out Supra with a scuffed bumper.

As he mounted the front steps, Riley said, "This should go better than last time."

"I'd fucking hope so," Andrew said.

The door was unlocked. The pair wandered into a living room fogged with chatter and green-smelling smoke, the quiet thump of music from another room. Sam called out, "You're late, boys!"

One couch ran along the wall next to the door. Another sat catty-corner to it on the far side of the room. Ethan and Luca were sprawled on the distant couch, her plump bare feet braced on his thigh. Riley crossed the room to drop himself on them with no regard for elbows or shins, earning two pitches of indignant squawk in response. Sam and two other plain-looking white men were passing a blunt on the other couch. Andrew accepted when the person on the end offered him a hit.

Sam leaned around his friend and waved, then said, "We ordered some pizza, but it takes a dick-year to deliver out here, so settle in. Hope you like supreme."

Without another option, he planted his ass on the arm of the couch next to the stranger and laid his arm along the backrest. The other man said, "I'm Ben, I think we met for a minute at the party. Your face looks like shit, dude."

Sam barked a laugh and said, "Hey now, you can't just tell a man he looks like shit."

"He's right though," Riley said.

"Big tough guy, isn't he," Ethan drawled.

Andrew grunted; something about Ethan's teasing tone wedged itself under his skin. Ethan cackled at his discomfort and Luca kicked him. Riley grabbed her ankle; she wriggled around while Ethan trailed off into a winded giggle, amusing himself. Once the trio righted themselves from their puppyish squirm, Luca tipped her head over the couch arm to look at him upside-down.

She said, "I couldn't get a straight story out of any of these ass-holes, which means something happened that none of them wants to admit to me. So, why don't you tell me what happened?"

The question flew into the wall of Andrew's privacy like a bird into glass and dropped dead. His stiff shoulders raised another notch. He'd spoken to Luca once, for two minutes, and the room was full of people he didn't know at all. For Luca, the arrangement was safely domestic, but for him it was lightning-charged.

Sam took over: "A couple of good ol' boys decided to shit-talk Ed in his earshot, I gather. Andrew here put them to rights, scrappy little thing that he obviously is."

Ben hummed an approval and Luca murmured, "Huh, all right." She turned her attention from him back to her couchmates, though he doubted she found that answer sufficient.

Andrew stared at the side of Sam's face, the small crimp of his lip that he read as *liar, liar*. Neither Riley nor Ethan contradicted him with the significant detail. No one was saying what had set him off—and he wondered if that was a matter of politeness, or if some of the men in the room might lose their sympathy real quick, given the truth. As he watched, Sam rolled his head back against the couch. The track of love-bites on the side of his throat had disappeared.

"I expected a more animated guy, given Ed's stories," the third man on the couch said.

"Shut up, Jacob," Sam said.

Andrew craned his neck to look at him and said, "Yeah, shut up."

Ethan chuckled again, as did Riley. He had the sense that they were laughing at him, or Sam, or the general situation. He ran his thumb in circles on the rough weave of the couch and listened to the pack rib each other. Observing them in close quarters would give him a better sense of the threat each of them might've posed, but to do that he had to sit and be social. His mouth had gone dry with anxious tension, unsure of how to insert himself into the conversation again without being obvious. His phone buzzed and he fished it out with relief at the distraction.

Thanks for getting coffee, said West.

Yeah, he sent, following up a moment later with *thanks for the review.*

Are you busy tonight?

He tossed the phone from hand to hand before responding— *Yeah*—and jammed it into his pocket again. West hadn't offered him enough information to draw him out from here, the place where Eddie would've been. Riley playfully tugged a long, kinked curl of Luca's hair while she wiggled into a more comfortable position with her legs fully kicked over both his and Ethan's. An unwelcome sense memory washed under Andrew's skin: his fingers grappling then tangling with Eddie's on the slick, smooth handholds of Del's bony hips, knuckles bruising against knuckles as he gripped tight without acknowledging the heat that spiked through his solar plexus. Mouthing the same places on her that Eddie had, seconds after, still wet from his lips.

"Bathroom?" Andrew asked with a slight tremble to his tone.

"Let me show you," Sam said, pushing free of the couch.

The bathroom was the first room on the right. Sam led him

past it to the end of the carpeted hall, then opened the last door, waving Andrew inside. The pile of clothes at the foot of the unmade bed, the faint smell of gasoline and oil, and the overflowing ashtray on the side table coasted a careful line between lived-in and dirty. On the windowsill a series of colorful model cars sat frozen in an unending chase.

"Sit," Sam said and pointed at the end of the bed.

"Why?"

"Because you're giving off some weird fucking vibes tonight, man." The setting sun, obscured by the trees surrounding the house, cast the whole room in strange lines of orange and taupe. Sam shut the door and leaned against it. "If you're going out with us, I've got to be sure you're good for it."

Andrew spread his feet and leaned forward. "What's that supposed to mean?"

"Jacob was right, I can't get a read on you. You're not the guy I was expecting to get to know, from Eddie and shit, and I protect my own. Among which you do not currently number," he finished with a pointedly raised eyebrow.

"Good of you to remember that," Andrew said.

"Answer the question," Sam said. "I get that you're fucked up right now, okay? Fine, great, that's your business. But if you're planning to lose your shit on someone else, this time on the road, that's not going to fly with me."

Andrew said in Eddie's drawl, "Anybody here tonight asking for an ass-whipping?"

Sam said, "No, kid, none of them are going to mess with you like that."

Before he could respond to the unexpected gentleness in Sam's voice, the doorbell rang. Sam opened the door and jerked his thumb toward the hall. He took the hint and ambled to the bathroom for a mostly unnecessary piss, appreciating the brief solitude, then zipped his jeans and returned to the pack. In his absence, a stack of pizza boxes and a chair from the kitchen had appeared. He took the extra seat without a word.

Jacob put a slice of pizza in his hand and said, "No offense meant."

The curious comfort faded as night descended, their meal reduced to an empty set of greasy cardboard boxes. Sam bounced his leg. Jacob whistled tunelessly under his breath. Ben sprawled on his corner of the couch like an indolent big cat. A soft roll of stomach peeked from underneath the high hem of his T-shirt. The trio on the other couch had drifted apart, no longer crowding the same square foot of space—and all of them had their eyes on him, the stranger in their midst.

"Dibs on the fresh meat," Luca said.

Ethan said, "Oh, that's unfair. I'm the best suited, our cars match."

"You match the Supra, and he's not driving the Supra," Riley said.

"We'll do this quick," Sam said. The group turned to him as one. "Set the pairs here, block the street, get it done before someone notices."

"Basic setup for his first time?" Ben asked.

"Far from my first time," Andrew said. He stood and stretched, back cracking, arms over his head. The lengthening of his chest masked the strain in his voice as he continued, "Between me and Eddie I'm the better driver."

"Let's put him through his paces, then," Sam said, slapping his stomach hard enough to crumple him. He thumped a loose fist on Sam's arm in response. The wolf-grin made a reappearance as Sam, knees spread in his kingly position on the couch, dragged his eyes up the length of Andrew, as hot and stinging as the four faint lines his fingers had left behind. "Keep up, princess."

The pack stood and gathered shoes, hats, ducked out for a last-minute piss. Andrew scrubbed the heel of his hand against the sting through his shirt, and Riley threw an arm over his shoulder, pulling him down to murmur next to his ear, "Welcome home."

Andrew flinched. The arm slipped off his shoulders, palm

glancing off the small of his back as Riley turned to his girlfriend and his—and Ethan. The trio were first out the door. Andrew hung at the tail end of the group with Sam, who stood on the top step of the porch to survey his crew. Andrew hopped off onto the lawn, and Sam tousled his hair from above. He stumbled two steps out of reach.

"You're still wound too tight," Sam observed.

No one had touched him so much in—weeks, months. Eddie had visited him at the end of the spring term and spent the whole five days manhandling him: scratching his scalp, digging thumbs into the knots of his trapezius muscles, rolling on top of him during naps, once gnawing absently on the knob of his wrist for a full five seconds during a movie. Eddie's touch was a careless claim that meant home, home, *home*. These knockoffs hadn't earned the right to handle him.

"You set the pairs?" Andrew asked.

"Consensus, I guess," he said. "Luca called your dibs, though. That's her car."

He pointed to the fox-body Mustang Andrew had noted at the gas station. Andrew almost hadn't expected her to mean it. Del hadn't been much for their sport.

"She had a bone to pick with Eddie about his attitude toward girls, and I'm sure she'd love to pick it with you too," Sam said.

"Shouldn't be hard to beat that car, unless she's packing something real impressive under the hood," he said.

"Cocky little shit," Sam said.

"What are you two gossiping about?" Riley shouted at them from the open window of his Mazda. "Hurry up, goddamn."

"All he does is bitch," Sam said with affection as he strode toward his WRX.

The roar of their motley crew careened off the hills. Andrew rode middle of the pack, the bulk of the Hellcat digging at the pavement. He pulled Eddie's hat onto his head and kept a thumb on the brim, elbow on the edge of the open window. The dying light tinged the evening gold. He ran his tongue over his teeth. A dog bayed once, distant and eerie.

The passenger seat pricked at the corner of his right eye—the same straw paper and discarded shirt from the first afternoon remained, nothing remarkable on second and third glance—but there was a *tug*. Ethan's taillights ahead guided him out of the hills alongside the rest of the pack, to an outlying suburb, then an unlit stretch of street leading into an industrial park. The grungy rumble of someone's muffled electronic loops ahead of him bounced against his eardrums. The road through the boxy nondescript buildings was deserted and straight and nakedly public. Eddie would've said, *kiss your plausible deniability goodbye*. But he'd have been smiling when he said it.

Andrew had missed this too, no matter his other reasons for being in the pack tonight.

Practiced as choreography, Ben pulled onto the shoulder a stretch down the road while the rest idled in wait. Music throbbed through open windows, guitar and percussion and electronic fog clashing from all sides. Streetlights cast shadows behind Ben's heels as he climbed out of his car with an actual orange cone in hand, like from high school gym class. He slapped it on the yellow line and bowed performatively at the group before hopping back in his Focus and reversing to meet them.

Sam hollered, "Let's get this done before we have company!"

The Mazda rolled ahead of the rest and purred in the lamplight. Andrew was unsurprised to see Ethan match Riley, goosing the engine once their noses were even. It reminded him of his own habitual match with Eddie, first and last no matter what happened between—until now. Ben jogged to stand between the cars with a hand raised. Desire flamed in Andrew as both cars shot off the mark to Ben's hand chopping the night air. The Supra's whine shrieked over the Mazda's lower register, plowing ahead first. Riley caught Ethan, though, at a too-abrupt shift. The Supra's tail end went loose, a brief but unsalvageable slip that let the Mazda skate past the cone. Brake lights spilled bloody red over the road.

The Mustang rolled up next to Andrew, and Luca shouted to him, "Ben and Jacob have it next, then it's us."

"Clear," he said.

The tattoo itched, a ring of tender prickling pain. Andrew rubbed his wrist on his jeans. Floater-specks danced at the edge of his vision while his nerves throbbed in asymmetrical tempo. The gunmetal WRX idled at the edge of the pack. Sam boosted himself to sit on the rim of his window, ass tucked into the notch of the door and one arm on the roof. Andrew was peripherally aware of the other pair squaring up with Ethan as their flagger.

The rest of him settled, attuned to the cigarette hanging from the corner of Sam's mouth. His sunburned neck led to the swell of his paler, naked shoulders, where a hint of black ink slipped loose at the collar of his tank top. It was shapeless but bold in the gloaming light, too distant to guess at. Sam noticed his attention and flicked his cigarette onto the ground. Andrew's hand lifted without his permission. He pointed a finger to his own chest and then at Sam. The bark of Sam's laugh carried over the noise of the other cars bursting from their stop.

On the other side, Luca said, "Keep it in your pants, Jesus."

Andrew twitched. She laughed when he turned from Sam, but it was good-natured, lighting her face. Her laugh gave him permission to look, but her seeing made him feel naked. High cheekbones, plump cheeks, the cloud of her hair wrangled free of her face with a toothed headband; the orange lipstick matched her short orange fingernails. He tried to imagine Del behind the wheel of her own car, doing her own work under the hood, and came up blank. Riley said Luca didn't care for most of Sam's friends, and neither did Ethan, but here they were: the core of the crew, the ones he should talk to more.

Thinking about that, he called back, "Next?"

"Yeah, I figure I've got a point to prove for our first head-to-head," she said.

"What's that?" Andrew asked.

"Got to demolish the new boy to keep him in his right place, like the rest of 'em," she said with a wink as she worked her left arm to roll her window up between them. The tint concealed her one mechanical inch at a time, smirking at him all the while. That was a brand of showmanship Andrew appreciated.

His spark of pleasure was unexpected, momentarily unbalancing. The outing he'd intended as an investigation kept distracting him with something close to fun. He thumbed the button for his windows and coasted to the line. The Hellcat rumbled under him. The interior hush, tinted windows cutting him off from the light, sparked at his fingers on the gearshift. The digital display changed as he shifted to sport drive, the 0.00 timer mode active. All tech, Eddie's car, compared to the classic machine Luca had chosen for her own, or his Supra, waiting at the house on Capitol for his next outing.

Sam strolled past the hood of the car, one proprietary hand trailing over the sleek, glossy paint. He nodded to Luca first, but then his whole focus shifted to Andrew, eyes on his, hand raised. Andrew held the clutch and eased onto the gas, pushing revs while the digital readout reminded him to hold it, wait for the right moment to explode. Sam's fingers touched the rim of the moon hanging in the sky. A shudder ripped across the bones of Andrew's forearms, terror and delight and the promise of risk bringing him to life.

Smashing forward into motion was as natural as breathing when Sam's bicep bunched and he chopped his hand at the ground. He felt his own heartbeat and the car's lurch off the line, pinning his stomach to his spine with sweet vertigo. At that precise moment, his pulse bit between his teeth, the flick of shadow *yanking* at the corner of his eye from the passenger seat distracted him—and he dropped the bridge of his foot too fast. Tires shrieked in the fractional second before his traction bit. Luca zipped ahead smooth as a shot, white smoke wafting in his trail as he fought to shift to catch her. Disorganized noise and adrenaline and the image of Halse's inked shoulder blade fought inside his head with the desire to *push* himself. No time to think; only time to react. The tach jumped to match his punishing acceleration. He shifted to second, then third almost instantaneously to boost his speed, a buzzing roar to fourth, but her taillights had barely begun to approach his grill and the orange cone was closing fast—

Zero to sixty in the Challenger was advertised below 3.0 seconds, but Andrew had fucked that up. The timer feature read 4.7 when Luca snapped over the line, a full car length ahead of him. The startling reality of his failure rattled him as he downshifted sloppily, while she blazed ahead to top out her speed in the distance before her brake lights flared, her horn blaring a cheery note as she rolled to a stop. The Challenger shook miserably at his rough handling. He dropped his head onto the wheel, panting from adrenaline and the increasing pressure around his wrists, behind his eyes. A hiss, too sibilant and muffled to understand, rattled from the gravity well of the passenger seat that had been sucking at his head all night. *Oh fuck,* he had time to think, before the blackness crawled up from the footwell in a hallucinatory blur, over the center console and across his legs.

He pawed at his seat belt and jerked it loose. His hands vibrated with fear, embarrassment, and guilt—he'd lost track of his purpose for a selfish moment in the excitement of the race, and the haunt had fucking noticed. He had to get the door open. The handle stuck. His revenant reared in patchy rotting fragments of oxidized light, pinned between him and the steering wheel in a manner impossible for a real living body, stinking with malevolence. He groaned in the base of his throat and shoved against the hard planes of the door, fingernails squeaking at the window glass. Eddie kept on breaking the rules in death, his shade manifesting without regard for witnesses, as unpredictable as he'd ever been—and growing stronger the more blood and desire and attention Andrew paid him. The static whisper rolling from between its unhinged jaw-bones sank into his ears like hot nails, jealous and unwilling to be forgotten. He caught the possibilities of words in the scratch of sound inside his skull—*can't* or *can* or *this* or *you*—and tore at the handle again. It opened with a click. Andrew tripped himself out of the car, crashed to his knees, and puked.

12

Riley's boots thumped on the pavement in a sprint as Andrew spat a last mouthful of stringy bile and saliva onto the ground. The asphalt scraped his palms as he swayed and gagged again, overwhelmed by the rancid stink. He used his cleanest hand to bunch his shirt up and scrub his face with it. Riley crouched next to the car, saying, "What the hell was that?"

"Bad timing," Andrew slurred.

The miasma clung to him in a tenacious film, prying at the cracks in his focus the moment he directed attention to Riley. The dead thing would not allow him to refuse it for much longer, each pull more vicious than the last. *I'm trying,* he wanted to scream.

"What's wrong with you? That felt like a goddamn bomb going off," he hissed. "None of them would know, but I can—"

Andrew staggered to the driver's seat and swung his feet back inside the car, wincing under the ghoulish pressure attempting to crack into his skull. "Tell them I've got a fucking head injury, I don't care."

"Andrew," Riley said again, grabbing the doorframe with trembling fingers in a last-ditch effort to stop him.

Touching wholesome, *living* Riley seemed like the worst option while ridden by a ravenous spirit; he recoiled when the other boy reached for him. Riley let his hand hover in midair. The haunt dug at Andrew's control, an insistent but unclear demand he had no resistance against—an incursion that prodded at his constant, habitual grip on the eerie *power* he'd shared with Eddie. As soon as he directed half a thought to it, the oily streaks in his blood pulsed to attention; the haunt blanketing his flesh reverberated in sympathy, prompting a revolting crawl across his skin. Riley flinched backward like a startled cat.

The longer Andrew stalled, the deeper the creature attempted to burrow, emboldened by the bonding communion he'd offered up on accident during his night of bad choices. It had bided its time for another shot at him, and the situation had spiraled out of his control. He jerked the door closed, even as white-faced Riley attempted to grab for the handle again. His phone hornet-buzzed in his pocket as he put the car in gear. He drove past Luca standing next to her Mustang and waving at him to stop. In his rearview, the confused pack mingled, Riley gesturing broadly at Sam as he jogged the distance to them.

The radio clicked on to aggressive white noise and the time on the digital display flickered—3:18, 9:30, 12:02—before blanking to a row of zeroes. His hands quivered on the shifter and the wheel, but he kept driving. The horror movie shit was flat unnecessary. He skated past frightened straight into furious at the intrusive, crawling thing attempting to wrest more and more life out of him. It wasn't Eddie, not in the ways that mattered; letting it eat at his pain and yearning wouldn't bring Eddie home, it would only strip him down to the bones. But he had to admit—alone, still devouring ground on a street he didn't recognize that was growing ever less populous—that on another level, it *was* Eddie, so it knew him inside and out. Knew his tells and his weaknesses, how to force him to see and hear and sacrifice. Nothing remotely close to this extravagant personal haunting had ever happened to him before, not even in the weeks after the cavern when the curse was fresh and awful. He was in uncharted territory.

The engine sputtered dead five minutes later, leaving him in the thick of nondescript empty land, a field of undergrowth on his left and a copse of young trees to his right. Andrew let the car coast to the side of the road. The radio had died too, small mercy, no longer filling the interior with raw static. No houses, no headlights on the road in either direction. He tried the starter button again and nothing happened.

With no options left, apparently, but to see the haunt's detour through to its intended conclusion, he got out of the car and stood in the center of the street. His phone vibrated again as he waited for the next spectral signal. He pulled it from his pocket, saw Sam's number, and tossed it on the driver's seat, where the accusatory glow lit up the dash from below. He crunched into the dry grass on the berm. The ground swam under his feet as he paced through trees, the sour taste of his mouth recalling his experience in the back seat of the Mazda—blanketed in the revenant and dreaming about possession.

The trees cleared again and he stuttered to a stop outside a collapsing square of iron fence overgrown with creeping plant life: saplings, vines, flowers. The gate, thigh-tall, hung loose. Age-polished gravestones tipped and trailed through the plot of land. The iron taste in his mouth intensified, and he unsealed his teeth from the protesting flesh of his lip, a drip of blood beading and falling from the split.

That drop struck funeral ground and a taut wire strung his lungs to the soil, taking him to his battered knees. One time, in a high school friend's basement for an illicit party, there had been a Ouija board amidst the cheap beer and plastic bong packed with someone's ditch weed. Andrew remembered Eddie's feral smile, *I know something they don't know,* and the nudge of their fingers together on the planchette. The other kids had shrieked with laughter and jostled to push the wooden pointer, spelling out girls' crushes and spooky movie threats. But then Eddie hummed one breathy sigh and loosened up on the indefinable dam inside himself, relaxing that fist-taut muscle and pricking a sympathetic twinge at the tip of Andrew's tongue. A chill nipped at their ears and fingers. Eddie's stare held steady as he trickled more and more of his corpse-cold *pressure* over the board. The giggles died as animal instinct rippled through the room in a fearful wave. And then the wood had cracked, provoking screams and a universal recoil like a bomb had detonated—except for Eddie, except for Andrew, touching separate halves of the fractured game piece.

Andrew felt like that planchette: broken open. He crawled across the boundary of the forgotten cemetery, each drop of blood striking the earth with the force of a church bell pealing. As his heels crossed the perimeter a rush of wind scoured through the trees. Leaves rattled overhead. He lay on his side, fingertips touching a smooth stone, a twig jammed against his scalp. Greyish mist seeped up from the earth with an unreal tinge like the afterimage from a lens flare, remnants heaving themselves free from their grave-plots to trickle up his wrist, enveloping his arm, his torso, his ankles, in a tingling embrace that was not illusory.

Breath rasped in his throat. Eddie's notes about his visit to a graveyard—*that was a fucking trip and a half*—had not prepared him for the marriage of terror and release that washed through him. Eddie had finally managed to force his hand after death, and as he'd always insisted, it felt *good* to let the power flow through him at will, tingling and illicit. When the phantom weight of an arm slung over his waist and an eerily solid hand gripped his outstretched wrist, when the murmur in his head magnified to a roar, that was also a relief. The horrible, comforting weight proved to him that he hadn't brought himself past the edge of control all on his own. He'd been drawn to this pit on purpose, pushed in. He caught a jumble of words in the distorted muttering: *letgoletgoletgo.*

A half hour prior he'd been calming his fluttering nerves while Halse petted the hood of the Challenger. Andrew tried to dredge that moment of vitality to the forefront of his head, but the shade hissed nastily and jerked on the loosened knot of energy filling him to the brim; the graveyard ghosts flared brighter as he groaned, slipping

out of his control once more. Surrounded by old death Andrew
was a less-than-human creature, strangled on the haunt's leash
while it fed off the battery of their curse. As he tilted forward into
unconsciousness, the shade dumped him, disoriented but partially
lucid, into the memory: the cavern. It had tried to pull him through
time to this moment over and over—their binding, their breach of
normal life. This time he let the dream take him.

He was a lanky boy with his friend's bloodied hand pressed
to his face. Crisp, limestone-rich water splashed under him as he
clasped the shivering palm when it flopped onto his shoulder. He
pressed it to his neck, heard himself whispering a mantra of "don't,
don't, come on, don't," in the pitch black. It was impossible to tell
the slickness of water from the slickness of blood. The moment
he looped Eddie's scrawny, limp arm over his shoulder, the scene
clipped through time and place as if he'd fallen through a trap-
door. Horror-logic, haunt-logic; the specter's dragging, shrieking
static filled his ears. He was still blind, but no longer in his child's
body living a familiar memory. He was in another body, living a
suffering he'd never known himself. Agony bloomed in a terrible
sawing stroke through his (not his) forearm, gouged a divot into
the bone of his (not his) wrist when the point caught wrong. *Eddie's
forearm,* he knew without thought, *Eddie's wrist,* without question.
Blood spilled out of him and carried life with it, vitality draining
into the dirt as he struggled. The revenant forced him to remain, to
experience, to understand how it died. Though he struggled to separate himself from the dying body with frantic, wordless, thrashing
begging, it held him, collared and pliant.

Don't make me see this. But the haunt's recollection rolled onward.
At the last moment—consumed with a primal rush of panic both
his own and remembered—he (Eddie) dug into the gated, controlled power that coiled eternal and patient inside him, a dearest
companion hissing promises of revival and salvation. But it slipped
through his (Eddie's) fingers, dripping out of him (not Andrew,
Eddie) along the path of the pouring blood instead of responding

to his call. Andrew's lucid struggle to escape the revenant stalled in shock.

The revenant's memories were muddled, distorted through dream logic and the trauma of death. The erratic lashing of Eddie's dissolving power was unable to suture his bone-deep wounds closed, despite his last-ditch effort to harness it to that end. Unstuck from him and tearing loose of its moorings, the oozing thing in his blood leapt desperately toward another person, the *only* other person who carried it, too far away—and Eddie's final coherent thought was, *help me.* The soil drank his sacrament and shot an echo into the world, an arrow that struck Andrew through the heart as he tore himself free of the mist with a shout, kicking leaf litter, mindless with the struggle to escape the married memories. Eddie's death, his failure to *connect* in his final moments, had been forced on Andrew in cinematic, visceral detail. The revenant made its accusation implicit: at the bitter end, Eddie hadn't wanted to die—Eddie tried to save himself, Eddie reached for Andrew. If Andrew had come home sooner—if he'd been there, to stop the whole thing—

When he staggered onto the road again, the moon had traveled farther across the almost-cerulean sky than he expected. Fresh dew beaded his hair, his clothes. Andrew Blur, the least willing of all to fuck with Eddie's dumb gothic bullshit, had spent the night passed out in the woods amidst unnamed graves, and his new acquaintances were no doubt after his ass for disappearing. He couldn't think of a single explanation that was going to make this seem reasonable. The true answer didn't seem like the smartest: *my best friend is dead, and I'm out of my fucking mind.*

The car started without a flinch as if it hadn't betrayed him hours prior, and he drove the considerable distance to Capitol Street without incident. The lights were on in the living room, casting a dull, homey glow onto the lawn. He braced himself as he mounted the steps to the porch. The door was unlocked and he kicked his shoes off in the foyer, aware of his roommate struggling to sit upright on the couch, squinting with sleep. He was too tired to argue, too worn-out to be upset, and too shattered to be angry. It was the most he'd felt in control of his life in a long time, like the calm after a storm.

Riley said, "What happened, where were you?"

Andrew said, "I waited it out."

"In a ditch?" Riley asked, gesturing to his dirt-smeared clothes.

Andrew stripped his shirt off. He left it and his jeans in a puddle on the floor without turning his back to Riley, digging through one of his trash bags of clothes for replacements. The pre-dawn quiet was almost as intimate as an apology. He might regret his silence after a real sleep, but Eddie's death looping on repeat inside his head kept his other feelings at bay. The repetitive bite of knife into bone turned his starving stomach on itself, a sensation no person was meant to remember.

"Seems like he's trying real goddamn hard to get your attention," Riley said.

Andrew ground his teeth as he strode past his roommate. He'd had a brief moment of forgetful enjoyment behind the wheel alongside the pack, and in response the ghoul had dragged him to a vulnerable place and forced him through the isolated misery of its death—violent and violating. But how Eddie had gotten to those final moments, desperate to survive, was no clearer. That was what he hadn't been able to explain to Riley: it was a haunt, and haunts didn't go around feeding *clues* to the living left behind.

Still, as he mounted the stairs, he replied, "You've read your Hamlet, man, what do you think happens if I give it?"

Riley didn't respond.

He climbed into the shower and scrubbed at his scabbing knees, head bowed into the hot spray. His core seethed with cold. Eddie had reached for him in those last moments, after violence was done to him, and Andrew hadn't been there—not to stop it from happening, not to rescue him as he begged for help. That was all the haunt really had to show him. He didn't blame it for rubbing that salt into his wounds.

Andrew untangled himself from Eddie's stale, sweat-damp sheets once the afternoon sun heated the room too much. A scab on his knuckle had come loose during his nap, and a tiny streak of dried blood graced the pillow next to his nose. He pulled on a pair of cutoff sweats, groggy and sore. Tiny threads tickled the crease of his knee as he sat at the desk, considering the laptop once more. On impulse, he stuck his hand under the desktop and ran it along the wood—until he bumped against a piece of paper.

"You little fucker," he muttered, peeling the taped paper off.

In Eddie's blockiest script, the torn scrap of notebook paper read *townsend2004*.

He tapped in the password and unlocked the screen, waited with clenched jaw while it ran through an update. The desktop background was matte black, with threads of night-sky blue and maroon cracking through it like veins. Aesthetic and unnerving, provoking a strange pulse in Andrew's skin. The visual reminded him of the ghastly instincts that rode his own blood. Four folders, all labeled with the names of spring courses, were stacked along the right side of the screen, while the left held programs—a handful of video and voice chat options, all of which they'd used, word processing, games, and so on.

With his guts crawling up to his throat, suffocating the memories the revenant had forced into his skull of the knife and the vulgar wounds, Andrew opened the word processor and clicked to the most recent documents. The first was labeled "bullshit." All of the file names listed beneath it appeared to be papers or assignments, with *Fulton* and a course number in their titles. He opened the document.

Stream of consciousness: a handful of cramped, single-spaced lines. He read,

Are you losing control, my good pal? The clock is ticking and you
can't put him off for much longer. If you can't hunt down this stuff
in time you're going to drag him into it, and if he responds to the
source the same way you are, it's going to be a disaster. How do
you think he'll thank you when he wakes up in the yard or fucking
hallucinates when he walks past an apartment where somebody
offed themselves? Not good. He'll freak. Get it together
   Not putting this in the journals

That was all. Had he gone through all that effort to hide one file,
one paragraph? Andrew sat back in the seat with one hand gripping
his chin, index finger over his mouth. He squeezed spasmodically
to feel the pressure on his gums and teeth through his lips. *Are
you losing control,* Eddie had asked himself, as private as possible—
keeping it out of his journals, out of his texts, out of his lies. And
he *had* lied. Eddie had lied to keep him away, keep them apart. He
clicked through the other documents but found nothing out of the
ordinary.

His haunt-memories had dragged him face-first through the
death, the undeniable cut wrists. No one had sliced him up after
he died of a fucking overdose or a fight or an accidental drowning
or whatever other wildness he might've fallen into. He'd been alive
for the cutting, and scared. But he'd been keeping Andrew apart
from him while he dug up his own history's bones for answers no
one needed, spending his time and attention on all these strange
men and their friends—keeping such a mountain of secrets. Had
he known Eddie at all, in the end? He rejected the wispy cloud of
a thought even as it returned to flit treacherously across his mind,
reminding himself that he was sure someone else had been the one
to inflict that violence on him.

Andrew shook free of the passing horror of his smothered, tiniest
doubts, abruptly needing to recenter himself with an alive person, a
real human, and lay out a concrete path again.

Downstairs, Riley sat cross-legged on the couch in a pair of bas-ketball shorts and a loose tank top, notebook open to one side and a stack of printouts on the other. His glasses were perched on the tip of his nose. Andrew's planner sat on the coffee table where he'd abandoned it days before. The calm of the night's trauma lingered, coating his brain in a thin patina of exhaustion. Riley spread his hands theatrically to welcome him to the room, taking one look at his face and offering, "You want a smoke?"

"Yeah," he agreed, hoarse.

Riley's knee popped when he slid off the couch. He disappeared up the stairs. Andrew sat in front of his own abandoned laptop and notes. He stuck the base of his pen in his mouth and gnawed, his knuckles sore and still faintly swollen, aggravated from typing and flexing. In his notebook, he scrawled as loosely as he could:

the phone
who was E with
enemies/fights?
research??
sam

After a split second, he amended the last line with *halse*. The few points he was able to list didn't add up to much. He had to keep considering the angles, keep looking for connections. Whether he wanted it to be or not, the fieldwork he'd heard about was part of it, as much as tracking the pack's involvement during Eddie's final hours.

"Here," Riley said as he rounded the corner, smoke billowing from his mouth.

Andrew took the blunt and pulled a long, deep drag. He passed it back as he exhaled, the smoke hanging lazy in the air. Andrew opened his laptop and logged in to his student email. Fifty-six un-read messages spilled down the page in a stream of bold black. Two were from West, plus one from Professor Troth that had arrived since his last look. The rest were announcements or push notifications from his courses. He deleted those and read West's most recent outreach from two days prior while listening to Riley's pen scratch on paper.

Hey Andrew,

Dr. Troth asked me to see if you've been getting her emails. She's looking to set up a review session with you to share her notes on Ed's research and to discuss the material she gave you. It would be in your best interest to keep her as your advisor if you're at all interested in the same subject—she was getting hands-on with Ed and would be a great asset to you, since she cares about the topic so much. Trust me, that doesn't always happen with a thesis advisor.

And let me know if you get this, too.

He fired off a quick acknowledgment before opening and skimming West's other email—nothing significant—then opening the message from Professor Troth. He agreed to the meeting she wanted, willing to give it another chance for more information about Eddie.

"Shit, I'm hogging," Riley said abruptly and handed him the blunt. Riley watched him as he took a drag, breathed out slow, ashed it, and took another hit. "Hey. Are you okay?"

He'd wondered how long the study session could last before they circled around to the night before. He said, "I'm pretty goddamn sore."

"Not really what I was referring to, but I've been thinking about what happened," Riley continued. He flopped against the back of the couch and spread his arms along it. "His ghost is fucking attached to you at the hip, and you're telling me it doesn't matter."

Andrew closed his laptop and stood.

"Don't—come on, please," Riley said.

"I can't," Andrew said.

Riley pitched forward to grip his own knees and said, forceful, "He told me he thought it was a waste of my potential to spend half my time making ends meet, instead of focusing on school. He said that when he'd known me for, what, a week? Two? I care about this, Andrew, I care about it a fucking lot. I want to help him, and you're being shitty."

Eddie hadn't told him why he'd offered to adopt Riley and create some little household. The thought that he'd made it so fucking tender, such a *meaningful offering*—

Andrew was speaking before he caught himself, almost spitting in automatic reaction, "He kept me from coming here and he lied to me about the shit he got up to, especially with you and your whole fucking crew, and it seems like it fucking killed him, so tell me *again* how I owe you something?"

The room dropped still after his last words, Riley's startled silence cushioned by the continued stream of music. Andrew's chest heaved as he caught his breath, winded from the sudden shouting. Apparently he wasn't too exhausted to lose his temper. Riley's tense mouth had gone slack.

"Shit, I'm sorry I asked," Riley whispered.

"Have a little respect, all right?" He tucked his laptop into his backpack.

The last thing he needed was to trap himself in this house, cycling through the same conversations he didn't want to have and accomplishing nothing. He hefted his bag over his shoulder. The sour ache at the small of his back twanged. As he crossed to the front room to find his shoes, the music cut off.

He had the doorknob in hand when Riley said, "He changed my whole life and it was nothing to him, pocket change. I don't think either of you could understand, but I can't get out from under that, and I don't take handouts. He isn't here for me to repay. I'm not judging whatever you were to each other, man, but at least let me try to make his generosity right by you."

"There's nothing to make right."

"Bullshit," Riley said. "I don't leave debts. Sam neither. You're here, we're here, Ed's not. And I really do think you need our help."

Eddie had left him this. Andrew rested his forehead on the doorframe for the space of a few heartbeats, then slipped out into the world again. It welcomed him with a sticky-hot burst of air and the rich ripe smell of cut grass left to bake in the sun. He hiked his bag higher and set off for the car in his sweatpants and running shoes, just another student in the grip of summer's end.

13

Stop fighting kids it's giving me grey hairs

And I'm too hot for that

Come over

Hey fuckass come over

Come here

Asshole

Answer me princess

"Jesus, Halse." Andrew swiped another text notification off the screen of his phone. The café buzzed with harried students and unhurried retirees. A half-finished drink sat sweating at his elbow, separating into layers of melted ice and cream and overpriced coffee.

He hadn't been home except to sleep and shower for three straight days. His head was full of music criticism and debates about the *future of the academy;* he'd begun to dip his toe into a survey of early American novels. He'd missed close to three-quarters of his course meetings without meaning to—time skittered past him so easily—and if he intended to pursue the path Eddie left behind and maintain his access to Troth and West through his patchy scholarship, catching up was a necessity.

And it gave him an excuse to take a breather, sort out his head, which he needed whether he liked it or not. He hadn't spoken to Riley or responded to the increasingly extravagant string of texts from Sam, though it was flagrantly obvious that progress would remain stalled until he reconnected. Halse and Riley were the ones who'd been with Eddie most when he hadn't seen fit to share the details of his entire life in Nashville with Andrew, and instead of talking to them, he was sitting in a suburban Starbucks twenty minutes outside of campus, reading articles he'd forget again by the next month. He had to admit that he felt raw, lost, stuck in the memory loop of the revenant's awful death, though it had remained absent—spent, maybe—since that incident. The schoolwork let him pretend he was making progress.

The morose urge to lie down in Eddie's bed and drift off to sleep for good washed over him like rain. He picked up his phone and opened his texts to fire off a quick response to Halse: *I'm working go away.*

Immediately, a response.

> No can do
>
> If I have to deal with my cousin sulking around my living room for one more night I'm going to beat your dumb ass
>
> Kiss and make up already

He closed the thread. After a moment spent swirling his drink into something more appetizing, he opened Eddie's Instagram again to stare at his last photo. The handsome man in the shot might pass for a stranger, a model, painted in sunset colors. Eddie had constructed a narrative of his life for Andrew instead of telling him the truth. Andrew's ineptitude at searching for information, and his growing awareness of the rift between them that Eddie had kept smooth with affection and encouragement, twined together in a hideous braid. The manipulation left him off-kilter.

His phone pinged that it was time to leave for class—the alarm a recent concession to the schedule Eddie had set for him. He shuffled his books into his bag and left in the Supra, having returned to driving it after the haunt had hijacked the Challenger. Avoiding a repeat performance was his top priority, though the revenant had not returned since its explosive intervention. Eddie's missing phone lingered at the back of his mind as he drove, and at a red light, he opened the quick-add recommended friends list for his own Snapchat.

Lo and behold: Ethan Jung, handle *jungian,* sat smack in the middle. He clicked the plus symbol and tossed his phone on the passenger seat. He had to start somewhere. He knew the pack were his best leads, but the cousins themselves were too difficult to address, too fraught. And based on his own altercation at the get-together, Ethan might have more of an insight to offer him than most if Eddie had got caught up in that mess too—given he actually was one of the men those shitty good ol' boys had a problem with. When his screen flashed he glanced at it, but the light turned green. He didn't check his notifications until he'd taken his seat in class.

Ethan had sent him two quick messages:

Sup man, you looking for some
SupraxSupra action?
Or am I a one track mind kind of guy

He responded, *Yeah I'm down for that.* Class kicked off around him and he handed in his response paper with the rest of the students. A frisson of relief washed over him, as if he'd clipped a red light exactly at the cutoff. He and Ethan traded messages, planning and prep, throughout the lecture. Ethan didn't mention Riley once, or Sam, which was what Andrew had hoped for.

Ethan met him in a gas station parking lot outside campus. When Andrew parked, Ethan boosted himself off of the hood of his car, a cheap iced coffee in each hand. He passed the untouched one through Andrew's window. Two wide gold rings on his middle fingers matched a chain that hung in a glittering, teasing loop over his upper chest. The magnetic glint of the chain drew attention to the scooped-neck shirt baring the expanse of his collarbones.

Andrew caught himself watching the curves of his mouth: a thin upper lip but a plump bottom lip, dimples at the sides of his smile. Ethan looked more high-end model than a law student.

Until he spoke: "Want to commit a series of misdemeanors, new friend?"

Andrew raised his eyebrows over a sip of his bracingly sweetened coffee and cream. Ethan scratched his upper thigh and adjusted his belt with a thumb. Nonchalant but eager, the faintest hint predatory: the same impression Andrew had gotten at the party, before his roommate had climbed the man like a tree. That image loitered in the basement of his brain, color-spattered and confused with yearning and fire and hurt.

"I'm free all evening, so what's a good time around here?"

Ethan grinned. "And to think Riley was concerned you weren't going to branch out, get some socializing in. You want to drive, or you want to party, or both? I'm guessing you need a break from the cousins, or you wouldn't have texted just me."

"If I were here with Eddie," he said, rolling each word off his tongue, "what all would we do tonight? Party, or drive?"

"I guess we'd do both," Ethan said, his voice softening.

"Then let's do both."

"Cool. Follow me and we'll get some fun in on the highway."

Breathless anticipation sluiced him from head to toe, unsurprising but unwelcome. This was, in a sense, research—about Halse, about the pack, about where Eddie *fit* into their messy web. Ethan's Supra turned over with a handsome purr. He'd asked the question he needed to ask: if I were Eddie, where would I be? Even spread across Andrew's fits and starts, that was more effort than the police had made. He felt weightlessly alien after the nights with the cousins, the brutality of the confrontation at the semester-opening party, and he didn't know if his current momentum would last. He had to continue to believe that Eddie hadn't done the deed himself, no matter how strange his life had become while he was alone in Nashville.

Once the pair made it onto the interstate, Andrew changed lanes to pull up alongside Ethan. Cars liberally dotted the four-lane highway. Familiar sport. Andrew revved his engine once and cut across to the far left lane at speed. In his sideview Ethan did the same, gaining velocity and slicing through traffic one smooth maneuver at a time. Adrenaline hummed as he wove through the impeding cars, nosing ahead of Ethan, then falling behind. The speedometer showed triple digits for a heartbeat but banked down to double behind a tangle of cars he couldn't get past. Ethan dodged in front of him. Andrew blurted an expletive, braking to avoid a high-speed collision. Another, more temperate flash of Ethan's brake lights prompted him to follow a turn signal to an exit ramp. They made their way through a scattering of stores into a neighborhood of middle-class homes with SUVs in driveways and the occasional concrete lawn ornament. When Ethan turned onto a side street to park, Andrew mirrored him.

"Not bad keeping up," Ethan said to him, bumping knuckles.

"Same to you."

The drive had only ratcheted his energy higher. Ethan, too, seemed to be vibrating in his shoes. "How do you feel about recreational drug use, my good man?"

"Neutral to positive," Andrew replied.

"Okay, great, cool. I'm in a seminar with this chick, Leah, and she has a bunch of molly. Her boyfriend is a mediocre DJ, the scene's very posh and suburban. So, that's what we're doing tonight." He snapped his fingers at his side twice, glancing at the house. "Eat some party drugs and dance in someone's basement."

"Law school, huh," Andrew murmured.

"Fuck off," he said pleasantly.

Inside, the house was muggy despite the air-conditioning. Bodies crowded the living room and kitchen, bare skin and summer dresses and high heels—more women than he'd seen in one place for months. Compared to Halse's gathering, the vibe was downright cosmopolitan. Andrew kept close to Ethan as he led the way to the back deck, where a handful of people splashed around in an aboveground pool. The thump of a bass beat from the basement rattled the wooden boards.

"Leah, my dear, my darling," Ethan crowed.

A young tanned woman in a bikini top and board shorts clambered out of the pool without using the ladder, also grinning, her hair streaming with water. "Ethan, hi there! You doing business with me tonight? Your pretty, pretty partners come too?"

"Nah, I brought another friend." He made finger-guns at Andrew.

"Like a friend, or a *friend*," Leah said, raking her gaze over Andrew from his eyes to approximately dick-level. He had to admire the lack of dissembling. "And where from?"

"Riley knows him, and just a friend." He planted a comedic smack of a kiss on her cheek. "Let's make his night nicer, yeah?"

"It's ten per, and each capsule is about point-one. Stuff the cash in my purse and help yourselves," she said.

Ethan grabbed his wallet and crossed the deck to the table with her bag on it. She leaned on the railing next to Andrew, the blue fairy lights strung around the porch emphasizing her water-beaded skin, and said, "You like girls, handsome?"

"That's direct," he replied.

"Never let it be said I'm not honest," she said.

"Leah, leave him be," Ethan called over.

She flipped her hair over her shoulder, still smiling, and took two sprinting steps before cannonballing messily into her pool. The other partygoers splashed at her when she resurfaced, cackling. The tousling pile of bodies in the pool struck him as remarkably wholesome, though he figured most of them were also high as hell. Andrew approached Ethan, and the other boy placed two capsules in his palm. He had two of his own.

"My treat, I'm the oldest," Ethan said.

Inside, the conversation and laughter were almost deafening. The music throbbing up from the basement made it worse. Andrew took a beer from a cooler in the kitchen and washed down his capsules. Ethan did the same. He had a half hour, he thought, before it hit him. Eddie hadn't been a big fan of MDMA, so they hadn't done it often, but this was for a purpose. At his elbow, Ethan shifted from foot to foot, scanning the crowd with a casual interest.

"I'm about to be just as direct as Leah, but tell me if I'm supposed to be wing-manning or something here. Glad to be of assistance if so," he said.

Andrew glanced at him, startled. Had Ethan helped Eddie get laid, was that what he would've gotten up to? Andrew had a hard time picturing the scenario that would lead the Eddie he knew to choose Ethan as his party companion.

But apparently he'd missed a lot in the six months Eddie spent trawling Nashville.

"No thanks," Andrew said.

Ethan grunted his understanding, fidgeted another minute or five, and then said, "Downstairs, music, yes?"

The steps descended into a close space lit by a star projector and nothing else, full of humans pressed flush against each other, moving in sync with the eardrum-splitting throb of EDM pouring from a set of cabinet speakers. Ethan grinned across at him, face streaked with neon color, before disappearing into the crowd. Andrew breathed in and out, stuck along the edges with his beer held above his head to keep from being jostled. The cold concrete wall braced him. He allowed himself the briefest thought of Eddie in the fray, filthy broad smile and a woman in his arms, moving with the music and the lights.

It occurred to him an indeterminate period of time later, bones liquid and fingers lax around his warm beer, dizzy sparklers of sensation pinging constantly, that Ethan had drastically miscalculated his dosage. He wheezed through his nose and rolled his skull against the wall, one quick sigh-and-gasp for air as the yank of concrete on his hair buzzed through his scalp. He felt fucking *good*. He'd forgotten how to feel good, and here it was, plowing him under.

A palm landed on his ribs and a mouth pressed damp against his cheek, speaking directly into his skin: "How is it?"

He pried his eyes open, unsure when he had shut them again. Ethan's blown pupils and cherry-liquor-smelling breath were the whole world for a disorienting second. His tongue lay unwieldy in his mouth. The strong fingers curving around his side burned with tender sensation, heavily present and approaching sensual. He managed, "Rolling my ass off."

Ethan's laugh was more a giggle. He notched their bodies closer together with a sinuous wriggle and shouted over the music, his thigh between Andrew's, "Christ, yeah, that cannot have been point-two. I'm gone."

The music pulsed. Ethan made a breathless but shattering sound into his ear and his hand slid to grip the firm divot of muscle at the middle of his back, leanly built torso shifting along Andrew's without an inch of free space. He swayed, an attempt at dancing, and unasked-for pleasure lashed up Andrew's melting spinal cord. Ethan's smooth, well-shaved cheek pressed to his own—same height, same build, *same*—and he tugged at Andrew's arm as if to encourage him to hold on. Instead, he fisted his hands in Ethan's shirt and pulled backward to separate their bodies, shivering head to toe and close to panting. Without Ethan's warmth blanketing him, the molly turned cold. The seam of his jeans pinned his responding dick to his thigh. He hated that he was aware of it, startled and undone and too high.

"Upstairs," he slurred.

Ethan blinked, comical realization and red flush crawling across his face at once, then let him go. They staggered from the corner to the stairs, the stairs to the kitchen, and the kitchen to the living room in a blur. Andrew kept his hand anchored in the hem of Ethan's shirt. The physical delight was blinding, swamping his brain's capacity to hold on to a thought for longer than three seconds before dissolving into pure starving sensation. Falling onto the blessedly abandoned couch together allowed Andrew an excuse to remain as close as his skin craved without making contact. He lolled his head onto the armrest, one leg hanging stretched out in a greedy sprawl. Ethan kicked his shoes off and put his feet up. A Solo cup hung precariously from his fingertips.

"Eddie come to these parties often?" Andrew asked, staring at the ceiling.

"Not as much as I'd have expected," Ethan said. "He kept his distance from most of us, to be honest. Sometimes he was cool, sometimes I thought it was like, too much for him, how we all were together. He didn't seem comfortable."

"Thought he was in the pack," Andrew said.

"Sure he was. But he was one of those guys, I doubt I've got to tell you this, who was more his own protagonist than a normal person." An eloquent shrug, a dazzled moment spent flexing his fingers and watching his rings flash. "When he was around he was king of the castle, and it made me forget to ask where the fuck he was the rest of the time. He paid enough attention to make you feel close without ever telling you shit."

Andrew said, "You didn't like him."

He heard the revelation in his own voice before it hit him. Ethan sighed noisily. "He was good to Riley and Halse, he had some kind of soft spot for them. The rest of us, man, I'm not sure he really saw us. And he had a fucking wild temper, so I didn't like that, no. Reminded me of too many DL frat boys, the staring and the weirdness and shit. I know I'm pretty, but I'm not that pretty, you know?"

Andrew had no idea what those words meant in that order, except he disliked the idea of Eddie staring enough to get noticed. The insistent buzz of molly kept him from accessing his roiling emotions, reflexive anger smothered under euphoric distraction.

He sorted through his words carefully before he asked, "Then how was he spending his time, it if wasn't with y'all and it wasn't with school? I don't know what he was even fucking doing here. I should know that."

He hadn't meant to say the last bit out loud. Ethan tipped himself closer on the couch, gripping the frame to settle in the middle with his toes jammed under Andrew's thigh. Andrew lifted his head. "He did spend time with us. Just not, like, separately and of his own volition. Wouldn't have caught *him* snapping me for a night out. He had his own shit to do. He and the cousins got along good enough. I mean, he made runs with Sam sometimes, and none of us ever got in that deep."

"Made runs?" he asked.

"Yeah, Sam's second job," he said. For clarity's sake, he mimed smoking a joint. "Sam's too protective of Riley to let him fuck up, so he's not allowed in on that shit, and I'm in law school, and Luca tolerates Sam at best. The extended company he keeps is kind of gross and scary, you know? And the rest of the kids are too casual of friends to be trapping with our boy on a Tuesday night. You get me?"

"But Eddie wasn't too casual," he said slowly.

"Nah." Ethan's mouth pursed as he considered his response. "Those two hit it off fast, nothing casual about it. It was sort of like watching some big dogs decide they didn't want to bite each other's faces off. There were a couple of times I wasn't sure if they'd decide otherwise."

"How do you mean?"

The toes still digging and flexing against his leg distracted him briefly. The room around them pulsed with life, the crowd fading in and out of his conscious awareness as he focused on them and then on Ethan and back again. He missed half of a sentence, tuned in again to hear, "—can't have two leaders, but Ed didn't want to lead, he just wanted to have his space I guess. He was more excited about his fucking social research or whatever than he was about selling drugs anyway."

Andrew grunted, confused. His high coasted to a peak. The music, even muffled from the basement, had a physical presence, a pressure on his ears and throat. Ethan's voice made a steady constant over the bass, narrating, tongue loosened with the chemicals in their blood and the paradoxical closeness of total strangers in the same place at the same time. *Same,* his blood beat. His rebellious fingers itched to wrap around Ethan's foot.

"He was collecting all those oral histories and ghost stories and nonsense," Ethan said. "Sam was after his ass to quit asking his customers about their haunted houses, like, all the time. He hates that shit. Their grandma was a real weirdo about it, if you didn't know, some kind of reformed hill witch who found Jesus and gave up her wickedness, et cetera et cetera."

"Well, shit," Andrew said. "I didn't."

"Yeah, he spent way more time haring around on his own harassing people for stories than he did hanging with us, Sam or no Sam," he said. "But to reiterate, he and Sam were a goddamn bonfire. We were all kind of hoping they'd blow each other and get it over with." Ethan cackled and slapped Andrew's upper thigh before collapsing onto the couch again. The stinging burn shocked straight through his belly as if Ethan had grabbed him by the crotch. Andrew's mouth hung open, the picture of those bodies in contact flashing behind his eyes in full, glorious, terrible detail before Ethan interrupted with, "Fuck, sorry, that was bad. Ignore that. I'm fucking high as shit."

It hit him, with the approximate force of a train, that they'd been talking about Eddie for minutes or hours as if catching up, as if they'd see him later. His heart crawled up into his throat. He didn't need to be here. None of these people had been with Eddie—not Ethan or his nameless, faceless law school friends. None of them had a reason to do whatever had been done to him.

"Hey," Ethan said. Fingers tugged at the hem of his jeans, wrapped around his ankle. A thumb massaged tickling, tingling circles on the knob of the bone. He kept staring at the ceiling. "Sorry. I'm sorry."

"I didn't know he got so close to Halse," he murmured.

Ethan let out a nervous chuckle. "It wasn't a thing, man, don't like—don't get upset, okay. I'm not trying to speak ill of the guy. He wasn't running game on you or something. He never even hit on Riley, and Riley's fine as fuck, yeah?"

Responding to that broader implication was impossible in the split second he had before Leah interrupted from behind the couch. "Your host has arrived, and requests thank-yous in the form of kisses."

She had a shirt on now, her hair damp and drying in a chlorine-tangle. Andrew wasn't expecting it when she planted a hand on the seatback and vaulted over onto the couch between them, her knee almost clocking him in the jaw. He yelped and toppled backward. Ethan laughed. She kissed Ethan first, a chaste peck on the mouth, then wriggled to kneel over Andrew's sprawled form. She, too, was bright-eyed, with the narrowest ring of green iris visible around her pupils.

"Say no if you want to say no," she said.

He found himself murmuring "No" against her plush, sweet-tasting mouth.

She stopped and sat back on her heels with a small frown. "Is it the girls thing, or just a no?"

"Just a no," he said. The skin contact felt all right, but his body wasn't strung toward her, not the same as—

"Apologies, but it's guys for me, as you're aware," Ethan said.

"No worries," she said. She patted Andrew's cheek and miraculously got up without kicking either of them again. "Forget it happened!"

"I'm going to go," Andrew said.

"Yeah, sure," Ethan said. He had a hangdog look on his elegant face. "My mouth got away from me. Sorry again."

"Thanks," Andrew said, and he was more thankful than Ethan knew, for revealing a fault line between Eddie and Halse that he hadn't been aware of before.

Sitting in his car, waiting to sober up enough to see the road, he checked his email. His skin buzzed, needy, with the ghost of confident, masculine hands grabbing him at leisure, mind spinning with the assumptions people kept making about him. Amongst the junk emails, Troth had sent him a confirmation for the review meeting tomorrow afternoon—and since it appeared that Halse was connected to the fieldwork too, not only the parties and related mischief, he'd chase that down. Easier than digging at the burgeoning, unsettling quandary of what had changed so much with Eddie that folks kept referring to Andrew, without a pause, as his—*boyfriend*. Andrew swallowed against his sandpapery case of dry mouth and, methodical with each keystroke, agreed to her proposed time before hitting send.

14

Avoiding a roommate was an art form, and Andrew's creativity had run dry. The front door opened a handful of minutes past three in the afternoon. Andrew, in his briefs and socks, eating applesauce directly from the container in front of the fridge, had the option to either stand his ground or flee to the yard. Neither was appealing, but the dull grey hangover of the molly he'd eaten the night before sapped the remainder of the motivation he needed to dodge Riley.

"Oh, hey," the other boy said, stopping short in the small vestibule between the kitchen and living room.

"I have a meeting with Troth this afternoon," Andrew said, gesturing aimlessly with the spoon and funneling another bite of fruit paste into his mouth.

The jar was running low, and the beer had disappeared from the bottom shelf. Aside from two packages of shredded cheese and a gallon of milk, it was a depressingly barren environment, befitting the home of two students.

"You still pissed at me?" Riley asked.

"I wasn't pissed."

"Hah, fuck you," Riley snorted. "You were. But if you're not, you're not, I'll let it go. I'm glad you're going to class. And I guess I'm glad you're getting social with my boyfriend, if that helps you sort yourself out."

He set off up the stairs and Andrew rapped his knuckles on the fridge, caught off-guard. His phone vibrated on the table. It was Del. *Please talk to someone.* He furrowed his brow and opened the actual thread. At some point in the night, he'd sent her a series of messages he didn't remember typing, mostly disorganized and unfinished:

> I don't know what's going on
>
> He wasn't spending his time where I thought he was hiding it from me and people think we were
>
> He changed his laptop password. What if he

Nothing to close the last line, more damning than the rest. He cringed.

As he read, another message came in: *I'm calling you.*

The phone rang a moment later. He set it on the table, leaving it to buzz its way across the smudged glass. Ethan had called Halse protective of his cousin. He wondered with a swoop how Halse had felt about Riley and Eddie's friendship—the house, the research, the ghost stories—and where protection might come into the argument. The specter had shown him its death stripped of context, which remained to be filled in despite his guilty misgivings. Eddie as he had carried himself through Nashville was an enigma to him, increasingly unknowable. Instead of answering Del, he fired off a fast message to Ethan: *How did Halse like Eddie and his cousin being friends?*

The response, *fine I guess,* wasn't much of an answer.

———

Andrew stubbed out his preparatory cigarette three-quarters smoked on the deck railing, shoes in hand and feet warm on the wood. He was due to meet Professor Troth in a half hour at her office. She had emailed him another reminder that morning, which was irksome but reasonable. As he bent to slip on his Converse, gravel crunched at the end of the alley. He glanced up. The gunmetal WRX rolled to a stop, blocking his car into its space. Halse climbed out, leaving the car idling in the middle of the drive.

He approached with arms swinging at his sides, hands loose, bearing a flat-lipped smile that presaged a storm. Aggression rolled off of his posture. He was hatless and wearing scuffed tan combat boots laced tight at his ankles. Andrew dropped his shoes onto the deck out of reflex. The muscles in his forearms bunched as he closed his fists.

"Riley texted me some interesting shit this morning, my friend," Halse said, and this was *Halse,* not Sam, though Andrew didn't realize he'd created the distinction.

"Define interesting," he responded.

Halse stopped at the base of the steps, nostrils flaring as he gave Andrew a caustic once-over. His bare toes curled into the deck. The feral part of Andrew paced its cage, alert and uncertain. All the paths he'd found, so far, led to Halse—but knowing that was a far cry from having a plan to confront him about it.

"To start, that Ed's phone has been missing this whole time, and you're all fucked up about not knowing what he was doing with which people, especially me. Which is an accusation I feel like I deserved to hear from your own fucking mouth," he said. "Put your shoes on. We're going on a trip."

Andrew's chest collapsed into a painful squeeze, and he blurted out, "Fuck off."

Measured, Halse repeated, "I said, put your shoes on."

"I'm not going anywhere with you," he said.

Squared shoulders and quickening breath recalled their first meeting, and the tension that had begun to bank between them after regular exposure. Andrew stood stock still, neither retreating to the house nor forcing his way down the steps. The series of rambling texts he'd sent Del, the thoughts he had trouble quashing, roared into the substrate of his brain: if someone else had hurt Eddie, had kicked off some violence that led to the ugly end the revenant had shown him, Halse was his prime candidate. Getting in a car alone with Halse while he visibly boiled with anger, no one around to notice or care where he disappeared to, seemed stupider than Andrew was willing to be.

But then Halse said, "Forget your plans. I know where they found him, and we're going."

Rational resistance crumbled in an instant and Andrew bounded down the steps in two strides; Halse held his ground. Nose to nose, glaring into Halse's auburn-flecked eyes from as close as he'd ever seen them, he snarled, "How do you know that?"

"Because I asked when it happened, you ungrateful dick, so put your shoes on and get in the damn car." Halse jammed his arm between their bodies, wrist bone and the blade of his hand shoving into Andrew's sternum.

Andrew staggered against the step and used it as an excuse to sit and yank his Converse on. Halse headed off across the path through the yard. *Got on like a bonfire,* he recalled, yanking his laces tight and double-knotting them. He had a dull pocketknife and the conviction of revenge if their unplanned field trip spiraled out of control, but nothing else. Eddie was a bigger, stronger man than Halse, but there was no telling how their fight might've started—who would have thrown the first hit, over which of a handful of possible triggers. Killing a man with a knife took some real intimacy, and while Halse and Eddie had spent a lot more time together while he was stuck up north than he and Halse had put in so far, Andrew figured he could manage if his skin was on the line.

Just to confirm, he called out, "Are you asking Riley to come with, then?"

"No, I'm not." Sam kicked the gate open, wire rattling on wire. "This is our business."

As he expected. Andrew's phone buzzed a gentle appointment reminder as he got up to follow, seating himself in the WRX and clicking his belt into place. He swiped the alarm silent. Halse, jaw set firm, rolled out of the alley onto the main street. The air conditioner whirred over the stifling silence. A yellow rubber duck sticker decorated the gearshift, worn and faded. There was a quality to their coexistence in the small space, sour and ragged, that made it hard to take a full breath. Andrew propped his elbow on the rim of the closed window and put his fingers to his temple.

"Talk," Halse said as he took a ramp to the I-40.

Andrew dug his thumb at the interior corner of his eye, strung high enough to vibrate in his seat. Having a conversation felt impossible, but he said, "I had a meeting."

"Do you care?"

Andrew shut his mouth again. Eddie would've been irked with him for his laissez-faire attitude to this program, his research—but not angry, given that he was faced with something larger. He wanted to believe that, if their positions were reversed, Eddie would have already drowned the necessary parties in the ocean of his loss. Instead, Andrew was stumbling blind from one failure to the next, hamstrung by his own destruction, a boy made of clumsy mismatched pieces. Running straight into the mouth of danger, after it found him and invited him along for a ride.

Halse said dryly, "It's an hour and a half drive, so it's going to be real boring if you sit there quiet the whole time."

"Hour and a half?" he questioned, turning a fraction toward him against his better judgment. "What the fuck?"

"They found him out in the woods, edge of a national park I guess," Sam said.

He kept a hand and one knee touching the wheel, the other hanging a measure above the gearshift. Traffic passed behind them at a steady clip, going the compulsory twelve miles per hour over the limit. Periodically his fingertips twitched to rub the edge of the peeling sticker.

When it became apparent that Andrew wouldn't continue, Halse said, "He had Riley listed as his emergency contact through Vandy. I guess the cops looked that up when some lady out walking her dog or whatever found him. I asked to see where, after they brought him back and called his parents and shit."

"Why?" Andrew asked, packing weight into that one word.

Sam said, shrugging, "Because I needed to know."

Sober and strained, the pair lapsed out of conversation. Andrew scrolled on his phone with nerves jangling, typed a brief email to Dr. Troth to apologize for missing their arranged time. Without his hat, Halse was a younger-looking man, still unfinished around the edges of his stubbled jawline and prominent cheekbones. The mantle of his persona hung looser on him than usual. Andrew swallowed a knot of uncertainty, his earlier aggression dissolving from the simple awkwardness of the situation and the lack of continued provocation.

Sam took his eyes off the road to catch Andrew staring and said, "I'm not stupid. I'm guessing you think something bad happened with him and us. Like we did something to help him along. Riley has buried himself ass-deep in guilt. He didn't see shit wrong, and I didn't either. Eddie was acting kind of manic at the end there, but who doesn't sometimes?"

The responses that rose to his mouth and died there formed a block of clutter. Andrew grunted and nodded instead of offering an explanation. Halse hadn't quite hit the nail on the head, but he was too close to the truth of the suspicions knocking around Andrew's skull. *Something bad* covered a whole manner of sins.

"It doesn't sit right with me that his phone is missing. Odds it's out there in the woods?" Sam asked.

The question sounded rhetorical, but Andrew said, "Not strong."

"Maybe it landed in someone's pocket," Sam said slowly, testing the idea.

"Yeah, maybe," he said to the man he thought might've taken it.

"You're crazy," Halse said. It didn't sound like a real disagreement.

After another drag of tense quiet, Sam turned on the radio and spun the dial to loud. Andrew sat gnawing his nails in sequence to pass the drive. He had come with Sam alone, friendless, far from the city, and he hadn't bothered to so much as text a person his whereabouts. Ethan's monologue lingered in Andrew's head: protective of his cousin, disapproving of the gothic obsession that selfsame cousin shared with Eddie, prone to clashing with Eddie bad enough that other people noticed. He recalled the scabs on Halse's jaw the first time they'd met, and West's observation about Eddie's fights. The fact that the pair of them had been running Halse's business routes together. All the secrets Eddie had hidden from Andrew. He was starting to feel like every one of Eddie's lies and evasions had something to do with Halse.

At a turnoff with a national parks sign, Sam spun the wheel and took a hairpin turn faster than he needed to, with a noisy scatter of gravel. He parked at a service road that said NO PARKING. Their doors slammed in the birdcall-split solitude of the wood's edge. The total absence of other humans was notable in the density of the quiet. His skin crawled. If Halse was the one responsible, despite his performed ignorance—

"Down here," Halse said as he set off walking, interrupting Andrew's uneasy hesitation.

Andrew followed him onto the hiking path. The trees closed over their heads, undergrowth lush on either side of the packed dirt track. At a sharp curve in the trail, split with a snarled ankle-thick root, Sam grabbed a tree branch for balance and clambered off the path. He waved an unconcerned hand through a dreamcatcher of a spider's web at face-level. Andrew picked through the underbrush at a more sedate pace. He drank in the gloaming-dimmed forest around him for signs, for some necromantic twinge, and scuffed his feet through the leaf litter in pursuit of more tangible evidence. Then Halse stopped. Andrew halted two feet behind him.

Halse laid his palm over the trunk of a broad, craggy white oak with its bottom branches curved almost to the ground. The tree was as broad as Sam's wingspan, Andrew guessed, a monster planted in the middle of a ring of skinnier growth. It had a certain poetic weight. He hated it with a fierce, scouring depth.

"Cops said here." Halse moved his hand from the trunk, un-covering a freshly scarred carving, *EF.* "Under this tree. Might've taken weeks to find him, if that dog hadn't helped."

Andrew swallowed. "Has Riley seen this?"

"No," Sam said. "I wouldn't bring him out here."

Without waiting for a response he turned and paced around the side of the tree to give Andrew some privacy, scuffing his boots through the ground cover, as Andrew had been doing on his ap-proach. He disappeared behind the trunk. Andrew sidled up to the tree with the caution he'd use for a skittish horse. The bark was rough and warm, but inert under his hands where he traced the scarred memorial letters he presumed Halse had left, the only other man to visit Eddie's resting place. Andrew expected to feel a stab of recognition, the riffling wail of his spectral hanger-on, but there was nothing—the cold knot inside him didn't even stir in response to the supposed site of Eddie's death.

Andrew pressed his palms harder and laid his forehead on the coarse wood, grinding it into his skin. In all his dreams, he'd never seen the tree, this broad spreading creature standing guard over a forest he wasn't sure the name of. The toes of his shoes touched the base of the roots, his shoulders rounding. The rustling steps on the other side of the trunk ranged farther out.

This didn't feel like it could be the place. He felt more death walking down any street of Nashville. Any tree in the forest would have the same tug of interest or knowledge—which was to say, none—even though the cops said Eddie's blood had watered this monster's roots. Andrew took a knee at the base of the trunk. One hand on the root nearest him, crawling free of the underbrush, and one on the packed earth, he closed his eyes. He had an idea of how to ask, if asking was the right word. It was precisely the depths to which he'd promised himself he'd never stoop, but Eddie had called to him in his desperate times, and he still felt the visceral memory of power lashing out.

"Fuck you," he said to himself, and to the boy who whispered in his dreams. Then he shoved mental fingers into the snake pit of creeping potential coiled in the base of his guts.

Disgusted and clumsy without practice, he woke the cold pulse into his veins and his tongue and the fingertips he curled into the dirt. Eddie had practiced drawing out the power; Andrew never had, not once. *Fuck you, Eddie, fuck you for making me do this,* he thought on a loop. Eddie would've crowed to see him. He'd been pushing so long for Andrew to embrace himself, their difference, their death-made-life. Andrew reached into the ground, and instead of Eddie's praise, fresh blood pulsed up from the otherwise summer-dried earth with a reverberating strike that knocked the wind out of Andrew's lungs. An unnatural gust stirred the leaves up in a tiny red-spattered cyclone around Andrew's wrist, his fingers, stinking of rot and life.

The vision he'd called for spilled up from the ground and into his flesh, bowing him face-first into the wet earth and forcing his hands deeper into the solid ground: cool lax limbs spread to their full length, knife lying suggestive at the knee, jaw hanging a fraction loose. Uncaring alien fingers adjusted the dead weight and thumbed the livid purpling bruises at the elbows, the wrists, chafed and burned around his matched tattoo. Andrew existed in that moment as both the dead man and himself, inside and outside, witness and victim all at once in an immense moment of confirmation—someone else *was* there. Another set of hands arranging the stiff corpse.

Violence hadn't found Eddie here in the forest, not at this resting place, quiet and green under the leaves that had scattered themselves on Andrew's call in a paroxysm of sacrifice. The land had known Eddie, had given him its rites, drunk the dregs of him down. He was one and the same as that earth. But the true death had happened elsewhere, not beneath the handsome tree in the woods far from home. The soil had so little spilled blood to give as offering to Andrew when he came for his inheritance.

Andrew came into his skin heaving, slumped on his side in the fetal position. The blood on his hands might've come from his cracked nails, but he knew otherwise. The dampness on his face might've been sweat or tears. Footsteps approached and paused at the side of the tree, and he scrubbed his fingers ineffectually on his shirt.

"I leave you for five minutes," Sam said, strained.

"He didn't die here," he slurred.

"Remember that thing I told you, about *not* fucking with things you shouldn't fuck with," Sam said. There was a subdued fury in his voice. "This is one of those things. What even were you doing?"

"I needed to be sure." He planted his back against the tree, legs spread. A tremor crept up from his hips to his heart. He was lying now in the same spot Eddie had been staged. Panic raced and spasmed. "Someone *killed* him, someone fucking—"

Halse grabbed his upper arm and hauled him to standing, grip like iron. Andrew staggered against him. "That's the real reason you've been asking around, huh? Asking questions about me and him? It didn't occur to you to wonder why Riley told me all that shit when he hadn't told me before? We all met up last night to talk about you, compared notes after your party with Ethan."

The blazing fire in his stare was the realest thing Andrew had seen in weeks.

"Say it to my face," Halse snarled. He released Andrew's arm and took a step and a half back, shaking his elbows out. "Fucking hell. Ask *me* if I did it, you fuck, come on."

"Fine." Nausea gripped his esophagus. "Was it you who killed him?"

Halse's fist caught him square in the stomach.

15

The second blow landed off-center, knuckles on his bottom ribs, and Andrew crumpled around the breath Sam drove out of him. He clawed a hand into the neck of the other man's T-shirt and grabbed his bicep with the other. The edge of Sam's jaw pressed into his temple as they grappled. Ragged, silent struggle took up the quiet calm of the spreading oak's embrace, broken by gasped breaths. Sam's clumsier free hand crashed into the meat of Andrew's upper back three times in quick succession. He wedged his palm around Sam's throat to push, up and out, separating their clinch. Sam choked as he staggered free. Spit flecked his cheek and mouth, viscous. Andrew wiped it with his forearm. He smelled blood and dirt. Skin-on-skin contact seared the chill from his bones.

The pair circled, hands hovering near collarbones in neutral loose fists. Andrew kept his attention on the winged movement of Halse's elbows, the taut corded muscle of his arms.

Halse said, "Get at me, come on."

Andrew dove for him. Halse accepted the tackle that bore him to the ground and flipped them in mid-fall, slamming Andrew into the dirt. One knee grounded Andrew's inner thigh to pin the leg while he attempted and failed to hook the other around Halse's waist. Andrew reared up savagely but Sam dodged the headbutt, then slapped him open-handed with the full weight of his arm behind it. Andrew's vision streamed with color. His ears rang. The burn seared from temple to jaw, spreading over the whole side of his face. As he reeled, Halse pinned his wrists, bringing them face to face.

"Fuck you for thinking I'd hurt him," Halse said.

Andrew went performatively limp, wheezing. Sam slid his knee off the meat of his leg to kneel straddled over him. A fraction at a time, he released his grip on Andrew's arms to settle at rest on his heels. Andrew scooted out from under him, still supine. The throbbing of his thigh ached worse than his face, radiating the phantom pain of Sam's weight crushing muscle to bone. The smack was just shocking, unlikely to leave a mark but disorienting all the same. Tension dispersed as Halse stared at his hands. The blood streaking their skin and clothes belonged to neither of them.

Sam said, "You're talking about actual murder. Not just someone messing with him, pushing him to off himself."

Someone killed him, he thought with a shameful burst of relief. The nightmares he'd had, the revenant shaking him in its teeth like a dog with a bone, clicked into place: how many times had he been forced to see the ragged wounds, the blood pouring out? All that hadn't been enough to quell a last miserable twang of uncertainty, raised through the lies and misdirection. Even after experiencing the desperation of Eddie reaching out to him at the end, he'd allowed himself to doubt—no surprise the haunt had pushed him, punished him.

"People don't get fucking murdered often, Andrew. That's a big jump from suicide. How can you be sure? You weren't even here."

Andrew hissed, "I just *saw* it. Believe me or don't, I'm goddamn certain."

"All right, then," Sam said, disgruntled but—Andrew noticed Sam hadn't stopped looking at his inexplicably bloodied hands— acquiescent.

In unspoken accord, Andrew took the hand Sam offered him a moment later. His ribs felt compressed. He spat a mouthful of phlegm on the ground. Sam lifted his own palm and examined the fresh print of red-black mud. The tiniest shiver shook his fingers. He wiped the evidence on his pants. Andrew remained at the tree as Sam took off for the path, tracing the initials one more time.

Maybe days after he had died, Sam had stood here with his pocket-knife and carved a spot to remember Eddie by.

At the car, Sam stood smoking. Two cigarette butts lay at his feet. The third glowed orange and crisp between his lips. Andrew plucked it from his mouth and burnt it to the filter with two hard drags that seared his lungs. Sam snorted and unlocked the car. Andrew considered the weight that had lifted from his shoulders, thinking: *I guess I believe him.* Neither of them spoke as each settled into their seats, prickly with the aftertaste of another physical boundary crossed.

Fifteen minutes into the quiet drive, Halse said, "I shouldn't have been taking him on errands with me. I get that. If someone killed him, for real, then maybe I'm the one who set that off. He didn't have the sense god gave a dog when it came to leaving people's business buried."

"Ethan told you I had questions," Andrew said.

"He told us he took you out, and that you asked about me and Ed while you were rolling, how we got along and all," he said. "You could've asked me. First time you met me, you could've just asked."

"Not if you did something," Andrew said.

"Glad you've got such a high opinion of me, Blur," he said.

"I didn't know you." He shifted in the constriction of the seat, belt digging at his ribs. He wasn't injured, but he was going to be bruised his whole time in Nashville at the rate he was going, wearing his hurt on his skin. "I might now, I guess."

"Didn't trust the drug dealer fuckup cousin after meeting the smart one, makes sense," he said.

"It wasn't like that."

Halse drummed his fingers on the steering wheel. His bitter grin flashed white in the streetlights. "I'm not stupid. I know what I am and I know what I'm not. I guess I'd have pegged me for trouble too."

The nakedness of that admission hit like stumbling into a

friend's bathroom without realizing they'd gotten in the shower. He hadn't seen a thing, but he was too close to revelation.

"I didn't kill him. But you're saying someone did, fuck," Sam marveled, horror and disbelief mingled in his voice, the same as they were inside Andrew's chest—enormous, impossible, with awful certainty.

The interstate spread in front and behind them. Night descended in degrees. Andrew watched shadows grow in the divots of Sam's wrists, his exposed collarbones. His belt buckle peeked from underneath the hem of his shirt.

"Ed was a good man," Sam said. "It doesn't matter how I feel about his extracurricular crazy shit, he did a bunch of things for Riley I couldn't have, even if I worked at it for ten more years. I tried to do for him in exchange, but he made shit difficult."

"Riley said he felt like he owed Eddie," Andrew said.

"I thought that before he died, sure as hell think it after."

Andrew said, "He wouldn't have agreed."

"Don't matter much, does it?"

"No, it surely doesn't."

The slip of Andrew's accent, dead and buried, threw him from the conversation. Eddie had never quite lost his. Riley's was cultured over, but still audible in the vowels. Halse, though—Sam Halse talked thick and dripping when he got into it, fat vowels and stretched consonants. He had come from here and he'd die here, that was clear. Halse had taken Eddie on his business runs, out to the hills, where Eddie met strangers and asked after their family secrets. He bet Eddie had sat on a dozen couches and two dozen porches, beer and a joint in hand, prodding grown men for ghost stories, digging up mischief and murders and feuds.

There would've been stiff rides back, Sam telling him to keep it to his damn self. Then Eddie took to going out on his own, like Ethan said. Eddie roaring down back roads in his car worth twenty acres of decent land, so fucking sure of himself. Somewhere between there and here, he'd gotten his wrists cut and his corpse laid out under a tree in the middle of nowhere. It wasn't unlike how they'd ended up trapped in the cavern as kids, with Eddie too clever and too stupid by halves—listening to his instincts, whether or not that was smart.

Sam let the silence hold until he pulled the hand brake in the familiar comfort of his garage. The door grated shut behind them to seal the small concrete space in darkness. Blindness lent plausible deniability to the fingers that swept across the line of Andrew's shoulder, the broad hand squeezing the nape of his neck. The thumb pressed under his ear had two owners in his mind, welcome and alien at once. Then Sam released him and clambered out of the car in a hurry.

Andrew thumped his head onto the seat. He'd spotted Riley's car on the side of the drive. He needed a minute before this conversation. Maybe Sam hadn't done the deed himself—but Andrew didn't think either of them had absolved him of guilt. Andrew still had more questions than answers. He heaved himself out of the bucket seat and slammed the door behind him, stumbling through the dimness. Short steps from the garage led into a messy laundry room with a laminate floor, past which was the kitchen. He crossed through toward the sound of quiet voices in the living room.

Riley gave him a once-over when he collapsed onto the couch opposite the cousins. He said, "I guess that advisor meeting got canceled, huh."

"Guess so," Andrew said.

He awkwardly checked his phone and tapped open Troth's response to his email.

Andrew,

I'm sorry to miss you. Would you be able to do the same time tomorrow, or if not/regardless, attend the faculty and student gathering I'm hosting later this week? You're welcome to bring along a partner as well, if you wish.

—Jane

He replaced the phone in his pocket without answering.

"What happened?" Riley asked, first to step over the invisible line.

Andrew said, "We went to the tree."

"Shit," Riley said. He glanced at Sam, like he wasn't sure how to proceed, then continued, "Well—how'd it sit with you, being there?"

"I saw something," Andrew said, but his throat locked up before he could explain.

How to put to words that he'd seen a stranger's hands arranging Eddie's corpse in a cruel parody of care, that knowing the truth recast his haunt-dreams from covetous punishments for his absence to stark evidence of his failing loyalties? The revenant had shown him in its crooked, horrible way, and he'd ignored its efforts. He jerkily shook his head at Riley's inquisitive noise.

"Ed's phone wasn't out there either, so we're gonna help him look for it," Sam added.

"I didn't ask for help," Andrew choked out.

Sam said, "Don't you know how to make friends, Blur? It goes like this: you meet them, you like them, you get to spending time with them, then your shit to deal with is their shit to deal with. Ed did that with us before you even showed up, so we have to help you out for his sake. Blame him if you're feeling fussy."

Unprompted vertigo struck him with a burst of sick-spit in his mouth. He bent to brace his forehead on the heel of his clammy, dirty hand. The sensation that he'd been hanging on to the edge of a cliff with his fingernails gave way abruptly, a scatter of debris into free fall. He stood unsteadily from the couch.

"What," Riley started, and Sam covered his mouth. Andrew made a beeline for the porch door. Breath stuttering in choppy bursts, he sat down hard against the exterior. The sob that wracked him, sudden and brutal, wasn't a surprise. He gripped the back of his skull with both hands, knees pressed to his eyes, and cried. Throughout, he was aware of them inside the house, close and ready if he were to call out. For a moment, he hadn't felt alone.

———

The door opened. Andrew propped himself up on his elbows, rising a meager amount from the long sprawl he'd taken up on the warm wooden deck. Riley handed him a paper towel with four strips of bacon on it. He grunted his thanks and popped half of one piece into his mouth. Riley leaned against the wall.

"Sam has work in the morning, figured I'd head out. You coming?" he asked.

The last time he'd spoken to his roommate, before this, had been about the fact that he'd been *getting social with his boyfriend.* The phrase still stuck in his head. The whole group knew, or understood, the dynamic between Riley and his—people. Andrew was starting to come around to the idea that the three of them weren't as much like the mess he and Eddie and Del had made of each other as he originally imagined, but he wasn't sure how else to understand it.

"I wanna ask about you and Ethan and Luca," he said.

"Been waiting for that, yep," Riley said, popping the last letter. "Questions, comments, concerns?"

"All three together, or just—" he trailed off and sketched a descriptive V-shape in the air.

Riley said, "Option two, for the most part. Ethan's not into women much, excepting special occasions where he's got a dude to engage with too. Me, for example."

"Okay. Okay," Andrew said, not sure where he intended to go with his questions. *Special occasions,* that was—something to review. He filed it away for the time being.

"So are you coming home, or was that, like, relevant somehow," Riley said.

Andrew stuffed another piece of bacon in his mouth. His face felt tight. He'd wiped his nose on the inside of his shirt enough to gross himself out, and he desperately needed a shower.

"Coming home," he said.

"Good," Riley replied with ease that belied the gravity of the night.

Andrew followed on his heels through the house, offering his casual goodbyes to Sam, who saw them off at the front door. Leaving Sam standing on the porch alone, the immensity of the spectral revelation weighing on his shoulders too, unsettled Andrew, but the urge to flee was stronger than his burgeoning desire to stay.

In the car, Riley asked lightly, "How'd you like Ethan's law school buddies, anyway?"

Andrew said, "Seemed like a lot of felonies for anyone who wants to be a lawyer."

"Right? Kids these days."

Andrew attempted a smile. Woods coasted along outside, lending their green smell to the humid breeze.

"Would've paid to see you rolling. Ethan said you were a real treat, all big eyes and flopping around like a sexy rag doll," Riley noted.

The tips of Andrew's ears went hot; he ignored the comment. The Mazda purred on the hill road, coasting fast toward the city. Andrew rubbed his eyes with his thumbs to grind the salt crust away. Better to pull the Band-Aid off before the ball of silence in his chest swelled to an expansive, choking burst. It was made easier, somehow, by Riley's rare lack of prying.

"While I was outside, did he tell you about what happened at the tree?"

Riley's throat worked in a sudden swallow. His grip on the steering wheel clenched; he said in an almost-whisper, "Yeah, but maybe you should too."

"He didn't die there." The tree branded with Eddie's initials would survive for more generations than Andrew had a sense of, roots stained with his death, even if only the afterimages of it. "I, uh, I . . ."

"You sensed it, whatever, that's fine." The dismissal rang false, but Andrew was grateful. "I can't fucking imagine what you're going through. This doesn't feel real."

"No, it doesn't," Andrew admitted.

"How'd Sam take it?"

"Told me to stop messing around with spooky bullshit."

"Sounds like him."

Andrew worked the stress-tensed muscles of his jaw with his thumbs. Should he apologize for suspecting the cousins, for continuing to harbor a smoldering coal of blame while accepting their help?

Before he solved that conundrum, Riley asked, "Trying to be delicate here, but—are you going to listen to, uh, the ghost, now that you know he's trying to communicate?"

Communicate, right. Andrew chewed his lip. He said, "No, there's a difference between . . . me using the shit I used, and giving a haunt free rein. It isn't *him,* don't mistake that. It doesn't care about us."

"But if it knows something about what happened to him, why not listen?" Riley insisted.

"It's not that simple." The end came out strangled; he cleared his throat of the blockage. "I'm more interested in the fact that Sam said he was taking Eddie on his errands, introducing him to people, and that he thinks he wasn't being smart about his mouth. You know about that?"

Riley nodded. Andrew felt as if he'd fallen out of his body, as if his roommate could see straight through him. After a night spent driving, crawling, fighting, and spilling confessions, he was a different version of himself than he had been that morning. It was rare to feel a shift so clearly. He wasn't sure he welcomed the defamiliarization.

"I mean, off the top of my head, I'm not sure who all he spoke to, but he took lots of notes in field interviews. He used Sam as the easy in for gathering his participants, so those chats and his research were one and the same," Riley said.

Andrew straightened in his seat and said, "I've gone through his notes some, but I hadn't seen a field journal, nothing that particular."

"No offense, but how thorough a search was that? Last time I checked, you weren't super into his whole business," Riley said with a gentle grin to ease the sting.

"I'm not, but—fuck." Andrew covered his face again. Riley wasn't wrong; he had no desire to dig through the minefield of papers again—not if he could ask a human instead. "Guess I'm going to have to be."

"We're going to figure this out," Riley said.

Andrew's mouth moved on its own, numb with the shock of remembering, and he said, "Someone cut his goddamn wrists for him and left him to bleed out alone. He died pissed off and scared and knowing it was happening, and I was so fucking far away."

"Jesus, Andrew," Riley said, sounding strangled.

Tears streaked the bridge of Andrew's nose, salt on his lips. He hiccupped with the force of stifling the broken, miserable wave of sobs that swept him under. Riley's deep, wet, nose-clogged breathing next to him was also hid from sight in the gloomy dark. Sam—sitting on his couch, maybe, or on his porch with a smoke—was probably mired in the same loss. And worse than the pain was the gladness lurking underneath, Andrew monstrously pleased to know he hadn't been cast off, hadn't been left behind, that Eddie still wanted him in his final moment, even if he'd failed him in the grandest possible sense. Eddie had tripped himself into some trouble that even he couldn't fix, had been taken from him.

The revenant was notably silent, absent, and Andrew's usual humming awareness of the ground under his feet had gone dormant too. As if he'd spent himself dry reaching into the roots of the burial tree to pull forth blood from nothing—*from stone, from water,* he thought with the tiniest flare of panic. Before he got too caught up in the horror of it, Riley parked the car behind their house and wiped his eyes on his sleeve. Two snot-clogged snuffles echoed in the enclosed space as he caught his breath. Though some barriers had crumbled in the face of grief, others remained upright; both men went to bed without speaking.

The first texts he saw in the morning were from Riley, asking: *you going to the faculty party tomorrow? i'll be there with luca. it'd be cool to go together maybe. you could ask Troth more about eddie*

I'll go, he agreed and sent Troth a similar email—because as West had said, and Sam too, Eddie had been asking people a lot of questions. Maybe too many.

16

Considering the nature of the event, Andrew wore a button-up and arrived an hour late—having napped through the afternoon, then loitered in bed, steeling himself for another hour. He hadn't met the hosting professor before, but his home was grand: three stories brightly lit from top to bottom, set far back from a clipped lawn with a half-oval drive. Andrew entered into a foyer alive with the social noise of a large gathering. A younger woman he recognized from his introductory course greeted him near the door and directed him through the living room to a spacious dining room, where the table was lined with copious, generous amounts of alcohol. He poured two fingers of bourbon over a spherical ice cube in a squat glass snagged from the sideboard.

"Mr. Blur, hello," greeted his intro seminar professor, Dr. Greene, from the kitchen across the way. "So glad to see you this evening."

He tipped his glass in greeting. "You too."

The cuffs of his shirt irritated his wrists, and his armpits had already begun to dampen. He paced the circular ground floor, passing through clusters of new students like himself, faculty, and the more senior cohort of students clumped *around* the faculty doing their dog-and-pony show with a mix of familiarity and desperation. He frowned, considering tactics for separating Dr. Troth off from the rest for a conversation. He made it almost back to the foyer before he found Riley and Luca, seated on a low couch in front of a bay window in the second den. The framed, ragged-edged original posters for silent films lining the den's walls formed a strange audience as a ruckus in the dining room called the attention of the other mingling guests.

"Hey there," Luca said.

She was wearing a cream blazer over a jet-black jumpsuit, belted at the waist with a gold cord. The cornflower blue of Riley's dress shirt, cuffed to his elbows, complemented his black slacks. Riley's smile lifted a notch.

"Glad you came, Andrew," he said.

Andrew planted one cheek of his ass on the couch arm and crossed his ankles. Riley flung an arm over the back of the sofa and angled himself so he could look up at his face. The subdued air between them rang with unspoken, unprocessed meaning. Luca leaned across Riley to tap the edge of her glass to Andrew's, a toast to nothing. She and Riley blended in to the posh get-together with a seamless prettiness that was at odds to the last time he'd seen them together: on the road, behind the wheel.

"How long am I expected to stay at these things again?" Andrew asked.

"I dunno, get comfortable and see how it goes," Riley replied.

"We'll duck out in a couple of hours—that's usually about how long I can take the general atmosphere as a plus-one. The flavor of rudeness is more subdued than at Sam's soirées, but a lot more . . . chilly, shall we say," Luca added under her breath, conspiratorial.

Andrew's phone buzzed. He slipped it from his pocket. Sam had texted, *Guess you're all being fancy tonight. Tell me if you get bored.*

"Andrew," called another voice from across the hall. West, displaying his usual mixture of sleek and tousled style from immaculate gleaming boots to a silver-threaded mauve shirt with two open buttons, stood framed in the doorway of the kitchen with a glass of wine loosely held at his side. "Did you just get here?"

"Yeah," he said, straightening from his slouched perch as the other man approached.

"Bored already?" West asked, lifting his glass for a sip with long fingers spread across the rim rather than the stem.

Andrew said, "Working on it. Got anything interesting to talk about?"

Riley snorted. West glanced at him, smiled a flat, crooked smile, then nodded to Luca with a warmer exchange of murmured hellos. Standing close, Andrew caught the scent of his cologne: cardamom-edged and musky. The cluster of their bodies at angles to one another, observed by the magnified faces of dead celebrities from the room's posters, carried a tense intimacy—and for once, the tension wasn't about Andrew. Or at least, he assumed not.

"How's your research going, Sowell?" West asked.

"Fine; revising my thesis proposal at the moment."

West watched Riley over the rim of his wine glass as he savored a slow mouthful. "I heard it was rejected at the end of last term, that must have been frustrating."

"Where'd that information come from?" Riley said.

"We all have our sources."

"Boys, behave yourselves in front of company," Luca said as she jerked a thumb surreptitiously toward the bustling chatter of faculty in the kitchen.

"Apologies," West conceded with a grin that said he knew he'd won that round.

"Sure, sure, you're right," Riley said, patting Luca's leg.

Andrew met Luca's eyes over the top of Riley's head. She rolled hers so dramatically that it almost made him snort while West and Riley bristled at each other and nursed their drinks. Andrew felt as if he were juggling three different lives and dropping the ball in all of them, but most of all this one. He had no place at ostentatious academic gatherings where people took thinly veiled potshots at each other's writing over wine. On impulse, he slipped his phone out to respond to Sam: *worse than bored*

Oh really. Well come over and we'll get drunk instead.

Despite his brief agreement, Riley opened his mouth again, like the words were being dragged out of him: "It was a request for revision, not a rejection. I agreed with the proposed narrowing of the research question. How's your dissertation? Ed told me he thought you stalled out over the summer."

Andrew's hackles rose at Riley's reference to Eddie, while West responded, "I'm not stalled, I'm investigating a fresh avenue for my third chapter my chair insisted on—"

A hand cupping his elbow startled him. He locked his phone screen with a twitch and Jane Troth laughed musically, recalling childhood memories of Eddie's mother in a loose silk shell top and trim slacks.

"Sorry to scare you," she said.

"Don't worry about it," he said.

"Hello, Dr. Troth," West said, the animation smoothing from his expression until his face was a polite mask. "How's your evening going?"

She glanced at him, then said to Andrew, "May I borrow you from your friends?"

Andrew nodded, surprised to see his problem solving itself. As she turned to leave the room, clearly expecting him to follow, he caught sight of Luca wrinkling her nose and West glowering with exhausted irritation at the professor's retreating back. Riley crimped his mouth too. *Subdued,* Luca had said, and he thought he maybe understood a glimmer of what she was trying to explain to him.

Nonetheless, he followed dutifully as she led him from the group. The upstairs study she retreated to possessed the signs of human life that the public spaces of the gathering lacked: a pair of discarded socks next to the desk; a closed Macbook on the blotter; a haphazard collection of coffee mugs lined up on the windowsill. Andrew inspected the books on the shelf without seeing the titles. Dr. Troth propped her hip on the desk.

"Eric won't mind, so long as we ignore the clutter. He offered the space so we could speak in private."

"Sorry I missed our meeting, things have been busy," Andrew said.

She gestured to the fading bruises along his jaw and asked, "Were you in an accident?"

"Yeah, and I've been catching up on assignments this week to make up for lost time. What did you want to talk to me about?"

Dr. Troth stood straight, pulled a folded square of paper from her trouser pocket, and passed it to him with a cool brush of fingertips. The edges, folded under themselves, formed an elegant packet. His thumb pressed the dense weave of the stationery into a hard ridge on the object it contained.

"Edward's ring," she said. "I found it, after, but I hadn't had the chance to meet with you without an audience, and I didn't think it would be appropriate to give you in public."

Andrew tucked the packet into his jeans without opening the flap, imagining the weight of the platinum burning a circle into his thigh. He flattened his palm against his leg to press an indentation of metal to flesh for a split second and said, "Where was it?"

"He'd come to my home for a small dinner party and helped with the dishes after. I found the ring next to the sink," she said.

"A dinner party?" Andrew repeated dumbly.

Troth swept her palms along the desk behind her, leaned back, and nodded. She was as earnest as a well-bred greyhound. He had a difficult time picturing his Eddie washing dishes at her sink, sleeves rolled, ring on the countertop—considering he'd seen him open beer bottles with the selfsame ring more than once—but the man had contained hidden multitudes, as Andrew so richly understood these days.

"I'm sure he didn't mention it to anyone, but I reached out to him when I saw his name on the roster, well before I realized how intriguing his research would be. I was an acquaintance of his parents, years ago," she said.

The content of their first uncomfortable office conversation stood out to him in chilling relief: her implicit knowledge of him and his past, the panic attack he'd heaved through in the stairwell.

Of course she knew Eddie's parents, that was his fucking luck—no wonder she had been acting weird about Andrew avoiding her.

"He hadn't told me that, no," he said instead.

She shifted her weight from one modest high heel to another, relieving the pressure in a minute human gesture. Even leaning against the desk, she had several inches on him. Andrew fought the urge to draw himself taller while she observed his discomfort with the conversation, his fingers itching to ground themselves on the ring in his pocket.

When he said no more, she continued: "The Fultons and the Troths are old families, you know, but both our lines have dwindled to almost nothing. He said the old Townsend house was still standing. I suppose it's yours now, as well. Have you been to see it?"

Prickling cool sweat spread across his scalp.

"No," he said.

His tongue stuck to the roof of his mouth; he took a sip of his ice-diluted bourbon to cover. He shook his head in a second *no*. His phone buzzed once, twice, three times in quick succession, each message a faint audible hum in the stock-still room. Another sip of bourbon. His fingers itched to see what he'd been sent, but Troth remained perched against the desktop, unfinished, considering him with a tilt of her chin.

"I apologize, local histories are a passion of mine. I'm sure you've been busy. But have you had a chance to read any of the texts I loaned you?" Before he found an answer, she cut her own question off: "Ah, I suppose not, with the accident. Proposals will be reviewed at the end of the term for initial approval, you're aware?"

"Yes," he said, lost in the chop of the conversation.

She sighed, cracked her knuckles, and said, "I'll be frank. I have an interest in working with the material Edward was gathering, but I don't think it would be appropriate for me to adopt it, given the circumstances. The optics would be poor, don't you think?"

Taking her dead student's research—Andrew allowed, "Maybe, yeah."

"So, let's you and I meet in the coming week. If you'd be willing to consider continuing in his footsteps, and would allow me to participate in a *hands-on* capacity, I'll do all within my power to assist. I'm aware this is unorthodox," she said. "But it feels almost like returning the ring. Since you're an heir yourself, after all, aren't you?"

The briefest flicker in her expression set him on edge. Something akin to disdain, there and gone. To her, was Andrew another scholarship kid, a different sort than Riley but a charity case all the same? She was old blood, watching him pick up the leftovers of a family hers had known for generations. He pressed his thumb to the edge of the ring in his pocket and thought, *hands-on means she'll know who he was talking to.*

"All right, I'm interested," he said.

"Perfect. I hope I haven't come across as rude; I don't mean to pressure you. It was a delight for me to help a Fulton research the Fultons. They've always had a famous connection to the supernatural, you know," she allowed, smiling like a conspirator.

Andrew finished his drink in a long gulp. The burn singed his healing gums. His phone buzzed again. Despite his scramble for ten total words in the entire conversation, she'd said more to him than she ever had to date. Maybe she'd been planning out her pitch, saving it up. Maybe he'd pissed her off by ignoring those emails, or maybe she was wine-drunk and feeling proprietary over the young wreck in front of her, connecting him to a namesake he'd never claim for himself.

The Fulton line, dwindled—a bitter taste in both their mouths.

"I imagine that fine, spooky history was what led you boys to tromp around the woods that summer. It's hard to believe I'm looking at the young man from the newspaper all grown up," she said. Andrew's hand spasmed on the glass. Weaker crystal might have cracked. Troth stepped from the desk and laid delicate fingers on his shoulder in passing. "I remember the search, because my youngest was your age then. Edward's parents were distraught. It was such a relief when you were both found."

She left before he had a chance to ask his questions, or calm his pounding heart. Her heels clacked across the hall, then down the staircase in a decrescendo. Andrew set the empty glass on the floor at his feet before he could throw it. White noise roared in his head. She'd hinted before, but proof that she really *knew* ripped him open like a row of unhealed stitches—that was why he hadn't wanted to be in Nashville, had argued with Eddie not to take him back to a place where people might remember him. And Troth had the gall to throw it at him while leaving a room.

When he passed through the den Luca called out to him, "Andrew, are you all right?"

"—and anyway, you're flat fucking wrong," Riley said with enthusiasm, gesticulating wildly at West as they stood toe-to-toe, refreshed wine glasses in hand. Riley's cheeks were red; West's eyes blazed.

"Listen, I'm not disagreeing the book is useful, but what I'm saying is—" West began in a rejoinder containing equal fervor.

"Sorry," Andrew said to Luca as he waved her off and walked straight toward the door.

"Wait," she called out.

Andrew didn't pause in his flight, unbuttoning his cuffs as he jogged down the short porch steps. He swung himself into his car—his real car, his Supra, with its ugly wrap and sticky transmission—and pushed the clutch as he turned the key. The messages on his phone, which he read while he waited for the frantic shaking in his hands to quit, read:

I've got whiskey and two blunts

One blunt

Zero blunts but more weed

Tell me you'd rather stay there and listen
to the nerds twist each other's pigtails

He almost sounded like Eddie. Andrew put the car in gear and sent, *what's your address,* then input it to his GPS as soon as he got a profanity-and-praise-laden response. The paper in his pocket jabbed into his thigh, pokey and unforgiving. He drove fast through the yellow-moonlit night, tracing steep hill roads to the house he was becoming familiar with. Troth was after him to fill Eddie's shoes for her, to complete his research with her, to dredge the accident up for her—she forced her way into things no one else understood, probing secrets he'd rather leave buried.

But he had questions to ask, and he needed her answers for some of them.

"Fuck," he barked, crunching to a stop on the gravel in front of Halse's garage.

He wasn't some whiskey-gentry scion playing historian for kicks, digging into his long-nursed wounds to find the festering bottom. He didn't belong at Vanderbilt, and he didn't belong in Troth's world either. He hadn't been groomed to inherit the Fulton name and legacy. He was just Andrew Blur. All he wanted to unearth was the truth of Eddie's last hours, to set things as right as he was able.

The front door opened as he climbed out of the car and Sam jogged down the steps, his fingers looped through a plastic-ringed sixer of Old English tallboys and a smile on his face.

"I've got you covered," Sam said.

Andrew met him halfway across the lawn and yanked a beer free. The rib-crushing squeeze in his chest hadn't abated, but the hiss-crack of the can opening eased it a fraction. Bitter malt liquor on his tongue settled him another inch. Sam snagged the can and stole a swig. Companionable silence settled between them, unbroken by Riley's chatter or the squabbling of other boys. It was the second time they'd been alone. In the ambient light, the square cut of Sam's jaw was ghostly familiar.

"Let's go for a drive," Sam said.

"Yours or mine?"

"Mine. I haven't gotten to show her off yet," Sam said.

Andrew grunted his agreement and moved his car to the side

of the drive while Halse cut through his house. He clasped the OE between his knees, since the can wouldn't fit in the console holder. With a clamoring grind, the garage rolled open to reveal the WRX, gunmetal and black chrome and anticipation. Andrew squeaked his thumb over the low spoiler, touching the car for the first time. Sam had left the bolts unpainted, bare metal.

"Get in," Sam said as he locked the door to the house.

The passenger door was already unlocked. Andrew glanced over his shoulder as he settled into the seat. The rear compartment was empty, bench seats removed. Halse snagged a hat from the scattered detritus, and Andrew passed him a tallboy from the sixer.

"Thanks, man," Sam said.

He planted his hand on the back of Andrew's seat as he turned in his own to reverse the length of the drive, fast enough to feel fun-sloppy, comfortable with his maneuvering. Upon executing a two-point turn onto the main road, he released Andrew's seat to face front—and somehow managed to skim the tips of his fingers across the join of Andrew's neck and shoulder, raising the hair on his nape in a bristling twitch. Opposite the direction of the city where Andrew had come from, the road climbed farther into the hills; Sam headed that direction, seeking distance from the rest of the world. Once he'd hit third gear at a maintenance speed, he cracked his beer open.

"So it sucked," he said.

Andrew nodded.

Sam hummed and passed his tallboy across the console. Andrew balanced it on his knee, dropping his head onto the seat rest when Sam thumbed the controls to roll their windows down. Fresh summer air filled his mouth with the taste of a forest in the hot dark. The engine revved and Sam laughed under his breath, laughed for himself. Andrew had done this more times than he could count, with a different man at his side. The road leveled out around the side of a hill, a track cut wide and long with a gentle curve and a precipitous drop past the steel barrier rail.

"Well, fuck 'em," Halse barked, and gunned it.

Acceleration flattened Andrew into his seat, pinning him. With eyes closed and lips popped open he allowed the vertigo to slam through him, cold beer spilling on his crotch when Sam pumped the brakes to corner hard around the curve. The tires slipped in a wild second of drift before he wrangled the car over the center line. Sam Halse drove with the confidence of a man who knew he was a king. Andrew lolled his head to the side and peeked at the broad set of his smile and his loose shoulders. The relaxed pleasure in his posture spoke to the fact that he'd taken this route a million times and would drive it blindfolded if someone asked. Andrew chugged the rest of his beer and tossed his crumpled empty over his shoulder.

There were no streetlamps. Sam's bluish headlights and the partial moon were all that illuminated the world. Trees towered mossy green, eerily verdant, from out of the blackness on either side of the road as they cut through a flatter strand of hillside. As their pace leveled, fast enough to entertain but slow enough to split his attention without the risk of death, Sam reclaimed his OE. He tilted it to the side of his mouth and watched the road while he sipped. Andrew watched his throat work, watched a trickle of sweat leaching into the collar of his shirt.

Andrew opened his mouth and said, "None of them ever shut up."

Sam snorted. "Let me guess. My cousin and that rich dude he's always getting irritable at sniped at each other about bullshit they technically agree on while Luca tried to smother their dumbass feud, and you hated every minute of it. Am I right, Blur?"

Andrew gulped another throat-challenging mouthful of OE in response. The grade of the road descended by degrees as they circled the other side of the hill. If Eddie were driving, he might've reached across the console to grab Andrew's knee. He'd have dug his thumb into the notch on the outside for a moment of grounding discomfort. Sam just drummed his fingers on the steering wheel, left arm flung briefly out the window to grab the breeze.

"Call me Andrew," he offered.

Without looking at him, Sam drawled, "All right, Andrew."

His name lay full on Sam's tongue, the two syllables spilling out rounder, less clipped than the one. The disembodiment of the department gathering, his pretense at scholar-gentleman, dropped away at Sam's slur on the -*drew*.

Switchback pavement led them to the base of the hill. In a creek-split holler between the rolling heights of the forest, draped with night and interrupted only by the porch light of one farmhouse set a far distance from the road, Sam coasted to a casual stop. Humid air danced through the windows. Sam wiped his forehead with his wrist, dislodging his hat. The pair of them finished their sixer, elbows out their windows and silent as old friends—the night had spackled over his cracking façade with watchful silence and purposeful adrenaline, offering the right comfort without making him ask for it.

After Sam tossed his last can in the back, he asked, "Ready to head home?"

17

Sam drove them up the hill again, climbing toward the moon resting in place overhead. A fierce urge to piss battled with his head-
fogging buzz. Something in his pocket jabbed the crease of his
groin as he shifted; he adjusted it, rediscovered the paper packet,
thumb finding the metal indent of the ring. Through the whole
drive home he left his thumb there, and only when Sam parked
them safe in the garage did he rouse from his distracted reverie.
Even as he tromped up the steps to the house, Andrew found he
wasn't ready to leave the night behind them. Sam gestured over his
shoulder, a crook of his index finger, without a word or a glance.
Building nerves dispersed as Andrew followed after him through
the kitchen, accepting a handful of mismatched blankets tossed at
him from the hall closet. He dumped them on the couch and sat
to unlace his high-tops, soaking in the intense release of pressure
around his sweaty ankles.

Across the room Sam braced his arm above his head at the entrance to the hall, worming his scuffed sneakers off without bending over. His right sock caught on the shoe and slid to mid-foot;
instead of fixing it, he kicked it free. His tattoo's bold edges hinted
from underneath the hem of his shirt as it rose above his waistline.
As he straightened he caught Andrew staring and flashed a smirk
before striding down the hall, one sock on and one sock off. A door
shut in the depths of the house, and Andrew released the breath
lodged in his chest from the abrupt eye contact.

Andrew availed himself of the bathroom and considered his
reflection in the unlit mirror: mouth slack with exhaustion and
drink, a hectic flush from cheeks to chest, hair a wind-snared mess.

The bruises on his face were healing through a spectrum of mottled flat colors, unlike the nasty green of the fresh one Sam had left on his thigh. On the couch he wrapped himself up in blankets to check his phone. From Riley, a series of questions, then silence once it became clear he wouldn't respond to them. Either that, or Sam had told him he'd collected their wayward charge. More surprising, three messages from Del:

> I've given you some space to sort through a few things. I'm checking in now because I'm worried, and I'd appreciate you letting me know you're okay.

> I know you don't want to talk about it, or about how you feel, but we were friends. I want to think we're still friends. It shouldn't be my job alone to make that happen.

> Love you Andrew

He responded with a brief, *Give me some more time. Love you too.* He didn't think he meant it, but it would give them both longer to sort out their relationship. For good measure he sent a quick message to his mother as well before shutting his phone off. Head turned into the couch cushions, he wondered if Eddie had slept where he was sleeping, if he'd driven those same roads and drank that same cheap liquor and passed out here with Halse. He hadn't told Andrew if he had—but it made sense, more sense than dinner parties, than washing professors' dishes. He pressed his thumbnail into his wrist bone over the tattoo, and felt the earth calling to his bones. There were answers somewhere out in these woods.

He slept easier than he'd expected.

The velvet twilight of the dream resounded with Eddie's voice: *further, come further, this way.* Andrew stumbled toward the sound of his call over roots and rocks, the shadows treacherously mislead-ing. Just as he glimpsed Eddie's silhouette through the trees, the ground collapsed under his unsteady heels. Pain sliced from hip to scapula as he fell, the breath punched out of him in a cracked shout. He scrabbled for a grip on the dirt walls as he tumbled with the rotten leaves, tearing a fingernail loose with a pop. His full weight landed on his left ankle, crunching it to the wrong side. Overhead the light waned as his vision swam.

That was how it had happened, and also not how it had hap-pened.

Further, he heard from within the cavern, across the dripping water and the rushing of a far-off stream. He crawled on elbows and knees, useless ankle stabbing at him. He'd lost someone, some-thing. Blind and blinder fumbling led him into chill emptiness, bloodied and hurting. As a child, he'd reached out and touched the heaving warmth of his friend's chest. This time he encountered a cool, slick, porous surface. Numbing tingles sparked up the length of his arm as the blood in his veins vibrated to life. His thumb slid around a strange, slick hollow, followed a ridge to a branching, rough length of—antler.

The hungering void lurched. Eddie's cracked murmur filled his ear—*further, you're getting there,* huskily intimate—whispering as the revenant had while dragging him through the graveyard, at-tempting to show him the truth. Hands closed over his, guiding his limp fingers to wrap around the damp-furred antlers. Power beat in a determined pulse at the base of his tongue. Reverberation pinioned him alive between the haunt's bones and the antlers—conducting from their hands on the stag's skull to the swelling ne-glected *thing* in Andrew's belly with an agonized ripple.

"Jesus fucking goddamn." Rough hands jerked under his arm-pit and around his waist. "Wake the *fuck* up, come on Andrew."

The antler in his hand was attached to a dead deer. Andrew recoiled in deranged panic, phantasm superimposed onto reality.

Halse dragged him farther from the animal's remains as he kicked at the ground and struggled to shove himself free. Coarse, gore-matted fur clung to the deer's corpse, its rot-eyed skull. Scavengers had begun their work long before he'd stumbled onto this dead thing in his sleep. The overpowering stench gagged him. The roiling cold the haunt had raised in his blood lashed toward the deer without his consent, pouring from his fingertips into the earth—and from there to the corpse, its sucking gravity drawing the spill.

Andrew swore a hoof twitched in response, or the shadow it cast did.

"You in there?" Sam said, crouching in front of him to block out the sight of the deer. He was wearing nothing but basketball shorts and house shoes.

Andrew resisted the hair-raising urge to peer around him and confirm the corpse *hadn't* moved, grunting out, "Fuck."

"So do you sleepwalk often," Sam said, flat.

His clothes stank. The brackish streaks on them, he realized with a burst of nausea, were almost certainly from lying near, or *on,* the rotting stag. He made a disgusted noise and pulled first one arm then the other into the shirt, careful to strip it over his head without turning it inside out.

"I heard the door open, figured it wasn't a big deal, and then remembered you're the poster child for doing insane shit when no one is looking," Sam said. "Took me like twenty minutes to find your dumb ass. Get up. I'm tired."

Andrew dropped the shirt on the ground and got to his feet. Sam turned from him. The glow of his phone cast eerie shadows from under his chin while he flicked the flashlight on, a bubble of white light cutting into the forest ahead. Sam started walking; Andrew stumbled after, footsore. Under muted moonlight, filtered through the leaf cover, the stark lines of his tattoo crawled in spiny, feathering geometric shadows across his pale back.

After a few steps he glanced over his shoulder and said, "I haven't charged this thing in like a day and a half, so get a move on before we end up lost in the woods."

The final brambles of the tattoo crawled under the waistband of his shorts.

Andrew winced at the bite of sticks and underbrush on his lacerated feet, each step stoking the hurt higher. He couldn't remember if he'd had a tetanus shot recently. Sam moved at a comfortable lope through the forest debris, tracking their dot on his phone's map until the vegetation cleared into his backyard. On the porch, under clearer gold light cast by a bulb studded with blundering moths, Andrew noticed that the tattoo lines curled between a scattering of thin, raised white scars. Sam opened the door and raked another look over his filthy body.

"I'm gonna shower," Andrew said, hoarse as a crow's caw.

"Yeah, I'll find you something to wear," Sam said. "A dead deer. Christ, man."

His tone was incredulous and disturbed, a pair of emotions Andrew could relate to. He stripped to his boxers and threw his pants onto the porch rail, resolving to add them to the list of things he wasn't going to deal with if he didn't have to. Sam called from the hall, "Dropped you some shorts in the bathroom. Figure you didn't want to touch them until you're clean."

An hour later, he sat at the kitchen table with a glass of bourbon and ice. He was scrubbed pink, ticks removed and peroxide liberally applied to all of his minor wounds. Sam sat across from him, watching Andrew over the rim of his own tumbler. Andrew had nothing to say for himself. Last time the revenant had hijacked him, it had at least shown him the death he deserved to see; he wasn't sure of the point of dragging him into the woods, which was almost more disturbing.

The stag's hoof had moved, he was sure of it.

"Here's some free advice for you," Sam said, turning his glass in his hands. His accent crept thicker as he spoke. "Our grandma,

Riley's and mine, she owned this house. She told us one thing from the time we were little: don't fuck with what's outside your scope. There's a lot of that weird shit out in these parts. Keep your hands off it, it's no good for no one. I told Ed and Riley the same thing, they just didn't listen."

"I hear you," Andrew muttered.

"Seems like you're smarter about it than those two chucklefucks, but I still keep catching you at it." He gulped the rest of his drink and stood. "C'mon."

Andrew carried his bourbon with him. Sam's tattoo moved with the defined muscles of his back, trailing from the complex physical machine of his shoulders across the sweep of his lats as he strode to his room. Andrew paused in the doorway, the quiet urge to *stay* catching him. Sam sprawled onto his bed with a creak of springs, arms over his head, ambient light from the window caught on the hollows of his knees and the central valley of his chest. He tilted his chin expectantly. Andrew knocked the door shut behind him with his heel, set his drink on the dresser, and considered the floor with its pile of laundry. He hadn't brought his blankets, but he grabbed a pillow off the bed and flopped onto the gritty roughness of the rug.

Sheets rustled; the bed frame creaked.

"Just get up here," Sam said.

Andrew blinked into the black space under the bed. He sat up. Sam had turned onto his side to face the far wall. The mattress was at least queen-sized—and he was allowed this one thing, he thought, after the fucking nightmare and the dead deer. He missed sleeping beside a warm, breathing body. Andrew tossed the pillow into its proper spot and laid stiffly on the cool twist of sheets, tucking his lacerated feet and calves under them as unobtrusively as possible. Sam sighed. Andrew breathed to his rhythm.

He woke up alone the next morning in an empty house and wore his borrowed shorts home to Capitol, unsettled by the fleeting, sleep-muddled recollection of Sam's knees pressed into the backs of his own, alive and sweat-damp. Underneath, the stirring whisper of *further, further, you're getting there.* Riley was standing in the kitchen cooking eggs when he opened the porch door and Andrew paused, feeling inexplicably naked in borrowed clothes that he knew Riley would recognize. His soiled jeans dangled from a plastic bag looped around his wrist. The ring was still in the pocket, in the professor's fancy paper packet. Riley glanced over at him, started to speak, then did a filmic double-take before shutting his mouth.

"Slept there, it was too late to get back," Andrew said, not addressing the fact that he'd been with Sam in the first place. If he didn't, he figured Riley wouldn't.

"Sure," Riley said, awkward. "Uh, how come you left after talking to Troth?"

"She gave me back Eddie's ring, and brought up all that stuff about his research, their families. Couldn't get a word in edgewise," he admitted.

"Overwhelming, huh," Riley said as he turned the burner off and scooped his scrambled eggs onto a plate.

Andrew sat at the table. The stag and the mud and the bones hadn't quite dispersed under the strong summer light. Riley plopped down across from him and tapped the tines of his fork on his plate a couple of times, chewing his bottom lip. Andrew raised an eyebrow.

"Okay, so, I got curious," Riley blurted out. "And I'm sorry, I know, but I went and dug out his notes in your room? I figured you were going through it so I'd help out. You didn't miss the field notes—they're *not there*. I can show you?"

Andrew let the whiplash range of emotions wash over him, from anger to exposure to reluctant interest; then he said, "Show me."

Riley dashed up the stairs, leaving his eggs unattended. Andrew stole a bite with his fingers, then snagged the bag of shredded cheese from the counter to snack out of. On his return, Riley thumped the stack of journals and pages onto the glass tabletop—looking eager to present his research. With a flourish he spread them out.

"This is all personal stuff—like, his journaling and planning and thinking, but not the ethnographic stuff like demographic data and transcriptions and shit. I remember seeing his field note-book; it was like, this grey Moleskine. If this is everything you found, there's a ton of shit missing," Riley said. "Have you checked his carrel?"

"I didn't know he had one to check," he replied.

"Well, shit."

The men stared at each other for a long moment.

"It's under both our names, but I haven't gone back since. He kept the spare key upstairs," Riley said. "It's reserved all through the semester."

"Then let's go see," Andrew said.

"Let me change," Riley said, cramming two bites of eggs into his mouth before jogging upstairs again.

Andrew bounced his leg, waiting. His phone had a text from West, asking him what had happened with Troth at the party, and he responded *she returned one of Eddie's rings to me and ambushed me about his research, I had to go after that*. West's typing bubble popped up, disappeared, popped up again. Riley returned before the message arrived, twirling keys around his finger and wearing a grey Henley, the bright butter-yellow of his sneakers offsetting black jeans. His glasses narrowed the lines of his face. Andrew was struck again at the chameleon effect of his roommate: one minute a grubby punk with an ugly, fast car, the next a svelte young academic. The contradiction made his skin crawl with sympathy. He had to fit in somehow.

"This might be nothing," Riley said, as if to convince himself.

They drove the short distance to campus in tense silence, and a feral energy pushed their pace striding across the weekend-emptied quad, dotted with a bare handful of students appreciating the weather. The carrels were located in the central library, up a few flights of well-trodden stairs. Overhead fluorescents hummed ominously across the rows of cubicle-esque box offices. Riley strode through the first row, took a turn, and cut across two more before he stopped in front of number 32. Andrew unclipped the small brass key and fit it into the petite lock, scarred from decades of clumsy student handling. It turned with an audible click.

Riley said, "I can go first, if you want."

"Wait out here," Andrew said.

He turned the knob and the door sagged into his grip, worn on its hinges. He let it swing open. The high walls of the carrel and the wan track lighting overhead turned the compact space into a chiaroscuro relief. He flicked on the lamps, one for each corner, and braced his hands on the solitary chair tucked under the desktop. The carrel had two long, pale wooden desks with drawers at one end, joined at the far corner in an L-shape.

Books, as he'd expected, scattered the far desk: historical survey texts, local journals, a lone mismatched graphic novel with an envelope sticking out of it as a bookmark. Two more composition books, flat and pristine, were tucked into the top corner. Andrew sat in the chair, laid his hands on the working desktop, and thought *where the fuck are these notes?*

"Riley," he said.

The other man peered around the edge of the door, a briefly disembodied head and one shoulder. "Sup?"

"What's missing?"

Riley pulled the door shut behind him as he crammed into the small space. The light flashed on his glasses as he turned his head to inspect the full range of the carrel. He said, "Check the drawers."

Andrew pulled out the bottom drawer and found a package of granola bars, unopened. The middle contained nothing but a binder clip and a pen, while the top offered a spiral-bound purple notebook, battered and dog-eared, but it had Riley's handwriting on the cover. The chair spun when he kicked the floor to face the other man again, empty-handed. Riley stood near his knees, leaning against the other desktop in the confined space. Neither spoke, but Riley's face had gone a hectic scarlet, scar standing out in silvery relief across his cheek and nose.

Andrew's hands clenched and unclenched on his knees. He'd almost expected to find Eddie's phone, his notes, a neat trail that said *met with a crazy old man in the woods, here's his address, he tells good stories.* Clean answers to an impossible situation. The disappointment outweighed his understanding that the lack of material was also significant.

"Andrew," Riley started, sounding on edge already.

He wasn't ready to be interrogated while his brain continued to spin its emotional gears, so he pointed to the bridge of his own nose at the same spot Riley's scar was and asked, "Where'd that come from again?"

"Someone hit me and I fell on some glass," he said, undeterred by the redirection. "Andrew, there's nothing here."

"Sam take care of that person for you?"

"There's nowhere else his notes should be," Riley said, doggedly having the conversation Andrew wasn't participating in.

"I'll ask Troth first thing on Monday, it doesn't . . . mean shit yet. Not yet," he said.

Riley shook his head. Andrew stood, curving his chest and hips to avoid contact in the one-person room.

"West said she wanted me to follow up with her, and she was talking about his research at the party, before she gave me the ring. She definitely wants me to keep working on it. The notes might be with her, might be somewhere else. Don't get your hopes up."

He was reminding himself as much as telling Riley, who nodded.

Next to the door, pinned to the cloth wall from top to desk, were a set of eight-year-old newspaper articles, some clipped, some printed, some scanned. *Local Boys Found After 72-Hour Search*, read one headline paired with a black-and-white photograph of two skinny-limbed kids in cargo shorts and sneakers posing for a camera. The picture had been taken at his twelfth birthday. Eddie had pushed him into the swimming pool with his flip-phone still in his pocket an hour later and they'd had a muddy fistfight in the yard. The other headlines weren't much different. He shoved his hands in his pockets to keep from tearing it all down.

18

Andrew lowered himself into the same cracked vinyl chair in front of Troth's desk from his last visit. The professor had left a note on the tiny square whiteboard hanging on her door: *Be back shortly!* As he waited, implications spooled out inside his head one after another, unforgiving like a corpse under hospital lighting, like how he'd seen Eddie in the identification photographs. Men who had violent squabbles over cocaine shot each other; someone desperate to cover up an overdose would pose a body, maybe. In neither of those scenarios would the perpetrator tie someone up, slit their wrists, and drive their corpse to a scenic location for a dog-walker to find. Nothing qualified him to investigate an actual murder, but if he took his handful of suspicions and bad dreams to a cop they'd pity-laugh him out of the room.

Something drastic was missing—maybe in the field notes, maybe in the phone. He didn't know what it would mean if Troth had the notes—it might mean nothing at all. But without access to the fieldwork he'd have to retrace Eddie's steps himself, and she could help with that better than anyone.

From the foyer Dr. Troth said, "Andrew, I'm glad you could make it."

"I'm sorry it's taken a while," he said as she entered the office.

He crossed one ankle over the other, attempting to loosen his posture to an approximation of normal. Professor Troth lowered herself into her utilitarian chair. She rested her wrists on the edge of the desk, fine-boned fingers interlocked, to regard him. Overhead vents kicked on with a muffled roar, and a burst of chilly air rattled the papers scattered over her blotter.

Andrew said, "Thanks for returning the ring."

"I couldn't have kept it, but you're welcome regardless," she said.

Here goes nothing, he thought, then said, "I read through some of Eddie's notes and stuff he left around the house, and you're right—it was, uh, interesting. How'd he present it to you?"

"Well, his general focus as I understood it was on folklore unique to the region: urban legends, ghost stories, that sort of thing. His study was comparative, and focused on placing local traditions within the broader context of Appalachian-South cultural studies."

While she spoke, she reached into the purse on the far corner of the desk. The same sort of brass keys he had on his belt loop cluttered her key ring. She thumbed one loop out of the clump and unlocked her top desk drawer. It slid free with a quiet hiss and she lifted a hook-ended manila folder from the hanging rack. The plastic tab at the top said *Fulton* in blue spidery script. She laid it flat and pushed it toward him. Andrew flipped the folder open, glancing at the tidy stack of printed pages.

She continued, "First is the mentoring file I'd been keeping, followed by Edward's own notes, in particular the sketches he'd been constructing of early Fulton history. I had intended to assist him with archival research from my own family library, before he passed."

"And you said you were hoping I'd take it up?" Andrew prompted.

Troth nodded, tucking her hair behind her ears studiously. "The project is unique, truly. Edward was able to speak with a . . . *type* of person whom I don't have access to or rapport with. But I encouraged him to pursue his unorthodox avenues of investigation—his reach revealed fresh information on stories I thought I'd known inside and out. I suppose old money talking to and about itself isn't nearly as interesting; significant facts are easily missed that way. I'd almost abandoned hope on continuing to pursue the avenues he opened up—until your arrival."

Andrew said, "I thought you said he mentioned I'd be coming here?"

"He had, but after his passing, you didn't reach out to confirm your enrollment with the department, or answer our correspondence. So your arrival came as a surprise," she admitted. "My husband also found Edward's methodology fascinating, but aside from difficulties accessing Edward's sources, it felt disrespectful for us to pursue further without him. And then, as I said, you arrived— which refreshed my interest."

"Opened the door again, huh. Can I look?" he asked with a gesture to the folder.

"Be my guest," she said.

Andrew slid the file onto his lap and read through the first few pages of her notes: *Edward has laid out a frame that balances academic inquiry into folklore with field research to trace the origins of stories, both familial and commonplace, that will allow him a unique ethnographic perspective on his subject.* Several pages further in, she continued: *the first set of interviews conducted in the field were inconclusive, but Edward seems nonplussed, eager to continue, and perhaps enamored with the process itself.*

"The material will certainly be publishable," she continued. "And more importantly, the original contribution to the field would have quite an impact. I act as advisor for several students in every cohort, but I don't often see work that catches my interest so thoroughly. Assisting your efforts, if you choose to pick up his project midstream, is a personal priority for me. Your first publication could come as a co-authored piece, with my assistance on the material."

Her motives slid into place, filling the logistical gap he'd been struggling with. It made no sense for something high-concept like loyalty to the Fulton legacy to drive her persistence when she'd known Eddie for less than six months. The opportunity to co-opt a student's labor to boost her own profile did—how neatly and smoothly she'd proposed he do the work and she take the credit. He gnawed his lip for a moment, glanced up at her from the notes, and prodded to confirm, "Not an entirely altruistic motive, then, bringing me on board?"

Her gallant smile had a playful edge, conspiratorial. She leaned onto her elbows and said, "No, you're right, my interest comes as much from personal desire as altruism alone. I hope that doesn't come across as ghoulish? Believe me, I was fond of Edward, and I truly do think that his work is worth the effort of preservation. I wasn't expecting to get a second opportunity."

"Publish or perish, huh," he said.

"Exactly that. I'm willing to admit, between the two of us here, that Edward's passing left me stuck on a professional level as well as a personal one," she said. "I wasn't able to fruitfully pick up where he left off, but he'd mentioned your interest and qualifications. And you also have access to his estate, correct?"

"Yeah," he agreed, distracted as he thumbed through the notes in the folder.

The pages were in Eddie's handwriting on loose-leaf paper with neat marginal annotations in her script. The first sheet read, *James Fulton settled the land that would become the estate in 1806 without incident or conflict. Found a family Bible that cuts out around 1910 when people stopped recording names in it, but the lineage is clear from the first guy to the last (aka, me).* Eddie's small aside was jarring, as if he were performing for the reader. Andrew frowned and shuffled through the pages—there were only around twenty-five.

"Do you have more than this, somewhere else in your files?" he asked.

"What do you mean?" she responded.

The notes she'd handed him were spartan, bland compared to the personal journals. Andrew sat the folder on the desk. Troth's interest might be ghoulish, but her angle on the whole mess was academic, oblique to his ultimate goal. It was an angle to exploit nonetheless.

"The field notes for his interviews are missing," Andrew said.

Troth tilted her head and said, "I don't have those, unfortunately. He provided me summaries where appropriate, not his originals or transcriptions."

"No, I mean they're just *gone*. I've dug through everything at home, in his car, and in his carrel. Everyone has mentioned them, but they're nowhere to be found."

After two beats of strained silence, with her blank stare pinning him to his stiff seat, Troth crossed the office to close the door. The air conditioner cut off. Andrew drummed his fingertips on the chair arm, watching her as she paused. Her grip rested loose on the door handle, and she cocked her head at him with a considering flat frown.

"And you've looked everywhere, you're sure?" she repeated.

"Yeah," he agreed.

"He did a full semester's worth of interviews; there should be at minimum one full notebook. We discussed the interviews in a general sense, and he referenced from them in our meetings, but the originals and the audio recordings should be with his other materials."

Andrew spread his hands in a gesture of supplication and said, "I was assuming, or maybe hoping, you'd have them."

The fine wrinkles at the corner of Troth's mouth lent a severity to her expression. He wouldn't have wanted that intensity turned on him in a course; he doubted she ever had trouble with boisterous underclassmen. All his leads pointed in the direction of those field excursions, alongside Sam or otherwise; the absent phone with its likely collection of audio recordings and the written notes both were too closely joined to the hallucinatory vision of the corpse posed under the oak tree. Troth clicked across the tile floor in her sensible heels to pull the second guest chair over to his elbow and sit.

"Here." She flipped the folder open once again between the two of them. Andrew shifted in his seat to face her. "While I don't have the interviews themselves, my notes reference a handful of them in greater detail."

She split the stack in half and handed him a pad of ruled Post-Its. The frown was ever-present as she skimmed through the first few pages. Andrew ran his thumb across his own page, unfocused, seeking names or locations instead of her long-form analysis of Eddie's writing style. At his side, her pen scratched on the Post-Its. He forced himself not to look.

Four pages in he happened upon a paragraph: *Rob and Lisa Mc-Cormick are an elderly couple who are located close to the boundaries of the Fulton estate and Edward expressed excitement at their agreement to speak with him soon. The majority of his subjects have been in their mid-thirties and are transplants to the area; the McCormicks are older, from a family long established in the region, and are familiar in passing with the Fulton line.* He snagged the pen and wrote their names under Troth's brief notation of *Eric Middleton,* a name snagged from her own stack of papers.

She checked his note and murmured, "I'm not certain he managed to arrange that meeting, with the couple. You might have better luck."

Each of them wrote two additional names, six total, before Troth flipped her final page facedown. Light slanted lower through the casement-style windows. Andrew cracked his knuckles. Troth returned to her chair, where she sat heavily and propped her chin on one hand. It was a less manicured gesture than he was growing used to from her. His phone kicked up an incessant vibration in his pocket, ringing, but he ignored it. He stuck the Post-It note to the outside of the file folder.

"Thanks," he said.

"You're sure the notes weren't in his carrel?" she asked.

"Positive."

"Those locks aren't particularly secure. I can't imagine someone breaking in to steal from him, though," she said.

Andrew balanced the file on one knee. "You said his research was good. And he'd have been talking about it to everyone, probably."

"An opportunistic researcher . . ." Her thumb pressed to her thin lips in thought.

Like you, he thought to himself.

"It must be frustrating, and insulting, to be forced to retrace his steps," she said. "I apologize. I'm hoping there's an explanation that doesn't implicate one of our students stooping to theft."

Troth didn't rise from behind the desk as Andrew stood. She continued absently tapping her thumbnail on the seam of her frown. He and Troth were both, he justified to himself, using each other for different ends.

"If I'm continuing the work, I'm going to have to piece it together to catch up to where he left things," he said, aware of the doubling of his words, the implications hiding underneath.

"Indeed you will, or so it seems." Troth glanced over at him, straightening her posture. "Edward started with a broad approach to local folklore, but he had begun to focus more on stories surrounding the Fultons before our meetings paused for the summer. The last time we spoke was at the dinner party, the day he left his ring behind. I remember his excitement about some recent discovery he'd made, but I never had a chance to find out what that entailed."

"Maybe I'll be able to unearth that, whatever it was," Andrew said.

"One hopes," she said. "Please come to me, as you continue. I'd like to avoid unduly influencing the dissertation you'd create, but I'm familiar with Edward's intentions and approach."

"And you'd like to guide us toward something usable," he acknowledged. *For your own sake* went unsaid.

The ghost of a smile returned to her mouth. A dramatic flick of the wrist that seemed to encompass *yes* and *don't mention it* was all he received in response. Instead, she said, "This land and the stories people tell about it are fascinating. Hauntings, massacres, dark magic—all that bloody business lingers underneath the surface of respectability. It's a grim, delicious contradiction. I appreciate those contradictions and what they reveal about us as humans."

Andrew hated that whole business, but he offered her the only agreement he could: "Eddie appreciated it, too."

"I know," she said. "He was an interesting young man."

Andrew let himself out and closed the door behind him, his nerves doing uncomfortable flips. He checked his phone. Two missed calls and a text, all from Riley. The text just said *call me asap.*

He headed for the parking garage absorbed in his thoughts, cognizant of the tightrope he had put his feet on. Eddie must've found something, stumbled on it like the eager stupid boy he was, but Andrew had no idea what that thing could even be. He was one step ahead of Troth at least, in knowing that Eddie wasn't so much interested in folklore as in explaining his own secrets to himself.

He texted Sam, *if I had a list of names could you tell me if they're people you know*

No response.

The lights were on at Capitol. He parked on the street in front and took the porch steps two at a time, Troth's folder pinched shut in his grip to keep the papers in. Holding it had started to make his palm twinge. He jiggled the knob to unlatch the door and shouldered his way inside. Riley jolted an inch in his seat on the couch, slopping water from a pint glass over his lap.

"Andrew," said Del from the other sofa.

"I'm going to go," his roommate said as he stood.

Del had her hair knotted up in a loose bun, like the one girl he'd seen at Sam's party. She held a full glass of water in both hands, elbows on her bare knees. Riley grabbed his shoes from next to the door, made frantic eyes at Andrew, and slipped outside. The soft click of the latch shut him in with her. He slapped the folder onto the side table and shrugged his bag off. She took a sip from the glass, staring at a point past his left ear.

"What are you doing here?" he asked.

"I needed to see for myself—this place, how you were living. If you were all right," she said.

Crossing the room to sit on the other couch was like swimming through syrup. Andrew picked up Riley's glass for a fortifying swallow of tepid water. The tendon that ran from Del's shoulder into her neck was taut as a whipcord. He stretched his legs, knees apart, and dropped his head back. The chastised feeling didn't dissipate as he waited in silence for her to speak.

"Remember why we broke up?" she asked.

"Because of the tattoo," he said.

She snorted and set the glass down with a click. He glanced at her as she rubbed her arms, then her legs, her familiar nervous tic. "No, that wasn't the reason. It was a symbol of the reason. The reason was Eddie and you, you and Eddie. And here we are with that again."

His thumb pressed to the ink on his wrist bone. Del flicked his hand and he let go. She took his wrist in her fingers, long and thin, to trace the band of faded dots. The touch was clinical. She edged closer and sighed a stranger's sigh, the briefest exhalation. The lamplight on her face cast her cheekbones in hard relief. In high school, people had treated her as one of the guys because of her butch face, because of her preferred companions, because of her oft-contested spot on the baseball team, a hundred other petty reasons. He'd been one of those people, and so had Eddie, until the three of them figured out another, more intimate option.

"The funny thing is I haven't missed you since you left, and I'm sad as fuck he's dead, but until then I hadn't missed him either," she said.

She dropped his wrist and he crossed his arms over his lap.

"Then why come?" he asked.

"I don't know. Because I already lost you to him once, when it might have mattered more," she said. "And I guess because I needed closure. This time I'm here for me, not for either of you."

Andrew's phone buzzed in his pocket, twice. His hand twitched to check if Sam had responded before he made himself relax, forced himself to keep considering her face. The separation had made them alien to one another, or maybe that had been happening for years and he'd ignored it. He'd kissed that mouth more times than he could count. He'd watched Eddie do the same.

"I wasn't the one who ended things," he said.

"I saw those fucking tattoos and all I could think was that he'd *marked* you. The three of us were supposed to be . . . working on something together, but neither of you would've ever thought to give me a goddamn tattoo. Neither of you really gave a shit about me except as a conduit for the feelings you weren't going to talk about." She heaved a breath and let it out. "You still don't, Andrew. So I guess I came to say goodbye."

19

Andrew rested his forehead on the edge of the refrigerator. In the other room, Del waited. The pit of guilty loathing in his gut was enough to swallow him whole. He hadn't missed her, either, but he wanted to argue all the same. He grabbed them each a beer from the case Riley had mercifully picked up. One tab cracked and then the next; he carried his can at his side and passed hers over with a sense of communion. He'd expected tears, recriminations, but her eyes were dry and she was calm.

She took a swallow before continuing, "Tell me the truth, for once: did you really never love me, or did you only love him more?"

"Fucking Jesus, it wasn't like that and you know it," he said—except everyone in Nashville had been speaking the same language to him since he arrived. This time, he let the dart strike a bullseye even if he denied it.

He was yours.

"Andrew, yes it was like that," she said.

He scrounged for something to say, and found a meager offering: "I did love you."

But I loved him more.

He couldn't bring that to life, not aloud, not with his own mouth.

"You know, I came to the dorm one night and let myself in, back when we were together, and he was in bed with you. You were asleep. He was running his hand through your hair and he had his mouth on your neck. He made some pretty serious eye contact. It wasn't friendly. I left. I don't know why I never brought it up until now."

"We never—" Andrew started, heart pounding in his chest.

The phantom image of Eddie kissing him in his sleep was doing something to his insides he didn't appreciate.

"Nah, you never touched his dick, I know." Her laugh was harsh. She smacked the can onto the coffee table hard enough to foam it and put her face in her hands. "Instead you fucked me, and then he fucked me, and then both of you fucked me together, and it was great until I realized you were using me like a goddamn sex doll. You two used me because he wouldn't admit what you were, and neither would you. He used me to be with you. I deserve better than that. I deserved better then, and I deserve better now. I'm a *person*, Andrew."

Did we do that? he thought. Out loud he asked, "How long have you been saving this up?"

"Years, probably. You fucked me up good."

He tipped the beer into his mouth, throat working as he chugged it. The words she'd slapped him with stung. The world was tilted off its axis, crooked from what he'd known before. He wanted to argue, but hard as he tried, he found nothing to say in defense of himself, and less in defense of Eddie.

"I'm not a bottomless well for you to throw your stress and your misery and your repression into," she said when he didn't respond.

"I thought it was good, with us," he said. "For a little while."

"If it was good, I would've stayed with you and made it work, Eddie or no Eddie. But 'no Eddie' never even crossed your mind. You're a selfish, entitled disaster of a person. And I'm sorry . . ." For the briefest second, her voice wavered. She lifted her beer for another sip and took a breath, staring up at the ceiling. He waited. "I'm sorry he died before you figured it out. For what it's worth, I think you might've eventually, without me there to displace your bullshit onto. He was head over heels for you, and everyone knew but you, and maybe him. No, I think he knew. I think he hated seeing you with me, so he got himself involved."

That wasn't how Andrew remembered it, the first time in the dorm: Eddie's arm around both of their shoulders as they sat against the wall. Eddie's mouth on Del's cheek. Her smiling and saying *yeah, okay*. He remembered their hands glancing on her hips and her ribs, one of them latched onto each nipple, the thrill of that, of touching her together while she yanked on their hair. Read through her lens, though, through the shock of her obvious hurt and his compounding horror of himself, that old scene was less of a beautiful coming-together and more an opportunity they'd taken advantage of. Andrew let himself study the narrow cut of her chest and hips, her rock-solid calves, her pale pink sandals and calloused heels, and at the present moment, he felt nothing.

He hadn't realized, and that was her whole point.

"So, yeah," she said. "I guess that was a lot. I've been in therapy, just as an FYI. It's helping. She thought it would be good for me to say all this in person. I thought it wouldn't be fair, as fucked up as you are right now, but she said it hadn't been fair before. So it wasn't my job to make it fair now."

"And I deserve that," he said finally.

"You do."

"I'm sorry."

He meant that.

Del shook her head, dusted her hands on her shorts and offered one to him. He took it and stood. The drowning sensation continued unabated. He walked her to the door with endless things to say, but none of them enough to fix what he'd broken. At the threshold she said, "Goodbye, Andrew. Get some help. He was a piece of work, and so are you, but I don't hate you. I just can't help you anymore."

The sandals slapped softly as she descended the stairs and set off across the sidewalk toward campus. Andrew sat on the porch until she was long gone. Eddie had whispered into his hair once, half-asleep, *fuck you for being so good*. He'd laughed and let it tie him into a giddy knot for days. That same week he'd watched Eddie punch a frat kid at a kegger, heard him snarling *who are you calling a faggot*, saw him leave with a girl whose name he didn't know.

Andrew had found his own companion for the night, pomegranate lip gloss his sole memory of the experience.

He'd always been with girls; he'd always fucked girls, and so had Eddie. Eddie was his best friend and then some, and maybe they'd been closer than the norm, but no one else could have understood what it meant to live with the ghosts and the haunt-dreams, the danger that lurked in cellars and attics of friends' homes, the endless throat-closing, loitering horrors that held off sleep for whole weeks during the most uncontrolled period of it. No one else had been there with him in the cavern for hours spread across days, freezing, terrified of encroaching death. No one else was Eddie, and no one else held him the same as Eddie had.

He gnawed on the sore patch of skin over his wrist bone and tried to pack it all into the box where he kept the things they didn't talk about, didn't even fucking think about, but it wouldn't go back neat.

He swiped the text alerts waiting for him away without looking and messaged Del, *I didn't mean to.*

She didn't respond. He didn't expect her to.

———

hey dude can I come home yet

she's gone

cool thanks

you okay?

Andrew rolled off of the couch. The two texts he'd received while Del was in the house weren't from Sam, who hadn't responded at all, but from West attempting to follow up on the meeting with Troth. He ignored them and texted Sam one more time, *I have a list to run down.* He wasn't going to ask for help more directly than that. After a moment's hesitation he picked the phone up one more time for another message: *going out tonight?*

The front door opened. He arranged his expression into the

closest approximation of blandness he was able to manage. Riley still winced, a performative grimace. "That bad, huh?"

"Troth didn't have the field journal either," he said.

"Nah, I meant—" Riley started. Andrew glowered, a bitter flashback to his first nights in the house, and Riley smoothly shifted course. "Moving right along, then. What did Troth have on hand?"

"Her own mentor notes and some basic shit he had written about his family history. She said he'd gotten on that track, which makes sense, since he was really looking for . . ."

"Stuff about himself," Riley finished helpfully.

"I told her the interviews were missing and she implied the carrels weren't exactly secure. She was irritated, I figure from losing access herself," he said.

Riley considered that, then echoed his sentiment: "Doesn't seem coincidental, his phone and his interview notes both going missing."

"Looks like someone's hiding something, doesn't it?" Andrew tossed him the Challenger's key fob. Riley smacked it out of the air in his attempted catch, launching it clattering into the foyer. "A while ago, like when we first met, she gave me a bunch of books she'd gotten for Eddie. She's been waiting for me to come to her, I guess. I told her I'd re-create the shit we were missing, and she said she'd help."

"Why's she been after you so much?" Riley asked as he chased down the lost fob.

"Wants her name on a published version of Eddie's work, sounds like," Andrew said.

Riley snorted. "Fuckin' faculty. You'd think she'd have her hands full with West right now, and it's not like she's hurting for acclaim. She's got tenure already."

"What do you mean about West?" Andrew asked, perking up.

"You hadn't heard?" Riley asked. He spun the fob around his index finger. "His revised draft got rejected, for the fourth time. He can't get his dissertation off the ground, and he's running out of time before the seven-year cap."

"He hadn't said—" Andrew's phone buzzed, one-two-three, Halse's number on the screen. Andrew answered. "Hey."

"I was at work, calm your thirst." Andrew removed his phone from his ear and stared at it. Sam's voice kept going, words indistinguishable but tone jocular. Riley raised his eyebrows. Andrew put the receiver to his ear again in time to hear, "I'll be there in fifteen."

"The fuck?" he asked.

"Get that list ready," he said and hung up.

Riley said, "So I guess Sam's lending a hand."

Andrew passed his phone from hand to hand, swallowed his pride, and said, "Guess so. Are you interested in putting some work in, too? Split things up, or something."

"Duh," Riley said with a feigned nonchalance.

"Found some names in Troth's file, going to compare them to Sam's business. In the meantime, I dunno, would you—read through his fucking notes, check out those books she foisted on me?"

His roommate glanced at the keys in his hand, visibly put the pieces together, confirmed that Andrew was genuinely offering him an in to help, and nodded his assent. Andrew would rather be struck dead than read those journals again, even if it meant exposing stories about himself to Riley. Raw vulnerability stung at his nerves, but he had to delegate.

"The books are in the car, stuck them in the back seat," he clarified.

Riley gently joked, "Put the nerd on the boring part of the case, I see how it is."

Anticipatory silence curtained the room. Andrew's head felt full of fiberglass, biting and insulating at once. The two unanswered texts from West waited in his messages folder, one reading *How was your meeting with Troth?* and the other *Would you like to unpack it with me later.* He opened the thread and wrote *having trouble with your research?* then deleted it, *what was your dissertation on again* and deleted that as well. He settled on *get coffee with me and we'll talk about the meeting.* Riley returned with the book-stuffed tote before he got a response. He dropped it next to the end table and picked up Troth's folder.

Andrew said, almost to himself, "There's got to be something to find if we look hard enough."

Riley crossed his arms over his stomach and shook his head. "None of this makes sense, man. Feels like it can't be real."

"What do you mean?"

Riley ran a hand through his dye-crisped hair. It stuck straight up and he smoothed it flat habitually a second later. He shoved the tote with his sneaker-tip. "What the fuck in any of this could possibly have been worth killing him for?"

The door slamming open a fraction of an inch from Riley's elbow startled them both. Sam paused on the threshold, looking them over. His buzz cut was growing in. Riley handed Andrew the Post-It note list, scooped up the research, and headed for the stairs without a word to either of them, but it felt natural; a granted pardon, rather than a dismissal.

Sam said, "Gimme that list. We're going driving."

Andrew handed it over. Sam scanned the Post-It while Andrew checked his phone; West had responded, *Tonight?* He typed a quick *maybe tomorrow.* Andrew followed Sam out of the house. Sam glanced back once, grinned to see him there, and started to whistle as he crossed the street to his car. The sound was tuneless, flat, carrying an aggressively jaunty rhythm. In sync, doors shut on either side, sealing them in the already-hot interior of the WRX.

"Half of those are people I've got on string, but the other half I don't recognize, so those are on you to figure out," Sam said. The engine turned over with a comforting growl. "You eaten today?"

"No," Andrew said.

He'd had a bagel from the campus coffee shop the previous afternoon, and before that a carton of fried rice he ate standing outside a restaurant. Food hadn't been much of a consideration since Columbus. His jawline was sharp enough to cut glass. The first thing Sam did was pull up to a Panera and say, "Stay put."

"Nothing sweet," he requested and Sam flapped an acknowledging hand behind him as he got out of the car.

He left it running for Andrew, air-conditioning valiantly fighting the heat, and returned a few minutes later with two sandwiches and two iced Americanos. Andrew unwrapped his sandwich. By the time Andrew took his second bite, Sam had crammed his down in six disturbingly fast bites, effortless and neat, then sucked down a third of his coffee in two long pulls. The sandwich, as with most things Andrew had tried to eat since the funeral, tasted like air and dust. But it was food.

"So, Riley texted me in a fucking panic when he couldn't get in touch with you," Sam said. "Something about your girlfriend or ex-girlfriend or whatever showing up at the house?"

"Yeah, that did happen." Andrew popped his knuckles against the door panel in an irritated snap. Of course he'd told Sam about it. Andrew wasn't sure why he hadn't expected to be confronted with the situation immediately.

"Okay, so it didn't go well," Sam prompted.

"Ex-girlfriend, and no, it did not."

The interstate opened up around them as he continued eating the sandwich Sam had gotten for him. It was easier to swallow when someone else provided for him.

"It's sorted out now?" Sam asked.

"Sorted," he confirmed. "It was old business about us and Eddie, and it's done for good, now."

Sam gave a quiet, satisfied hum of understanding. Andrew wondered if West had texted him again already, mind bouncing from one uncomfortable topic to the next. The ring of ink on his wrist kept catching his eye almost as if it were fresh, a scribbled signature that crossed time and space to remind him of his place, one half of a whole. He saw it how Del saw it, for a moment: a claim, not a bond. While Andrew sat deep in thought, Sam braced the wheel with his knee and snagged his snapback from behind the seats. He pulled it on and thumbed the brim up to the perfect spot, framing his face with afternoon-sun shadow.

"We're going to go out to the Masterson place," Sam said over the crumpling of Andrew's empty sandwich wrapper. "Beck is a decent dude, I'm sure he's got nothing to do with whatever happened, but he said he'd chat."

Andrew had six names, and Beck Masterson was one of them. Sam wasn't going to make him beg for help. Andrew threw the wrapper out the window and drank the first bracing, bitter mouthful of coffee while they drove in silence.

———

Beck Masterson was a nice enough man a bare few years older than Eddie himself, willing to express his condolences and share a bowl from the weed he bought off of Sam. He had precisely one spooky story to tell while reminiscing about the questions "Sam's friend" had asked, but the story he shared was run-of-the-mill, a great-grandfather's ghost out back making moonshine from beyond the grave. He even said it like that, *from beyond the grave*. Andrew hadn't sensed more death from the property than usual, though—no great-grandpa lurking as far as he could tell.

Sam dropped him off at the house no more informed than he'd been when they started, but far more exhausted. He'd learned nothing useful about Eddie, though he supposed expecting answers on the first attempt was a reach. Sam left him with a promise to call the other two names he knew to set up meetings; in the meantime, he needed to tackle his own share. Without Eddie's phone or his records, though, that was a challenge in and of itself.

On the back porch steps, the plastic bag with his ruined jeans sat sweltering and stinking. He held his breath long enough to gingerly remove the paper packet from the pocket, then kicked the bag into the corner to throw in the garbage later. He collapsed into the desk chair with an overstimulated groan and dumped the ring out of the packet.

Platinum refracted moonlight as it rolled across the desktop. Andrew caught the cold metal under his thumb, sitting sprawled and barefoot. For a moment, he rolled it to and fro, considering: one more piece of Eddie returned to him, to try to fit into his life. Nowhere near sufficient. He let the ring clink onto its side and unbuckled his belt, thumbed open the button and zipper of his jeans. He hesitated with a hand splayed over his hip bone, fingertips dipping under the waistband of his briefs. The heel of his hand pressed a bruise over his stomach, speckled in the shape of Sam's knuckles.

With a groan, he stripped to his underwear and sprawled on the bed. The stale mess of sheets stuck grimy to his summer-salted skin. He kicked them to the end of the mattress, flopped onto his front. The air conditioner hummed. Eddie's clock read 1:19 A.M. Exhaustion fogged his head, but the constant conflict of the past week left him wired: the vision at the tree, and connecting with Troth, and Del's axis-wrecking goodbye speech all together, stacked against a whole afternoon spent with Sam—Sam feeding him, and refusing to let him fade out of conversations, and *constantly* touching him. Light from his phone caught his eye, a soundless notification. He snagged it from the bedside table and held it at an angle above his head at the strained end of the charging cable. Sam had texted him:

Sorry that was a bust

What's your theory

The reason someone would commit

murder over any of this

He responded *that's what I'm trying to figure out* and turned the phone off. After another defeated, miserable span of minutes, he lifted his ass enough to fit his hand down his briefs, pinned between his weight and the mattress. The tacky heat of his soft dick filled his palm, skin silky and loose, faintly damp from a long day's confinement. He pressed his thumb at the base and kneaded his fingers against his balls, holding the whole package more for comfort than pleasure. No response from his traitorous, anxious body; he stayed limp. The pillow smelled as much like old spit as Eddie's lingering hair product. He let go of himself and rolled onto his side, facing the far wall.

At 3:05 A.M. he threw the pillow on the floor and padded in his underwear to the kitchen table with notebook in hand. The air-conditioning prickled goose bumps over his thighs. Beer at his elbow, he wrote:

> *The car was with him so someone drove it there. Notes are missing—so's his phone. Bet someone's name is in both. How'd he find*

He stopped. His notes were sparse and his text blocky, uneven, ugly compared to Eddie's wild meandering journals with their colorful ink, doodles, erratic trains of thought. Utilitarian at best. He closed the notebook with the pen still uncapped inside and took his beer outside to sit in the pitch-dark lee side of the porch. He wasn't cut out for the life he'd inherited. It should've been him, not Eddie, in the ground.

20

A sedate robotic recording asked him to leave a message. The tone pinged.

"Where are you," he said, one hand tucked in his back pocket, and hung up.

It wasn't the most politic of voicemails, but he'd sent West three texts already, waiting out front of the campus café for almost an hour. The sun stabbed at his insomnia-sanded eyes through his shades. In the mood for a fight but without a contender, he grumbled a mashed-up curse containing the skeleton of *fuckinggoddamnasshole* and went inside to order himself a drink. The barista grimaced sympathetically at his expression.

"Exams, or worse?" the barista said.

Their hair was cotton-candy pink streaked with silver, complemented by a tiny silver nose ring and a light smattering of blond stubble on their upper lip. Signals crossed in his brain between *pretty* and *handsome* as Andrew struggled through a distracted pause to say, "Worse than that. Triple-shot iced chai, please."

As he reached for his card, they said, "Nah, on the house."

They turned from the counter to snag a cup for his drink, and he noticed from behind how the apron ties cinched their oversized shirt in close to reveal a tantalizingly narrow waist—petite enough for larger hands to wrap most of the way around. Would he have paid attention to them at all, before Nashville? They tossed him another winsome smile as he moved down the counter line. The other barista at the end handed him the finished drink as he muddled through his irritation with West and with himself, jamming his untimely insecurity about noticing and being noticed *by* the cute stranger in the basement of his brain where it belonged.

He finished the sugar-bomb concoction at a corner table, phone unresponsive at his elbow. Class started in fifteen minutes; West had ghosted him. He strode outside and threw the cup of melting ice into a trash can so hard that a man walking past flinched. Instead of heading for the humanities building, he made for the garage, tired and furious and unfit for human consumption. As he squeezed the steering wheel of the Challenger, another connection to the man he needed to be to get through this, he got a text.

Riley had said, *meet me at the carrel in ten?*

fine

Riley was drumming his fingers on the desktop when Andrew opened the carrel's door. Documents spread across both desks, with the loaner texts from Troth in a stack next to the crumpled tote bag. Post-It notes and placeholder tabs bristled from pages of composition books and hardcovers alike.

"Take a look," Riley said, handing him an open notebook.

Andrew read in Eddie's scrawl, *Hard to tell if West is trying to help or poach my shit. There are questions and there are Questions. He asks too many fucking Questions. And that he said/she said with him and Troth over their Novel article isn't confidence inspiring either. Keeping him away from the actual research for sure.* He went on to discourse at length on a disappointing collection of Southern-themed horror short fiction.

"What the hell is that about?" Andrew asked.

"I think he's referring to this." Riley handed over his phone, which was logged into the university's library database and open to an article. "Troubled Lineage: Curses in American Gothic Literature" was authored by Jane Troth, with a first-line acknowledgement to Thom West for his assistance. "The article reads like his work, but it's got her name on it. That's something to fight about, especially if she's going to keep rejecting his diss revisions and diverting all her attention to a first-year. And uh, the optics, you know? Rich ol' white Tennessee lady versus the Black student from up North, et cetera. I wouldn't put it past her to have some secondary motivations for fucking him over, frankly. We've never been close enough for me to ask about that."

"Seems petty to be a reason to lash out at Eddie though," Andrew said.

Riley choked on a laugh and said, "When isn't this academic shit petty?"

"Four rejected revisions," he repeated.

He ran through his interactions with Troth and West in his head, the usual shades of deference and direction between student and professor taking on an entirely different tone under the light of a previous conflict. West's efforts to connect the professor and Andrew took on a compulsive edge. Troth's ghastly, undaunted appetite for Eddie's research, even though she thought him to be a suicide, spoke for itself. And she had a real obvious, uncritical hard-on for her *family histories,* which even Andrew had an inkling might indicate some tension between her and a Black student from Massachusetts.

"Not a lot of recourse for a student with a fucked-up power dynamic under his advisor, especially an institution as, let's say, *traditional* as this one," Riley said with a sneer. "Plus he obviously didn't succeed at calling her out before."

Andrew handed him the notebook. His heel bounced frantically where he stood, jiggling his leg and redirecting the burgeoning swell of energy out of his body to keep from sprinting across campus to find his supposed mentor. "Troth said she approached Eddie first because of his name; her family knew his. He didn't initiate contact with her."

Riley whistled and said, "Like, I feel bad for the dude, but if I'm West and I'm already having a rough time with this lady, trouble getting independent research off the ground, then this fucking legacy asshole shows up and she loses interest in me—"

"Petty as fuck," he repeated again.

"She's kept him here years longer than he needed, and his job prospects are dwindling. People have done worse for a whole lot less," Riley said.

"West missed our meeting this afternoon, but it's the first one he's missed. Otherwise, he's worked real hard to get friendly with me," Andrew said.

Riley chewed his thumbnail, spinning the chair in quarter circles back and forth. Andrew shifted his weight to his other foot and raked his gaze over the pile of materials again. Compared to the red-line tachometer at two in the morning and a snarling smile, the filtered murmur of a university library held less obvious danger. None of this academic shit seemed worth killing someone over, but nothing ultimately did, in the grand scheme of things. If he put his mind to it, the death he'd expect for himself and Eddie would be an accident, a collision or flare-up, never purposeful violence. Both of them were spoiled enough to assume they'd be their own undoing, he guessed, but Eddie had paid the price.

His phone vibrated and he checked it, said, "Speak of the devil, it's West," and answered with a curt "Hey."

"I'm sorry, Andrew, a meeting with Troth ran long. I didn't mean to miss you. Are you in class?"

"No, I skipped it," he said.

Riley steepled his fingers, grimacing as he listened.

"All right. Is it too early in the afternoon to meet me for a drink?" West asked.

"I'm fine with a drink. Where?" he asked, stilted.

West's harried tone wasn't any less short when he said, "How about the Red Door?"

"Be there in fifteen," he said and hung up.

"Is that a good idea?" Riley asked.

"Best idea I've had all day."

"Peace then." Riley flashed him a quick V sign as he left.

If Eddie had died for some goddamn research into haunted

houses and family histories, if *that* was the stupid reason Eddie's life had been cut short, he didn't know what he'd do. Nothing West had shown him indicated the temperament to harm someone else, but none of his other leads had gone anywhere. Tightness sang up his arms, and he realized he was clenching his fists hard enough to make his fingers go numb. The last time he'd had a second to relax was probably—the long drive and the companionable solitude after the faculty gathering, before the incident with the deer carcass.

Crossing campus, he texted Sam.

> chill later?

> Sorry princess, got work tonight
> Unless you just need to get free then the
> key's under the rock next to the steps
> crash on the couch.

The relief that clawed from toes to sternum paused him on the threshold of the bar, hand on the door, staring at his phone. Country woods weren't his favorite place to be, but Sam's offer meant something; depending on how the conversation went with West, he'd need to have a breather outside of the rooms Eddie had left behind, and Sam was giving him somewhere to be. No one would fuck with him out at Sam's, and there would be room to think through whatever he learned. He hated that it sounded so good.

"Andrew," called his mentor from across the bar.

He slipped his phone into his pocket. Tinted bar windows completed the time dilation that haunted his afternoon, plunging the table into an almost-twilight as he sat across from West. The other man looked severe and troubled, divots pinching at the sides of his mouth and a crease wrinkling his brow. One of his wrists crossed the other loosely on the tabletop, but his fingers were tense. Foam rings crept down the interior of the almost-empty pint glass in front of him.

"What was your long-ass meeting about?" Andrew asked.

"Everything, nothing. You'll get it when you're six years in. What do you want to drink? On me," West offered.

"PBR is fine," he said.

West got up and approached the dead bar, one other patron at the far side of the space their only company. Andrew heard West add his beer to the tab as clearly as the speaker quietly piping in The Ataris overhead. Not the most private space to have a harsh conversation, but not the least either. *How much, exactly, did Eddie fuck up your life.* He took the tallboy he was handed as West scooted his chair close to the table once again. Dim tinted bar-glow brought out the russet undertones of his skin, in handsome contrast to his silver rings and thin, short necklace. Once again, Andrew caught himself *seeing*.

"I've got to apologize one more time," West said. He lifted his own glass in salute. "I'm usually punctual, but when she calls, I come running. I'm buried in diss work, and her schedule is tight, as I'm sure you've noticed."

"I don't know, she's made a lot of time for me. She's real interested in Eddie's work," Andrew said.

"She has been since day one," West said with an unsmiling quirk to the side of his mouth.

Andrew took the risk and said, "To use for herself, so far as I can tell. Which I guess you're familiar with."

West took one long gulp of his beer, maintaining eye contact, before responding, "Was that a question, or a statement?"

"I think it could be a question, if you have an answer. Or a story," he said.

"Sounds like you've heard some gossip about her and me, the whole ugly situation."

"Clear it up for me," Andrew said without confirming or explaining.

The song overhead switched to a Top 40 pop jangle. West reclined in his chair. Fine wrinkles edged his narrowed eyes. "I handed her the material for her *Novel* article as part of my first dissertation proposal. To be direct, she stole that research. When I brought it up, she threatened to accuse me of plagiarism in turn; the department swept it under the rug, with a strong hint that it'd be best if I stopped rocking the boat, lest I find myself dumped overboard. All implicit, of course. That answer your question?"

"But you're still working with her," he said. "Doesn't that piss you off?"

"Who else would I work with?" The pint glass clunked against the table as West scoffed at him. "After selecting my committee and working with the same advisor for years, it's a bad look to suddenly request a change. And, furthermore, if an accusation I had *evidence* for was dismissed, how do you expect they'd receive my request to change advisors? You've got the same stroke of luck with her Eddie did. She's interested right now, but I'd advise you finish quick before she gets distracted."

"Like she got distracted from you when Eddie showed up?" Andrew asked, frowning.

"Exactly. Use her interest while it lasts, or you'll be fighting for every inch of cooperation," he said, brittle and warning as he cast Andrew a pointed look. "Or maybe you won't. Both of you have something *else* in common with her that I don't benefit from, if you get my drift."

"Guess the meeting didn't go well," Andrew ventured, pushing another inch.

"No, funnily enough it was mostly about you," West snapped— the crack he'd been hoping for. "You and Eddie. She had pointed questions about his missing notes, as if I'm the one with a history of stealing research. Frankly, I'd have thought she had them."

"So you didn't take it on yourself to keep his notes, instead of her," Andrew said. The tips of West's ears flushed a deep mauvered as he stared Andrew down over the table, then pushed his almost finished pint to the side.

"No, I didn't. Thanks for asking as if I weren't aware of the implications of the question. I'm getting out of here. Sorry again for missing our meeting—I'm sure Doctor Troth can catch you up better than me."

He stood with a shriek of his chair on the tile.

"Wait," Andrew said.

West strode with purpose toward the door and straight out of it, bell jingling merrily overhead. In profile, obscured by the tinted window, he snarled something inaudible and took off, away from the campus.

The bartender said, "He didn't close the tab."

"I'll sign for it," Andrew said.

He left his unfinished beer on the table and a seventy-five percent tip on West's dime. Trekking from the bar through campus to the garage took him past the entrance to the humanities building. He considered the lit windows on the top floor, unable to pinpoint which might be Troth's. Instead of going upstairs, he dropped his backpack on the lawn and sprawled next to it, breathing in the living smell of crushed grass. He typed a quick email to the professor on his phone to summarize his conversation with Masterson and his plans to continue pursuing the list over the course of the week. To close, he added, *Would it be productive for me to share my findings with Thom as I retrace these steps? I understand that his research area is similar to Ed's and mine but am unfamiliar with his work.* Baiting a trap or sticking his fingers in one, he wasn't sure which he was doing.

Phone on his chest and limbs splayed on the grass, Andrew observed the endless blue sky streaked with wisps of shredded clouds. The spread was so cavernously wide it compressed his lungs. The anger that had fueled him through the afternoon crackled, derailing his attempts to find his center and reorganize his thoughts. What could a person do out of desperation, driven to the brink out of fear for their career and their future—backed into a shitty corner by the whole system? He heard West's voice: *everything, nothing.* Eddie had spent time alone with him. Eddie had bought him drinks and listened to him complain about their advisor, but his trust hadn't run so far as to share the details of his work. Andrew rolled onto his side, scooping his bag strap over his shoulder as he stood.

In the garage, the Challenger welcomed him with the pungent, humid stink of leather and boy. He needed a change of clothes if he planned on crashing at Sam's. That was as far as he let his skittish brain run before he pressed his thumb to the starter, waking its familiar purr. As he reached for the shifter, his hand passed into a patch of incongruous and impossible chill. He flinched out of it, startled. The same Misfits song that had been playing when he picked the car up from the impound lot burst from the speakers, crooning about skulls, and a casual stroke of fingernails scraped up his raised forearm before the spectral hand gripped his wrist. No time to escape, even less to scream, before the phantom settled on top of and *through* him, mimicking the posture of his slouch, bony knees spread on either side of the wheel in a mismatched fit—him inside the revenant inside him in terrible recursion. The garage wall pulsed and swam as his vision fogged; he arched forward to separate his chest from the ghost's. His heart restarted as he escaped its rib cage, pounded hot and struggling and alive.

As he heaved a painful breath the specter disappeared, gone the instant it arrived, knocking him off his momentarily complacent pedestal. Based on the pattern of prior grim engagements, he'd drawn its attention somehow—but what had he done this time to tempt its casual and pervasive torment? The meeting with West, maybe, but what about it? He wiped his leaking nose with his forearm, panting through his mouth, then swallowed the fresh blood oozing down his throat from his sinuses in response to the traumatic visitation.

The campus garage in broad afternoon light didn't seem like much of a locus point for the revenant's manifestation. But—if he ignored the bedroom visitations, most of the haunt's worst interference had occurred inside the Challenger. Someone had left it at the trailhead while dumping Eddie's corpse—and he hadn't put much thought into the logistical implications of that, of the car being found with the body, of the revenant's *attachment* to the car being more than just a lingering affectation from life. Once his nose stopped bleeding onto his wadded shirt collar he shifted into gear, tires chirping as he passed the red light at the garage exit with unnecessary force. No one parked in the gravel alley behind Capitol except for him and Riley, and Riley wasn't home when he arrived. Andrew set the brake, steeled himself for the possibilities, and pushed the button to pop the trunk. Why hadn't he thought of that before, when searching for the phone the first time?

For an extended moment he loitered at the open driver's door with an arm braced on the roof, convincing himself that he needed to push through his fear and look, one way or another. Breeze nipped around his ankles, scattering dried grass clippings from the yard. The abandoned alley held an eerie solitude. His haunting's abrupt reminder that he had a constant shade dogging his heels left him on edge, but the sun drifting toward the horizon marked a time limit he wasn't keen to test.

Gravel crunched as he rounded the tail end of the car. The trunk hung an inch open. He almost expected, when he slipped his fingers under the rim and lifted it, to find some gaping maw. Instead, the trunk contained a spare tire and a discarded spray bottle of Armor All with a greasy rag tied around it. Same as at the oak tree, Andrew wished he had a better option to get his answers, but—

Equally eager as it had been the first and last time he let it loose on purpose, the knotted spool of *potential* that pulsed in his veins responded with a vital, ugly spark the moment he nudged at it. He resisted the urge to push it back down as it unfurled beneath his bones. It was a leeching, corpse-cold thing; he wasn't going to think of it as a real part of himself. It spread from its home in his belly through his veins, his teeth, his fingernails. The corpse of the neighbor's house cat, buried three feet behind him in the yard under fresh-turned dirt, gave a homing pulse. Andrew jerked his attention from the welcoming rot and instead planted his hands against the trunk's rough upholstery.

Barbs hooked through his palms on contact, echo calling to echo, blood answering blood. Slippery gore welled from the carpet as he crumpled over the trunk rim, sliding in the mess and struck stupid with borrowed agonies. His mouth filled with a taste that crossed old meat with the sick-sweet ooze of a cold sore. He gagged. If the vision at the tree had been hallucinatory, the trunk had no time for illusions. Images smashed through him, reeling like film stock and pulling like muscle memory.

A tarp filled the trunk and the slack, sluggishly bleeding body toppled into its plastic embrace. The remnant that had once been Eddie clung to its recent flesh, claws sunk into the inert matter of the corpse, unwilling to separate. One hand flopped loose over the rim of the trunk, the wound below gaping raw and wet; the ravaging memories of pain lanced through the remnant and the vision and Andrew. The dead hand was lifted and dropped on the corpse's chest with distaste, like a marionette gone limp.

The sound of Andrew's shoes sliding on gravel faded into the rush of his pulse in his ears as he lost consciousness.

21

"Almost there," Eddie's whisper vibrated in his ear.

Aged floorboards moaned threateningly under each cautious step. Twilight hung in the foyer, gathered in the folds of disintegrating curtains and wrapped around the collapsed banister of the grand stair. Andrew had no recollection of arriving, and that knocked him lucid enough to understand the rotting grandeur surrounding him wasn't *real*. The front room had aged to nothingness in shades of grey and taupe, all other color drained to dust. Andrew struggled to determine if he knew the house, but the pernicious doubling between himself and revenant and imagination and memory made it familiar. As soon as he thought of the specter, he realized that the thing was him, that he *was* the thing, Eddie's hands within his hands and feet within his feet as he moved through the cobwebbed mausoleum of a home.

Rooms yawned from the hall, dark and cold; no life scurried underfoot, not so much as an ant. No longer in possession of himself, Andrew stepped over a hole broken through the old warped boards, a dead-alive creature being dragged along toward some fresh revelation. The drawing room was black as starless night, its gaping shadows corroding the relentless grey pallor of the foyer, the long hallway. Though the haunt hadn't shown him this dream before, a forebodingly similar aura of rot and ruin hung suffocating in the still air, familiar from the cavern and the stag's skull in the mud. Ahead stood a locked door; he understood without attempting the knob that the door was barred, blocked off from him—unless he *desired* it open.

"Here," the revenant said with their mouth, to him and through him.

As he reached for the knob, his sight blurred. He made contact with the icy brass and the pulse of power that rolled off of it knocked the haunt loose from his bones; abruptly, he occupied his body alone, with sole control of his limbs and nerves and tongue. His chest heaved for breath, heart solid and unmoving as a stone. Slickly cold, the doorknob slipped out of his grasp as he collapsed to his knees.

The tender grasp of a bony fist knotting in his hair choked off another breathless gasp. Andrew allowed the hand to tilt his chin while his mouth worked like a fish drowning in air, leaned his head on the revenant's too-solid hip. Kneeling on the ground before the creature, he stared up at hollow sockets regarding him with all the warmth of a grave. His vision wavered again, popping with white sparks; the haunt grew denser and richer as vital heat leeched from Andrew's skull, from the press of his nose and cheek on its femur.

"Through the door," it said.

As borrowed life colored in the revenant's edges, its tattered wrists began to ooze fresh red. Andrew saw that his, too, were shorn open to the bone, gushing with slow, determined pulses— matched and matching, in death as in life. *No wonder I'm cold,* he thought with a horrified clarity.

Biting, gagging cold, struck his face and forced up his nose. He woke with a shock, gasping, flailing. He banged his knee on metal. Water soaked his shirt and hair. He blinked to shed the skin of the nightmare superimposing itself over Riley, who stood astride him in the alley with an empty plastic pitcher in his hand. His eyes were wide in his wan face. His mouth moved, but the sound passed along like wind: unparseable noise. Coughing and sputtering, Andrew fumbled to shift his leaden body. Ice cubes tumbled loose from the creases of his shirt. While struggling to sit up, he planted one hand on the gravel and a bolt of liquid pain seared through him. The arm refused to take his weight and he flopped to the side.

"What is it?" Riley bent to grip his hand.

From his palm to nearly his elbow, a fresh furrow dripped sluggishly. All of the bright red blood spattered on the gravel was his. White patches spread fuzzy over his sight. He heard himself mutter, "What the fuck?" as if from outside a room, eerie and distant.

"It's fine, it's okay, you're okay," Riley chanted. Sturdy hands scooped under his armpits, forced him to sit up. "It's not deep, stop looking at it. Please don't pass out, dude, I can't drag you into the house, and I do not fucking want to call Sam about this."

"Yeah," Andrew rasped with a swollen throat.

On the long ride from the place where he'd died to the oak tree, already stripped of his power, Eddie's hideous spectral remainder had sheared itself off from his corpse in the trunk of the Challenger. Those oily leftovers had clung to the interior, and Andrew had opened himself up to them. He'd forgotten the danger of *knowing*, given into the temptation, and paid the price. An unnatural breeze rose around him as he thought about the haunt, a cold, hungry touch brushing over two warm-blooded creatures.

"Oh, hell no," Riley said, hauling him on his ass toward the house.

At the fence he helped drag himself to his feet using the chainlink, heels sliding, listing onto Riley's shoulder like a drunk—not so different from the last time they'd done this dance. Pounding agony in his skull eclipsed his dread. Night loitered in the shaded basement stairs and the silhouette of the house on the grass, waiting to descend. He didn't want to be outside when that happened. The ripe possibilities of a horror movie chased their heels on their shuffling struggle up the porch steps, despite nothing being technically present to spook them.

Riley left the door hanging open and dumped him on a kitchen chair, then skidded over to the pantry. He grabbed the blue container of table salt and popped the spigot. Andrew turned his throbbing arms over on his thighs, palms up in benediction, gouges still glistening with lymph and clotting blood. No flesh under his short nails; the wounds bloomed stigmata-like from his skin. He looked up at the sound of a rushing hiss. Riley paced a circle around his chair, a blue container of table salt pouring a trail behind him. The sight struck him as patently and suddenly hilarious. He choked on an inappropriate guffaw.

"Shut up." Riley finished the circle, stared at it for two seconds, and threw the salt container out the door before kicking it shut. "Salt is a thing, right? I'm making this up as I go along."

"What is this, an episode of *Supernatural?*"

"Looks just like one," he agreed without humor.

Andrew angled to the side and tucked into a hunch to better support his own sagging weight. Exhaustion dragged his muscles loose. The quiver that rippled from his sacrum set up shop in his molars. One messy salt circle made no difference to him.

"Bed, please," he requested.

"Hang on." Riley had his phone in his hand. He tapped the screen a few times and lifted it to his ear, then said, "Hi babe, it's me. I have a weird favor to ask." Silence. "Bring some groceries over, most especially a motherfucking big container of salt? Andrew's sick, so I'm gonna cook him dinner. And we're out of salt. Okay, good. Thanks." He hung up.

Andrew cracked one eye to regard his flagrant, stilted falsehood with disdain. "Which one was that?"

"Ethan, I ain't stupid enough to pull that kind of thing on Luca. She'd see through it and have my ass," he said.

"Good for her," Andrew grunted.

He slipped into helpless drowsing until damp fingers touched his palm. The chair skidded an inch with the power of his reflexive jerk. Riley sat crouched outside the salt line with a first-aid kit, watching him. Andrew allowed him to wipe the wounds with antibacterial cleansing cloths, alcohol stinging as the beginnings of scabs flaked off. The gouges were shallow, as Riley has said, but also long and grislier for it. Riley smeared ointment on them before wrapping gauze over the whole mess. White cloth on tan skin, as if he were mummified.

Andrew flexed his fingers. "I'm going to lie down."

"Not in his bed, you're fucking not," Riley said.

"I'll sleep in mine," he said. "This circle thing isn't going to do much, even if it was real."

"Why not?" Riley challenged him.

Andrew scuffed his shoe through the line, scattering salt. The present, constant heartbeat in his chest thumped a steady reminder. He said, "I'm the conduit, it's coming from inside me. I don't think drawing a circle around me is going to keep the thing out."

Needing assistance up the stairs galled him, but it was either lean on Riley's shoulders, hips bumping each other and the banisters, or crawl to his room. The synaptic feedback from brain to limbs was on the fritz. He fumbled the doorknob on first attempt, roommate's arm around his waist, though he succeeded on the second attempt. Stale air wafted out in a gush.

"Text if you need me," Riley said.

Andrew rolled to the center of the mattress, toed off his sneakers, and grabbed one edge of the comforter. The door shut with a creak as he bundled himself in. Soft pillows surrounded his face. Eddie's final dissolution had come in the trunk of his car, wrapped in a cheap tarp with his own blood soaking his clothes. The oak tree, in comparison, made for a serene place to rest.

Not two minutes later a text from Riley arrived: *you were convulsing and i couldn't wake you so i got the pitcher from the kitchen. i don't know how long you'd been laying there. getting kinda tired of playing nurse so take it easy*

The clock on his phone read 7:48. Startled fear sloshed across his nerves. If he'd finished meeting with West around five-thirty, and Riley found him closer to seven-thirty, that was two hours

unaccounted for. Two hours spent in haunted limbo, collapsed behind his fucking house unresponsive to the world, shaking apart at
the atomic level. It wasn't the first or even second time he'd been
rescued from himself or the revenant by one cousin or the other.
He'd set a hell of a pattern, and it was getting nastier each time.

Six nights after their return from the cavern he'd climbed on
top of Eddie in his neighboring twin bed, buried his face against
his slender neck, and sobbed until it hurt while eerie hissing shadows clawed at the corners of the bedroom. Eddie had murmured
it's nothing, just pretend it's not there, it can't bother you. He had gotten
used to their curse and what it could do in the years since, and
that had made him complacent, but now he was scared again.
The version of Eddie lingering under the rattling of the window-
panes, the hush of the air conditioner, offered no succor and kept
no promises to him. The bandages on his itching arms proved that.

———

> Expected to see you when I got in from
> work
>
> You good?
>
> Got one more interview lined up for you
> later

Andrew considered the messages Sam had texted him in the
middle of the night, and decided to sort himself out before he answered, rolling himself free of his pillow nest to face the morning.
Under harsh bathroom lighting, the unwrapped gouges scrawled
across his forearms spelled a message of violence. He ran his thumb
along the edge of one, a millimeter short of the soft scab. Firm
pressure worsened the itching. Long sleeves in the miserable heat
of summer's last gasp would provide camouflage if not comfort, so
he crossed the hall to Eddie's room and snagged a lightweight, pas-
tel green Henley from the closet. Fabric caught on the scabs with
miniscule stinging yanks. He rolled the sleeves up to his elbow.

Aside from the revenant waiting to drag him under, what else might be hiding in the Challenger that he hadn't noticed before? Bodies left traces behind; he'd listened to enough true crime podcasts to know that. The house was empty when he descended the stairs. Another quick tap on his phone screen to remind himself of the day of the week; on determining the date, he realized he was due in class later in the afternoon, if he so chose. With practiced motions, he turned on the single-serve coffee machine, filled a glass with ice from the dispenser, popped a pod of grounds in place, and tapped the button for OVER ICE.

While it rumbled through the brewing process, he dug the list of names out of his pocket and booted up his laptop. Sam had left him three to research; two had bullshit nondescript names he had no idea how to locate, but the older couple—the last ones, the ones Eddie had missed out on—seemed easier. Sure enough, some lazy social media stalking and googling led him to their contact info in the digital phonebook by the time the coffee maker beeped completion. His arms burned as he scribbled the number onto the Post-It.

No part of the *investigation* process seemed particularly real to him, but digging up some elderly couple's phone number through their Facebook accounts was exceptionally weird. Sorting through a script in his head for what he'd say, he grabbed his iced coffee and stepped onto the porch. Grim and sleek, the Challenger waited behind the house, a blot on the greenery of the alley under the broad blue sky. Before he approached, he texted Sam: *I'm fine. going to reach out to some people on my list.*

Daylight rendered the haunt *marginally* more inert, or so he had to hope, despite recent encounters. After a bracing sip of bitter, watery coffee—homemade, never as good—he popped the trunk again. Trepidation slowed his crunching steps across the gravel; he set the glass off to the side, wedging a little hollow into the rocks to support it, and bumped the lid all the way open. As before, he saw the spare tire and the Armor All, streaked now with a crust of dried gore from his indiscreet supernatural bullshit.

"Well, shit," he grunted.

If Eddie's murderer had left real traces behind, his own attempts had covered them over with fresh, gruesome leavings. Andrew sat on his ass on the gravel, then flopped backward, letting the searing pebbles dig into the meat of his shoulders and legs. *What the fuck am I doing,* he thought.

One task left for the morning. He let the crest of his miserable irritation drive him to tap in the McCormicks' number. To his surprise, after three rings, a woman picked up with a friendly, "Hello, this is Lisa."

"Uh, hi," he sputtered, sitting up straight. The sun beat hard on his long-sleeved shirt. "My name is Andrew, I'm—sorry, this is going to sound dumb, but did a guy named Eddie Fulton reach out to you about doing some interviews? Local folk stories?"

She hummed on the other end, responding, "Yes, actually, about a month ago. What's this about?"

"I'm a friend of his, and he—well, he passed, and I'm trying to finish up his work?"

"Oh," she said, obviously startled. "I'm so sorry to hear that."

"Yeah, thanks."

A long pause hung between them.

"Would you be willing to talk to me instead?" he asked.

"Sure, sure, hon," she said. "I've got nothing else going on this afternoon, would you like to speak to me and my husband then?"

Clarifying that she had a man around the house, Andrew realized wryly. "That sounds great. Thank you."

After another awkward pause, he wrote the address she gave him on his Post-It and hung up. He wasn't cut out for police work. He grabbed his coffee and fled inside out of the heat, sweating from armpits to knees. In the fridge he found an assortment of pre-packaged salads, deli lunchmeats, and a plastic carryout container full of chicken wings with an electric blue sticky note on top that said "eat these Andrew." He'd never laid eyes on such bounty at Capitol Street. While microwaving the wings, because the idea of preheating the oven to wait for them to crisp again amounted to torture, he opened his university email. Troth waited at the top of the inbox.

Hello Andrew,

I would advise speaking with me directly about your continuing research as Thom is busy in his own process at the moment. I did not want him and Edward to influence each other or be in competition, and have in the past guided them both toward separate arenas. I've instructed him to pass along relevant questions to me and to focus on his own dissertation. I'm happy to work with you as he pursues his own projects.

Best,
Jane Troth

The front door banged open at the same time the microwave beeped. Andrew stood in the center of the room with brow furrowed, re-reading her email and ignoring both, until Sam called out, "Hey, princess, you here?"

Andrew stuck his phone in his mouth and jerked both shirtsleeves down to his wrists as footsteps approached the kitchen. He took one long leap to the microwave. Sam rounded the corner of the doorway. Andrew sat his container of wings on the table and took his phone from between his teeth. One glossy patch of spit streaked the screen.

"Hey," he said, belated and stiff.

"It's your house, so I'm not judging." Sam's eyes glittered with mirth. "Perfectly good table right there to put your phone on though, just saying."

Andrew picked up a chicken wing, stomach sour with hunger and nerves. "I texted you."

"I was already heading over," Sam said. "What's the plan? I'm off work, at your disposal all afternoon."

Andrew said, "I set up an interview, with the last people Eddie was supposed to talk to. You coming?"

Sam took the address from his hand and said, "That's a hell of a drive, huh. But yeah, sure, why not."

"Now?" Andrew swallowed his relief with a mouthful of chicken.

"Bring those," Sam said with a gesture to the box of wings.

Five minutes later he was in the passenger seat of the WRX eating his second piece of chicken, air on full blast, speakers blaring a hideously distorted EDM track. Sam stole a wing from the container on his lap and ate it in two motions, one tearing gnash of teeth for the thickest chunk of meat and a complex suction maneuver that pulled the rest off the bone. A straggling bit of sinew was all that remained when he popped the bone free and tossed the scraps out his cracked window. Effortless and practiced. He waggled his fingers, and Andrew lifted the container to let him steal another.

There was no need to speak. Pressure receded from behind Andrew's eyes, the tension he carried from his blackout easing a fraction. Sam drove while he finished the leftovers. Whenever he let himself slow down, the monumental weight of his unanswered questions started to crush him to dust, so the drive and his company for it were both a relief and a torture. After an hour on the interstate, Sam punched in an address on his GPS.

The same highway led to the park with the oak tree, but this time, the route took them off an exit and through a cluster of trailers by a gas station. The red line on the GPS wound deeper into sparsely forested nothingness, a rural road spitting out the occasional unmarked driveway to either side, some paved and some dirt. The McCormick mailbox whipped past them around a blind curve, and Sam had to slam on the brakes and put the car in reverse.

The double-wide at the end of the drive had a painted tan deck and yellow window trimmings, with box planters full of flowers on the stoop. A mid-nineties Chevy pickup sat out front. One big tree shaded the whole house.

Andrew said, "All I told them is I was a friend of Eddie's, that he'd died, and that I still wanted to come talk to them about shit. These people were supposed to be his next interview, but he put them off for some reason—found something else, I guess."

"I hear you," Sam said as they mounted the steps.

The doorbell pinged, audible from the porch, and a woman's voice hollered, "Just a minute!"

Andrew stuck his hands in his pockets, Sam loitering behind him with his best good ol' boy smile buttered onto his lips. The door opened, leaving the storm glass pane between them and a lady in her seventies at minimum, white hair in tight gramma curls around a plump tanned face. Appliqué flamingos dotted the breast pocket of her pink shirt.

"Hi, ma'am," Sam said.

"I called this afternoon," Andrew clarified, as if she couldn't guess.

With a nod she opened the storm door and gestured them inside, smiling. "You boys are here to get the good gossip, huh?"

The den had a big television and a small couch, barely more than a loveseat, with a handful of homemade throw pillows on it. Andrew and Sam perched there with equally delicate discomfort, broad shoulders and unruly knees all wrong in the cozy space. Lisa McCormick planted one hand on her hip to look them up and down.

"Y'all want something to drink?"

"I'm good," Andrew said.

"Yeah, please," Sam said.

"All right, let me get Rob too." She went farther into the house. "Hey hon, those boys who called are here!"

Andrew wasn't too accustomed to dealing with the elderly. He hadn't visited his surviving grandfather in months. Last time he

had, it was with Eddie in tow to take the old man from his condo
to a Hooters for his birthday. Riley said Sam had been raised up by
their grandmother, though, which didn't explain his tense seat on
the edge of the couch. Maybe he was bad with strangers. It was odd
to see him polite and almost demure. The sound of a sliding door
opening and shutting came from the other room.

An older man who must've been Rob entered the den in the
midst of wiping his hands on his jean shorts. "Hey there. Was out
picking tomatoes, we got too many growing this summer to keep
up with."

His wife popped her head around the corner and said, "Come
sit at the table where we can all see each other."

"Yes, ma'am," Sam said.

He stood first. The low ceiling of the double-wide made him
appear taller. Andrew wracked his brain for his segue, his conversation points, and realized he had none. Other than that they'd
known the Fultons, and their land backed up to the estate, he
didn't know what the hell Eddie would've asked them about.

Sun streaming in through the glass doors to the yard lit the
kitchen-slash-dining room brightly. The garden out back was full
of tomato bushes and cabbages and zucchini. Sam and Andrew
sat across the table from the McCormicks. Lisa handed Sam a tall
glass of tea and kept another for herself.

"What relation are you to that young man from before, again?"
Lisa said.

"Eddie and I grew up together, he was my best friend," Andrew
said. "There was an accident and I'm following up on some things
he meant to do, before he passed."

Sam nudged him, boot-tip to ankle, under the table. The Mc-
Cormicks made sympathetic noises with twin frowns, the way cou-
ples do who've been together for decades, separate faces with the
same expression.

"I'm damn sorry to hear that, with as young as y'all are. You in
school too?" Rob asked.

"Yeah," Andrew said.

"And what about you, son?" he said to Sam.

"I'm a mechanic, sir," he said. "Also a friend of Ed's."

"My name's Andrew," he added. "And this is Sam."

"Oh, hell, I remember that face now," Lisa said. She propped her chin on her hand. "You and the Fulton boy were the ones that got in trouble out in the woods back there, weren't you? He said he was curious about his family, and we've been here for years, my mama and her mama before that."

Andrew nodded, glancing out the doors again. A steep hill rose up at the edge of the yard, shale sticking out of the crumbling dirt and grass, straggling trees tumbling and growing on the slope. A curious tremble ran up his fingers into his sore arms.

"So I guess you're here about the curse too, then," she said.

22

"Curse?" Sam asked first.

"The Fulton curse," Lisa McCormick repeated. She sipped her tea and glanced between the boys at her table. "It's a grim subject though, considering your friend's accident."

"No, I want to hear," Andrew said.

"He asked us to meet a little while back, but then he rescheduled. I think he had some detail or another on the family history he wanted to chase down before he interviewed us," Rob interjected.

"There's a couple different versions of the story," she said. "I heard it from my mama, who must've heard it from someone else, and so on. But I guess it's too backwoods for people to be putting in books."

Andrew crossed and recrossed his arms on the table, finding the safest angle to support his wounds. He settled with a thumb tucked into the crease of his elbow on one side and the other hand resting on his bicep. Sweat prickled the divot of his pectorals. Sam and Mrs. McCormick sipped their tea.

Andrew said, "What's the curse about, then?"

"Well, it's more or less what you'd expect, but it's a good story. Legend has it," she started, hill-rolled accent deepening, "that the second son of James Fulton fell head over heels for a delicate girl from up north he met when he was at schooling. So against the family's judgment, given he had prospects down here, he marries the girl and brings her home to the estate his daddy built."

Mrs. McCormick gestured out past the slope of their yard. The sympathetic tingle in Andrew's skin rippled. He was closer to the Fulton land than he'd been in eight years. When he'd checked a

GPS map before the drive, he realized that the McCormick forest joined the Fulton forest some distance from the trailer with its flower boxes. He owned the land across that invisible line. He wondered if he'd recognize the moment he stepped across the divide.

"What happens to the wife?" Sam asked, his posture unsticking as he listened.

"Good question," Mrs. McCormick said. "She was delicate, like I said, and she got sick from the trip. And they're only your age, might as well be babies. The second son puts her up in that big plantation and gets her all the best care money can buy, but she doesn't get better. She catches fevers and won't eat, and she wastes down to skin and bones."

"The Fultons had a plantation?" Andrew cut in.

"Of course! I bet the old house is still standing out there, but you wouldn't know it. The ones that came back after the war moved to the opposite end of their land and built fresh," she said.

On some level Andrew had forgotten, spending his years as a teen and then a young man in northern Ohio, that histories had a longer and uglier reach where he was from. His mind turned straight to the fat zeroes in his accounts, the estate he'd inherited and the implications of where it came from, with a creeping dread. Of *course* the Fultons had owned a fucking plantation—how else had he imagined them getting rich?

"Sounds like something out of a book already," Sam said, oblivious to his ongoing internal reckoning.

Mrs. McCormick laughed, a brief pealing sound. Her husband chuckled as well. His fond approval radiated from the attention he paid her as she spoke. Andrew noted their openness, then asked, troubled, "What happened next? After she got sick?"

"This is where it gets interesting. The second son loves this girl so much he decides to step onto an unholy path. Now the story varies, but in the one my mama told me, he makes a deal. He takes his youngest sister, goes out to a crossroad on the property past the witching hour, and he waits until some evil comes to him. He looks that evil square in the face and offers it his sister in return for his wife."

Despite her warning of grimness, her face was alight with the pleasure of spinning out the tale, leading them from one beat to the next. He supposed she hadn't had much occasion to tell it. He hadn't noticed pictures on the mantles or the walls, not of children or grandchildren.

"He kills his sister," Sam guessed.

"Of course he does," Mr. McCormick said.

"Naturally," his wife confirmed. "He slashes her throat and she bleeds out onto the crossroads. Right where they put the marker of the estate, if you're feeling symbolic. It's old land anyway, land that's had people doing their deeds on it for a long time before the Fultons decided to own it. So he sheds her blood, then he opens his wrist and gives it some of his, and he makes a deal that if he can have power over his wife's death, he'll keep giving the land more."

Andrew stopped breathing, hands gone tense around his arms. Blood for blood, offered to the earth—wasn't that a familiar story, one that lived curled up at the core of him.

"The wife lives," Mr. McCormick said, glancing between Andrew and Sam. "He blames the sister's murder on another man. But the land's alive, after that, because his sacrifice woke up whatever thing had been sleeping there."

"And deals with the devil aren't ever equal, which is where the curse comes in," his wife continued, trading the telling to and fro between them.

Sam's boot heel ground into his toes so hard Andrew jerked. Mrs. McCormick gave him a curious look and said, "Oh, are you all right?"

He said, "Sorry, cold chill."

He forced himself to take a breath, then another, and another. His heart pounded fit to burst through his ribs. Eddie's notebooks had been full of references to families and land and sacrifice. And the things that had happened in the cavern—

"The important part is that the deal doesn't miracle-cure his wife. Instead, he gets some sort of terrible gift to manipulate death itself, and it drives him mad. His brothers end up locking him up in the big house along with his wife, who ain't right either. They grow and die together. The brothers raise their children as their own. It was a scandal and a shame to the whole bunch of them," the old woman wrapped up with panache, crossing her arms over her pink-flamingoed bosom in pride.

"Damn, that's wild," Sam said. He slathered his vowels out like welcoming honey, boot grinding constant and careful onto the top of Andrew's foot. The minor, grounding pain sparking on those fine bones kept Andrew from rocketing out of the trailer in a blind panic. "That story hit all the notes I'd want and then some."

"Thanks hon. Lot of Fultons follow after that, but—" Mrs. Mc-Cormick glanced at Andrew once in sympathy before continuing at a more sedate volume, "Their line's cursed with death. Almost all of 'em died in the Civil War, and the handful that built the estate up after, kept it going, they had the worst luck. The story has it that even those who don't try to wrangle the curse, like the second son who brought it on them, it wrangles them in the end regardless. The land's hungry, and it gets its due, one way or another."

"Thank you. He's right, that's a hell of a story." Andrew fumbled for his phone under the pretense of checking the time. "Hey, don't you have to get to work?"

"Yeah, probably got to get going," Sam said as he pushed his chair out.

"Was that useful?" Mrs. McCormick said. She gathered up the glasses to bustle them over to the sink. Mr. McCormick stayed seated. "I hope it wasn't too upsetting."

"No, no, it's real interesting," Andrew said.

"I'm from around here, I'm surprised I hadn't heard it before," Sam added.

"I might reach out again," Andrew said.

"Of course, please do," she replied.

He blanked out for the walk to the car. He found himself struggling with the seat belt; lining up the buckle with the receiver might as well have been brain surgery. His mouth was full of spit, nostrils flaring with each taut, panicked breath. Sam smacked his knuckles, latched the buckle for him, then grabbed the base of his skull for a squeeze.

"Hush, dude, you're good. It's done," he said. His palm and fingers were broad, thumb pressed under one ear and nails scratching near the crown of Andrew's scalp.

"What the fuck," he whispered.

"Why are you so freaked?"

"Get me out of here."

The loss of the grounding pressure on his scalp when Sam switched his hand to the gearshift almost spun him off the face of the earth. He dug the heels of his hands into his eye sockets while the car purred around him. The grand staircase flashed in his mind, unfamiliar but familiar. He remembered the gaping cave of the drawing room and the forbidding, locked door that stood between him and the dark inheritance his revenant so wished for him to embrace.

"His parents died in a wreck, you know that? Slid right off the road head-on into a tree. Happened on the property," Andrew said into the silence.

"It's just another story, Andrew," Sam said.

In lieu of a response, he opened his phone's notes app to painstakingly type the McCormicks' version of the Fulton curse with his thumbs. The tale had all the hallmarks of Eddie's favorite Southern gothics: a devil's bargain, a damned lineage, an eldritch power resurrected. Except the tale belonged to him, the scion of a cursed house moldering in the woods, answering a question he'd been asking for almost a decade—the one Andrew had strenuously avoided for just as long.

But Eddie had never made it out to interview the McCormicks. He'd found some other record of the curse to hunt down in his final days. Troth said he'd mentioned some breakthrough at her dinner party, the last outing he'd attended. Without his notes, Andrew had no idea what he'd discovered or where, only that between his lucky find and the interview he'd intended to do with the McCormicks, trouble had found him and the land had taken its due.

As Andrew's thumb hovered over the keyboard, partway through a sentence about the hubris of the second Fulton son, an incoming call took over the screen, phone vibrating angrily in his hand. He fumbled to answer with a brief, "Hey."

"Found something kind of weird. Where you at?" Riley asked.

"With your cousin, running down an interview from that list of names." Sam shot him a look, curious. He switched the phone to his left hand, angling his torso toward the window to escape observation in the close space. "What is it?"

"Okay so, near the last pages of the journal he writes about finding a mention of the Fultons in a genealogical history—and that mention referenced another book, get this, a monograph from the late forties about supernatural lore and folk magic in rural Tennessee," he said in a rush.

"Maybe that's the breakthrough he told people about. Did he find the monograph?"

"Here's where that gets a little weird. I went looking for the monograph, because it's obvious he found it given the timeline of his notes, but the damn thing has disappeared into thin air. It's not with his materials or in the carrel, and the library system says it's checked out. I've spent the whole fucking afternoon combing shelves to see if it got misplaced or something, but nada. I know it's minor, but given everything else, it strikes me as off."

"Yeah, more of his shit going missing fits in with the rest." Andrew struggled to connect the dots as his thoughts chased themselves in circles. The McCormicks' tale was trope-filled and appropriately spooky, but didn't seem too special on the outside—unless someone knew, like Eddie did, that it held a kernel more truth than most.

"It's either correlated with the phone and the notes or the worst coincidence in hell. The question I've got now is: was it the research someone got after, or something he found *in* the research?"

Andrew grunted his neutral agreement with Riley's train of thought. "See if you can find another copy of that monograph, and I guess we'll find out."

"On it, boss man," he said with a tinge of snark and hung up.

Window glass propped up his forehead, cool and soothing. After the initial burst of adrenaline faded, he felt emptied out. The sedation of rhythmic movement and enclosed silence dragged Andrew's eyelids down in swooping blinks as he drifted between sleep and consciousness. Sam turned on his stereo system and spun the volume knob to a faint murmur.

The ratchet of the parking brake startled Andrew alert. He straightened out his kinked back, disoriented and cotton-mouthed, fighting to process the sight of a garage wall plastered with band posters. He croaked, "Your place?"

"Yeah," Sam said. He drummed his fingers on the steering wheel. "Leave Riley out of this, going forward. He doesn't need to be fucking with it."

Addled from his impromptu nap, he said, "What?"

"I don't see this curse business turning up rainbows, Andrew, so leave him out of it," he repeated. "Find that shit yourself, don't send him looking for it. I don't want him involved any further."

"He's a grown man," Andrew said.

A muscle in Sam's jaw twitched. He let a breath out through his nose and opened his car door, stuck one leg out, then said, "I'm not asking your opinion."

"What is your problem—" he started.

Sam slammed his door midsentence. Andrew sat in the car as Sam mounted the steps into the house, leaving the interior door hanging open behind him as an obvious demand. Andrew swallowed his pride and got out to follow. At the kitchen table he took the unoccupied seat in front of a neat glass of bourbon and faced

Sam, already sprawled in his chair, indolent, radiating displeasure. His glass dangled from his fingers. Andrew sipped while looking right at him, waiting as the silence stretched.

"Why can't you be the one to tell him?" Andrew asked when it became clear Sam wasn't going to start the fight. "You have the problem, so you can tell him to back off."

"The last thing he's interested in is me parenting him," Sam said.

"Then don't parent him," Andrew replied, unprepared for how adult he felt.

"He still needs it, and he deserves to make something of himself without getting pulled into this wreck of a situation," Sam said with a broad gesture in his general direction. "In case you missed it, the last person doing the research you just asked him to do is dead. Have you thought enough about that?"

"Riley was Eddie's friend," he said.

"Yeah, and so was I. Look where that got us. This is our problem to solve, you and me. I'm not going to ask you again," he said.

The weight of the preceding weeks crashed onto Andrew in a tumult, filling him up to bursting and straining all his existing fissures. Andrew leaned forward with both elbows braced on the table to snap, "I'm not your bitch, so tell him yourself."

Violence crackled between them despite the calmness of the kitchen, the shared drink, the loose posture. Riley's involvement was tangential to Andrew's anger; he wasn't sure what about the situation made him so fucking furious, but his temper was not about to slow down. The last time a man had the gall to tell him *I'm not going to ask you again,* it had been Eddie. He'd been telling Andrew to shut up about coming to Nashville in the spring, earlier than planned. Andrew didn't take those kinds of orders from Sam.

Sam got up and rounded the table, saying, "I know your spoiled ass doesn't understand what it's like to claw your way out of awful shit, and neither did Ed. So I'm going to tell you this once"— mid-sentence, he shoved Andrew's chair out cockeyed with a foot on one wooden leg; Andrew caught himself with a heel on the ground before he tipped over—"and you're damn well going to listen. That kid has had it hard enough already, and I will not fucking tolerate any threat to him or his success. Not from you, not from Ed, not from myself. You got me?"

"You think I don't know what that's like, huh," Andrew said.

Sam's shinbone ground against his calf, boot still planted on his chair leg. Andrew grasped the table and leveraged himself to standing, nose to nose with Sam, invading his space in turn. From other nights, fire nights, he knew the taste of the fight about to unfurl between them. Swift and brutal, to assume the least.

"Yeah, I do. Everything's been handed to you. You live in your own fucking world, and all you see is you and him," Sam accused, breath reeking of liquor, his glare just as scouring.

Andrew said, "I see you, Sam. You don't see me, though, if you think that's true."

"Ain't it? Prove me wrong," Sam demanded.

He splayed his hand on Andrew's sternum. Andrew grabbed his wrist to pin him still, the fingertips digging into his pectoral muscle as if Sam could scoop out his beating heart. He squeezed the thick wrist in his grip until his healing forearm hurt from the strain. Sam took it, unimpressed, forcing him a step backward until the edge of the chair bumped the backs of his knees. Seconds dragged out as the room fell silent, each watching the other, skin to skin.

Andrew spilled over first: "When we were kids, I followed Ed into the woods. He was feeling something weird. He had to figure out what it was. When it started getting dark, I asked him to go back. He said no. We got a minute or two farther in and fell down a fucking sinkhole." The confession scalded him from the inside out. "I broke my ankle, he concussed himself. We couldn't climb out. I broke all my fingernails trying to get up the dirt. The sun went down. He was delirious, bleeding goddamn everywhere. I'd cut myself from ass to shoulder on a root. You want me to keep going?"

"You're not dead," Sam said.

"Yeah, fucking fancy that."

Sam broke Andrew's grip with a simple twist of his wrist, as if he'd only been waiting for the right moment. In the process he caught the start of the raw brown-red scab Andrew's sleeve failed to cover. One additional step to the side broke their clinch. Sam gestured to his arm and Andrew realized his cover was blown.

"What'd you do?" Sam asked.

"I thought you didn't want to get involved with my weird shit," he said.

"I really don't," he said, "but you're going to tell me anyway."

One thing at a time, Andrew thought, rancor simmering at Sam for thinking he was soft and spoiled. "You want me to finish the other story first or not?"

Sam gulped the last of his bourbon in two huge swallows and bared his teeth in a sinus-clearing gasp of relief. Trees loomed outside the kitchen windows in the settling night. Andrew felt a desperate call to speak, maddened by the unstoppable fractures spreading from his past to his present; he was the sole living person who knew the tale he was about to tell from front to finish. After he told it, he wouldn't be alone.

"Fine," Sam said. "Porch. Let's go."

23

Andrew sat on the edge of the porch with his legs dangling behind the bushes and Sam settled down next to him, one big hand planted on the concrete between his spread thighs. The minutely grating seam of the concrete sank into Andrew's hamstrings, a distracting line of pressure. Fireflies blinked through the gloom of later evening, brief lights there and gone. Starting again after the fight had stalled out felt wrong, so Andrew offered, "You want to see the scar?"

"Guess it's fair, I know you saw mine," Sam said.

Andrew skinned his shirt over his head, the mop of his hair collapsing around his face in disarray as the collar pulled it. Sam leaned back on his hands to have a long look and whistled through his teeth, then said, "Got you deep, huh?"

Andrew often forgot about the long weal of white, puckered skin that ran up the left-middle of his back, until he caught sight of it in an angled mirror; at a glance, it looked like someone had tried to pull his spine through his skin crooked.

"The paramedics were surprised I hadn't bled out," he said.

"Mine are shallow, but there's more of 'em," Sam said. "If we're trading here."

Andrew balled the shirt up in his fist and turned his arms to hide the scabs, his belly plumping to little rolls as he bent forward over his thighs. Sam stayed reclined, giving him the illusion of privacy as he began to speak.

"I passed out. When I came to, Eddie had wandered off. The sinkhole was attached to some big cave system under the forest. By then, it was nighttime, so once I got a foot inside I lost the moon and I couldn't see a fucking thing. No light at all, that's the part I still . . . dream about a lot."

"Horror movie shit," Sam said.

Andrew snorted, but he was right: crawling through the pooled, brackish water, pawing at slick stones, banging his sore knees and throbbing broken ankle and stinging bloodied hands, wound pulling on his shoulders and hips. Surrounded in his blindness by a whispering susurrus, the illusion of movement in the black. The *wrongness* of the cavern. His fingers bumping into the limp hot warmth of Eddie's leg and grasping it, shaking it, to no response. Not being able to wake him. Horror movie shit, truly, and it had stuck to him for almost a decade.

"I had to crawl through the cave, felt like forever," he continued. "And I found him, but in bad shape. There was something in there with us, man. It never felt like we'd had an accident, no matter what people said. The thing in the cave wanted us there, I think, and it especially wanted him."

"Fulton curse," Sam said.

Andrew paused to orient himself and scratched at the scabs on his left arm. Sam smacked his hand loose to make him quit it. He finally said, "The story gets weirder from here, if you want me to stop."

"When I was fifteen, my dad knocked me through the glass of the storm door," Sam said. "Cut my ass up. Little less spooky, more domestic, I guess. That was the first time Mom had to take me to the hospital after something he did. Mamaw picked me up from the hospital, brought me here, and I never saw either of them again. Not one time, not even for fucking Christmas. She was a hard old bitch, but she was sure about keeping her grandbabies safe."

"Well, shit," Andrew said.

"Riley's parents aren't violent, but they're real religious. His mom wouldn't let him change his name. He came out here too after he got his ass whipped at school too many times." He let out a breath.

"Fifteen is the year for moving in with your grandmother, in our family."

Sharing the grisly truth was easier if he didn't have to acknowledge the shit being said, if each of them just—spoke out loud, to be heard without being dug at. So in turn, Andrew said, "Eddie wasn't himself when I did find him," though that was nowhere near the whole truth of it.

He remembered Eddie's skinny arm crossing his shoulder and the sharp shock of Eddie's fingers curling into his lacerated back, bringing the beastly muttering of the curse into his ears. Remembered pain bowing him, fresh blood rolling in fat drops from his armpit to his elbow to his wrist and then to the fingers supporting Eddie's limp head. When the blood touched Eddie's hair his neck turned, an unnatural jerk, and he flicked his tongue over Andrew's wet skin. Dizziness struck Andrew while the mouth dragged up his arm, as if it was lapping up more than the blood alone; he collapsed facedown in the chill water, gasping and choking when it got into his mouth. Eddie loomed over him and palmed his cheek to turn his face out of the water, letting him swallow and spasm. One corpse-cold hand tilted his chin and squeezed his jaw open while the other slid bloodied fingers into his mouth, gagging him as it reached deep down his throat to make him consume, in turn, as he had been consumed.

The warmth had drained out of him into the ground. Eddie curled up around his inert flesh, whispering the cavern's toneless whispers in his ear, words he had no recollection of later, except that he'd felt them changing him to his bones. The curse tied him to the ground and to the blood coating his throat, reached past the boundaries of his skin and turned him inside out. The edges of his flesh, split like an overripe tomato, pulled along the length of his back; under the cold, coagulating gore, the abrupt itch of healing stung.

He struggled to articulate even a portion of those memories, the violation of them, and managed only, "He did some fucked up stuff. Made me drink his blood. The Fulton curse, that shit's real.

I laid there all night, with him on me, and when the sun came up I like—*felt* it. I felt the ground warming up. Daybreak brought him around, back to normal, and he didn't remember a thing. And then it still took two more fucking days for them to find us."

Andrew stuck his thumbnail between his teeth and started to gnaw, curled on himself, too awkward to wriggle into the shirt again but feeling utterly naked. Sam lay a hand on his shoulder, one squeeze.

"So, as a kid, you knew you were going to die," he said.

"Yeah, I did, after that first night. I thought I had died already." That part, he'd never said aloud, not once—not even to Eddie. "I thought I was some sort of really visible ghost, for a whole week after. Took burning myself on the stove making tomato soup to realize I was still kind of alive. After we got out, we both, we weren't . . ." *normal.* He couldn't say that, couldn't keep talking. His offering to Sam dried up.

"I kept raising Riley out here, after our grandmother died," Sam offered in return. "On paper, all I am is a good-for-nothing piece of shit mechanic who gets drunk four nights a week and lives in his dead mamaw's house. But Riley's better than that. He's the only one in our family who's gotten to college, and he deserves to get out from under all our history. That kid's the reason I've kept it together."

Andrew said, "That's all good, but he deserves to live how he likes too. And coming from outside, that age difference between y'all seems like nothing. He's just another guy to me."

"To me he's always going to be the kid that came here with a backpack and nothing else, and asked me to shave his head in the bathroom. I'm responsible for him," Sam said.

"Except he's grown," Andrew repeated with care, "and you're not his father."

Sam stood, knees cracking. "Fine, I'll be the one to talk to him, but I'd still prefer you not pull him in deeper. The pair of us, that's different, we can handle it. Just keep him on the edges."

Andrew kept sitting, lost in thought, though he jolted when Sam palmed the topmost point of his scar as he brushed past— glancing, curious. The hydraulic stop on the screen door released with a hiss when Sam went inside. Drained from the conversation and the argument preceding it, Andrew was glad to be alone for a minute or thirty. The unlit living room welcomed him later on with sustained quiet and a pile of blankets on the couch, all for him and offered without comment.

———

Andrew let himself into the house on Capitol at 7:30 A.M., buzzed on gas station coffee and Sam's good-morning blunt, and was relieved to find that the other cousin wasn't waiting for him on the couch like a sitcom dad. Andrew showered, washed a few dishes, swept the dirt outdoors, spending the first hours of the morning on mechanical tasks to distract him while he twisted the information he'd gathered into mental knots and then unpicked them again, trying to find a clearer angle of approach. There was a curse on the Fultons, their land or their line or both, and Eddie had been searching for an explanation—a search that seemed to also be connected to his murder, no matter the angle Andrew held his internal puzzle at. If he found the monograph, that might point him in the right direction, since it was Eddie's last stop too.

After he took the garbage out to the cans, he gripped the frame of the back door and used it to stretch, popping his shoulders, rolling his neck. Sleeping on a couch wasn't the most comfortable experience, but the reprieve from bad dreams left him more rested anyway. He felt scoured from the intimate conversation, occupied by the picture of a miserable teenage Sam Halse tumbling through a single-pane glass door ass-first, bleeding on the upholstery of some cheap sedan on a long ride to a hospital. Mundane, personal, and monumental at the same time.

"Hey," said Riley from the stairs.

Andrew jumped, fingers slipping off of the lintel. His roommate squinted at the clean kitchen in his boxers, bedhead puffed out in crowning glory. Andrew dragged his glance past the scars on his bare chest, caught out the moment he met Riley's eyes.

"Stayed with Sam again?" Riley asked.

Andrew said, "It was closer."

"Sure, yeah." Riley patted his waist companionably as he shuffled past him to the fridge. "Good for you, putting yourself out there. Also, I'm feeling charitable this morning, so if you want to ask me a set of invasive, personal questions you've been stocking up, now's the time."

Andrew paused, then asked: "Are the glasses only for aesthetics?"

Riley burst into surprised laughter and thumped his forehead onto the fridge door, continuing to chuckle for a long moment after. Andrew had questions, but as he crossed to the living room and flopped onto the couch, he thought he'd made the right choice not to ask them. His firm limit on hard conversations per month had been exceeded multiple times over, and the one with Del lingered like a leviathan under the rest. Riley joined him a few minutes later with two mugs of coffee. He offered the second to Andrew as he asked, "How long has it been since you actually made it to class?"

Rather than answering, Andrew sipped his coffee too soon and seared his taste buds.

"Okay, uh, consider fixing that before you can't. If you want to, that is," Riley said.

"Message received," he said.

With the rest of the bullshit going on, time passed fast and loose, but he'd managed a couple of course meetings for each class so far, and had turned in a few assignments, sort of on schedule. He had to get it together, he couldn't afford to lose his access to Troth and her ilk while he kept searching. Riley got up and scratched his flat, lightly furred lower stomach; Andrew looked elsewhere a second late.

"I'm heading out, morning class to teach and all. Hit me up if you're on campus later," Riley said.

He carried his coffee upstairs, floorboards creaking overhead as he prepared for the day. Andrew logged onto his student email, laptop precariously balanced on one thigh and coffee in his free hand. Two from West, the unanswered warning from Troth, and several from his courses. He responded to Troth first: *I had an interesting breakthrough with the McCormicks, can we meet to discuss? Free this afternoon.* The emails from his mentor came from five minutes after their ill-advised beer and then the previous night at 11 P.M.

West's first email was brief:

Hey Andrew,
    Sorry for the abrupt departure. Full disclosure, I was already pissed about Troth spending half of our first dissertation meeting in a month going on about you and Ed and that missing notebook. I can't pretend to be in a good place about it. The problems I have with her aren't yours to deal with, though, so again, apologies.
                                                                —West

The second email, sent after Andrew had missed the class he shared with West and Riley to go off hunting stories with Sam, read,

Hey Andrew,
    I haven't seen you in class. Troth asked me about our mentorship meetings and I had to admit we hadn't had one in forever. Let's meet this week?
                                                                —West

Andrew popped another sliver off the ragged edge of his thumbnail with his eyeteeth. His cursor blinked at the start of an unwritten response. During the vision, or haunting, from the trunk—the scabs on his arms ached as he remembered—the person had been strong enough to lift and drop Eddie's body into the trunk. That narrowed the field considerably. Out of the minuscule list of potentially culpable parties in Andrew's head, West ticked the boxes for access, ability, and motive. The relationship between West and Troth had been fraught before Eddie came into the picture, and worsened after—suggestive in a way that his other options, all suspect due to circumstance or opportunism, weren't.

He typed, *Yeah sure, when's good?* and received another message almost instantaneously, this one from Troth: *Come to my office this afternoon around 3pm, if you're able?* Andrew responded with a quick agreement. The shower's hiss traveled through the vents. He ducked upstairs to change into another lightweight shirt with long sleeves, and scribbled a note for his roommate that he slapped on the closed bathroom door. It read *going to look for the monograph myself text me the title.*

The requested text arrived fifteen minutes later as he parked on campus: *Appalachian Folk Knowledge and History* by E. Gerson, circa 1943. In the hours following, he combed the library stacks one shelf at a time, repeating Riley's work, looking across the full spectrum of reasonably related shelves—tedious, eye-straining work that turned up nothing. The alarm on his phone rang at 2:45. He crossed campus to Troth's office, sore-eyed from the fluorescent lighting and towering, shaded shelves.

She greeted him from her desk. "Welcome, Mr. Blur. I hope you're having a productive afternoon?"

"Something like that," he said, taking his accustomed uncomfortable seat.

"Let me get the door." She pushed it closed, the thick wood muffling the enclosed space in an instant. "You said you'd had a breakthrough?"

"Yeah—or, I guess I caught up to the breakthrough Eddie made at the end? I talked to the McCormicks," he said.

"And what came of that?" she asked with laced fingers, elbows propped on the desktop.

Andrew spread his hands on his knees and sat deeper into the vinyl chair. Their distinct postures, her leaning in and him withdrawing, struck him. "So, the last thing Eddie was looking into was the Fulton family curse itself. Mrs. McCormick knew a version of that ghost story, and she told it to me. She said he postponed their interview because he found another version somewhere else."

Troth smiled, uncomfortably eager, and said, "Excellent, to be making progress so soon. Were you able to record the interview for transcription? I'd like to hear the original, as soon as possible."

Andrew winced; that hadn't occurred to him, but he knew it was proper procedure. "I didn't get audio, no, but I'll send over the notes I took. The setup was more casual, and I haven't done an interview since my thesis. The story doesn't stand out much from, you know, the standards of the genre, but it's about his own family, so I'm sure it had special interest."

Her manicured nail tapped her first knuckle on the opposite hand, a hint of agitation cracking through her veneer of concerned care. "Of course. Next time, do make a recording; it would be good to return and request an oral history from the participants. Otherwise, it doesn't count much for the archival record. And while I'm sure the text Edward found was fascinating enough for him, an original interview contributes more to the field than any rehash of prior work."

The concept of returning to the McCormicks and sitting through that tale again, with his phone recording as they sat around their sunny table, made him feel sick. Troth needed to wrangle a publication out of the mess, but that was beyond Andrew's scope or interests, and he wouldn't be derailed.

"Sure, but if the other version he told them he found is out there, I'd appreciate seeing it for comparison's sake," he said.

"Certainly, and I wouldn't want to discourage good research habits. If you'll send me the title, I'll look into it as well." As he started to respond, half a consonant out of his mouth, she cut him off to continue, "I'd also intended to extend you an invitation to a small gathering of students and faculty at our home this Friday, but lost track of time. Would you be able to attend?"

"That's tomorrow," Andrew said.

"Yes, I apologize for the short notice, but I believe you'd benefit from speaking with my partner. He might prove most helpful on your research into family lore. And you are my advisee, after all. If you'd care to, bring the notes along and tell us both the tale. We'll offer feedback on avenues worth pursuing. I believe Mr. Sowell and some of your other cohort-mates will be attending," she said.

Andrew hesitated. The invitation was forceful and abrupt, and she hadn't extended it to him at the same time as the rest of her students. But, an opportunity was an opportunity.

"All right, sure, sounds useful," he agreed.

"Perfect. I'll email the invitation with the address, and the gathering begins at seven. I do have a course to prepare for, though—if you'll excuse me?" She gestured him to the door.

Steamrolled, he got up and crossed the room without another word. As he pulled the door shut between them, sweating palm slipping on the cold door handle, she pressed the bridge of her joined hands to her mouth, giving him no further notice.

24

The bottle of top-shelf bourbon Riley clasped by the neck was their contribution to the get-together. He cleaned up well, as usual: hair styled in an artful side part, glasses perched on his nose, a grey sweater-vest over a black Oxford. Andrew's combination of persistently stubbled jawline, rumpled Henley, and black jeans were shabby in comparison, but he doubted it mattered. Impressing the faculty and making it through to graduation weren't his driving motivations.

"I don't dig this place," Riley said under his breath as he rang the doorbell.

The house was grand, ancient, about an hour from campus. Cars speckled the paved drive. Extensive lawns spoke to the builders' life of leisure, as did the ostentatious columned veranda and the house's two tall stories that sprawled far in either direction. The ancestral home creaked at the seams with the weight of contained histories, a constant pressure that ached in his nail-beds and molars. While Andrew hadn't run across much detail about the Troths during his perusal of Eddie's research, he bet with enough dedicated attention he'd unearth their ghosts as well; no old families around these parts came without some monstrous history. He scratched at the seam of his jeans to soothe the soreness of his fingertips.

Another student opened the door for them with a smile, a perky young woman whose face he vaguely recognized but couldn't put to a name.

She said, "Hi there, come on in!"

The entrance hall ceiling soared to the full height of the house, chandelier casting eerie gold light in pools through the bannister of a sweeping staircase. Their classmate walked into a room on the right, French doors thrown wide. Andrew followed with Riley at his elbow. Sedate conversation filled the handsome space, electric sconces on the walls dim enough to articulate the idea of gas without the need for fuming poison. Two long couches and a sideboard loaded with drinks took up most of the drawing room's floor space. Gleaming, rich hardwood paneling spread underfoot with no rugs to obscure its lavish shine. The handful of faculty attendees were in their fifties or older, scattered with a sparse number of students. There were no staff to speak of.

Aside from the outfits, he felt as if he'd stepped backward in time. The persistent, phantom itching ramped up; Andrew fought off the urge to gnaw on his fingernails. Jane Troth, seated on the far corner of one sofa, lifted her hand in an inclusive wave.

"Hello there, gentlemen," she said.

"Hi," Andrew replied.

Riley lifted his bottle in greeting before adding it to the array. Andrew had bought it without checking the cost, but he assumed it would work well enough. While he approached the couch to curious glances from the assorted guests, Riley poured them each two fingers in squat crystal glasses. Professor Troth stood up and smoothed her dress around her middle, then waved to her vacated seat.

"Take my spot, and I'll go see if Mark is feeling well enough to speak to you about the project," she said.

Andrew gingerly took the warmed corner cushion and Riley wedged himself into the middle space, their thighs pressed together, handing him his drink with a faintly spooked grimace. To Riley's right sat an older white woman in a mauve blazer and corduroy slacks, chatting up the same student who'd led them inside. Andrew rearranged himself to tuck the arm of the sofa under his elbow and angle his body toward Riley, who leaned to murmur in his ear, "Are you, uh, feeling this place too?"

The tingling itch that had started the moment he set foot on the property marched along his elbow joints, merrily aggravating. Andrew closed his eyes slowly, looking inward, tugging on the roiling chill in his gut that was—suddenly responsive, so very eager, starved perhaps, for his attention. His whole body twitched. The faux gas lights flickered at the corners of his vision like the shadows might crawl up to snuff them.

Riley pinched his leg savagely and hissed, "Do fucking *not*. Whatever you just almost did, do not."

"Sorry," he muttered, cramming the messy tendrils of the curse-gift back into their metaphorical lockbox. He felt like some kind of idiot, trying to explore his *magic*.

"Christ almighty," Riley said.

The house seethed around them, responding to his nudge. The anxious strangeness dogging his heels since his arrival resolved into a juxtaposition of realities: the boards under his feet were steeped in death, stained to the foundations with knowledge and time. Reverberations echoed for miles around, as if he stood at the center of a welcoming necropolis.

"Are you talking about the house?" said the young woman on the other end of the couch, startling Andrew.

Riley covered for him and said, "Yeah, just that I didn't expect it to be so big."

"It's the original Troth plantation home. Been here, what, more than a hundred seventy years?" she continued, a little too starry-eyed considering the topic.

Riley's nose scrunched in disgust before he schooled his face into polite boredom.

"A piece of the past," the older woman interjected, turning to face them as well. "Nice to meet you, boys, I'm Dr. Koerner. Which program are you from?"

"American studies," Andrew said.

"Oh, wonderful," she said.

"We're here to meet with Dr. Troth and her husband," Riley said.

Andrew nodded as the room continued to tilt and warp at the edges of his vision. He didn't care for strangers on a good night, let alone with the lurking, fatal mass of the house and its dead pressing on him from above and below. He snuck a swallow of bourbon large enough to qualify as a shot, and the caustic burn settled him, drawing him back into his real, living skin. If Troth had possessed even the slightest portion of his or Riley's affinity for the dead, he was sure the malevolence of the place would've driven her right out of the countryside.

"Andrew," Troth said from the entrance to the drawing room, as if summoning him.

"Be right back," he murmured to Riley, guiltily leaving him to his conversation.

"Mark is, I must warn you, in ill health, and wasn't feeling up to the party," Troth said when he caught up to her in the foyer. Her low heels clacked resolutely on the wood of the grand staircase. "Would you be amenable to telling us both the story, however you heard it from the McCormicks? It might give him a lift."

"Okay, I can do that." Photograph after photograph lined the upstairs hall, most featuring a younger version of Jane Troth with the man he presumed was Mark. In some, there were two young girls, but one vanished as the family got older. His nape prickled with premonition. "Is West coming tonight? I'm surprised not to see him here."

"Ah, well, he doesn't prefer to venture out of Nashville proper. I thought it'd be better not to split my attention tonight regardless." She frowned in thought. "He was rather irritated at my questions about Edward's missing research earlier this week, but I'd be a fool not to ask the one other person besides myself who had shown an interest. I hope you don't mind that I brought it to his attention?"

The question couldn't be unasked; what else was there to say but, "No, it's fine."

Troth turned down the hall to the left, lit dimly by the light from a far room. The darkened remainder of the hall stretched off to the right, cast under full shadow, a darkness that pulled at Andrew's attention with a sweet whisper—unlike his revenant, but a presence nonetheless. Recalling the animate shadows that had oozed from the Challenger's footwells, he forced himself to ignore the call. Troth led him to a bright, modern study out of place amongst the preservation chic of the house at large: Macbook on a pale wood and glass desk, sky-blue rugs on the hardwood floor, white cube shelving. An older man reclined on a chaise longue with a book open in his hand, lean and balding with prominent cheekbones.

Ghostly miasma pooled around him, stinking of premature rot. A retching spasm squeezed the back of Andrew's throat. *Ill health* was a drastic understatement; he'd only encountered a handful of people so close to death in his years post-cavern, and he usually hightailed it away from them. He knocked back a fortifying swallow of bourbon to cover the pulse of his gag reflex and coughed, waving his hand as an apology. The man chuckled at him.

"Watch yourself, there," he said, glancing at his wife. "Your student Andrew, I presume?"

"Yes, the one and only," she responded, sitting at the end of the couch, her fine creamy-peach dress a contrast to his unfashionable sweater and sock feet.

She touched his exposed ankle with a tender fingertip, intimate, and then settled with wrists crossed daintily over the couch arm. Andrew hovered, awkwardly looming over the two of them on the reclined sofa.

Mark pointed to his desk chair. "Have a seat there, roll it over if you want."

Andrew grasped the chair arm and scooted it closer to the couple. Writhing tendrils of impending death kept snagging his attention: shadows dripped over the man's clavicle, fluttered at the hinge of his jaw. Hunger within Andrew crouched in eagerness, straining to reach out. Nothing good was going to come of that impulse, so he smothered it. The revenant's continual interference over the past weeks had frayed his collapsing self-discipline, and Jane Troth's husband was far enough along to taste and smell and *provoke* like a thing already dead. Andrew's whole skeleton throbbed under his skin.

Mark said, "I'm sorry for your loss, Andrew. Edward was a great guy; we smoked cigars and shot the shit over scary stories a few times, my favorite kind of student. He fit right in, here."

"Thanks," Andrew said inadequately.

"I'd offer you the same, but I'm banned from smoking at the moment. Had a bad relapse last month and here we are," he said. His polite smile never reached his eyes, though Andrew hardly blamed him. "Cancer's a bitch. I've got some time left, though, so tell me this scary story while there's still a chance."

"Please do," Jane said.

Her posture yearned toward the man on the couch, though she tried to lean away and keep him in her sight. The magnetism between them was strung tight as a spiderweb. Andrew propped a heel on the chair leg, forearm on his knee to support his glass. It unnerved him to witness Troth's oncoming, inevitable hurt.

"The way the McCormicks told it to me, the second son of the Fulton family married young and his wife got sick, so he sacrificed his sister to the land the estate's on as part of a, uh, sort of deal with death to keep her going." He didn't have the gift for spinning the yarn, not how Lisa McCormick did. "The version I heard has it that the power was already there, sleeping in the land, and he woke it up. It goes on that the wife does survive, but the power drives them both mad, and the family's been cursed by the deal ever since."

"That's it, huh," Mark said with a sardonic raised eyebrow.

Andrew said, "Sorry, I'm not a great storyteller. The McCormicks made the land itself seem the most important part of the story, not so much the Fultons in particular. They were like, collateral damage for the existing power they tied themselves to. It's a little different than the usual devil's bargain story, because the devil isn't personified, and because the curse is still out there haunting the remaining descendants."

"The bit about the young husband is familiar. People will go far for love, further than you'd expect," Professor Troth said.

Her husband murmured, "And who wouldn't want to be able to stave off death, right? Hell, what I'd do for that, curse or no curse."

Her hands held each other on the couch arm, twisted tight enough to turn her knuckles white. Andrew looked out the window across the broad lawns to the edge of encroaching forest, the gloom of the settling evening as the stars came out. Troth knew her husband wasn't going to see through another winter, and he felt a kinship with her over that—Eddie wouldn't be seeing snow either, not even the wet slush that Nashville got in place of Columbus's frozen tundra. Neither of them would be scrambling over the tiny ice-mountains scattered across parking lots up north, or shoving cold hands under each other's shirts.

"I'll write it down better than I told it," he said. "But I'm looking for a book, too, to fill the story out some more. *Appalachian Folk Knowledge and History* from an E. Gerson, published in the forties."

"Huh, haven't read it, but the title sounds familiar. Have you tried the library?" Mark said.

"It's not there, I've looked," Andrew said.

Silence settled for one beat, dragged into a second and a third. Mark hummed, a bit dismissive, without taking his eyes off of Andrew; the continued attention seemed too intense, paired with his noncommittal response.

Dr. Troth tapped her husband's ankle again as Andrew sat caught-rabbit still, and he cast a long glance up at her. "Sorry darling, getting tired. I might be done for tonight."

"I'm sure, dear, I understand. We'll let you rest," she replied, gesturing Andrew out.

He waited for her far enough into the hall to avoid eavesdropping on their goodbyes. Troth joined him minutes later, standing in front of one of the photos on the wall: a husband and wife, a pair of young children. Her face crumpled, pinched, as a crimson flush of emotion colored her paper-white skin brighter than her hair.

"Shit," she said, strained.

Andrew cleared his throat and asked, "Those your kids?"

Her throat bobbed as she swallowed, gathering herself. In her heels, when she turned to look at him, she must've topped six feet; he lifted his chin to meet her eyes. "Yes, I believe I mentioned them once before. The oldest is at Cambridge for her doctorate currently; the youngest would've been your age."

Below them, a door creaked, then shut with a snap. Troth frowned in the direction of the noise, chandelier-light catching on the creases of her face—immediately as remote as she'd been before her brief flare of naked feeling.

"That's the library downstairs," she said. "I'd rather not have guests spilling wine on the family papers, if you'll pardon me."

The nude bumps of her uppermost vertebrae showed above the draped, elegant neckline of her gown as she strode away. On impulse, Andrew slipped his phone out of his pocket and texted Riley: *if that's you leave she noticed.* His inbox held two texts from West and seven from Sam. He descended the stairs behind Troth, jogging to catch up to her fast clip. As her heel touched the final step, the imposing door on the far side of the hall opened to divulge Riley.

With a dazzling smile, academic charm at its full wattage, he said, "Andrew, I was looking for you—Sam's having car trouble and needs a ride. I thought you'd be in there but you weren't, my mistake. Nice library, Dr. Troth, really impressive."

"Of course, thank you," she said coolly and turned to Andrew, laying a hand on his arm. "Will you be going already, then?"

Riley said, "Andrew drove, but if we need to stay longer I can ask Sam to wait."

His perfect amiable mask didn't slip an inch. *Chameleon,* Andrew thought again with admiration. Troth looked between them without a word as Riley waited for a response, not one single bit of unease written on his face.

"Let's go get him," Andrew said. "Dr. Troth, I'll email you the write-up as soon as I finish it. I'm sorry the story wasn't what your husband was looking for."

"No, it's not your fault, it was perfectly intriguing. If you'd spoken to Mark a month ago, before the downturn, his response would've been far more enthusiastic. And you're right, most devil's bargain stories don't treat supernatural gifts as hereditary or landed, that's worth further research," she said.

Civilized chatter and clinking glasses emanated from the drawing room as the trio stood outside the warming boundaries of its influence. Troth's premiere hostess guise had firmly reassembled; vanished were the personal agonies Andrew had witnessed five minutes prior.

She offered them both another manicured smile and said, "Thank you for coming."

On the front steps, the moment the door slammed shut, Riley turned to him with a grimace. He said, "First of all, fuck that creepy-ass house full of *only* white people, Christ. You caught me before I finished, I only had a second, but her library is chock-full of fucked up occult shit, spook-factor top to bottom."

"Huh," Andrew murmured, casting a long glance over his shoulder at the hulk of the house retreating behind them as he strode toward the Supra. "More than you'd expect? I mean, she does research it."

Riley gave another grim shake of his head. "No, I'm talking super bad vibes, dude. Not real surprised she's excited about a weird death curse; that library felt like it'd seen a few of its own. Maybe go on and add her to your list."

25

Does the internet tell me true that your birthday is in two days

Andrew is it about to be your birthday

Andrew

We're celebrating

Save the fucking date

Also are you coming over tonight

Text me later

sam what the fuck

and yeah that's my birthday

Andrew scrolled up and down the message thread as he stalked across the quad to the library. He left the thread from West unopened, the first handful of words visible: *Did you get my email* . . . Troth hadn't invited West to the gathering. Her suspicion was another red mark, though the leap from possible plagiarism to straight-up murder was vast. Missing puzzle pieces lodged in Andrew's throat. The more he uncovered, the less he understood. Before he saw his erstwhile mentor again, he needed an angle of approach.

At the door to the library he slid past an anonymous, scarf-wrapped woman on her way out. Murmuring paper-scented quiet enveloped him. Since his immersion in Professor Troth's terrible, looming mansion and exposure to her corpselike husband, his control continued to creak—his hold on the curse weak and weaker. Eerie potential, for a haunt or worse, pressed at the edges of his head. The revenant was silent for the time being, but constantly biding, never forgotten. The time between hauntings got shorter every time it sank its teeth in. He jogged up the steps to the research floor two at a time, working his legs for the sake of grounding himself in his body.

Fluorescents buzzed overhead. He fit the brass key into the scratched lock of Eddie's carrel and jiggled it to get the tumblers to fall. When he entered the enclosed space, the pinboard of news clippings lurked at his elbow. The curse had picked its last Fulton victim and lured him to his first death, friend in tow as a side dish. Andrew collapsed into the chair to stare at the clippings Eddie had assembled to chart the public narrative of their shared trauma. Faded photos of two tanned boys, summer sons, gazed into the family camera with hapless eagerness.

They'd survived, but not unscathed. The unruly, ghoulish power that streaked through his veins marked him as an heir to the Fulton lineage, more than he ever wanted to be. The haunt seemed determined to drag him over the threshold and make him embrace the curse.

Footsteps approached and paused in front of the carrel; a fumbling metal-on-metal clink sounded as the lock turned over, rattled, and turned once more.

"Riley—" Andrew started.

West froze as the handle slipped from his grip, door yawning open on its loose hinges. A single key with a tiny metal loop-tag dangled from his fingers, carrel number written on it.

Shock and rage exploded across Andrew's body in a blistering wash, propelling him forward to ball his fist in West's cream-pale polo. With a wrenching spin and a shove he forced the other man into the carrel.

"Hey, watch it," West blurted as he staggered against the far desktop, catching the edge on the backs of his legs with a dull thud. Andrew hooked the door shut with his foot. The slam was loud on the quiet floor. "What are you doing here?"

Andrew shoved a finger in his face and snarled, "No, what the fuck are *you* doing here?"

With a pursed mouth, he smacked Andrew's hand aside and edged farther onto the desk, bracing his shoulders on the wall with his knees apart—as far from Andrew as he could get in the enclosed space. His messenger bag hung crooked at his hip, rucking up his shirt.

"Oh, come on. I heard about the get-together at Troth's," West said with a glower of his own. "How'd you like that, her undivided attention?"

"Not much," he said. "But you've got Eddie's fucking key and thirty fucking seconds to explain yourself."

On the heels of a frustrated sigh, West said, "I came to give you something, but you need to hear me out before losing your temper."

"I'm all ears," Andrew said, turning his hand in the air in a get-on-with-it gesture.

"I wasn't expecting to find you here, since you've stopped attending class so far as I can see," West said. He tossed his hair in an agitated shake, though the short fall of locs immediately resettled over his forehead, and shifted in place on the desktop. "I was going to leave a note. Look, I can't put up with your bullshit and hers at the same time without failing this dissertation on timeline alone, and she's just lapping it up from you, this wounded animal routine."

"Fuck you," Andrew said, driven closer by furious instinct.

Sparking temper flared to life at the corners of West's flat-lined frown. He dropped both hands on Andrew's shoulders for a shove, then planted his Chelsea-boot heel above Andrew's knee when he staggered away—holding him at a safe distance despite West's disadvantage. Their mutual vitriol tainted the stagnant air of the cube. West forced him an additional step toward the door. Andrew winced at the sharp spike of pain the heel-edge drove through his leg and retreated out of reach of the shoe entirely while West yanked the clasp of his bag open.

"I took this." He stood at his full height and smacked a notebook against Andrew's midsection. Andrew grabbed his wrist, thumb over the rabbiting beat of West's pulse. Cardboard edges dug into his navel. "But I grabbed it *after* he died. Insurance against Troth and her games, a way to catch her if she stole his work too. Except it clearly doesn't matter one way or another, does it? She'll screw me over regardless."

Andrew released his arm and caught the notebook, letting it fall open in his palm. Eddie's handwriting filled the pages, spangled with bullet notes and pointy asterisks, the top corners labeled with names and dates. The field journal. He tossed it onto the desktop, where it skidded cockeyed to a stop. West glanced at his own hands while he popped his wrist, his jaw muscles clenched. His contrapposto stance at the far corner of the carrel, designed to fit one grown man with comfort and not two in conflict, showed discomfort but no guilt.

"How much did you want him gone?" Andrew asked.

"None of this was about him," West responded. "And it certainly isn't about you."

"Bullshit it wasn't," Andrew said. "Eddie came along and stole your mentor's attention, guaranteeing you another year stuck at Vanderbilt. Now he's dead, and you're standing there with his notebook."

"What's your point? I've returned his notes to their rightful owner." West's voice dropped, colored by guilt. "Though I'd appreciate the consideration if you kept from telling Troth where you located them."

Andrew said, "Forget the fucking notes, West. Out of all these motherfuckers, you're the one person who had a reason to get rid of Eddie. He was in your way, whether you admit that or not."

West crossed his arms, his shoulders dropping an inch. Ragged exhaustion showed on his face for the briefest second. He glanced from the news clippings on the far wall to Andrew's face, but instead of escalating he let the flames between them gutter with an expression of—*pity*.

"Is that what this is all about? You think I drove him to . . . what happened? We weren't even friends, Andrew. How could I have influenced Eddie?" West looked sad and resentful as he continued. "It's tragic what Eddie did to himself, but it doesn't have anything to do with me. My world doesn't revolve around him, or you for that matter. Troth's conflict with me predates Ed by years, and is a symptom of a systemic problem in the whole department. My big mistake was sticking with it, thinking I'd be able to put up with her and this institution both, long enough to defend. Have you even noticed that I'm the only Black student in the program? Our issues here have nothing in common, frankly. Troth has miles of give for her white legacy students, but I get the sense she'd rather I hadn't been admitted in the first place."

Given what he'd seen of Troth's parties, her home, and her interactions with them both, Andrew couldn't disagree with West's assessment—but he had been spending so much time with Riley and Sam that he'd almost forgotten the prevailing narrative was suicide. He asked, "Did you take any books, or just the notes?"

The other man gave a short shake of his head. "No, nothing else. I asked for a copy of the key when he passed because I assumed she'd get to it if I didn't. I needed her to drop Ed's line of inquiry so she would focus on my dissertation. She wouldn't do the work herself, so if it was gone, my problem was solved."

Andrew thought out loud, piecing the timeline together, "Then it would've been in your best interest for me to defer, keep her attention off me. Or, barring that, to fail."

"Of course I'd rather you deferred, but that wasn't entirely selfish," West said. "You are, actually, failing of your own accord. My advice wasn't wrong there."

The door handle dug into Andrew's side. He'd relaxed enough to loosen his posture. The whole interrogation left him with one remaining question, though he suspected he wasn't going to get much use out of the answer.

"Where were you when he disappeared?" he asked.

"At home with family in Boston. As in, Massachusetts. I get out of Tennessee the moment I'm free every summer. Sowell called me when he was found, out of courtesy, but I hadn't seen or spoken to him in weeks," West said freely.

The adrenaline fueling Andrew sputtered out, at last, with that verifiable proof. An alibi that big was simple to confirm, so he doubted West would lie, and the tale he laid out gave him no reason to. The sense-memory of careless strong hands toppling Eddie's corpse into the trunk stung him, and Andrew rode ghostly shotgun toward the old oak tree. West shifted on his feet, fabric-on-fabric rustle breaking their silent reverie.

"I'm done with mentoring, all right?" West asked. "She forced me to keep after you, but we're done."

"All right, fair," Andrew agreed, picking up the missing notebook with the sour edge of disappointed expectations.

West stepped past him, pausing to rest a hand on his shoulder in comfort. He said, "There's no shame in quitting if you're struggling. I'm sure you're beginning to realize how goddamn unwelcoming this place is, no matter their public image. If I'd left sooner . . ." He trailed off. "Well, no telling what would've changed for me. Get out from under her thumb, Andrew, and don't let her use your labor."

Andrew shrugged his hand off and leaned on the desk corner to allow West to pass. He swung the door closed behind him with a resounding click of finality. Andrew had lost his only suspect, for the most mundane of reasons. It might be life or death for West, but Troth plagiarizing Eddie's work wasn't a problem he cared about.

He dropped into the rolling chair and buried both hands in his hair. Skeletal fingers laced with his in the knotted mess of his curls. The whisper of his name drifted through the air like dust. The phantom draped over his crumpled form, offering the relief of an ice-bath after a distance run. He'd been expecting a visitation for so long, the real thing was anticlimactic; he shook the haunt off, standing through the churning cold, and set off from the carrel with notebook in hand.

Music greeted him at Capitol when he entered through the back door, echoing from farther in the house. He stole a few gulps of juice from the container in the fridge door, fruit punch with questionable relation to actual fruit.

"West wasn't even in the state last month," Andrew announced as he entered the living room.

Riley looked up from his book, fingertips marking his place. Notes and texts littered the couch and coffee table in a semicircle, most pertaining to his actual coursework. His phone, facedown, blared *Get Stoked On It*. Andrew braced his hands on the doorframe above his head for a necessary stretch. The left shoulder popped.

"He's not going to mentor me anymore, either," he said.

"Well, fuck," Riley said.

Andrew flopped lengthwise over the arm of the empty couch, legs propped up at the knee. He felt like a starter that wouldn't turn over, coughing and whining and straining, fuel lines flooded. The research explosion bracketed Riley off on the second couch, but he leaned over to tousle Andrew's hair, one firm ruffle that contained a comfort words couldn't begin to provide.

That made it easier for Andrew to admit, "He did steal the field notes, though. Gave them to me this afternoon, had it out with him about the whole thing."

"Holy shit," Riley said, startled. "Well, damn, hand them over—what are you waiting for?"

Andrew heaved himself to sitting on the couch, grabbed the journal out of his messenger bag, and threw it to Riley. While his roommate fumbled to catch it, he covered his face with both hands, pressing onto his orbital bones to relieve a building stress headache. Continually smashing himself against walls—picking up a clue here or there, reaching dead end after dead end—had drained him to the point of surrender. Pages rustled on the other couch.

Riley said, "His Rolodex is the final few pages, looks like."

Andrew executed a combined roll and bounce onto his stomach, sticking out a hand for the journal. He skimmed the list of names, addresses, and phone numbers with a quivering chill, each of them a possible contender. Would their interviews rule them out? Page numbers correlated to each person, a total of twenty-three participants including the last addition, Lisa McCormick. Andrew paged to the right spot and found a blank page. Eddie had begun the entry with her details at the top, then added a big, fat asterisk that said *review the Gerson first to compare, schedule 8/9??* His immediately preceding annotations were, judging by a fast skim, from an interview with one of Sam's customers that was mostly about the *Blair Witch Project*.

"Another reference to the fucking monograph," Andrew said.

Riley stole the notebook back with a frown and did some paging through of his own, nearer to the front. Andrew watched him chew his thin lower lip, incisors peeking out along with his front teeth. His brow furrowed.

"I figured," he said, turning the pages toward Andrew.

The notation at the top said *Jane Troth (follow with Mark [Troth??] later)*.

"She said he interviewed her about her family shit early on," Andrew confirmed.

"Dude, he only filled a page and a half on her, they barely talked about anything," he said. "That strikes me as a little weird, yeah? Given her goddamn cursed house."

"Noted. You want to add reading those interviews to your helping-hand research?" Andrew asked—offering him an opportunity to assist them that wouldn't put him out in the field, a minor concession to Sam's demand.

"Sure, I guess." Riley gave him a confused look, as if he wanted to ask *why are you not more excited about this,* but the thought of reading a whole book of Eddie's handwritten ghost stories made his skin crawl. "Wanna smoke?"

"God, yeah," Andrew said.

Riley peeled a page flag from the minuscule dispenser to keep his spot and disappeared upstairs. While Andrew waited he texted

Sam, *crossed out the one real lead I had*. Professor Troth and her husband spooked the shit out of him but, given her rail-thin build and his state of illness ten weeks or so after Eddie's death, neither of them were prime candidates to handle Eddie's six-foot-plus frame, even after he bled out. They could be connected, but how? Missing pieces taunted him, twisted him up on himself. Riley's bare feet slapped the wood of the stairs as he returned, blunt in hand, and blew smoke in Andrew's face. He breathed it in and let Riley stick the blunt in his mouth, lopsided. Filling his lungs with sweet, weighty burning calmed his nerves instantly, a fully Pavlovian reflex.

"I'm still searching for a copy of that monograph," Riley said.

"West told me he didn't take the book, just the notes, and only to keep Troth from doing it first." Andrew lifted the blunt into the air blindly and Riley snagged it back from him. "Who else would've known about the book, though?"

"Honestly? Literally anyone who talked to Eddie in that last week. He was running his mouth off to everyone, from Troth to his interviews to . . . whoever," Riley said.

"Square one," Andrew said.

Riley sighed, agreement without needing to agree. Andrew's phone buzzed on his chest and he picked it up to read Sam's response: *I'm off tonight, you're off every night, let's get the boys together.* A text alert cut through the music from his roommate's phone a moment later. He tipped his head back and their eyes met. Riley smirked, knowing.

"Sam?" Andrew asked.

Riley checked his phone and said, "Yep."

fine, he texted back.

Star-white gas station lamps threw bottomless shadows between the gaudy finery of the waiting pack. Andrew circled his thumb around the knob of the Supra's gearshift as he coasted on neutral into the space between the WRX and the Mazda, conspicuously unoccupied. The interior of his own car was almost alien to him, stripped to its necessities aside from the red LEDs he'd added aftermarket. Compared to the broad bulk of the Challenger or the spacious interior of Sam's altered WRX, his Supra molded around him like a second skin. He pulled the brake and slid out.

"Nice seeing you, princess," Sam called out.

Andrew flipped him off with a casual turn of the wrist and went inside to grab a bottle of water and a candy bar. Standing at the register, he stared out the ad-laden glass doors at their cars. He marked Luca and Riley and Sam and Ethan first, the rest second, far less material to him. A bare handful of weeks ago he'd run into them here, at this same gas station, knowing nothing but that he might punch Halse across his smug mouth at the first wrong step. Now he knew their faces, their habits, and in the case of the cousins, had begun to form something that felt like ease. His wrapped Supra fit in perfectly between their cars, right at home, oozing red to mauve to purple in the washed-out light.

"Three fifty-nine," the cashier drawled.

Andrew paid him in singles. The door jingled cheerily overhead. He glanced for the blacked-out prowl of the Challenger, from habit and a different hunger, one that would remain unsated for as long as it lingered. He was about to turn twenty-three, and Eddie wasn't going to see it happen.

"Let's go," he shouted to Halse as he strode past his bumper.

Luca and Ethan hooted in response, dropping into their cars. Riley cussed at him good-naturedly. Through his tinted passenger-side window, he saw Sam toss him a sketchy, kingly wave before his engine turned over. His phone buzzed with a group text, Halse and Riley and a handful of unsaved numbers, that read simply *Roll on 65*. The Supra leapt to life under his heels and hands. He was first to back out, the WRX falling in behind him, and he led pace to the on-ramp outside the neighborhood.

In his rearview the pack spread out behind him, late-night traffic sparse and the long stretch of lanes as close to abandoned as I-65 ever got. Andrew wasn't used to leading a crew. He plugged his phone into the aux, spun the volume knob high. A filthy grinding bass loop pulsed from the lightweight speakers. The WRX rolled up on his left, revved aggressively, lurched ahead a length, then fell flirtatiously to his side again. Andrew lifted his tattoo to his mouth for a good-luck kiss, unseen and free to follow the instinct.

His MPH climbed as the Supra plunged through to fifth gear on a spear of adrenaline. To his right, the purple Mustang over-took him briefly before getting sidetracked in a game of chase with the other Supra, splitting off from the group and merging to the last left lanes on their lonesome. He ignored their reflections in his side mirror, focused on Sam pacing him as the speedometer continued to rise. Andrew's anxious heart kick-tripped in his chest, woken from the disappointed stupor that dragged him under after his confrontation with West. Ahead, a semitruck's taillights approached at speed. Nudging the wheel ghosted him onto the shoulder, illegally passing the trailer to the right, abandoning the lane beside the WRX for a brief moment.

Cut loose, Sam blazed past the semi. Andrew growled at the provocation; his tach climbed closer to the red six. Sam bumped his brakes to allow him to return alongside, teasing, testing. *Princess,* Andrew heard in his head, the best sort of hateful—dripping with challenge he gleefully accepted. He and Sam Halse hadn't faced each other on the road since their first time, that death-taunting hill sprint with the oncoming headlights in his eyes. That night, he'd allowed Sam to drive off toward the horizon without him. To-night he intended to follow as far as necessary. The endless throb of *missing Eddie* kept on pulsing, but as he paced Sam in a pavement-eating game of tag, the pain banked a fraction.

At least until his engine temperature rose past the warning line. He laid off the accelerator with a swear, downshifting while he coasted closer to the speed limit. Quashing his fears, the WRX fell in line alongside instead of tearing off into the sprawling night. No one else hung behind, leaving him and Sam in the dust of their taillights, alone together. Andrew signaled for the next exit, unsurprised that Sam followed him to the first gas station he found. He climbed out beside a fuel pump. Sweat stuck his shirt to his chest. The air-conditioning wasn't working, and the engine running hot rendered the car a sweltering oven.

"Sup?" Halse said from the pump opposite, seat belt unbuckled and leaning over his console to brace his hands on the passenger windowsill. "Got trouble or just need gas?"

"Overheating. Where'd our associates get to?" he asked.

"Well, three of them probably had enough foreplay and decided to go fuck each other, ideally not in my house," he said.

Andrew rolled his eyes and popped the hood of the Supra. "I'm going to let this cool off. Smells like burning oil."

"Hey," Sam said.

Andrew leaned against his rear bumper. "Yeah?"

"I got something planned for you tomorrow, so don't disappear on me."

A mom in a pickup truck pulled up behind him, two kids hollering in the back seat. Their conversation paused. She clambered out of the truck and cast them a judgmental, hassled look, proceeding to viciously input her zip code at the credit card swipe. Andrew braced himself on the WRX's open passenger window as Sam sat back into his seat. The inside of the car smelled ripe and inviting, musky with weed and the scent he was starting to think of as Sam.

"What is it?"

"A surprise, birthday boy," he said, quieter than Andrew expected, smiling.

His throat worked around a dry swallow, suddenly parched. "All right."

"I got work in the morning," Sam said. His tank top scooped low on his chest and stretched against his pecs as he rolled his shoulders in a shimmy. "But I'll come over after, around nine. Be there."

Andrew smacked the inside of the door once in agreement and returned to the Supra. When he started it, the temperature gauge read closer to normal. If he didn't act an ass, he'd get home fine. He gave Sam a thumbs-up and watched him roll out, disappearing into the night with the familiar stink of exhaust.

26

Andrew sat on the end of Eddie's bed, working his fingers against one another, thumbs digging into the meat of his palms. His phone stuck out from the folds of the comforter. Curtains billowed in the breeze from the open window. The faint crispness of oncoming fall lingered in the gust of cool air. Summer's end. Nights that felt open with possibility, weather for a hoodie with the sleeves rolled up, cigarettes and bourbon to fight off the hint of winter rolling in from the north. It came earlier in Columbus. For his twenty-second birthday he and Eddie had gotten kicked out of four bars in succession and ended up unconscious in a stranger's yard, three-quarters of the way home. Freezing dew and predawn light had woken him, dappling his eyelashes. He found his phone, wallet, and keys in his snapback turned upside down like a bowl at his elbow. Eddie's leg, thrown over his shins, had cut off the circulation to his tingling feet. One of Eddie's hands had rested on top of his head, gripping his hair loosely; surrounded from all angles. He'd lain there, listening to Eddie breathe in his ear wheezy and slow, for an extra thirty minutes. He'd only woken Eddie when he started to shiver in his jacket.

A text alert lit up his phone.

Sup?

home

Good, stay there

Andrew stopped in the bathroom to piss without closing the door—Riley wasn't home. He brushed his teeth without inspecting himself in the mirror. Worming, suggestive tension knotted his muscles. Was Sam going to take him out, like Eddie had? He hadn't gone to a bar in Nashville since he'd moved. He spat in the sink and grimaced at the streaks of pink from his gums. He needed less coffee, more food, less liquor. The house murmured creakily as he descended the stairs.

"Don't, thanks," he said out loud. The sounds settled.

He wasn't sure if he'd rather that be a product of his imagination or not.

Scrolling on his phone passed the time as he fought to tamp down the swelling tide of memories and miseries. The kitchen door opened and shut. More than one set of footsteps came in.

"Happy birthday," Sam yelled.

The fridge opened. Glass clinked on glass. Sam rounded the corner with the tall woman from his party at his elbow. She grinned and waved before flopping next to him on the couch. Andrew glanced from her face to Sam's as he sat on her opposite side and passed them each a beer.

"Hi there, name's Irene." She took his hand in an awkward shake. Her skinny jeans hugged her thighs and a side-slashed cutoff revealed a neon green sports bra. "Nice work at Halse's little get-together, by the way, we all appreciated the show."

"Sure," he said, confused.

Sam tipped his beer in salute. "Irene and I were chatting about it being your birthday."

Her arm looped around Andrew's shoulder with a casual masculine grace, sneaker nudging against his. Sam wormed his arm between her back and the couch to rest his fingertips on the patch of bare skin between Andrew's belt and shirt. The small proprietary touch connected the three of them on one plane of contact.

Irene swigged from her beer and said, "Don't get the wrong idea, I'm very much not Sam's birthday present to his buddy."

"Then what's going on?" Andrew asked while Sam's questing fingertips wedged into the gap at the waistband of his jeans.

Irene laughed a husky laugh as she placed her bottle on the coffee table, then angled herself to press one cute, firm tit to his arm and her mouth to his ear. "Sam kept mentioning his hot new bestie to me, and maybe he also mentioned how bad you needed some attention. I'm a fan of threeways, plus it just so *happens* to be your birthday. We're all consenting adults."

Andrew dropped his arm out of the way as Irene swung a knee over his lap to fit her narrow, muscular frame neatly on top of him. No longer trapped behind her, Sam's hand ventured beneath Andrew's shirt, sliding over his rib cage until his middle finger brushed the edge of an areola. Andrew's lungs seized in his chest, forcing out a breathless grunt; Sam dug that fingernail into his nipple while Irene caught his chin in hand to kiss him. Weight pinned his thighs and steady hands forced his shoulders into the couch, her tongue in his mouth searing hot. His eyes shut without his permission.

The sofa springs creaked under the first testing grind of her hips, pressure sliding over the bulge of his trapped dick. Sam cupped the base of his skull and crossed one foot over his to pull his legs open with one hard jerk, startling a moan out of him into Irene's mouth.

"Oh, he likes that," Irene growled.

His hands floundered for a place to rest. The cushion skidded with a leather squeak under his palm; the other hand twisted in the hem of Sam's shirt for a lifeline. He'd held on like this before, but he'd never been so aware of the reason. Now he was starting to understand where the instinct to grab for Sam came from, and the resulting vertiginous swoop in his belly. Del's calm accusation played through the base of his skull, *I'm a person, Andrew, not a stand in for something else*—and then Sam tugged on his hair.

"I heard this was maybe your thing," Sam murmured against the side of his neck, closely eager. The thumb he dug into Andrew's pulse point said *control*. "I owe Riley a beer for guessing you right."

"Me too," Irene laughed breathily.

"Wait," Andrew grunted. She paused when he pushed at her legs.

"You okay?" she asked as she lifted her body off of him—furrowed brow, kiss-wet mouth glistening.

"No, let me up," he managed, pitch cracking with panic.

"Hey," Sam said. Irene scooted onto the couch arm. Andrew stumbled to his feet, banging his shin on the coffee table and tripping over Sam's legs. The memory of Sam's grip tingled across his scalp as he grabbed the banister and mounted the stairs in a frantic bid to get away.

From the living room, Sam said, "I gotta handle this—sorry, dude."

With no small measure of irritation, Irene replied, "No worries, but maybe ask him beforehand next time. Call me, or whatever."

Two bounding footsteps thumped the hardwood behind him and a hand caught his wrist, lurching them to a stop in the stairwell. Andrew snapped his arm to the side to yank loose from the grip. Momentum and desperation collided, along with their knees. Sam crowded him into the corner of the landing, his concerned, breathless expression half in shadow, lit by the small window onto the side alley. The kitchen door slammed. Cinders of need burned savage at the base of Andrew's throat, where Sam had spoken to his skin, glanced against him with his lips. The hand on his wrist slid up his forearm, past the tattoo, to settle around his bicep.

"What's wrong," Sam demanded, hoarse. "Tell me what's wrong."

Andrew lay his forehead on Sam's collarbone. Sam went still, his breath stirring the hair over Andrew's ear. The solid, undeniable strength caging Andrew against the wall provoked a stunning hunger, and his shirt smelled *good,* smelled right. Andrew arced against the wall to shove his whole body onto Sam's, sinking his teeth with moderate force and immense desire into the join of his neck and shoulder. The reaction was instant: a thigh forced between his legs, Sam's startled grunt in his ear. Firm muscle filled his mouth as he clamped his jaw and moaned at the taste, salt and skin. Sam grabbed the longer hair at the crown of his head and pulled; the burn raced across his scalp. Andrew ran his tongue-tip over the divots his teeth had left, the other man shifting restlessly against him from head to toe. Nothing from the past, here, no steps to retread—the fresh lightness of that almost made him laugh, but instead he gripped Sam's outside leg and slotted their bodies together. The unmistakable swell of dick pressed at the vulnerable notch of his hip and, before he had the chance to second-guess the fire burning at the pit of his spine, he reached between them to grab hold through rough denim. One careful stroking squeeze mapped the width at the base, partway to hard, filling his palm full.

Andrew smothered a reflexive groan in Sam's T-shirt. That, too, felt *good.*

"Holy shit," Sam whispered against the side of his head. His sneakers chirped on the wood as he moved into a better angle. "Fuck, Andrew."

Sam bent his knees and hitched Andrew's leg to the side to grind against him. The maneuver compressed Andrew's hand, wrist bent at an angle and knuckles bruising his own hip bone. Sam's shoulder clipped his chin. He tasted blood from his own pinched tongue. They struggled together, rough-edged, with the explosive purpose of a race or a fistfight. Sam worked his hand past Andrew's belt and underwear. His calloused palm and sticky, dry grip were more than enough after so long untouched, and for the first time, like this. Andrew lost himself, frantic gasping in the stairwell, fucking without finesse into the tight hole Sam made with his fingers. As he came he caught Sam's bottom lip between his teeth, moaning. The small cruelty melded into a sloppy kiss. Stubble scraped his philtrum. Sam made a voluptuous, aching sound into his mouth. The inside of his head rang clean and clear with shocked delight. Sam dragged his hand out of Andrew's jeans, smeared with his come, and the sight of that glistening mess made his dick twitch again in his tacky briefs.

"More, get to the bed," Andrew demanded, high on the rush.

Sam steered them to Riley's door with a ghost of a laugh. A cramp of guilt twisted inside Andrew then disappeared quick as it came. He wasn't going to do this in Eddie's bed, and even his own bedroom was a gift from Eddie. The release that cracked his sternum was a consummation of a long-held urge, but not a replacement for anything. He hadn't known how bad he'd wanted this, before, but—he guessed he *had*. Sam was alight with matched, devastating need under the moonlight streaming through the windows. He stripped the comforter from the bed and pulled his shirt off behind his head, one-handed. The developed muscles of his chest and stomach, cushioned by a layer of inviting softness, drew Andrew closer, desperate to touch without restraint. He planted a damp palm over the dusting of hair on Sam's belly, breath shallow.

"Made you come in your pants like a teenager," Sam said.

Andrew grabbed his ass, digging his thumbs into the swell of muscle at the top of Sam's glutes, then said, "Shut up, Halse."

The second time he kissed a man, he meant to do it, reeling Sam in with the grip on his ass and catching his thin lips. The arm that went around his waist forced him onto his toes, a bear hug that made him feel scared and turned the fuck on—something about the rarity of being smaller, though not by much. The pair toppled onto the bed, Sam rolling him onto the bottom of their clinch like he had in the woods and manhandling him out of his shirt, undoing his belt.

Sam knelt above him, looming. No mistaking how hard he was at this angle, the fat swell of his cock bulging at the thigh-seam of his jeans. Andrew palmed the length, groped at the heat of his balls through the denim.

"You're fucking thirsty for it, huh," Sam said with a laugh and grabbed his hand, holding it in place to grind into the grip suggestively. "Done any of this before, Andrew?"

"No," he said, shifting to skim his own pants off while Sam did the same, racing against his clamoring fear of the immensity of the moment. His briefs were soaked and slimy; he tossed them off the bed and adjusted his cock, stuck at the uncomfortable period between soft and hard. "Have you?"

"A few times," Sam said with a wicked smile, batting his hand free and closing a big, hot fist around Andrew's package.

He flexed his fingers in a rippling squeeze. Andrew yelped, hips jumping with streaks of painful pleasure, overstimulated. Sam had his underwear on, and Andrew fumbled for it, tugging the band down without finesse. His dick bounced free. He hesitated, ankle knocking against Sam's shin, unsure of where to move.

"How do you want it, then?" Sam asked.

"Fuck, I don't know," he said, staring. He swallowed, hyperaware of his tongue, his spit, all the porn he'd ever watched in his life. "Put it in my mouth?"

Sam lay on his back and pulled him, gripping hair and shoulder, down between his legs. "Do what comes natural, then, princess. Unless you want me to fuck your pretty face?"

"Jesus, god," Andrew muttered, shaking, so *hot* it hurt to breathe.

His hands mapped out the velvety-slick length, base to tip and carefully down again, tracing a path for his mouth to follow. Sam was uncut, extra skin he didn't entirely understand how to maneuver. The hand around the side of his jaw offered a helpful guide, and he went down, thinking for the briefest, sharpest moment about first times and lost chances.

———

Birdsong and skewed covers greeted him in the morning, like a movie scene, alone in his roommate's bed. The fitted sheet was strangling him. He sat up and considered the mess of his scattered clothes, the washcloth dried out on the hardwood floor, his nakedness. He snorted a slightly hysterical laugh and rose from the bed. His calves cramped at the press of his feet on the floor; he stretched through the pain. Noise from the kitchen filtered through the vents, a running sink and music. In the shower he catalogued the bruises that bloomed across his ribs, the odd passion of a bite mark imprinted over his knee, the raw soreness on the inside of his lips. His cock, chafed tender. He expected to feel ashamed, or frightened, or like he didn't know himself. Instead he floundered in a curious free-falling simplicity, almost pleasant.

The fact that his clothes mostly lived in trash bags in the foyer remained an issue. He came downstairs with a towel wrapped around his waist. At the base of the steps he stopped. Sam stood shirtless in last night's boxer briefs, washing dishes, suds to the middle of his forearms. His tan highlighted the massive, tooth-bruised hickey on his neck. Though he glanced over, he let Andrew take a quiet minute to catalogue him without interruption, from shorn buzz cut to the dense swell of his biceps to the faint roll of flesh at the band of his underwear. He had unexpectedly bony, large feet.

"You good?" Sam asked.

"I think I am, yeah," Andrew said.

He knotted the towel secure. Sam's posture held an uncertain wariness, which he supposed was natural, given the circumstances. Andrew fortified himself with a held breath and cupped his hand around the other man's waist, nakedly intimate. He closed the remaining distance to lean deliberately against Sam's broad, inked back. The catch of his left nipple against skin hurt, but a sweet sort of hurt, sore from thorough abuse.

Sam said, "I'm waiting for you to flip out, but I'd rather you didn't."

"Haven't yet, think we're in the clear," Andrew mumbled, partially joking.

"Good," he said, packing the word with expectation and vulnerability, far from on-brand for his provocative kingship.

Andrew inhaled again. He was twenty-three, Eddie was dead but lingering, and he'd fucked his friend Sam. *What next,* he thought once more.

The door croaked open; a comedic stillness swept through the room. Sam dropped the glass he was washing into the water with a plop.

"Oh Jesus, Mary, and goddamn Joseph," Riley said.

"You're not even Catholic," Sam replied.

Riley passed them with his hands over his face and stumbled up the steps.

The quiver in Sam's shoulders evolved into sniggering laughter. He leaned into Andrew and whispered, "Five seconds til—"

"Get the fuck out of my house, Sam!" Riley shrieked from his room.

Sam cackled with childish glee. Andrew ignored the reflexive burn of dampness that sprang to his eyes at the domesticity of the morning in favor of the fresh wonder of smooth skin under his cheek, magnetic and allowed. Life coursed through him with each thud of his pulse. He had no idea what he was doing, except that it fit. Sam pulled him apart one notch at a time to release the horror he held under his skin.

"What's your next move?" Sam asked.

Ghosts lingered in the gaps of the house on Capitol, and in Andrew too. Maybe Sam could exorcise some of them without judgment.

"We figure out who else Eddie told about the Fultons."

———

After Sam left with a smarmy reminder that he actually had a job and a brash, smacking kiss to the corner of Andrew's mouth, he'd gotten dressed in the front room. The brief, semi-public nudity in the pool of sun shining through the front windows made his touch-sensitized skin tingle. Listening to Riley thump around upstairs kept the tips of his ears burning. With purpose, he searched the living room for his car keys. A swoosh-thud sound startled him as he dug the Supra's fob from between the couch cushions. When he lifted his head, a blush scorched to his collarbones at the sight of Riley's bundled bedsheets and his underwear waiting at the foot of the staircase.

"If you don't put those in the wash before you leave, I am going to smother you in your sleep," Riley shouted to him.

No response needed. With shaking hands, he carried the bundle to the basement, tossed it in the machine, and escaped to the privacy of his car. Andrew was left alone in his head, Sam gone and Riley occupied. Partial thoughts and images chased themselves across his mind's eye—fighting with West, the list of interviewees to run through, the presence of Troth at the corners of all the spooky shit, the knowledge that Eddie was gone for good, the sour taste in his mouth from failing to brush his teeth after swallowing another man's come. The fact that he was continuing on—that he was changing, as the night before proved, growing past the static moment in time the revenant would always be trapped inside. The phase shifts were all overwhelming, impossible to encompass.

For a moment Andrew considered letting Riley chase down the academic angles on his own while he took a breather to let last night and everything else settle. But shame pricked him the instant he had the thought; if the act itself hadn't been a betrayal of Eddie, putting his purpose aside to wallow in it, selfish and indulgent, might be. Without direction, he set off for a drive. First stop, a Starbucks drive-through; second stop, lunch. His car was one of two in the Chinese restaurant's parking lot at 11:13 A.M. on a weekday. The "open" sign lit above the door read N W S RVING. Dead vowels lay dormant. He stabbed his plastic fork into the carton of take-out lo mein braced between his knees and hung his free arm out the window. Checking his phone revealed that Sam had texted him one time: *Called Irene and she said no harm no foul but not to hit her up again for awhile lol* as if that supremely awkward *lol* had the ability to defuse the real tension.

Fair enough, Andrew thought, stuffing a last bite of noodles in his mouth before tossing the container out in the parking lot. Oily sweetness lodged in his throat. He snagged his iced coffee for a bracing gulp. He had no one to tell about what he'd done—aside from the remainder of Eddie, which seemed like the worst idea. Aching to talk to a person, he sent a text to his mother with a brief message: *All his estate stuff is finished, I have the old house now and am settling in. You need anything?* She answered him as he drove; he snuck a read with the phone held in front of the steering wheel.

No thanks, hon, be safe.

Before the cavern, he'd been close with his parents. After, he'd been close with Eddie. The patterns set between them during Andrew's adolescence—distance, dismissal, without even the conflict of rebellion—held strong. He felt right at home with the cousins and their estranged families; his barely knew him. As he shifted in the seat, his belt dug into the blade of his hip, recalling with a burst of sensation the restraining heel of Sam's hand. Decisions he had made and would make again given the opportunity looped under the surface. Putting aside what it *meant,* desire had come as natural as breathing once he'd gotten Sam's body on his—as if the last decade of his life had been secretly leading to that moment, and when the time came to choose, he had no trouble letting go.

Riley's car was gone when he returned to Capitol. Andrew bounded up the stairs without a pause at the landing, promising himself he'd move the bedding to the dryer later. Eddie's room, stale sheets and old laundry funk, stood unchanged as he stepped inside. Dust coated the secondary monitor and gaming headphones hanging from their stand. The stillness of Eddie's paused life decomposed with each passing week, eaten away as the reality settled in. No one was coming home. The basket of clothes would remain unwashed, the guitar silent, the beer cans moldering. That immensity was the force that drove dogs to waste to death on their masters' graves. Whether he believed it was smart or not, he eased his pressure on the thing within himself, allowing the eldritch inheritance to bleed into the dead air.

If he was careful, then he'd be fine. But he needed to see something of Eddie.

He sat, and the mattress dipped behind him with phantom weight as the bell-toll of his power filled out the form of his ghost. The revenant settled spine to spine with him, stiff against the subtle movement of his breath while the sun loomed high outside. He could feel it inviting him to give more, the weeping edges of its outline chewing at the little taste of *being* he was feeding it clumsily, his barriers trembling against the urge to *let go*. Only one set of ribs lifted and fell; there was no bridging the gap across time, unless he let loose the way he had in the forest or standing over the trunk of the Challenger. An impression of indefinite fingers sieved through his onto the rucked sheets. Ghastly cold settled brittle in his joints. Breath misted in front of his face. As he considered confessing his indiscretion to the remnant, the haunt vanished with an abrupt pop, reminiscent of adjusting eardrums on an airplane.

The fingers of his left hand had gone white with a tinge of blue. He tucked them under his leg to warm and wiped his damp face on his shirt. Once he regained the feeling in his hand, he picked up the ring from the desk, playing it along his palm. Eddie might fade from the world, but he had a handful of things left to hold close. Platinum meant forever; he wasn't sure if he intended his gesture as an apology to the friend he'd loved or a reminder of his responsibility to him. The band slid snug onto his left ring finger, as if made to match the hand Eddie had held on the dorm balcony years before, when he'd been marked a second time.

The moment the platinum met the base of his finger it throbbed a spike of brutal, eldritch strength straight through the bones of his hand; his tenuous control shattered in an instant. The oceanic drag of that power rolled him under from the inside out. He fumbled at the ring but couldn't remove it as blackness ate at the corners of his vision. He staggered to his feet, concentration fractured as his blood throbbed with an answering grave-hungry desire.

Floorboards smacked his knees, the mattress soft under his cheek. Eddie's remnant scraped inside his skull, at once inescapable and immaterial, not as gone as he'd thought. He'd called it out of loneliness, and he was paying the price under the crush of its starvation, its jealousy, its anger. Andrew toppled to the side, a rag doll, confused to see his arm lift without his consent. His fingers hung limp, but his wrist straightened. Ring and tattoo both seethed with the absence of color, as if the specter had wrapped itself around them. His heartbeat skipped and stuttered with painful jolts—then hung at a standstill.

He clenched his fist, or tried to. His fingers remained motionless, arm hanging sore at an inhuman angle. His chest cavity seized, spasming. Looped, distorted sound chewing inside his ears cleared into a toneless repetition of *comehomeI'llbewaiting*. Consciousness fluttered in tatters. With an effort born of fervent terror, he fought loose of the revenant's grip long enough to slam the back of his head against the floor. Color burst in a halo across his vision, pushing at the dark; his arm dropped to his chest. Free for a moment, he heaved a gasp. His pulse kicked sluggishly for three uneven squeezes, then double-timed into a frantic sprint. Blood burned in his veins, coursing with unleashed potential at full tilt. He shoved the gush of energetic *power* into the ground beneath the house and the land past that, ripples like sonar pinging him with impressions of all the bodies of dead things, human and otherwise, scattered for miles around.

That explosive push redirected the river-rushing flow, and he visualized clenching a fist tight inside him, tighter, boxing shut what remained of the seething mass. The buzz faded, haunt dissolving with a shredded hiss into the afternoon sun once again. He rolled over and crawled to the bathroom to run the tap for the tub as hot as he thought safe, wrestling out of his jeans to climb in, still wearing briefs, T-shirt and socks. He spat a filthy litany of curses as he waited for his muscles to unlock in the broiling water. When the shivering stopped, he said to the dead space, "Are you trying to kill me?"

Nothing answered.

27

Hello Andrew,

Have you been successful in your attempt to access the monograph you mentioned? I've been unable to locate a copy with colleagues. Additionally, how is your write-up coming along? I'm eager to read the full transcription of the interview.

—Jane

Hello Andrew,

Thom informed me during our morning meeting that he's resigned from mentoring you after a disagreement over Edward's research materials. I was unaware of your recent absences. Please reach out as soon as possible to discuss your situation. If you need to withdraw and defer, I'll assist with the process; we'll continue with the research regardless, if you're willing.

Please allow me to help you.

Best,
Jane

The third and final email in his inbox from Dr. Troth, time-stamped to 11:45 P.M. from the prior night, was short and simple:

Hello Andrew,

I'm growing concerned, as I haven't heard from you. Are you all right?

—Jane

Sam finished reading and said, "So y'all think something's off about her?"

"Yeah, but him dying fucked her over too," Andrew said.

Sam leaned on the arm of the couch and Andrew sat square in the middle. Rain pattered on the roof. Tested patiences weighted the air in the room like damp humidity. The distraction of Sam in thin sweatpants and a white undershirt, tired from his afternoon at the garage but clean-smelling from a quick shower, dragged at animal parts of Andrew that had lain smothered for months, or years. Bleak longing of another sort bided its time, his loitering shade casting its pall over their shoulders. The lump on the back of his head reminded him of its constant threat. With each successive slip-up his control grew weaker and less efficient; at this point a menacing chill clung to his bones whether he fought loose of the phantom's influence or not.

"What about your lost lead?" Sam asked.

"West didn't do it, he wasn't even in the state. But Troth was using him and Eddie both, so it wouldn't make sense for her to kill him. Eddie disappearing just threw a wrench in her plagiarism plans," he said.

"Now she's getting pushier because she thinks you're going to give up before she gets hers," Sam said.

Andrew sighed. "Yeah, so there has to be someone else. One of those other interviews, or just—something we're totally missing."

Sam hummed his understanding. He wormed his foot behind Andrew's calf. Andrew swallowed and cast a glance to the side. Sam drew one knee onto the couch, letting his legs fall open with his thumb on his waistband. The sweatpants clung to an enticing bulge, and he allowed himself to notice. Andrew's eyes tracked up from that imprint, across the wrinkles of Sam's shirt and the pebbled bumps of his nipples to the divot of his throat, then at last met his welcoming stare. Caught and catching in turn. Thunder rolled overhead. The close call from the day before, his corpse-puppet hand hanging in the air, flashed through him like lightning. His jaw clenched around the impulse to warn Sam about the haunt, the risk he'd taken laying his hands on Andrew, the risk he'd be taking again if that really was what had kicked off the last, nastiest altercation—

"C'mere," Sam said, cutting through his turmoil.

Andrew went, wordless. He ended up crouched over Sam in an ungainly hover, sneakers wedged between the couch arm and the cushion. Sam spread his thighs open to brace across Andrew's, corded-taut hamstrings exerting a sturdy pressure above his knees. His outside heel hooked over Andrew's calf while his other leg stayed pressed to the couch cushions. Andrew planted a hand on the seatback to support himself.

"I'm bigger than you, dumbass, just get in here." Sam tugged Andrew close by his shirt collar, mashing their bodies together. The kiss landed off-center, noses bumping. Front teeth clacked. Sam grunted and moved Andrew's head with a hand on his jaw, licking into his mouth. Andrew twitched with surprised, blazing pleasure. Such simple touches threw him. Sam said, muffled against his lips but undeniably eager, "Yeah, there we go."

The house creaked with the storm. Andrew rocked in an unsteady rhythm, teased with friction but unsatisfied, fed with biting kisses. His hands gripped the couch while Sam's nails dug stinging furrows into the gaps of his rib cage. Pain and desire sparked to a warm burn in the cold hollow of his belly, the cave of loss his revenant had dug out for itself filling instead with life. Sam's hands dropped to his ass for an aggressive groping squeeze at the fat of his cheeks, fingertips pressing at the crease. The shocked flash of heat that bolted through Andrew in response had him choking on a whine. Forget spending the night talking in circles around Troth and the research, getting nowhere, he *wanted*—

A white flash cracked outside the big windows of the living room. The lamp on the table cut out, plunging the room into a darkness that radiated menace. Andrew froze. Sam paused as well, panting in the quiet against his slack mouth. The band around his ring finger radiated a bitter cold he hadn't noticed until it contrasted with the fever Sam stoked in him.

"Andrew," Sam breathed.

Static crackled from the surround-sound system. Sam gripped his waist spasmodically. The porchlight stayed dead. He held his breath. The hissing from the speakers hooked into his ears with the faintest hint of consonance, and a solid spike of pain drove into his head. He reared to a sitting position while static filled the room from end to end. A speaker popped. Sam grabbed his rising left hand and smacked him across the face with the other, as if attempting to wake him from the living nightmare unfolding around them. Andrew yelped, high and afraid.

The front door slammed open, rebounding from the wall it impacted, and the punishing shriek of the speakers cut short. A lamp flicked on to cast its welcoming glow. Riley stood soaked and furious in the doorframe with a bag dangling from his wrist. He bounded across the room, wrenched Andrew's hand from Sam's, and pulled the ring off, only to drop it immediately as if it burned. With a mundane clack, the band fell to the floor. Sam took Riley's hand and turned his palm to the light. A blister marked where he'd touched the platinum. Andrew's finger was hale and whole, unmarred.

"Where in god's name did you get that thing," Riley said, staring at the innocuous ring on the floor. "Can you not tell something is wrong with it? Like, seriously, extremely wrong with it?"

"It was Eddie's," Andrew said.

"Of *course* it was," Sam said.

He struggled out from under Andrew's unresisting form, kicking him in the thigh during his escape. As he leapt off of the couch, away from Andrew, he stepped with careful precision over the ring lying between their bodies.

Riley said, "Get me a towel or something."

Sam disappeared into the kitchen. Riley's clothes clung to him, water dripping from his flattened hair. The rich brown of his roots made a dual-color line in the dye. He held a hand out for the rag Sam passed him a moment later. The remaining tingles of fear and desire faded in the face of Riley's intrusion and Sam's—*disappointment,* maybe anger, Andrew wasn't sure.

"Let me handle it," Andrew said as he swung his legs off the sofa.

"Nah, that's cool, man," Riley said with a distinct lack of enthusiasm. "Frankly, I don't think it should be in the same room as you. Seriously, you can't tell?"

"Just get rid of it," Sam said.

With great reluctance, Riley crouched and scooped the ring onto the rag, which he knotted into a pouch. Sam plucked it from him like a bag of dog shit. He left the room again and a kitchen drawer shut with a forceful wood-on-wood collision. The storm of his displeasure outdid the rain lashing the windows. Andrew shook his head and massaged his temples, a creeping ache settling into the sockets of his eyes.

"Don't play games with him, Andrew," Riley whispered so low as to be almost inaudible.

Before Andrew could respond, Sam called from the kitchen, "What are you doing here so early, cousin of mine?"

The fridge slammed. Riley glanced at Andrew and responded in a raised voice, "I finally got my hands on a copy of that monograph, but Andrew wasn't home when I got back to show it to him and neither of y'all answered my texts. So, I figured he was probably out here with you."

The kitchen light cast Sam in a dull yellow halo, beer in hand and barefoot, as he stopped on the threshold between rooms to regard the tail-tucked pair standing across from him. Andrew recalled their earlier fight in abrupt, scorching detail. He didn't know if Sam had spoken with Riley or not in the interim—if he'd told him to stop looking, after Andrew hadn't said a word.

"You should be glad I interrupted," Riley grumbled.

"I got that ring straight from Jane Troth," Andrew said.

"Table the spooky shit for a second." Sam cut him off with deceptive calm. "I thought we talked, boys. I thought we each had a clear and cogent discussion about risk management. So how'd you go and end up being the person who found that book, Riley?"

"Sam, do we need to do this right now?" Riley said, agitated.

"Yeah, I think we do," Sam replied.

Riley said, "I called around to a ton of used bookstores and libraries, nothing fancy, nothing dangerous. Calm your bullshit." His hand flapped in the direction of the front door, where his bag lay abandoned. Rain wetted the porch up to the storm door, splattering on the glass. "But I did skim through it in the store, and—"

"Fuck you is it bullshit." Sam pointed a finger at his cousin from around the neck of his bottle. "The last guy we know who read that book is dead, and we don't know who the fuck killed him, so I'd appreciate some more caution on your part."

The room tilted on its axis as Andrew put one careful foot behind him after another until he bumped against the couch, taking a seat. Sam and Riley continued their bitter stare-down without noticing his wilting to the side.

Riley argued back, "I'm the only one who *could* have found this book, not that either of you were trying. While I was tracking it down, you idiots were warming up for a really, very, *extremely* bad hookup because neither of you had a clue that ring is, like, cursed. Please don't talk at me about dangerous when I'm taking care of the boring shit neither of you want to handle."

Wrenching, eerie hissing continued to twist and knot in the seams of Andrew's skull. The energy was stymied, but it hadn't vanished from the room. He interrupted the cousins' bickering to ask, "What's in the book? I assume there's something, if you drove all the way out here on the off chance I'd be around when you couldn't get me on the phone."

"So, I don't think the dissertation or his research were the reason someone stole that book from his shit, and I also don't think it's why they killed him anymore," Riley said, irritated expression melting into excitement. "Based on the monograph? I think maybe he was killed for the curse *itself.*"

"What the fuck does that mean?" Andrew said.

"I'm not done with what we were talking about," Sam snapped at them as he took a step toward the couch.

Riley reeled on him and said, "I swear to god, you are not my dad." He stepped up to meet Sam in the center of the room and stole the beer from his hand, knocking a swig of it down. "I told you I'd keep a low profile, and I have been, but this shit is too important for me to sit it out. I'm going to class, I'm teaching, and I'm a straight-A student, so please let me do my thing. I haven't asked you to quit trapping."

Sam jammed his hands into the pockets of his sweatpants. He asked, "What if I said I was going to?"

Riley shouted through his teeth, a gear-grinding sound, and stalked back across the room to grab the bag. He dug the book out and tossed it underhand to Andrew, who had melted into the embrace of the couch cushions under the weight of his migraine. He fumbled the catch, book thumping onto his sternum, anxious anticipation making him shake. The monograph fit neatly into one palm: taupe with frayed corners, the stitched binding loose from the board backing. A bright pink page-flag stuck out at a jaunty angle.

"How about we have that argument again *after* we get him fixed," Riley said to Sam as Andrew opened the book to the marked page. "Because I'm not sure if you're blind or something, but the ghost stuff, it's getting worse. It's like, hurting him."

"I had to dig his ass out of a deer carcass he cuddled up with a couple weeks ago," Sam said. "I think I'm aware of the situation."

"What the fuck?" Riley asked, both existential and specific.

Andrew read: *Elias Fulton is the center of the tale, though differing versions of the story disagree on the specific points of his culpability. There are, though, shared elements: in each version, Elias embraces the curse. In each version, the larger family appear to have agreed he was mad, and to have imprisoned him in their ancestral home. Madness is, after all, often displaced onto supernatural causes. Furthermore, the*

Fulton curse narratives as a whole deviate from traditional folkloric norms in their emphasis on heredity, bloodlines, and land ownership over and above individual fault or hubris. While the element of the supernatural bargain itself is a familiar motif, the nature of the deal shifts across the various tellings available to us. In one version, perhaps the most urbane, Elias bargains for his wife Tiffany Fulton's life, and their descendants are cursed. In another, he bargains for power over her death, with a similar outcome. But in the last, he bargains instead for an affinity to death and to the dying, becoming a sort of sorcerer—and it is in this story that he preserves her life, not by using his gift on his wife, but by sharing it with her and inducting her into the heredity of the power. She is, through a witchcraft that is not recorded, made blood of his blood and inheritor of the curse. It is the transferral that either heals her illness or makes it moot, as a secondary effect.

She hadn't been born a Fulton, and marriage hadn't made her one, but blood had done the job in the end. Andrew recalled the coating of rotten copper that had clung to his gums even as the fire-and-rescue team scooped him up, whisked him from the darkness of the cavern: the reminder that no matter what came afterward, he belonged to Eddie in flesh and spirit. He hadn't asked for that inheritance, but he'd gotten it regardless. His breath lodged in his throat in a wheeze.

"Andrew," Sam barked, startling him out of his spiral.

He snapped the book shut in his hand, face stiff and hot. Juxtaposed against the version he'd gathered from the McCormicks, one shared point stood out: the fact that the curse wasn't tied to the born-and-bred Fultons alone, but wove like a fat thread across their land and their blood, ready to stitch a fresh inheritor in at will—or, maybe, at knifepoint.

"You see what I'm seeing, yeah?" Riley asked.

Andrew nodded slowly, attempting to find the words to summarize. He said finally, "If the curse was just a hereditary problem for the Fultons, none of this would matter, but it isn't. People can be brought in from the outside, and they might wanna be, because it *works*."

Riley replied, "If it's not actually a curse in the 'all bad, no good, oops you made a mistake' sense, but more like a magical inheritance that comes with a price, and if you could pass that power on to someone else consensually . . ."

"Or nonconsensually," Andrew finished. "Someone might be able to force the issue, try to take it from you, if they knew. If they had reason to believe it was real."

Sam shuddered with discomfort and swigged from his beer while the three of them tried that thought on for size. A motive that might've seemed far-fetched weeks ago slid into place with an ugly, neat click in Andrew's head. The specter's constant efforts to drag him into his power made more sense, at least in part, if he was generous to the creature.

"Except Eddie wasn't the only one carrying it, last Fulton or not. And that wasn't exactly common knowledge," he admitted.

"I don't like the fucking sound of any of that," Sam said.

"Of course you don't," Riley snapped. "But what other leads do you have for us to follow?"

Sam held his hands up in deflection. "I didn't say y'all were wrong, it just sounds like some nasty fucking business. And from the outside, I've got to say, I don't like how that professor fits into this mess. She gave you back his ring when she shouldn't have had it at all, if we're being real, and Riley and you both seem to agree there's something off about it. But I thought you said she just wanted his research, like to publish, some petty insider shit?"

Riley and Andrew regarded each other, separately parsing the same set of details and implications. Riley said first, "I'm not so sure about that anymore, but it doesn't add up either way with the other shit we know about them."

"Like, neither of them, Troth or her husband, would've been strong enough to handle Eddie's body at the end," Andrew said.

"There's got to be someone else in the picture with them. We need more information."

"Their library was a trip though, and she keeps popping up. Plus, how much do you really know about the husband? Even if he's sick right now, maybe he wasn't as bad off over the summer," Riley said.

Andrew grunted his agreement, turning the monograph between his palms while he wracked his aching brain. Eddie had found his answer, though. The pinboard of articles on their disappearance in the carrel, the haunted-house stories, the cemetery visits and late-night communions with the dead; all of that mess led him to one long paragraph in an old monograph. He'd worried at it like a sore tooth until he unearthed the rotten core. If Troth's interest was more than academic—

"Wait," Andrew said. "Was there more in this, like about *her* family?"

Riley cocked his head. "Uh, I dove straight into the index, read that Fulton bit, and booked it over here to share."

"She talked up that fuckin' library being full of her family's stories, and you said it was massive—but when I mentioned this one book, she and her husband both pretended not to know shit about it," Andrew said while he paged through the index.

Damp, aged-paper stink wafted off the print; he ran his thumbnail through the T section until he saw *Troth, 32–41* with a series of subheadings: *plantation, witchcraft, ritual magic, Civil War, genealogy.* Ten pages in such a short collection meant a full chapter, a significant fraction of the material. What were the odds that she and the rest of her predecessors had missed out on the monograph for the last sixty years? It was circumstantial, but joined an increasing pile of bad coincidences surrounding her.

Unless her concern wasn't the research, as Riley suggested, but getting at the curse.

"Can I ask you something?" Riley murmured, splitting the tension.

Andrew lifted his chin and found both cousins watching him, one sympathetic and the other upset, with the same flat set to their mouths. His incisors had marred Sam's neck with their imprints; a matched pair of thumbprint bruises sat at the upper notch of his biceps. He'd put those there when he grabbed on for dear life. He remembered how his vocal cords had cracked on a startled sound he'd not made before.

"Okay," he said slowly, holding Sam's judging stare.

"If he passed the curse on, like you implied, you're the . . . carrier, I guess?"

"No shit," Andrew said.

"Then I think maybe we need to go out to Townsend, to *your* estate," Riley said.

"No chance."

"Hear me out." Riley paced closer with cautious deference. Sam crossed his arms. Riley laid the back of his hand on Andrew's forehead, swaying on his feet with his brow scrunched like a television psychic. After another second passed he let his hand drop and continued, "I'm not hot shit at the sixth-sense stuff, but that thing is eating you alive. Your aura is like a broken bone, it hurts to look at, and it's getting worse all the time."

Sam lowered himself to sit on the other end of the couch and wedged his foot under Andrew's thigh. With them crowded in close and human he breathed easier, the atmospheric pressure crushing his chest lessening by degrees.

"It has gotten worse," he admitted.

"What if it's getting worse *because* you're ignoring the whole thing? You could embrace it, like the book says Elias did, and get control," Riley said with an animated gesture toward the hills outside. "We go to the old place, you commune with the land or whatever needs doing to set all the broken parts whole, and then—maybe once you've got your death power on lock, you use it to ask Eddie who killed him or something?"

Before Andrew could process the absolute revulsion he felt at

Riley's suggestion, Sam grabbed his forearm and turned it over to show the scabs. "No, fuck no. Look at these. You think asking for more of the same is going to help? The story said this gift drove the Fulton guy off the fucking deep end."

Riley huffed. "I think we're running short on time, and it might eat him before we find out who killed Eddie, so we gotta find a solution that solves both problems."

Getting rid of the curse entirely, Andrew thought, would solve his problem. Eight long summers had passed since the cavern, since his life leaching into the earth with Eddie's blood in his mouth. The poetic circularity was compelling, that the thing he'd avoided at greatest length would continue to be the cause of his worst problems. He flexed his hand. His haunt pushed at him with increasing force, *come home come home come home*. When he listened to it—

Fluttering chill burst to life in his finger bones. Riley flinched away. Muscle and tendon rippled as he rolled his wrist to break Sam's grip. Eddie had written that he felt stronger the closer he got to the land, but that he was still missing something that needed to be set into place. During his last haunt-dream, the revenant had shown him a decrepit estate and a locked room, invited him to pry loose the door. And at the same time, it had tried to stop his heart and had cut his wrists from stem to stern. Embracing his inheritance felt like accepting the grave. Sam twisted loose fingers into the hair at the crown of his head.

"I won't do that," he said. "It's a goddamn trap."

"Fine, shit," Riley said. "Then what's your plan?"

"Focus on Troth, find where her stories don't line up. She's got to be involved," he said, tapping the monograph cover again.

"I'll help," Riley offered instantly.

"No," Sam said. "Absolutely not."

"Seriously, fucking quit that," Riley said.

Andrew leaned forward against the burning grip on his scalp; Sam cinched his fist another fraction tighter, provoking a short, grunting gasp. Sensation helped settle him into his bones again, alive. Riley made an uncomfortable sound, but before he could respond to their affection, his phone rang—a charming melody of bell tones.

He answered with a hostile, curious, "Hi, West, this is Sowell speaking." The frown morphed into a curled lip. He held out the phone and said, "Call for you, Andrew."

28

"I'm in Dr. Troth's office," West said.

Andrew tapped the speakerphone icon and balanced the phone on his palm, saying, "Tell her hello from me."

West continued, "She stepped out for a minute. I tried your phone but no answer. She's pushing me to explain to her what you're doing, and she seems mad. I don't find the tone of this conversation pleasant, Andrew. Help me out here."

Specks of color swam across his field of vision, pounding to the tempo of his heartbeat. He said, "Fuck it, tell her I said I'm going to drop out. That'll get her off both of our backs, won't it?"

"You're sure I should pass that on?" he asked, voice flat through the phone line.

Riley made a violent throat-cutting gesture and sketched a set of negative slashes in the air—but Troth had given him the ring, with its nasty psychic rider. Her eagerness for him to retrace Eddie's steps and report them to her might be sinister, or it might not, but it made her as good a suspect as he had to date. Plus, his radio silence had her pissed enough to involve a resistant third party once again, and that wasn't normal.

Andrew was finished with letting things happen to him out of pure coincidence. He had a trap of his own to bait, this time; if she was involved, she surely wouldn't let him slip from her grasp without a fight. Like she'd said, he was the heir now.

He said, "Yeah, tell her," and hung up.

"Let's get it," Sam drawled.

Riley threw his hands up and said, "What was that supposed to achieve, how are we going to question her now?"

"He's playing the game, trying to provoke her," Sam answered for him.

"If she's pissed, she'll be off her stride," Andrew confirmed. "What, did you expect me to ask if she killed Eddie during office hours?"

"You're going to need me, still," Riley said, gesturing to the monograph on the sofa. "Give me that and I'll start digging into her fucking family, too."

Sam started in with, "I said—"

"Thank you for helping." Andrew cut him off.

The cousins shut up. He dropped the phone and rubbed his face with both hands. If he paid close attention to the air currents wafting through the house, he could feel a faint pulse drag at him from the kitchen. He focused on it and reached his hand out while he tried to grab on to the *strangeness*. Foul, sucking tendrils reached for him through the wall, his own cold, clear power flickering out in turn—or so he pictured it behind his eyelids. On contact, the two ghastly energies skittered off each other. His breath caught at the crawling, clashing sensation.

"Stop it," Riley said, shaken.

Andrew made a fist to cut his clumsy outreach short. Lamplight dazzled him when he blinked the room into focus again, squinting at the pale fright on his roommate's face. Though the ring recognized him, its taste was alien compared to the familiar rot of his haunts. It carried more intention, though he was hard-pressed to explain the difference. He'd spent his whole life repressing the inheritance Eddie had inflicted on him out of careless adoration; using it on purpose was like learning another set of limbs.

"Y'all shouldn't be messing with that shit. Nothing good comes of it," Sam reminded him.

"I don't think I've got a choice," Andrew said.

"He needs to settle the haunting eventually," Riley agreed.

Andrew thumped a hand on his shoulder twice, and said, "Go to class, hold down the fort, and don't draw her attention. Eddie didn't want you to waste your potential either, he'd be pissed if I fucked that up on his behalf. We'll handle the haunting fine."

"Sam hates spooky shit," Riley said.

"Sam does hate spooky shit," the man himself said. "So take me serious this time. Keep out and keep safe. I swear I'm not disrespecting you, Riley, it's just the right choice."

Understanding passed between the cousins for a wordless moment. Riley's concession followed in the form of a shrug, no more. Andrew heaved a sigh and thumbed at the monograph—such a small book for such a big guess to ride on.

He said, working through his thoughts aloud, "West stole his notes, but he said he didn't take the book, and I'm hard-pressed to see a reason for him to lie about that. I never found the phone, either. But Troth said Eddie mentioned a breakthrough to her over dinner, at the same time he supposedly left his ring behind—sounds convenient, huh?"

"So you're thinking, what, he shares his findings and she makes the leap to 'if I murder him I'll get superpowers'? Because I'm not sure that adds up either, it sounds nuts," Riley said.

"Yeah, I don't know, but I guess we'll find out. Wonder how long she'll wait to get in touch," Andrew said. "God, my head hurts so bad."

Sam rose from the couch and said, "Go home, y'all. Night's been long enough."

Andrew hesitated on the couch—he'd still assumed he was sleeping over. When he opened his mouth to ask, Sam bent and planted a hard kiss on his parted lips, then abandoned him in the living room. Riley shifted awkwardly. Andrew grabbed the book and his phone and his stung pride to escape out the front door without another word.

Rain-thick night welcomed him, condensation clinging to his skin. Riley hopped into his Mazda, giving him puppy-dog sympathy eyes. Andrew stood at the open door of the Supra, not ready to leave. He tilted his chin and let drizzle soak his hair, his shirt.

Warm lights glowed inside the homestead. Sam's silhouette passed across the living room windows. Andrew collapsed into the driver's seat and focused all his scattered thoughts on the drive to Capitol.

When he came in through the kitchen door, his roommate was drinking a beer at the open fridge. He elbowed him aside to grab one for himself. In companionable silence, the pair stood drinking, glances half-catching. Riley crushed his can with a refreshed sigh and tossed it in the garbage. Andrew leaned against the table, his free hand braced on the dirty glass top.

"Sam hasn't been, like, serious with anyone before. Just so you're aware. I'm not labeling the thing you're doing with him, but he spends more time with you than he does with me and it doesn't feel casual to, I assume, let him give you your first dick," Riley said. He ran a nervous hand through his fringe, rain-frizzed hair sticking up in all directions. Andrew felt his face go red as fire, mouth open but no words coming out. Riley continued, "He's spent so much time on me he didn't bother with his own shit, until now. He deserves a good thing to happen to him, Andrew. I do like you, but I don't know if you're a good thing."

"I don't either," he said finally.

Riley nodded twice, punched his shoulder with a loose fist, and mounted the stairs to his room. Andrew watched him go. As he lay on the couch with a pillow and his comforter, his phone buzzed with a single message.

> I don't want to share not even with a
> dead man

At a quarter to eleven the following morning, Sam texted *Called in to the garage, omw.*

Andrew tapped a quick *okay* and ate another bite of cereal, seated at the kitchen table with Riley like siblings. He'd expected to wake to an email or five from Troth, but his inbox disappointed him: nothing so far. Of unspoken accord, the cousins were keeping him company instead of going to their respective jobs for the afternoon—just in case she reached out, or to help him figure a follow-up if she didn't.

"I read the chapter on her creepy ancestors," Riley said through a soggy mouthful.

"Yeah?"

"No more fucked up than yours, but that's not saying much," he replied.

"Eddie's, not mine," Andrew said out of habit.

Riley cocked one brow. Andrew crammed another bite of cereal in his mouth for cover, because he knew better—whether he accepted it or not, Eddie had left him all the Fulton wealth and a Fulton curse to boot. On the tabletop his phone began to buzz, rattling the glass raucously. He fumbled for it, not recognizing the number, then answered with a blank "Hello?"

"Mr. Blur," Jane Troth said on the other end of the line.

The paste of cereal and milk almost lodged in his throat as he swallowed too soon, saying, "Hey, hello."

"I apologize for calling uninvited, but there's something I need to share with you and it was not appropriate for our university email server." Strain pulled her voice thin around the edges. "It appears Mark has a copy of the text you were looking for, and more besides, that I wasn't aware he'd collected. I have concerns to discuss."

"What concerns?"

Riley watched him with a hawk's focus, gripping the rim of the table.

Troth hesitated for so long that, without the sound of her breathing, he'd have thought the call had dropped. "I'm worried that my husband might have interfered with Edward, to a degree. Would you be willing to come to the house to speak with me, as soon as possible?"

Interfered was a polite, euphemistic turn of phrase.

Andrew's skin shivered with suspicion. "I could be there in an hour or two."

"Thank you, I'll be waiting," she said and hung up.

Andrew laid his phone flat on the glass, goose bumps prickling along his arms.

Riley asked succinctly, "What the hell?"

"Troth thinks her husband did something to Eddie," Andrew said, slow and testing. "She wants me to come out to her place, said she found the monograph."

"That's too fucking perfect," Riley said.

"The timing is a little much, ain't it?" he said.

"You're not going alone," Riley said.

"No, Sam's on his way."

To warn him ahead of time, Andrew texted:

> she took the bait, said she found the
> book in her house
>
> thinks her husband might have done it
>
> will you come with me to her place this
> afternoon for a chat?

Sure

What a coincidence, her figuring that out

all the sudden

But probably not huh

The instant Sam opened the porch door twenty minutes later, Riley pre-empted his hello: "Let me go with you."

"Dude," Andrew said, clinking his spoon on the rim of his long-finished bowl.

Sam had a cardboard carrier of iced coffees for the three of them balanced on his left hand. The door swung wide, letting the air-conditioning out, while he sat the drinks on the table and clapped a hand on his cousin's shoulder.

"Upstairs," he said, hauling Riley to his feet. "Let's have a chat just the two of us."

While the pair of them tromped up the steps, Andrew paced the ground floor, straightening objects and generally fidgeting with the detritus of daily life that unfolded over their tables, couches, front room floor. From the end table he snagged Eddie's double black-and-red key fob. Two of the keys on the ring didn't fit the doors at Capitol, both cold iron, battered and tarnished. Andrew flicked them to and fro with his thumb, waiting while the murmur of Sam and Riley's low-grade argument filtered through the vents. Keys to the old home he assumed, his full inheritance lurking out in the overgrown countryside, just like the Troth estate he was about to head for.

The coffees sat sweating on the table when he returned to the kitchen, a welcome courtesy from his—courtesy of Sam. Footsteps thumped in the hall above him. Riley said down the stairwell, "You're going to need help once you're there, if she's the one that fucked with that ring. Neither of you is a sensitive or whatever like me."

"Then what am I?" Andrew hollered to them.

Sam jogged down the steps in shorts and desert boots, caught Andrew's waist in one big hand and snagged his coffee from the carrier. The casual touch felt like forgiveness, or an allowance. Riley followed at a more sedate pace and rolled his eyes at Andrew, collapsing onto his usual chair in a petulant pile of tawny limbs.

"You're not psychic, man, you're something else entirely. Especially if that book is right," he said.

Sam grunted, not agreement or argument. The golden, sunscattered kitchen was homey. Nothing cast a real shadow. Andrew picked up his own coffee, paler brown than the two straight black pours, and took one sip. "Has it occurred to either of you that you're not the only ones worried?" Riley asked. He kicked one foot up onto the table. "I'm real worried. This whole time I've been acting as the voice of reason and restraint for both of you, and now you're treating me like a kid trying to eat dish soap."

"That was one time, but it was memorable," Sam shot back with deflecting humor.

"Shut up, dude, I'm not joking," Riley said.

"We'll be fine," Andrew said. "What are you worried she could even do to the two of us, in broad daylight?"

"Arrogance," Riley said, "is not attractive."

"She's a professor, she's pushing late sixties, her husband is wasted to skin and bones, and she has no idea if we told someone where we were going," Andrew said.

"Even so, you're the only one of us who has aspirations, some goals and shit," Sam gestured with his coffee. "I'd rather we triage according to who's got the most to lose."

Riley groaned, "As if you're not worth worrying over, you dick. Text me the entire fucking time, please."

Sam tapped Andrew on the ass with the flat of his hand. Riley barked a laugh at the startled glance Andrew shot him. Sam ducked out the back door before Riley finished chuckling. Outside, Sam spun on his heel and walked backward toward the WRX, maintaining a steady and damning eye contact. Andrew followed, messenger bag thumping against his thigh, heavy with notebooks and the monograph; all of Eddie's research that he thought might be relevant to a conversation with Troth.

Once in the car, Andrew asked, "You sure about doing this with me?"

"Don't say dumb shit. You're one of mine, Blur, and we're going to get you sorted out fine, okay?" Sam said as the engine growled to life.

Andrew shut his mouth. *One of mine*—that had a ring to it, and so did the promise of safety, of being taken in hand. If Riley had tried to slap a label on the thing budding between them, he'd have rejected it out of hand, because nothing encompassed the particular set of feelings he might sum up as *owned*. What did it mean that he found that comforting, still, now that Eddie was gone?

Anticipatory quiet stretched between them as the trip unspooled ahead, interstate spreading out before them with heat-shimmer as Sam merged onto it. After he hit fourth gear, Sam's hand slipped briefly from the shifter to wrap around Andrew's thigh, squeezing once before retreating again. The shape of his palm lay branded there. Spinning thoughts raced through Andrew's head. The trap he'd set had sprung: the professor calling, dangling a morsel to drag him out to her, hinting at knowledge about Eddie's death. He'd made her desperate. Maybe, in that desperation, she'd done some research of her own that had set her on the same trail as him—and that was his most generous interpretation.

"They said her husband's relapse was recent, at the faculty party." Andrew shared the thought as he happened upon it. "Wonder how recent. You think he'd have been strong enough a couple months ago, if he wasn't as sick?"

"Or he paid someone," Sam said. "A family like the Troths would have the money."

Andrew gnawed the edge of his thumbnail, bitten almost to the quick. "I don't feel like this should fall into our lap so easy."

"Nah, but maybe we can use her, if she isn't bullshitting us for her own reasons," he said.

Andrew nodded. A muffled cloak of unreality settled over him as their pleasant sunny drive took them farther from Nashville, mimicking an afternoon excursion. Green forest and fields on either side of the highway were split up with billboards, exits to suburbs and neighborhoods, truck stops with McDonald's attached. Even driving toward the Troth land, so close to Townsend, he had never felt further from the stifling horror of the caverns. A mad part of him wanted to beg Sam to pull over, get out and take in the scenery, have a quick fuck in the dirt and grass.

But he said nothing. The work he'd done, that the cousins had helped him with despite their misgivings and his intractability, crumbled like dry soil through his fingers when he tried to mold it into a logical whole. Looming at the center of a set of jagged spokes sat the curse, connected to the hollers and to the university alike, thanks to Eddie—to study carrels and double-wide trailers and interstates at night. The curse was his and Eddie's bond; maybe it was an answer too, if he found the right question and put it to the right person.

"I got your text last night," Andrew said as the road continued to unspool ahead.

Sam hummed, noncommittal.

"He's dead, Sam."

"I know that. He's not gone, though. Look at us right this minute. Half the conversations we have, he's in them. I was going to fuck you wearing his ring on your wedding finger."

The hot flash that washed over him held discomfort and hunger in equal measure.

"Sorry—" he started.

"Don't be," Sam cut him short. "It's a choice I made, getting in this thing with you, whatever it is. But don't mistake me, I'm not interested in filling in for a ghost."

"You aren't," Andrew said.

Inadequate, but a start all the same.

Sam took the exit suggested by the GPS and Andrew stopped chewing his cuticles, the faint taste of blood in his mouth. After another few minutes of coasting past unoccupied, verdant land, the Troth house rose up at the end of its paved drive, cream and yellow. Less imposing in the daytime, though still grand. The restless dead of the estate lay sleeping under the sunlight. The WRX rolled to a stop in front of the veranda's broad steps.

"Damn," Sam said, an arm draped over his steering wheel to peer out through the windshield. "Big-ass house she's got."

"Come in with me," he said.

"No shit." Sam got out and popped his back, rolled his shoulders. His nervous energy had a feral tint. "I don't trust her."

They mounted the steps all the same, Sam a prowling creature one step behind him. A multitoned, mellifluous doorbell chimed when he pressed the button. The tall wood door swung open mere seconds later, as if Troth had simply been waiting a few feet away in the sitting room for him to arrive. Wearing a lilac sweater with the sleeves rolled up to her elbows, Troth blinked, sun-dazzled, at the two young men on her porch.

"Hello, Andrew. And who's this?" she asked.

"Sam Halse." He offered his hand to shake.

She took it with a professional firmness as Andrew said, "Riley Sowell's cousin. We're planning to run an errand in this neck of the woods afterward, so he came with."

"I understand," she said, stepping aside to welcome them in with a sweeping wave.

"What did you find?" Andrew asked.

Troth's mouth flattened into a frown. Her thin face was bare of makeup and carried a small collection of fine lines and summer freckles.

"Come with me," she said.

Sam glanced at him for confirmation as she turned into the grand hall; Andrew nodded assent. She led them deep into the house, their sneakers squeaking across the polished wood floor. Sam cast Andrew a puckered grimace at the sight of the chandelier overhead. The trio stopped in an extravagantly furnished kitchen with a large Chemex steaming on one marble countertop, coffee silken and almost black in the sun pouring from the bay of windows overlooking the yard. A glazed blue-and-purple ceramic mug sat to one side, prepared just on time, an impeccable hostess despite the circumstances. Troth gestured them to the table and rummaged for two more mugs in her cabinet, looping her fingers through the handles as she grabbed hers from the counter.

"Cream, sugar?" she asked.

"Cream, if you could," Sam said.

His accent thickened when he was being polite, maybe in response to being so sorely out of place in his grease-flecked boots among the finery. Andrew took the seat across from him and rested one forearm on the blond wood while Troth, in her immaculate leisure outfit, poured them each a generous serving. It occurred to him with an uncomfortable shock that he had the funds to step into a life like this, spending afternoons off in a historic home, lazing in the air-conditioning and drinking fancy coffee with cream poured from a tiny ceramic carafe.

Sam didn't. His face telegraphed the fact.

Troth pushed their finished coffees toward them across the tabletop before claiming the seat across from them. She warmed her palms on her mug, glancing from Andrew to Sam. "Are you all right with me discussing this in company, or would you rather we do so alone?"

"He's okay to talk in front of," Andrew said.

Troth nodded and sipped. Andrew did the same. The coffee, hot and bitter, stung his mouth. She was pushing for time, he realized. Sorting her words.

"When his health began deteriorating again, Mark developed a fascination with folktales dealing in methods for staving off death." Her tone approached clinical, gaze resting on neither of her guests but on the far wall. "I understand his reason. It breaks my heart, of course—how could it not? But I do understand."

"And how does that connect to Eddie?" Andrew prompted her.

"I believe the Fulton curse might have been of greater interest to Mark than was good for him, and I was unaware that he and Edward had been in contact without me," she said. "I found books I recognized from Edward's reports, copious notes in Mark's hand. The tone in the notes is not appropriate. I thought you should see for yourself; I'm not able to be objective."

"Okay, I'll look them over," Andrew said.

"In a moment," Troth said. "This is very difficult for me. He's upstairs, sleeping. I can't imagine him harming someone, but I will feel responsible for him if he pushed Edward too far in a fragile state."

Andrew's biceps bunched and his free hand flexed into a fist on his knee under the table. She might be lying or stretching the truth—he didn't doubt she'd do anything to protect her husband. He held his breath to keep from charging straight up the staircase to drag a dying man out of his bed. And he wasn't sure he believed her version of events, either.

Troth said to Sam, "I apologize for the distraction from your afternoon. Do you want something else to drink?"

Sam tipped his mug for a long swallow and said, "Coffee's good, thank you."

"To the library, then?" Troth asked.

"Yeah," Andrew said. He finished the dregs and set his mug on the table. "Sam, I'll be back in a minute."

Troth's tense posture loosened. She motioned for him to follow, and he cut narrowed eyes to Sam as she turned away. Sam nodded as they left the room. Andrew thought he might fare better than Riley at slipping through the vast, underoccupied ex-plantation without being noticed. Troth glanced over her shoulder as she opened the doors to the library, and despite the manicured cleanliness of the house, a crawling grime washed over Andrew. He stepped across the threshold.

It was a windowless room. Lamps glowed white and harsh in each corner, illuminating paired plush reading chairs and three walls of built-in bookshelves. In the center of the room, a glass-topped display case stood—ornate, heavy-paneled, antique. Troth padded across the twilight-purple rug. The corner of the display case held an irregular stack of books with a familiar monograph on top, and as he approached, he saw that the glass protected a collection of heirlooms: combs, a worn Bible, folio-bound papers. A disarticulated set of human finger bones. Mourning hair lockets fizzing with malevolence, an old knife with a pitched aura of darkness seeping off of it. The hair rose on the back of his neck; he braced a hand on the lacquered wood. Troth touched his knuckles.

"My family kept their history close. Mark married in, but it's the Troth name that carries on. I've got quite a collection," she said.

"You found the monograph?" he asked, zeroing in on the book—the one missing from campus, given the library sticker on the spine.

"Yes, and as you suggested, it has much more information on the Fulton curse. Mark must have borrowed Eddie's copy; neither of them told me about it," she said.

He picked up the petite hardcover with numb, tingling fingers. His tongue sat heavy in his mouth. The weight of age and haunting in the room pricked at him, plucking sore nerves, and waves crowded the edges of his vision. His phone buzzed in his pocket twice.

He said, voice thick, "You said there were notes, too?"

"Let me just get them for you." She crossed the room to the far shelving. "I'm surprised to see you're not still wearing his ring, Andrew."

"Still?" he asked with a swoop in his stomach that tipped him against the table. Sourceless sound rushed in his ears. He fumbled out his phone. Sam's text was a garbled smash of letters. Fine shivering in his fingers wobbled the already-fuzzed screen, and the phone clattered onto the glass. His thigh muscles locked, then turned liquid as the carpet rushed up to meet him, fibers soft as silk on his cheek.

"The other one's passed out in the front room," a man's voice said.

"I was worried about the dosage. I didn't expect another guest," Troth said.

His phantom flickered in the basement of his skull, hissing with helpless rage, a miserable, useless warning. Euphoria and terror swirled, disconnected, while his fingers twitched. He grasped the table leg and kicked out, dragging one shoe across the carpet. An attempt to speak came out as a slurred moan. He got his knees under him, forehead still on the carpet and head lolling.

"Poor thing," Troth said.

A gentle shove of her sneaker to his side sent him sprawling. Light dazzled his eyes, fractal patterns that spread and swam. Miasma covered him as her husband crouched alongside and pressed skeletal fingers to the pulse point in his throat. Oncoming death punched through the contact. He blacked out.

29

Static crashed *wake up wake up wake up* onto his eardrums. Andrew's head bobbed on his strained neck. His hands and feet were numb; he sagged against the cord looped around his chest and arms. The seat under his ass was solid, hard wood. Drool slicked his chin and lips. He gagged. Flares popped behind his closed eyelids in starbursts. The brush of spectral fingers on his jaw made him flinch against a hard, slatted seatback, skull braced on the wood at an awkward angle. With slitted eyes, he saw his wrists were bound to the chair arms so tight his palms had turned a worrisome shade of maroon. His vision streamed like a ruined watercolor.

"Troth," he muttered in an anesthetized slur.

Sam had followed him into the house. Sam had drunk the coffee out of polite discomfort, surrounded on all sides by wealth he'd never touch. He'd done it all because of Andrew. Coherency fled as chemical disorientation brought more spit to his swollen, dry tongue. He retched. Bile and coffee burned his esophagus, splattered his shirt.

"Andrew," she said from a distance. "You're awake."

He forced the muscles in his face to squint through the throbbing, shifting room around him, a broad open space with a dirt floor, dimly lit, hay and tarps and chain. The sedate breathing of animals.

"I keep horses," Jane Troth explained, as calm as if she'd taken him on a tour of the grounds. Her cold hand cupped his chin, lifting his head; her distant expression wavered in and out of focus as he blinked sluggishly. "Thank you for putting the ring on. I needed to be sure of your role, verify you were the vessel he'd chosen—which

I hadn't expected, or I'd have approached the whole situation quite differently from the start."

Before Andrew mastered his tongue again, she left him with his head lolling under the weight of his skull. A sliding door creaked, rolled, slammed. The specter's freezing palms petted his exposed, scabbed forearms. His unleashed, starving power hooked him to Eddie's specter, but he had no grip over their connection. Drugged as he was, the unstable frequency thrummed uselessly. Nightfall loomed hours or minutes from the horizon. He'd come full circle, back to the kid trapped in a cavern with a broken ankle, waiting to die, best friend in his arms.

But Eddie wasn't his only company, not in this reprise of his nightmares. He pried his eyes open. The gloom of the barn wreaked havoc on his no-doubt blown pupils as he waited for the blurring to resolve. Tilting his chin allowed him to measure the length of the stalls to his side. He froze at the sight of a sprawled body at the far corner. His heart tripped. Sam wasn't moving. His hands lay cuffed in front of him, ankles tied to one of the posts. No one would tie up a corpse. Andrew sipped minute breaths to keep himself from vomiting again.

"Sam," he croaked.

Eddie had left him a mess of clues to follow, but he'd stepped straight into the trap with the same blind confidence that had gotten them to the caverns the first time. Except he'd been the one to drag Sam along with him, unwilling but dedicated, repeating the cycle of his inheritance. The haunt continued to paw at him, cold flecks dusting across his nape and over his throat as if begging entrance. The rolling door opened. Neither Jane nor Mark spared him a glance as they crossed the barn floor together. She laid a canvas bag a few feet from Andrew, then unfolded a nylon tailgating chair closer to Sam. Her husband sat gingerly in it, wearing a thick sweater despite the sultry heat of the evening.

With him settled, she pecked a kiss on her husband's forehead and returned to her bag. Andrew's attention split between the heap of Sam and the woman unzipping a tote in front of him. As she removed a bowl and a set of small, stoppered vials, she began to speak: "I'm sure it doesn't comfort you, but I hadn't originally intended to kill Edward, and I do regret that I'm doing this."

"Then don't," Andrew managed.

Troth's smile was grim. "You're my one chance to keep my partner alive, and I'm finding there are few limits on what I'd do to save him."

"Sorry," Mark contributed with an unnecessarily chipper tone.

She gave him a sour glance and said, "If you would, please, don't be rude."

Silence as she mixed her ingredients in the bowl, kneeling elegantly on the packed-dirt floor. Sunset called to Andrew from a distance, as if reaching through time for him. His bones ached alongside the draining dusk while his revenant passenger whispered another phrase to him, indistinguishable though forceful, before seeping into the dirt with a pulse of communion that reverberated into the soles of his feet. The death-laden earth of the Troth estate was the revenant's home, as much as the trunk of the Challenger and more so than the oak tree in the park. Eddie's blood had spilled here in a corruptive consecration. Ghoul joined ground, and a taste as fetid as rot seized the base of Andrew's tongue. If he were able to draw out another moment, another hour—

"Why did you kill him?" he asked.

"I remember the night when the curse came to life again. It woke me out of a dead sleep," she said. "I dreamed of a black wave that rose up and up and crashed over us all. Both my daughters were crying in their rooms. I saw you two in the newspaper, and I wondered, but when your parents moved you and Edward away I thought I'd never learn the truth. Imagine my surprise when the prodigal Fulton son returned all those years later, searching for answers to his special gift. And then Mark took a turn for the worse, so I made a decision."

"He didn't tell you he was looking for the curse," Andrew said.

"Of course not, but he wasn't careful about the hints he gave me, or suspicious about the interest I showed. A very self-centered young man, Edward."

The drugs were either wearing off or he was acclimating to the dosage, judging from the increased responsiveness of his tongue behind his teeth. He gave silent, hysterical thanks to Eddie's bad habits and his own lack of survival instinct. Troth hadn't planned for two of them, and she wasn't that kind of doctor. He was willing to bet she hadn't accounted for his and Sam's wealth of experience functioning under the influence. She drew a knife from the bag, swirling it through the contents of the bowl. Recognition rocked him at the sight. That edge had bit through Eddie's flesh first. He remembered its touch from his nightmares.

"His power should've passed to me, according to the ritual I researched. I was surprised—and upset—that it slipped through my fingers, that even death didn't cut it loose from him," Troth explained. "The only possible explanation was that Edward wasn't the sole heir, that he shared custody of the gift. His portion escaped the moment I tried to take it."

She laid her knife lengthwise across the bowl to stand, dusting off her knees. He shifted in his bonds but was pinned immobile as she drew her thumb along his tattooed bracelet. He said, "He'd have given it to you if you asked. He'd have helped."

"No, he wouldn't have," she said.

"For good reason," Mark contributed. "I'm alarmed by this whole process myself."

"You share so much with him; I could tell the moment you stepped into my office," Troth said. "You thought you were hunting me, but you were being herded along."

Andrew peeled his lips from his teeth.

"I'll need your cooperation to bond the halves of the curse he fractured, before the ritual will function. I don't have any reservations about harming you, or your friend, more than would be necessary to ensure that I get it. Do you understand?"

"Fuck you," he said.

"I expected as much," Troth replied.

Bowl in hand, she approached him. The substance she'd created was murky, gelatinous, and flecked with dried plant matter. She scooped up two fingers of the oily sludge to smear across his forehead, his lips, the palms of his hands. With clinical detachment, she rucked up his shirt and added a dab above his belt-line.

"Open up," she said.

Andrew stared at her and then shook his head once.

"I will make you," she said.

He clenched his teeth shut and she gave a disappointed sigh—before grabbing his face in both hands and jamming her thumbs into the joints of his jaw. Weak from the drugs, Andrew felt his mouth pop open a fraction. She stuffed two fingers straight to the base of his tongue. The points of her manicure stabbed at his gag reflex. He swallowed convulsively, tongue forcing her nails against his soft palate. She withdrew fast, while he was still reeling, not giving him a chance to bite. The paste clung to the inside of his throat, coarse and stale, after she removed her hand.

"I'm not certain you swallowing is necessary, but I'd rather not skip a step to find out," she said.

"Are you going to narrate the whole thing?" he rasped.

"Yes," she said. "It's soothing for me. I'd rather consider this as theory instead of practice."

This being his murder, he realized.

From across the room he heard a brief scuff and a hoarse groan. The entirety of Andrew's being rocked in Sam's direction within the restriction of his bonds. Troth glanced over his shoulder. The knife dangled from her left hand, smeared with the ritual concoction.

"Keep an eye on him, darling," she called to Mark.

"Will do," he responded.

Sam scrabbled through the pile of hay scraps to roll onto his side with a heaving gasp for air. Andrew strained for him once more, cord sawing at his skin. He cursed through his teeth when Troth knotted a fist in his hair and wrenched his head toward her.

"It's better if you focus on me," she said. "Remember that I don't need him, except to keep you cooperative. You can earn my kindness."

His nostrils flared with the force of his breath. He expected nothing to be revealed on her face—but the pinched frown marring her expression hinted at some internal struggle. She transferred the knife to her dominant hand. The veneer of respectability slipped further for a moment as she tracked her stare from his head to his feet.

"To think that an old bloodline ends here, with someone like you. At least no one will be overly concerned about your disappearance—or his, from what I assume," she murmured.

Helpless rage made Andrew scuff his toes against the dirt, as much movement as he had left, while her left hand took hold of his forearm and spread the skin around his scab with the air of a clinician. The knife pricked pristine flesh an inch above the existing wound. Despite himself he groaned, strangled, as the blade split him open. His skin separated in a searing line as she bisected the scab efficiently, shallower than the memory he'd received from Eddie's specter. Her careful cut overlapped with strong hands that had filleted him to the bone.

Shallower, but more than deep enough. Blood welled and spilled over the pale sick line of white. Her palm smeared through the mess, tearing another unwilling yelp from his chest. She dabbed her tongue to her fingers with a crinkled nose. The spectral chill he'd grown used to rose in undulating spirals around his trapped ankles, rustling his clothes and hers.

"I'll need you to welcome him in, Andrew. Let Edward come to you. I'm surprised you've refused him so long already," she said.

The knife found his other wrist. Andrew tossed his head and

screamed as she cut him again. The pain was intimate. She shushed him out of reflex, squeezing his swollen hand for a split second. Behind him, Sam shouted a blurry invective. Rope creaked. Andrew's blood pooled in the hollows of his elbows, dripped from his fingers. The haunt croaked with renewed desire as it wrapped around his shaking calves, climbed his thighs toward his wounds. The sorcerers in stories all fed ghosts blood to bring them life, and in this version, he was summoner and sacrifice at the same time.

"There we are," Troth said.

She folded herself cross-legged on the ground in front of him. The tributaries of his gore soaked her jeans as she began to chant a sibilant alien language as familiar as his Social Security number. The revenant shade settled inside him, skin with skin and bone with bone, its hands upturned, its mouth panting in mimicry of his own, while Andrew resisted. His heartbeat stuttered, off-kilter. He gathered his ragged control to stem the pour of his inheritance onto the starving ground, holding the power inside, preventing the union of his phantom and his flesh through force of will alone. If she wanted that consummation, he would thwart it as long as he was capable.

"He's struggling. Mark, if you could please make a point for me about how much more unpleasant this could be," Troth said in a normal voice.

"Pocketknife will do?" he queried. She murmured an agreement.

The fabric chair rustled. Troth grabbed Andrew's chin, forcing him to watch as her husband approached Sam, prone and trembling in the barn dirt. Mark knelt with a flip-knife in his hand and laid it against the apple of Sam's cheek. Sam kept his eyes and mouth pressed shut. He made no sound.

"Don't," Andrew said.

"Do as I ask," she said, "and we won't."

Andrew released his fervent resistance with a pop like cracking knuckles. The remainder of the power he'd used to barricade himself gushed into the dirt and the waiting haunt. Without that final barrier holding it away from the deepest parts of him, the revenant rushed in and filled him to the brim. Troth's expression went slack with surprise. She lifted a hand to the air in front of him, grasping at something he was unable to sense through the haze of reunification. He had become a passenger in his flesh, one half of a whole, as he'd thought of himself for so long.

Eddie stretched at the boundaries of his being with a tearing discomfort. Their union was not the pleasure he'd imagined it might be. Andrew's pulse struggled to beat, erratic. The knife glistened in Troth's hand, droplets of *Andrew* plunking to the ground beneath their feet.

The sun set, and the revenant stilled, the taut pause of a predator.

Their inheritance was strong—not Andrew's thought, though it occupied his head. A concentric ripple washed from the site of his unmaking, his possession, through the earth and dust and bones the plantation was built on. The thing that had been Eddie was him, and he had become it as well. The crush of their beings slid home together, filling the gaps and crannies he had left, coursing through his blood and occupying his wounds. The pain lessened in his arms.

"Now give it over to me," Troth commanded.

He remained silent. She drove her thumbs into the meat of his arms; he shrieked again. One of the horses whinnied in empathetic distress. Another kicked the stall. The witch-lights of Troth's own power, some other eldritch thing with its own unwritten histories, set her eyes aglow with desire.

"Fuck," gasped her husband across the room.

Sam snarled with the wildness of a trapped bear. Andrew heard a choked, wet gagging and a thump. Troth glanced up, startled, and her expression morphed into a mask of desperate fury. She released Andrew, scooping her knife from the floor mid-stride. Sam and his captor were struggling in the dirt, the sick man's legs kicking while the handcuff chain sliced across his throat like a garrote.

Sam buried his face into the bony hollow of the man's shoulders as he scratched and slapped, clumsy with loss of oxygen. The nervous horses whinnied and bickered. Troth sprinted across the barn with her weapon at the ready as Sam rolled onto his back, Mark's spasming form shielding his chest and face. He maintained the choke-chain pressure.

Troth grabbed one of Sam's forearms and angled her knife at his unprotected side, but he twisted to slam their combined weight into her, throwing her aim. Her stab skidded harmlessly across the dirt. Three bodies writhed in violent tandem, indistinguishable. The revenant that was Andrew wrested himself an inch left and an inch right, straining at his ropes without loosening them. Troth slashed at the meat of Sam's thigh, splitting denim and skin. His blood mingled with the same earth that had drunk Andrew's, and Eddie's, feeding the growing storm beneath it—and as if called, the rush of death beat through the room like a hundred pairs of wings. Mark had gone limp.

Troth wailed, grasping at her husband's fragile torso as Sam crowed a hoarse laugh. Her hand raised again, knife held high. Sam freed the handcuff chain in time to deflect the blade with a metallic ring, but the tip caught his face on the altered path with a spray of red. Andrew jolted at Sam's punched-out yowl of shocked agony.

He'd never heard someone make a sound like that before. The disorienting wonderment of a fresh kill on the air coalesced with his own frantic need to help Sam. If he'd found the richness of his fully realized power intoxicating before, the added burst of sustenance made him and the revenant feel like a small god in their new flesh. Filmy, auric impressions radiated from Sam—and from Troth, who throbbed with the malevolence of a siren. He recognized the ochre sourness of her magic from the ring, the baited gift she'd used to confirm him as her next target. But, he realized with a grim flowering of determination, she'd made a miscalculation—leaving him unattended, as if he occupied a limited human body.

Ropes weren't sufficient to restrain the thing she'd forced him to become. Troth's knife lifted and Sam fumbled to free himself of her husband's corpse, bound at ankles and arms. He wouldn't get loose in time. The revenant wrapped their starvation tight around the oil-stained vibration of her power, with the same instinct as a python testing the size of its prey.

Eddie's remainder murmured with Andrew's mouth, "She's ours."

The wind that lashed through the barn frightened the horses into a shrieking frenzy as he poured himself into Mark's responsive corpse, now twitching it like a marionette. Things inside Andrew wrenched, and Mark's limp arm flopped up to catch the next stab Troth aimed at Sam's throat. Her knife stuck on bone. He severed the connection and the arm dropped, twisting the hilt loose from her flinching hand.

Compared to the darkness of Troth's void, Halse burned bright as an ember in their unearthly sight. His life was precious; on that, he and the remnant agreed. The doubled creature returned their attention to the viscous sore that was Troth, and Andrew followed his animal instinct—allowing the revenant to tear in with abandon, gnawing through the foul source of her magic.

Troth made a curious noise, pausing mid-reach for her blade. Her balance wavered where she knelt above her husband's corpse. Incomprehension washed across her expression. She toppled to the side. Andrew saw the terror twisting her face and hesitated as she seized on the ground. The revenant didn't hesitate. The revenant was the one who sank fangs into her core and shredded and shredded, until only the finest thread connected her flesh to her being.

"Andrew," Sam wheezed—scared and hurting.

Driven by the recollection of Eddie's pain and the fresh insult of Sam's, Andrew bit through that remaining psychic tendon and swallowed the force that had been Troth whole. After a hanging second spent casting around for further threat and finding none, their stacked power drained into the earth again, sated.

Andrew wrestled into control of himself once more. His skin stretched around the haunt, though it curled inside him with cautious stillness. Scattered memories cluttered his brain, his own and Eddie's, twinned: giving himself the tattoo with broader hands and a frantically pumping heart, while at the same time holding his breath and riding the stinging pain out for the sake of the marker. The vulnerable beat of his pulse and the bumps of his vertebra, held within the cup of Eddie's palm, silken skin under a sweeping thumb; his own soothed lull at the grounding weight, the squeeze, the welcome reminder of his belonging. Their alternate perspectives notched like puzzle pieces, building a whole. Eddie, bound to this chair, flinging their gift to Andrew in hopes that he'd latch on and tearing himself asunder in the process.

Movement caught his attention. Sam crawled from the pile of bodies, grabbed the knife, and sawed through the rope around his ankles. His cuffed wrists bled sluggishly. His breath came in sobs. With a shock, Andrew realized that the mask of blood on his face covered his eye, stuck shut with gore. Sam cut the ropes around Andrew's wrists first. He tried to lift his arms, experiencing a lag as the possession that controlled his flesh caught up to his impulse and assisted in the movement. It was now the work of two minds to move his body. The high whine of terror that slipped out of his throat was all his own.

Sam finished working him loose and dragged him off the chair, spilling his unresisting form out on the ground. He huddled around him to touch his wounded forearms, his bruised face. The slashes had closed themselves a little—perhaps enough to keep him living for another night. The phone that appeared in Sam's hand was incongruous in its mundanity. He watched Sam dial 911.

"Help," he rasped into the receiver.

The ghost and Andrew made a fist in Sam's shirt at his solar plexus. Sam's lips shook as he gasped disjointed chunks of information into the phone. His teeth were tinted red. He tossed the phone aside while the operator continued speaking. Sweat dappled his sallow brow. The splayed gash ran from the middle of his left cheek to his hairline; Andrew forced himself to acknowledge that Troth's knife had crossed deep over the eyelid. His gorge rose. Sam had suffered that for him.

"Your eye," he whispered.

"It hurts," Sam said, voice so small that it made goose bumps rise on Andrew's arms.

"Fuck," he sobbed. The revenant reduced itself to a passenger as he wrested control of his limbs and eased Sam onto his side. He ran bloodied fingers over his wrists to the cuffs that were cinched tight to his skin. "Fuck, I'm so sorry."

The tip of his nail slipped under the edge of the metal cuff. Sam's furnace heat, indisputably alive, intoxicated him as he held it within his palms. Sam stiffened. The faintest pop of connection sparked as their blood mingled, prickling at Andrew and the cavernous shadow of the haunt riding shotgun.

"Don't," Sam said. "Don't make me like you."

"I wouldn't, I didn't mean—"

"You killed her with that."

Andrew withdrew an inch from Sam to put distance between their skin, more than he could bear but the least he needed to prevent the transmission his instincts clamored for. Sam let him go, lying flat on his back, cuffed hands clasped on his chest as if offering benediction.

Troth's self, her lineage, the collected histories and magics and inheritances not dissimilar from his own, weighed like a stone in Andrew's belly. He'd *eaten* her, whole and struggling—and it had gifted him a stolen vitality, knitted his flesh, and settled his haunt-half. None of the books had mentioned this. What else could he do, as a whole monster, if he went to the old manor from his dreams and kept digging?

"It's no different than what you did," he said quietly.

Sam said, "Stop."

Andrew stopped. Neither man had to shift an inch for the gap between their skin to widen into a fissure. The sound of their shallow, labored breathing filled the silence as they waited for rescue.

30

"Thank you for your cooperation, Mr. Blur," the plainclothes detective said. She locked the screen of her tablet and tucked it into her almost-subtle tactical bag. "We'll release the effects recovered from the scene to you once the case has wrapped."

"Okay," he croaked.

The scratch in his throat had come with the passenger occupying his flesh, making him perpetually hoarse. He lifted his hand in dismissal as she stepped out of his hospital room. His doctor, a Hispanic woman in her late fifties, entered a moment later. She had strong hands and a brusque but pleasant manner that reminded him of his late grandmother.

"I'd prefer not to release you yet," she said. "The drugs are out of your system, but I'm concerned with the test results for your heart and kidneys. I'd also appreciate it if you'd speak with the psychiatrist instead of ignoring him."

Andrew shrugged as grandly as he could with an IV taped to his arm, tucked into his raised bed as if he were a child. "No thanks."

"Suit yourself," she said with a frown.

"How's Sam?"

"I can't discuss another patient's status with you," she said for the seventeenth time.

"When will I get out?"

"We have you another three days for observation, at least."

He grunted and closed his eyes. At some point later, she left, taking her vibrating *human* presence with her. Sam was ignoring his messages. He'd spoken to the detectives about his defensive killing of Mark Troth, Andrew knew via Riley, their strained go-between.

According to the coroner's report, Jane Troth had suffered a sudden stoppage of her heart at the height of her frenetic madness. He knew otherwise; Sam knew otherwise. That secret lay between them, in all its ugliness, festering. Sam's rejection—of him, of what he'd become, of what he'd done, or all of those things—filled him with a sour, slow drip of misery. After Troth had stitched Andrew's disarticulated portion of the inheritance to Eddie's haunting remains, carried within him now, he was less sure than he'd ever been of the neatness of his humanity. Maybe Sam was right to pull away.

The hospital rippled on all sides with human struggle, little flames guttering and flickering outside his grasp. He had to keep a constant curious need to seek contact with those burning specks in check—curb the part of him that hungered for life, death. His ghoul petted the interior of his skull, soothing his mind. Sleep, or something like it, swallowed him. He tumbled through a blur of memories doubled at the seams, *the dew-spangled lawn and the silk of Andrew's hair knotted in his fist, the gross patch of drool spreading on his chest, watching the sun come up and thinking fierce as devotion* this is mine forever *until sleep sucked him under again*

watching Eddie snore with a leaf stuck to the side of his neck and the cold damp grass soaking him as he fought to sit still, not shiver, not disturb the perfect moment of being that the pair of them occupied in sleep, in innocence, in dumb happiness

beer and foam spilled in an erotic embarrassing stream across the plane of Andrew's chest into the band of his swim trunks, Eddie's urge to put his mouth there and taste

Eddie stretching on the floating dock, the midday sun turning him into a bronze god of a boy with muscle from neck to ass to calves, untouchable and unbreakable, savage and timeless

the night before junior prom both of them dressed in their suits sharing stolen wine coolers alone and pretending, pretending without speaking, that they could be there together

"Hey," Riley said.

Andrew jerked out of his communion with a confused snort, room spinning around him. His arm stung nauseously where he'd tugged at the IV. His roommate sat in the bedside chair, haggard, wearing glasses and sweats, same as the past two visits.

"Sorry," Andrew said.

Riley gestured to his head and asked, "Has it gotten easier, the sharing?"

Andrew grappled with his desire to hide from that question. He'd known Eddie to the bone, or so he thought. But having Eddie's memories inside of him was different. The tender awfulness of remembering himself through Eddie's eyes, beautiful and cherished and wanted with raw confused intensity, with ownership, a sublimated tangled connection that Eddie had never spoken or unpacked, though it loomed so large—that understanding was an answer to the things about himself Del had made him confront, that he'd started figuring out with Halse, but it didn't help. Having been loved wasn't the same as being loved.

Eventually, he answered, "No, it hasn't."

"I'm sorry, Andrew," Riley said.

"And Sam?"

Riley's expression morphed through four versions of chagrin before he settled on an apologetic one and said, "The surgery saved the eye, but he isn't getting his sight back in it. Too much damage. He's dealing."

Andrew nodded without asking for more; he wasn't sure he wanted to hear the answer.

"He cares, dude, I swear he does care. He asked after you too," Riley said.

"Let me handle his bills at least."

"He'll be pissed," Riley warned approvingly.

"Let him be," Andrew replied. "Can't make things worse, can it?"

"Nah, and it'll take away his excuse to keep working that second gig, which has been my end goal," Riley said.

"Help me sort it," he said, weakening as the conversation dragged on. The pain meds made him drowsy, knotted his stomach. "Give them my card or something."

"Gotcha," Riley said. "Glad you're not fucking dead, okay?"

"You say that every time," he grumbled, but the comfort mattered.

On the bedside table, his phone began to vibrate. The number on the display was foreign to him but had a local area code. He ignored the call. Police had taken his statement more than once and had informed him in person of the evidence unearthed at the crime scene—the shattered remains of Eddie's phone in a spare bedroom storage chest, his hair and blood recovered from the barn. Nurses weren't going to call his phone to get in touch. Nothing else much was worth his energy. His roommate pulled a book from his messenger bag and curled up in the visitor's chair, despite it clearly being designed to prevent people from doing so. The end result was a contorted sprawl with one leg tucked through the arm gap, the other bent tight against his chest.

The phone rang again. And again. And again. As soon as Riley glanced at the table in consternation, his own phone pinged with texts, three in rapid succession, while Andrew's lit up with messages. The group chat that remained active from their one celebratory drive had come to life with a text from Ethan:

> \<link\>Vanderbilt Professors Implicated in Occult Murder, Slain in Self Defense
> HEY WHAT THE FUCK
> WHY Y'ALL NOT TELL US YOU ALMOST GOT ACTUALLY MURDERED
> WHAT IS GODDAMN WRONG WITH YOU

"That's not good," Riley murmured. He tapped his screen. Andrew muted his phone. "The article has details leaked from police reports, it's salacious as hell, and it names you. Eddie, too."

Mom lit up the incoming call alert. He answered without pre-amble, "I guess the news got there."

"Oh my god," she said. Those three words held an operatic implication. "Andrew Thomas Blur, I can't believe it, you're okay?"

"I'm fine, Mom," he said.

"You're not fine," she said. "And Eddie, my god. Oh my god."

"I gotta go, I'm in the hospital," he said—too tired for this. "Sorry, Mom."

"Baby, don't hang up on me, please," she said.

Riley set his book facedown, split open, on his vacated seat. He left the room with his phone in hand, grimacing as he texted with manic energy. As Andrew listened to his mother cry on the other end of the line, he realized that neither of the cousins had told the group without asking him. The world where he was some sort of living ghoul, where he carried a curse that allowed him to murder with a thought, felt impossible juxtaposed against a sterile Nashville hospital room, a roommate doing homework during his visiting hours, and a sobbing parent.

Dislocation threw him so badly that he repeated, "Please, I swear I'll call. I have to go."

She let him hang up with an outpouring of relief and affection. Once he tapped the END CALL button, he squeezed his phone until it hurt his stitched wrists. At least he'd finished Eddie's work. He'd solved their decade-long riddle, uncovered a generational legacy of violence and terror. That, and scattered remains, were all he had left. Riley knocked, slipping inside after a beat of silence. He thumped his forehead onto Andrew's gown-clad shoulder as he heaved a sigh, then stood straight.

"You need to get some rest. I'll come tomorrow. Also, I'm sure those calls are reporters, so turn your phone off," he said.

Andrew did as he was told.

Riley continued to visit, but Sam never did. Three afternoons later Andrew allowed himself to be wheeled out of the hospital in the change of clothes Riley brought him and driven to Capitol in the Mazda, his stitches itching fiercely. The specter kept him from scratching at the knitting skin, though he tried with increasing frustration, trapped in the passenger seat of his own body. He could tell Riley felt the struggle. He avoided looking Andrew in the face, as if he were afraid of seeing a different person there. Given the shock of surviving the reprisal of all his worst dreams, he felt ungrateful for wishing that he'd died.

What now? he thought.

"Holy shit," Riley said from the living room.

Andrew carried their mugs of coffee around the corner from the kitchen. Riley turned his laptop and pointed at the screen. The headline read, *Local Graduate Student Sues for Misconduct.*

"I never thought I'd be glad to read about West," Riley said. "But given how Troth got outed as a spooky goddamn murderer, he's taking the university to court over their handling of his and Troth's research dispute. God bless that bastard, he deserves some recompense."

"I'm going to go to Sam's," Andrew said.

Dumb consternation colored Riley's tiny "Oh."

"It's been enough time," Andrew said.

Riley sighed and pinched the bridge of his nose. "I can't stop you. I can tell you it hasn't been enough time, and he's not okay right now, and you're half the reason he isn't."

"It wasn't—I didn't *do* anything to him," Andrew said.

"He murdered a man with his hands after watching that dude's wife slit your wrists, and then"—he gestured sidelong at the mess that was Andrew, encompassing the broken remainder of his haunting, feral and barely controlled and part of him—"the ghost shit happened. I don't know if you've noticed, but Sam gives and gives all the time, and he doesn't get much in return. Have some patience if he's being selfish. He seems tough as nails, but he almost died."

"So did I," he said.

"Funny how different y'all feel about that."

The specter lifted their hand to hold the mug for warmth. Color drained from Riley's face. The other boy's laptop suddenly merited his dedicated attention. Instead of saying *but I miss him,* Andrew bolted the hot coffee in three gulping swallows, grabbed the Supra's key ring from the table, and left.

The comfortable embrace of fall was working on the trees in the neighborhood, orange and red creeping in from the edges of leaves, a carpet of discarded foliage on lawns and porches. Time soldiered on without his agreement. The drive to the ranch house in the hills reminded him of childhood field trips. His revenant offered him a burst of twinned recognition and delight at the crisp breeze.

The WRX sat parked in the drive. Andrew carried himself and his passenger up the steps, listening with half an ear to the impression of *missing–welcome–fun–irritation* it offered at the sight of Sam's place. He knocked on the frame of the storm door, then waited. Without much ado the main door opened. The sight of Halse standing barefoot, with bandages bright white against his tan face, settled and unsettled him at the same time.

Andrew broke the brittle silence: "I'm here."

Sam said, "Fuck, shit," and closed the door again.

"Halse," he croaked. He banged on the frame again. "Sam, c'mere. Let me set this right."

A muffled, "Go home."

"Talk to me first."

Seeing the bandages for a second time dropped his stomach to his toes. Sam flicked the storm door latch and pushed it open, forcing Andrew to step to the side. He stood in the frame with the door propped on one arm. Thin scabs ringed his wrists. He favored his right leg, another bandage peeking from under the hem of his basketball shorts. The bruises on his ribs matched Andrew's. He said nothing, but his stare made demands.

Andrew said, pouring his conflict and longing into it, "I'm *sorry*."

"Don't give me that," Sam said. He sounded unbearably exhausted. "Not after what we had to do, both of us. Don't be fucking sorry about it."

The nip of fall skittered past in a gust of storm-tasting wind. Andrew stuffed his hands in his pockets and leaned against the wall to watch Sam sidelong. The specter scratched inside his skin, inches too big in all directions for his body to hold comfortably. For the briefest flicker, Sam's attention cast around as if he saw the same smoky presence Riley did. His frown turned rock-solid.

Andrew asked, "Can you see it?"

"Yeah, at the corners," he said. "So, that, be sorry for that if you've got to pick something. I didn't want to join your cursed-haunted-bullshit club."

They'd comingled blood, Andrew remembered in a vertiginous swoop of guilt. He hadn't spoken the words or finished the ritual, but he'd done enough with his fingernails under the handcuffs, the desperate hook of connection he'd cast. "That was an accident."

"I bet you say that to all the guys," Sam said without much humor.

Andrew reached across the distance between them but hesitated halfway. Sam made no motion to close the gap. The limp flop of Andrew's hand back to his thigh went unacknowledged, until he said, "What are we doing?"

The question loomed.

Sam said, "Nothing, at this minute. That all right with you?"

"No," Andrew forced himself to admit.

"Give me some consideration, Blur. If you're going to be married to a fucking ghost, I'm not going to be your affair," Sam said. His jaw clenched, one visible eye blazing at the challenge. The dead man abiding in Andrew's bones hissed, displeased, and it drew a violent shudder across Andrew's own nerves. His response stalled out as he regained control of his flesh. Sam said, "The debt's clear, between me and Ed, and the thing with you and me has nowhere to go. With due respect and all, fuck off for a while. You already got what you wanted from me."

The door swooshed open, caught in the breeze when Sam shoved it free of his bracing arm. Andrew stood dumb on the porch as the main door slammed shut, lock turning with a clack. The haunt chittered sympathetic nothingness at him and took clumsy control to maneuver him to the car. He was miles from the house before he regained himself enough to skip the on-ramp and pursue the route in the opposite direction of Sam's place, following the track of the hills toward the swollen-bellied sun on the horizon.

One time. He and Sam had managed one night together. His whole being remembered the stretch of his jaw and the grip of broad fingers on the base of his skull, thighs solid under his palms, sheets tangled around his knees. An abyssal gulf opened in him at the thought that he had wrecked the potential for that to happen again. The endless taunting text messages and the raw late nights, fistfights and firelight, the one bright savage thing he'd gained from all the loss since the turn of summer—nothing else kindled him to human, eager life. Sam Halse wasn't going to be another *almost*. He'd made that mistake over and over in total ignorance for almost a decade, and he wasn't going to do it again.

He whipped a U-turn, returning to the house on Capitol in the gloaming hours. His roommate sat on the couch where he'd left him, buried in homework, fanning himself with a book in languid flaps while he typed one-handed on the laptop at his side. Three crushed cans of High Life cluttered the coffee table alongside a discarded lighter and pair of sunglasses.

"I need your help," Andrew said.

Riley dropped his book, bolting upright from his slouch. The leftovers of Eddie Fulton roiled, toneless and agitated and dead. Andrew swallowed against the lump in his throat, choking off the bitter curiosity about what he and the revenant could become together, as he waited for an answer.

Then Riley said, "Of course."

31

The lock at Townsend had rusted through. Andrew fought the creaking grind of the key against the tumblers. Exerting so much torque strained his stitches. Riley thumbed his baseball cap higher on his forehead as he watched. Tall grass rustled in the overgrown field of the Fulton yard, swishing and swirling, topped with grains. Despite the burnished gold light of afternoon, bleak shade crept at the corners of the porch and behind the age-grimed glass of the house's tall windows. The lock gave abruptly with a shower of corroded metal. Andrew swung the door open on its hinges. The fourth board past the old welcome mat croaked with his weight, as it had when he and Eddie were kids playing hide-and-seek. His heart soared and crashed all at once. Sheets eaten through in patches hung over the abandoned furniture. Haphazard packing revealed gaps, losses, the final lingering pieces of the family's life from a near-decade before.

"You grew up here," Riley said.

"The suburb on the other side of the woods," he said.

"Nice house."

"This isn't the house that matters, I don't think," Andrew said.

Riley cast him a grim look. "The one from your dream, then, the old plantation?"

Andrew closed his eyes and let the power creep out around his ankles in a spill, the revenant dragging with it to slide past memories. As boys they'd been happy here, together, and he felt scraps of the lifelong yearning Eddie had dragged to his grave with him. Riley smothered a shriek when the haunt lapped across him. Andrew recoiled at the faint, bitter taste of his friend's remarkable aura in his throat.

Riley said, shaken after the brush, "You sure it's safe to use your, whatever, powers after what happened to Troth?"

He said, "I did what I did for Sam."

The spreading power retracted once more into the film of shade cloaking Andrew head to toe. He'd found nothing in the house worth pursuing further—it was as inert as it could be. He'd expected as much, but he had to find out for sure, leave no corner unchecked.

Riley removed his hat and tugged at his hair before he said, "I know that. It doesn't seem fair to insist on thanking you for saving him, when I know it cost you something to get him out of there, and you're not going to tell me how much."

"Will you come with me to the plantation?" he asked, changing the subject.

Riley allowed it, responding, "How do we find it?"

"I think I just walk," he said.

Riley grimaced. Andrew clenched his fists on his next exhale and relaxed his control again. Denied free rein once already during their outing, at his second offer the ghoul overtook him with such urgency it felt as if his ribs might crack from the pressure, the sluggish beat of his pulse smothered beneath its stagnation. He pictured the dreaming vision of the house he'd suffered through previously in detail, feeding that image to the spectral operator of his flesh. The ghoul walked them out of the home from their childhood at once. Riley followed in his wake, with the hot fear of one candle in a vast darkness.

The woods were deep. No person had disturbed the undergrowth in years, but the expected rattle and skitter of small animal life was absent. Riley struggled to beat a path, Andrew nominally in control of his feet and elbows—his ghastly driver had not gotten the hang of his height, his reach. After almost an hour, a faint homing drone rose up from the earth. Andrew hesitated at the same time his roommate recoiled.

"That's really unpleasant," Riley choked out.

"It's that obvious?" Andrew pressed out through clumsy lips.

"Hard to miss, yeah. Like a big ugly lighthouse."

The trees thinned. Light dappled the green bushes and twisting ivy across their path. Andrew burst free into a clearing, almost swallowing his own tongue at the shock of resonance that struck him. The dilapidated plantation home was grandiose in death: sagging veranda, gaping windows like hollow sockets, rotten wood and worse aura. The sun made no dent in its malicious shadows.

"Oh, fuck that," Riley said an octave higher than his usual.

"The library," Andrew said. "We need the library, that's the room I dreamed about, there's got to be something on how to lay him to rest."

"If the house doesn't eat us first."

"It won't, it wants me to come learn from it," said the revenant with his vocal cords. Riley trilled a whine at the back of his throat. Andrew said, "Sorry, Christ."

"Do not ever do that again," Riley said, spooked to the whites of his eyes.

To be fair, Eddie's dismembered voice coming out of Andrew's body wasn't Andrew's favorite thing, either. The inheritance he'd taken up was nothing but poisoned ashes. It held only a fraction, a splinter, of Eddie's adoration and anger and need. Sometimes he imagined an alternate future, him and Eddie in Nashville without Troth, growing freer under the influence of the pack. Maybe one night, Eddie would've seen him right at sunset all doused in gold and grabbed him with both hands, and put their mouths together. Maybe he wouldn't have. And even if he had, maybe he'd have been a fucked-up, controlling, monstrous disaster of a partner. Andrew had to accept that he was going to take that *maybe* to his grave.

Andrew entered the house through the busted window on the groaning porch. The images and impressions from his vision rushed at him in greyscale, identical from the hole in the floorboards to the terrible age of the house itself moldering around them. The miasma of the Troth estate was nothing compared to the Fultons' original home, itself a dead creature and the locus of constant horrors. The manor resonated on the same frequency as the alien curse-gift latched to his insides—his to claim, if he would just accept the mantle of power and the cruelty that came with it. He shuddered, sick to his stomach.

"You can wait there," he said over his shoulder to Riley, who was loitering outside with a pale face and clenched fists.

"No, I need to see it," he said as if to convince himself. "Plus, if it fucking eats you, I'll be stuck waiting out here after nightfall."

Andrew entered the hall, which continued to match his vision. Eddie must've come here before his murder for the memories to be so fresh. Or maybe Eddie's ghost had visited on its own, autonomously; he didn't know if that was even possible. Earth crooned at him in welcome from an invisible cellar underfoot. His ghost fluttered in sympathetic vibration. Riley caught tiny, desperate breaths, almost sobs. The house clutched around them. Andrew put his hand on the library doorknob and twisted as Riley's fist snagged at the hem of his shirt. The door swung loose on crying hinges. A stinking wave wafted out of the hot dark room, mildewed paper choking the air. He lifted his phone flashlight to inspect the tall shelving on all sides, the antebellum chairs and rugs.

"Go check there—I'll cover these." Andrew directed Riley with a gesture to the far shelves.

Riley began to run his own flashlight over spines of books. Andrew inspected novels and collections of poems, children's books, all the Fulton family's gathered texts from their rich and awful life. Then, on impulse, he lifted the light to the topmost shelf for a flash of titles: *The Oldest Ways and The Ruined Gods, Witchcraft in Salem,* and more. The predictability might've been comical if it hadn't stoked his crippling terror higher with each passing second. But alongside the fear came a worse impulse: interest, the temptation to give in. If Sam rejected him again, if this bought him nothing, he'd lose the last connection he had to Eddie and to his line.

That thought—wasn't *his*. But it prompted his hand to pet across the looming books without his consent. He snatched his hand to his chest again as the hair rose on his nape. The remembered bitter sweetness of Troth's soul clogged the base of his throat.

"Change of plans. We need to get rid of all this. Burn it," he said. *Otherwise I might stop resisting.* And would the Fultons have collected information on willfully relinquishing their power, anyway?

"Let me take a couple of those books, I've never seen them before," Riley said.

"No—no, but I'll give you the research I've already got. For your dissertation. Just not these, we don't need to keep these," he rambled, tense as a hunting dog on point.

The house groaned again, purposeful. The cellar under the floorboards offered a barbed, engaging promise of *more more more,* as if there were bones buried there calling for him to come pay tribute. The haunt slavered in response. His power *wanted* to become stronger; he struggled to keep his feet from moving closer to the shelves again. He was not as in control of the situation as he'd hoped.

"Andrew?" Riley whispered uneasily.

With a herculean effort he turned himself toward the door and gasped out, "Run."

Riley bolted fast as a rabbit, and he followed at a pell-mell stagger out of the library, into the rotted foyer, and out the broken window again. Andrew tripped over his own feet in the grass and fell. Riley tumbled next to him on purpose, smacking a hand onto his chest twice.

"Haunted fucking houses, dear fucking god," he said.

Catching his breath while crushing the irritable revenant beneath his frayed will, he said, "I have some gas in the trunk. I figured we'd probably need to take care of it."

"Are you getting more psychic, or what," Riley tried to joke.

Finding the path to the car, then returning to the plantation with canisters of gasoline and his matchbooks and lighters, ate another two hours. The sun had crossed to the edge of the sky overhead. Andrew poured gas around the crumbling foundations, steeling himself before hopping onto the veranda again.

"Come get me if I'm not back fast," he said, then vaulted through the window to sprint for the library.

The land's offer tugged at him as he splashed fuel across the lightless barren hell the Fultons had created, preparing to put the past to rest along with the books. Eddie had left him this, all of this, but keeping it—allowing its horror to continue to thrive for another generation—struck him to the core as wrong. He would get closure, by force if need be. When the can was empty, four more striding leaps back through the rotting house carried him outside, safe and hale. Together he and his roommate set a respectable fire at the foundations, flames licking hot and glowing into the homestead's recesses.

The expansive, roaring catch of the fire dazzled them both with its ferocity and heat, as if it were burning off the contagion along with the aged wood and plaster. Fire wouldn't cleanse the history from that earth, but maybe it could put the bones to rest.

Though within him, the haunt pressed at Andrew, unchanged.

Riley said, "I grabbed the ring from Sam's. You still think you need it to do the rest?"

"Yeah, I do," Andrew said.

The land seethed with death and need under his hands. He dug his fingers into the dirt, recalling the idea he'd had the night before. In his mind he turned the thought on end and breathed through the revenant's instinctive resistance, waiting for that to pass, then held out a hand to Riley regardless when it didn't. Impulse and Eddie's damned memories told him symbolism was half the engine of magic. His roommate dropped the curse-tinged platinum band onto his palm. The revenant latched onto the metal it recognized in a heartbeat, despite its unwillingness to abandon him.

"This is yours," he whispered inside himself and outside at once.

Riley remained at the edge of the conflagration, a safe but eerie distance as the wooden frame cracked and collapsed. Andrew walked into the woods with the fire at his back, casting his writhing shadow into the tree-shade. The sinkhole was closer than he remembered. His legs were longer now. Unnatural chill rose from the gaping edge, the entrance to the caverns and the site of his first death. Eddie's, too. Andrew slipped the ring on and lifted it to his mouth. Metal stung his lips with cold. He urged the slithering weight of the haunt out of his flesh, cramming it into the band. Unpracticed though he was, Eddie had made him powerful— powerful enough to control a haunt, though he hated the idea of forcing him out. *Come on. I love you, but this is no life.* And, for once, it cooperated. His acquired memories slithered free with a mournful pang.

"Goodbye," he said.

Then he pulled the ring off his finger and pitched it into the hole. The cuticle-rip of the haunt tearing loose kneecapped him. Spit filled his mouth until he gagged. His forehead rested on the ground. Frantic with loss, he reached for the hole, about to fling himself in to recover the ring and the last vestiges it housed—but before instinct could transmute to action he forced himself to hold fast. He caught a sobbing breath. Knowing it was the right thing to do, to preserve the memory of Eddie as he'd really been, rather than what he'd become, didn't fix how bad it hurt to be well and truly alone. When the first wave of the dispossession's ache abated, he rose to his feet and edged back from the cavern, one step at a time, by himself.

Eddie's remnant had let him go, but the vibration of their bloody inheritance remained in his veins, sensitive to the sucking pressure of the caverns regardless of the resolution of his more personal nightmare. Curses weren't as simple to put aside as a ghost willing to be laid to rest; that grim weight would nest inside of him until the end of his life. Andrew trudged through howling winds toward the glowing blaze of the fire. Each crunch of forest debris under his shoes put another foot of distance between the person he had been and the person he thought he might become. Eddie had left him this, also: a future to see through.

———————

In Eddie's old bedroom, Andrew sat at the edge of the bare mattress. The sheets at his feet were destined for the washing machine. The final clean load of Eddie's clothes lay spread on the bed. He wasn't sure whether to keep or donate them, but the small constant pain of cleaning Eddie's space, putting to rest the mundane remains of his lost companion, kept him grounded. Without the haunt dogging his steps, the process of grieving was mechanical but raw.

He came downstairs and collapsed onto the sofa. Riley pulled on his high-tops, smoke leaking out around the blunt pinched between his lips. Luca and Ethan were horsing around in the kitchen in preparation for a night out; he'd been spending more time with them, since the hospital. Luca's sense of humor made him smile four times out of five, and he needed that. Tonight they were celebrating. The review committee had accepted Riley's thesis proposal, revised to adapt Eddie's unfinished work on folklore studies.

Andrew swilled the remains of his beer and texted Sam three times, dropping more stones into the well:

> laid him to rest and burnt the old house down
>
> it's just me in here
>
> and i'm ready whenever

He didn't expect a response, but he got one five minutes later as he shut the front door behind their cadre of rolling mischief. *See you tonight.* He stared at his phone for a beat before meeting Riley's gaze.

"Don't fuck it up," Riley said.

"I won't," he said, but he wasn't sure he knew how to keep the promise.

Riley led his group of four to their cars, as gaudy and unruly as ever, including the Supra, which still sported its hideous reddish mauve wrap. Their pack met at a gas station on the opposite side of the neighborhood this time. Andrew parked next to Ethan, who flicked him finger-guns when he went inside for his requisite candy bar and bottled water. The clerk eyeballed the fresh pink weals tracking up his wrists to his elbows with disdain.

Andrew curled his lip and said, "Got a problem?"

"No way, man," the clerk said.

He crammed a quarter of the Payday in his mouth on the way out the door. Caramel stuck inside the cracks of his teeth in a stinging rush. Riley called out, "Leading tonight, Blur?"

"Yeah, sure," he agreed thoughtlessly, then heard a familiar engine.

The WRX rolled over the bump of the entrance curb and coasted past the service station door in front of Andrew. He swigged a mouthful from his water to wash down peanut-grit, covering his burst of conflicted nerve-biting emotion. Sam parked next to his cousin and rolled his window down, languid, unmarked perfection as seen from the left side.

"Good news, I'm not blind," he said. "I can still drive."

"Bad joke," Riley said.

"Who said it was a joke?" he fired right back.

Andrew approached them, breathless for no reason and drinking in the sight of Sam, in his car where he belonged, like a parched man in a desert. A matte black patch covered one half of Sam's arresting stare, but the visible eye regarded him with the ferocity he had been missing.

"Y'all go on," Andrew said to Riley as he strode past the Mazda. "We'll text and catch up, after."

He didn't wait to see if his direction was followed, just opened the passenger door of the WRX and flopped inside, the closest he'd been to Sam in far too long. Time and distance hadn't cooled his interest while he settled into himself as a single man. The passenger seat was as comfortable as he remembered.

Sam scratched his own chin, nails scraping over stubble with a rasp, and said, "You got something to tell me?"

"Yeah, I do." Andrew chewed the inside of his cheek. Words piled up in his throat. He hadn't explained himself much to Sam since he'd moved to Nashville, but this was the one time he needed to be direct. He fought the urge to blurt out a grandiose, ill-conceived, revealing offer, *do you want to open a garage together,* or something like that. Instead he said, "I thought about the whole thing, start to finish. How much you did for me and how much I didn't do for you, just kept taking. And I know I want to do shit for you, with you. I do." He sipped a quick shaken breath and finished with crushing simplicity. "You're worth it to me."

Sam said, "I'm not jealous of him, it was never about that. It's about reciprocity."

"I can do better."

"Prove it," Sam said.

Andrew leaned across the gearshift. Sam stopped him with an open hand to the sternum that slid up, firm and sure, to the base of his throat. Fingers spread careful but grounding across the width of his neck; a thumb notched onto his pulse on the other side. Andrew's eyes traced over Sam's scarred brow, his narrow cheeks and evening stubble. Possibilities swirled in the smell of gasoline and the crisp October night. He swallowed, throat bobbing against the webbing of Sam's thumb joint. His stare rested on Sam's mouth—telegraphing his intentions, though the other man held him at a careful distance. Tension shivered between them.

Then Sam said, with more gentleness than Andrew expected, "Nah, we're a while from doing that again. Get back in your ride, Blur. Let's try to start fresh."

Andrew collapsed back against the passenger seat, Sam's nails drawing faint stinging lines across his skin with the suddenness of his retreat. He shuddered, swallowing again. After another moment stolen to calm his racing heart he opened the passenger door, casting a last glance at Sam—and found him staring. Their gazes met, sparked, split again with equal speed. Andrew returned to the embrace of his Supra with a flushed, hot face. The engine turned over, a rumbling whine, as it had countless other nights and would for countless more to come. Sam rolled out first. Andrew followed after him under the fog-yellow glow of streetlights, on the heels of their pack.

ACKNOWLEDGMENTS

Summer Sons wouldn't exist without the affection and patience tons of people poured out for me, over several years. Endless gratitude to Dave for reading at least one hundred drafts and providing never-ending enthusiasm with his valuable feedback, and to my big gay fam—Brett, Emilie, Em, Olivia, Alex—for supporting me through some weird situations across the writing of this project. I treasure y'all to the ends of the earth. Also, I appreciate you putting up with (or enthusiastically contributing to) all the horny bullshit I bring to the table of life.

Thanks to Carl Engle-Laird for seeing the same book in these pages I saw, then helping bring it to fruition; thanks similarly to Tara Gilbert for her work as my agent. And of course there are all the talented members of the Tordotcom team involved in making the book and getting it into your hands: Irene Gallo, Oliver Dougherty, Mordicai Knode, Amanda Melfi, Lauren Anesta, Megan Kiddoo, Steven Bucsok, Jim Kapp, and Christine Foltzer—as well as our absolutely awesome cover artist, Sasha Vinogradova. Thanks also to The Wonder Years for granting me permission to include a lyric from "Local Man Ruins Everything," as Riley's tattoo.

Furthermore, I owe a nod to all of the people in the field across the last decade whose support has been invaluable: the ones who offered me bylines, published stories from me, stood me dinners and drinks, gave strong critiques, held me accountable for acting right, hired me for editorial positions, and believed in the words I brought along with me. To my Lexington-and-adjacent writer's group: keep it up, team, you're golden.

Last but far from least, nerdy special thanks to BTS for providing comfort, energy, and healing with your music during exceptionally trying times. Your kindness, clarity, and strong friendship shine through for me as a model for what masculinity *can* be. Plus, I listened to RM's *mono* nonstop during the first revisions of the book; couldn't have done it without you.

And it isn't precisely a thanks, but: pour one out for all the boys who got lost—even the ones who got *me* lost. At least, maybe, I learned something from you.

ABOUT THE AUTHOR

LEE MANDELO is a writer, critic, and occasional editor whose fields of interest include speculative and queer fiction, especially when the two coincide. They have been a past nominee for various awards including the Nebula, Lambda, and Hugo; their work can be found in magazines such as *Uncanny, Clarkesworld,* and *Nightmare* and on *Tor.com*. Aside from a brief stint overseas learning to speak Scouse, Mandelo has spent their life ranging across Kentucky, currently living in Lexington and pursuing a Ph.D. at the University of Kentucky.